THE TARGET

A Novel by:

Dean Arden

The Target

A novel by Dean Arden

This is a work of fiction. Names, characters, places, incidents and events are the product of the author's imagination or are used fictitiously. Any resemblance to actual persons, living or dead, incidents, events, or locals are entirely coincidental.

Website: www.CRMmediaentertainment.com
Contact the publisher at: MDL@CRMmediaentertainment.com

Visit the author's website at: www.DeanArden.com
Contact the author at: authorDeanArden@gmail.com

Cover design by Alexandria Melone
Edited by Nick May

Manufactured in the United States of America.

ISBN 978-0-578-20286-0

FIRST EDITION

In appreciation to my family and friends
who inspire and support me.

A special thanks to Frank,
who told me to, *stop talking about it
and just write the damn thing.*

CHAPTER ONE

LUIS Afanador, a gentle and quiet man, leaned forward, his arms resting on his knees as he watched the network news. The anchor and his guest, a former Federal Reserve chairman, were discussing Freddie Mac's recent announcement that it would no longer purchase subprime loans and mortgage-related securities. As the euphoria of Wall Street slowly gave way to concerns over the latest business and financial news, the stock market had begun a decline that was quickly extinguishing the gains of the last few years. The truths about subprime lending, the securitization of mortgage-backed instruments, and weak monetary policy, were now being exposed. There was talk about widespread fraud in the banking industry, and the financial market—once fueled by a period of low interest rates, relaxed credit standards, risky investment products, and little government oversight—was suddenly on the verge of collapse.

As Luis listened to a discussion that he knew very little about, his two boys ran into the living room arguing loudly, which drowned out the TV. He reached for the remote on the coffee table before him and raised the volume. Although he did not know this Freddy Mac person or understand what was being said about the rise in mortgage foreclosure rates, a housing bubble, and the effects of deregulation, he guessed that, all in all, it didn't sound good. To anyone other than Luis Afanador it would have been clear—the proverbial shit was about to hit the fan, and there was nothing anyone could do to stop it.

Luis was four months behind on his own mortgage, and he knew for certain that wasn't good. The bank had demanded payment, and he was concerned about what it would do next. On top of that, he feared his wife would soon find out about their financial situation. He continued to watch the news, sitting motionless on the sofa as the boys ran around the room. The baby followed them in and stood nearby, holding onto the furniture as she attempted to make her way to her father.

Teresa watched their daughter from the small kitchen as she prepared dinner on the aged, tarnished stove that had come with the house. From the smell of it, Luis guessed she was making arroz con pollo, a traditional Colombian dish of chicken, rice, and black beans. Three-year-old Luisa tried to stand on the boys' soccer ball, only to tip backward and land on her backside. She looked at her father and, failing to elicit any sympathy or even a response from him, began to cry. Unaffected by the commotion around him, Luis continued to watch the TV, nervously wrenching his hands. Teresa put down the wooden ladle and darted into the living room. Lifting their daughter from the floor, she carried her into the kitchen, wiping the tears from her face with the palm of her hand. After placing the child in her highchair and returning to the stove, she could see that Luis looked worried. She wondered what was bothering her husband, but before she could ask, he got up and walked into the bedroom, shutting the door behind him. Teresa suspected something was wrong, and whatever it was, she sensed it was not good.

———◆———

It was a few years earlier that a close friend referred Luis and his wife to Carlos Perron about an apartment for rent. Although it was forty dollars more a month, a sum they could afford to pay, the young couple was still uneasy about the added expense. The apartment did, however, have a second bedroom for the boys, which they needed desperately because Teresa was pregnant again. They decided to see Perron at his office the next night, as was suggested. He greeted them warmly at the front door of a building that did not appear to be a real estate office. They wondered if they were even in the right place.

Speaking in Spanish, he immediately put them at ease. He sat with the couple politely asking questions about their home in Colombia, the trek to the United States, and their family in New Jersey. All the while he listened, absorbed, and assessed. He offered Teresa a cup of coffee and Luis a Corona. He joked and laughed with them. He was engaging—charming even. At some point during the evening, he called in his secretary, Katarina, from the other room and asked her to join them. She quickly came in with more beer and coffee, and Luis thought she was very young, perhaps too young to be working this late in an office alone with no one else around other than her boss.

When prompted by Perron, she told them that she was also from Colombia. This brought a smile to the couple's faces, setting off a five-minute discussion about their shared heritage. Carlos sat back quietly, allowing this warm exchange to take place. It was all part of the plan.

Getting down to business he asked, "Luis dónde trabajas?" *Luis where do you work?*

"Restaurante Cartagena. Yo trabajo en la cocina. Algun tiempo el Lunas, mi dia libre, yo trabajo con un amigo, Marlin. El limpia casas para gente rica, quien nos paga en efectivo." *Restaurant Cartagena. I work in the kitchen. Sometimes on Monday, my regular day off, I work with a friend, Marlin. He cleans houses for rich people. They pay us cash.*

Turning to Teresa, Carlos, now speaking in English, asked, "Teresa, you work, too?"

Teresa hesitated and said, "Arreglo la ropa, pantalonos de dobladillo, vestidos . . . todo lo que traen lo arreglo." *I fix clothes, hem pants, dresses . . . anything they bring, I fix.*

Smiling, Perron asked, "Cash?"

She nodded, "Si."

It seemed as if they were there for only ten or fifteen minutes, but more than an hour had passed before Perron even approached the subject of the apartment. He suggested that instead of renting an apartment, why not buy a house—telling them that they could do it with no money down. He claimed that he knew the perfect place for them. Best of all, the mortgage payment would be only thirty dollars more than they were already prepared to pay for rent on the much smaller apartment. He told them they happened to show up at the perfect time, and that they were incredibly lucky—the house was not even on the market yet. Luis agreed, now caught up in the idea of owning a home. Perron emphasized that it would be better for the children. They would have their own bedrooms and a backyard to play in. He said the seller would pay ten thousand dollars for their closing costs, and that it would cost them nothing to do this.

He shouted out to Katarina, who had returned to the outer room, commanding her to come back into his office. She walked in with two more beers. He told her to sit, that they were going to take a loan application. He directed her to come around the desk and substitute herself before the computer. Getting up from his seat, he allowed her to sit, purposefully brushing himself against her. He then moved his hand downward across her bottom, feigning an effort to help her sit.

Katarina grimaced at the unwelcomed touch but tolerated it like she had done numerous times before, only because she needed this job, desperately. Despite what Perron may have thought, his actions did not go unnoticed by Luis, who said and did nothing, continuing to sip his beer, waiting to be told what to do next.

Standing behind his secretary, Perron held onto her shoulders, watching as she pulled up a 1003 loan application form and began to fill in the blank fields with information he provided. He instructed her to put Luis on the application alone, but to use all the money from him and Teresa in the total income column. He went on to explain to the customers now sitting before him that the bank only cared about whether they could afford the monthly payment. He told Luis, "We put all the money under the restaurant job. It's ok because the bank doesn't ask. They don't care. They only care about you making the payment. That's all."

Luis shrugged his shoulders, took a swig of beer and said, "Si, Carlos. Gracias."

Katarina asked, "What do you do?"

Perron interjected, "Put down chef—just chef."

Luis immediately corrected, "I no chef, Kenny chef. I work kitchen, wash dishes, make salad, appetizer, clean the—"

"Just put assistant chef." Katarina typed in assistant chef on the *work position* line of the 1003, as instructed. Luis just shook his head yes, and drank what beer remained in his bottle, placing the empty on the desk in front of him. Perron grabbed the Corona bottle and walked into the other room taking two more beers from a small refrigerator that was conveniently tucked away behind a set of filing cabinets full of his customers' closed mortgage files. He walked back into the office where they continued to complete the loan application, handing Luis another beer.

Teresa sat quietly watching, wanting to ask her husband if he was sure this was the right thing to do. Instead, she thought about it and kept silent. She was not certain that what Carlos Perron was telling them was true, but she allowed the notion to slip her mind, as the idea of owning a home was now very appealing to her. Excited, Teresa did her best not to show it, as she tried to listen to what the men were saying.

Perron suggested that they come back in the morning. He would take them to the house himself; the owner was a friend who had given him a key. Luis and Teresa were not sure, protesting a little. He insisted. Although he was moving fast, he was very hard to resist, and so they agreed to be back at the office at 10:00 a.m.

Carlos Perron, who was a short, balding, and chubby man, smiled at his new friends, and said, "Bueno, Bueno."

He walked them to the curb, and standing there, bidding them a good night, he lit a cigarette. He stood watching as they began the three-block walk to the bus stop. Luis and Teresa had spent more than two hours in the Bender Capital Lending Hoboken office that night, although it didn't feel like it at all. They were excited and looked forward to meeting the next morning. The couple did not know it at the time, but they were already hooked, Perron was certain of it. He would have the office manager run the credit in the morning before they arrived to make sure he was good to go. He could tweak the application afterward, as needed, but he had no doubt Luis would get a loan. After all he easily passed the *mirror test*, the first obstacle in the home loan process. It merely required an applicant to fog up a mirror, the net result of which meant he or she was breathing and likely to qualify for a mortgage. If that wasn't enough, the equally difficult *pulse test* usually followed right after.

———————◆———————

Luis decided to call Carlos one more time. He left the bedroom and walked into the kitchen. Grabbing the phone off the wall, he dialed, hoping to get through to him. He had left four messages over the last week, explaining in each one that he was having difficulty paying the mortgage since the monthly payment had gone up a second time in just three years. It was now almost double the original amount, a payment they could no longer afford. The phone rang numerous times before going to voicemail; this time he did not leave a message. Luis walked back into the living room and sat on the edge of the sofa until Teresa called him for dinner. He got up, smiled at his wife, and began rough-housing with the boys, who giggled their way into the kitchen, eventually settling down at the dinner table. The family was altogether, as they were on most Monday evenings, Luis' only day off. Before eating, they joined hands and bowed their heads to say a short prayer of thanks. Luis held onto Teresa's hand a little longer than usual, silently asking for God's assistance in their struggles to come.

———————◆———————

Perron looked at his cellphone and saw the name Luis Afanador on the screen. This is probably the fifth or sixth phone call this week, he thought, allowing the phone to ring until it went into voicemail. He knew exactly why Luis was calling. He knew three years ago that this day would come, as it happened with all the others before him. In each instance, he anticipated the calls, the panicked pleas for help, the desperation, the anger, the hollow threats, the brief resistance, and the reluctant but inevitable submission. Carlos Perron knew that Luis' fate would end the same way as it did with the other families before him. He had been doing this for a long time, almost nine years now, and knew very well how this would play out, how it always played out. He would eventually call Luis and offer to help him and his family with a proposal he would have no choice but to accept. Perron would take the house from them and pay the mortgage, pointing out the generosity of his offer. He would tell Luis not to worry, that they could stay and pay him rent. A lawyer would prepare the deed transferring ownership of the home, and Perron would pay absolutely nothing for all their troubles. He and his partners would then eventually sell it to another Bender customer for a nice profit a few months later. They might even make a few repairs along the way, if only to earn more profits. After all, housing prices had been on the rise the past ten years, and there was no reason to believe that anything would change that. Once the house was sold, Luis, Teresa, and the kids would be forced out to an apartment that he and his partners owned. He had done this hundreds of times before, with many families before the Afanador family. In each instance, Perron and his partners made a lot of money. It was all part of the plan. He never thought of the families as victims but instead saw them as victims of circumstances, never feeling badly for any of them.

He would call Luis in a few days. Right now, he had a game of dominos waiting for him at his house and saw no reason to expend any more time thinking about Luis Afanador. Before going home, he stopped at a liquor store near the office to pick up a cold case of Corona. The clerk, Mr. Rashad, an elderly gentleman from Pakistan, was excited to see his new friend. He thanked him again, as he had countless of other times, for finding his family a house and securing a home loan on their behalf. It had been almost two years, but Perron remembered every detail of the transaction—what Rashad had paid for the house, the loan amount, the commission he had earned as the loan officer, and the profit he and his partners had received from the sale of a house they had acquired only four months earlier. Smiling he said, "You're welcome." He then wondered where he would go in six months to pick up beer when Rashad's mortgage rate adjusted, and he couldn't make the payments anymore. Suddenly, Perron began to smile, remembering the store on Federal Street. Pulling the case of beer from the counter, he said, "Gracias," forgetting that he was speaking Spanish. Rashad smiled back and said, "Good night my friend, and may Allah continue to bestow His blessing upon you."

CHAPTER TWO

THE light of the waning moon flickered on the water's black surface like an old Charlie Chaplin kaleidoscope reel. Michael Dolan could see himself standing on the muddy embankment, watching the water breaking on rocks scattered throughout the winding channel. He observed the man being carried by the river's rapids toward a deafening sound that grew louder with every turn of the twisting banks. Michael, began to grow restless, twisting and turning, as the waterway ended abruptly, and the force of the water sent the man downward into the darkness of a waterfall's abyss. Sinking deep into the churning pool, the man struggled to make his way back to the surface. His mouth began to fill with water and as he gasped for air, Michael stirred, now agitated. As soon as the man broke the water's surface, filling his lungs with air, Michael anxiously woke to the sound of running water and the smell of freshly brewed coffee. His dream abruptly came to an end as he groggily began to separate the fading imagery from the reality of the brand-new day.

He lifted his head from the pillow and glanced at the open bathroom door from where the sound was coming. Diana, who had gotten up long before him, went for a short jog and upon her return, set the coffeemaker on brew and headed for the shower, as she did every morning. He instinctively sensed the coffee was now ready. It would be strong. It always was. Although he had not always liked it that way, over the years he had become accustomed to the potent blend, now even enjoying it.

The aroma stirred him out of bed, sending him downstairs for his first cup of the morning. He poured himself and Diana a cup each, his light with cream and hers with just a touch. He put her cup down while he sipped coffee from his own. It was slightly bitter but oddly satisfying, as the caffeine provided a momentary jolt that released him from his lingering fatigue, his eyes no longer heavy and expressionless.

A few more sips and he was fully awake. He savored the coffee, puckering his lips as he drank from the cup. Enjoying the early morning solitude, he stepped through the French doors onto the patio.

Standing there, Michael tipped his head upward and closed his eyes, allowing the warmth of the sun to permeate his face. He lingered only briefly, taking a deep breath and filling his lungs with the morning's chilly air as he tried to search for a meaning to the somewhat disturbing dream that he was having far too often lately. Oddly, it always ended the same way, with the man barely escaping a suffocating, drowning death. Dismissing his thoughts about the dream for the moment, he quickly returned to the kitchen, grabbed the steaming cup from the counter and headed back upstairs.

Michael strolled into the bathroom as Diana was stepping out of the shower with a towel wrapped around her body and another atop her shoulder-length auburn hair. Without a word, he placed the cup of coffee on the vanity nearby. He then walked out of the room to check on Christina, their daughter, who was asleep in the bedroom just down the hall. She wouldn't be awake for another hour, or at least not until Michael was ready to dress and feed her. He would eventually take her down the road to Tiny Tikes Preschool before heading off to work himself.

Arriving at her door, he opened it slowly, so as not to wake her. Peeking in, he could see that she was still asleep. Without hesitation, he silently drifted to the bed and pulled the covers around her, gently pushing a few strands of soft, long brown hair away from her face. Diana had given Christina a bath the night before and was likely the reason why her hair now felt so soft and appeared so shiny. Before turning to leave the bedroom, he looked at her one more time. *She is all her mother—her eyes, hair, lips, and dimpled cheeks.* She also had a similar personality—a pleasant and friendly demeanor; one that made them both so very likable and relatable to others. *No doubt about it, all her mother,* he reflected again. Bending down, he kissed her forehead, and whispered, "Daddy loves you." He sensed Diana wanted another baby, hinting about it several times, and although not completely opposed to the idea, he was also not totally there yet. At least not until he was more settled in his new position as chief compliance officer at Bender Capital Lending.

As Michael walked out of the bedroom, he thought that Christina being asleep was a good thing. It would give him time to shower and have another cup of coffee before starting the day. He returned to the bathroom to find Diana finishing her hair and about to start on her makeup.

He walked over to her as she leaned forward over the vanity. Seeing him, she smiled, straightened, and turned to him. She grabbed his shoulders and drew him near, giving him a kiss that pleasantly lingered for too brief a moment.

"Good morning," he said, drinking his coffee. "How was your run?"

"It was good. Thanks for asking," she said, pausing momentarily. "You should start running again. Why don't you run with me? It'll be a good thing, you know. You've been a little stressed lately." Looking at him in the mirror she added, "You've gained a little weight . . . in your belly." Smiling at him, she turned and poked him in the stomach. She then turned her attention back to putting on her makeup, leaving the comment to awkwardly hang there like mistletoe at a Christmas office party.

What, I gained weight? He looked at himself in the mirror, lifting his t-shirt and putting his hand on what he believed to be a rock-hard stomach.

Quickly returning his attention to Diana, he said, "Yeah, ok I will. But I've been just so busy the last couple of months. Gerry doesn't make things easy. He thinks we're back at college and wants to go out for two-hour lunches almost every day. On the days we don't, he wants to meet for drinks after work. It seems he's never in a hurry to get back to the office or go home." He waited for a reaction and not getting one continued, "Sometimes his dad will join us for lunch, and it becomes a real 'business meeting' at that point," stopping to raise his hands in the air on either side of his head with two fingers extended to emphasize.

"Anyway, I can't get away. And you know Wallace, he likes to eat," continued Michael. "You can't help but gain weight going out to lunch with him. Believe me I'm not trying to make excuses, but . . . do you really think I gained weight?"

He was clearly distressed by her comment.

Diana, trying to avoid a big overblown discussion, looked at him in the mirror and shrugged saying, "Just a little," as she continued to get herself ready.

Looking at her, he hesitated and picked up where he left off saying, "Wallace is so intense; a few martinis and he will not shut up. He wants to reminisce about how far they've come, how much further he wants to go, what we need to do to get there, and some of it I just don't agree with. Usually I sit there thinking all I want to do is to get the hell out of here and get back to work."

Michael looked to Diana who was busy checking herself in the mirror and continued, "I'm having some difficulty wrapping my head around what Tesler was doing in compliance before he jumped to Nationwide Mortgage. I've got to figure it out. Something just doesn't feel right." He said this with a sideway glance, searching for a reaction from Diana. She, however, focused more intently on her makeup, mumbling a nearly imperceptible reply that sounded like "ok."

"But anyway," he said, shaking his head, "I'll do it, start running again, once things settle down." He was now staring intently at himself in the mirror and talking more to himself than Diana, who had moved on to her lipstick. Stopping his nearly obsessive search for belly fat, he turned and exclaimed, "It's not just this new position, though. It's everything else that's going on in the industry. It's nuts. Hard to stay on top of things . . . you know?" He looked to her again for some sort of reaction. Without saying a word, she nodded her head in agreement and went back to the mirror as she finished applying her lipstick.

Michael stopped talking and put his coffee cup down on the white marble vanity, almost forgetting what he was saying, as he suddenly noticed that Diana had put back on a silken nightgown after her shower. As she leaned forward, the nightgown rode up her backside, exposing her round, firm bottom and a sheer red thong underneath. Michael leaned back and silently praised Diana with an unflinching stare of her ass. He then came up behind his wife, grabbing her butt with both of his hands in a playful, but hopeful, manner. She looked at him in one of the two large square vanity mirrors that hung over each sink, and instantly reacted.

"Michael, come on. I'm finishing my makeup," she protested, with a tone and smirk that said she could care less about how she looked at that moment.

It was all the encouragement he needed, and moving Diana's hair from her right shoulder, he began to kiss her neck, inhaling the scent of sweet perfume and body wash. She moaned and turned her head to the left further exposing her neck, hoping that he would continue. Diana's breathing quickened and grew heavier as he kissed her. Her skin tingled with every touch of his lips. His hands were all over her body as she closed her eyes, now willingly surrendering herself to him. Sensing Diana's desire, Michael quickly moved his hands underneath the nightgown around her hips and onto her waist, momentarily stopping on her hard, flat stomach.

Moving upward he began to caress her breasts and press himself against her. She eagerly attempted to drop the nightgown straps from her body as Michael dropped a hand and began to pull down her nightgown, while at the same time attempting to peel off her panties. He kissed her more passionately, as Diana could now feel his growing enthusiasm against her.

Unexpectedly, from down the hallway, came a faint cry of "Mommy," immediately followed by a louder and even clearer call of "Daddy." Of course, Christina picked this moment to wake up from her usual restful sleep. Michael tried to ignore her, thinking, *Shit not now*, as Diana promptly straightened up and pushed herself away from the vanity, quickly pulling up her straps one at a time to cover her exposed body. Michael continued to struggle against her, realizing the moment was fading fast.

Turning to face him Diana whispered, "Michael, stop," and tipping her head toward the bathroom door, shouted, "Mommy is coming honey."

As she began to move, he tried to grope her one last time, catching the bottom edge of her nightgown with the tips of his fingers, his frustration apparent. Diana scurried out of the bedroom down the hallway toward their daughter's room, her displeasure not as apparent, but present nonetheless.

Several moments later, Michael grabbed his cup, drank the remaining lukewarm coffee, and walked out of the bathroom down the hall to his daughter's room. He followed Diana to see what was going on with Christina and why she was up so early, today of all days. When he arrived at her room, Diana had their four-year-old daughter cradled in her arms who, when she saw Michael, screamed, "Daddy," and stretched out her arms toward him. Diana quickly handed her off.

"Good morning my darling, are you still sheepy?" he asked playfully, now forgetting about his own disappointment. "Do you want to come downstairs with Daddy and get some breakfast?"

Christina nodded her head, softly saying, "yes," as she buried her face onto Michael's shoulder. He carried her downstairs to the kitchen while Diana returned to the bathroom to finish getting herself ready for work.

———◆———

Diana, a senior auditor at the accounting firm of Updike, Miller, Rollen & Hazlet, LLP, loved her job. The work required long hours and by her own doing, early morning arrivals. Diana's dedication and her work ethic were the reasons why she was almost always the first out of bed and out of the house in the morning. Although the work was demanding, she couldn't wait to get to the office every day. Diana was one of those rare people who was very happy in her career choice and was extremely good at what she did. Working in Stamford, less than twenty minutes away from home, also made things a little easier for her when it came to a career and taking care of the home and her family.

After graduating with an accounting degree from Boston College, she had quickly landed a job in the company's audit department. This coming on the heels of a yearlong internship with the firm at its downtown Boston office. Diana's intellect, abilities, and strong work ethic had earned her recognition by one of the founding partners, Kelly Updike. She liked and respected him very much, and after working with him for only a brief time, she decided that a career in auditing would be a good fit for her. Kelly had sensed that Diana possessed a very analytical mind and inquisitive nature, and he believed these traits would help her become a very good accountant someday. The two became good friends as he reminded Diana of her own father, who she had lost to a massive heart attack during her senior year of college. She was touched by how kind everyone had been to her at the firm, especially Kelly, who was the only senior partner to attend the funeral. When the offer for an entry level accounting position came, Diana jumped at it. Six months later, the partners announced that Kelly would oversee the opening and operation of a small office in Connecticut. Diana quickly decided she would go along. So, just like that and much to the dismay of her mother, twenty-three-year-old Diana Caruso left Boston and her family behind to begin a new life, almost four hours away in Stamford, Connecticut.

It was nearly a year later when she met Michael Dolan one night at a local bar, an authentic Irish pub, one that she and her co-workers sometimes frequented. He was tall, handsome, and charming, as Diana felt an immediate attraction to him. Michael had just recently accepted a position in the legal department at a small Manhattan investment brokerage firm. A recent graduate from City College Law School, he and several friends had been out celebrating his new job that night. Michael was immediately drawn to Diana, the two groups of friends merging into one.

It was obvious, at least to Michael's former college roommate, Gerald Bender, that he and Diana were in a world all their own as soon as they met.

It came as no surprise to him when eight months later, Michael and Diana announced their engagement, the wedding taking place shortly afterward. The couple quickly settled in Norwalk, purchasing a house close to Michael's childhood home. The city, a mostly blue-collar town, was filled with the post–World War II tract home neighborhoods, containing small to moderately sized houses neatly stacked on quarter acre lots. In contrast, it was surrounded by many affluent communities with large McMansion type houses situated on sprawling estates, appointed with poolside cabanas that served as home to the hedge fund moguls, the Wall Street financiers, and the generally well-to-do. Norwalk was a fifty-minute train ride from New York City, making for a comfortable commute to the Franklin Family Fund investment firm offices in Manhattan where Michael had been recently hired to work on SEC regulatory and compliance matters.

———————◆———————

Almost seven years later, Michael Dolan was now rushing to get out of the shower, after having prepared and fed his daughter a French-toast breakfast. He quickly blew dry his thick black hair, shaved, and brushed his teeth while rinsing with mouthwash, obviously in a hurry. It was 6:50 a.m., and Diana had dressed Christina, getting her ready for school. She sat in the kitchen waiting for him to be done, anxious to leave for work.

He called downstairs to her, "Hon, I'm just finishing now. Can you wait a minute?"

"I got time," was her reply.

Michael quickly wiped clean his bathroom sink and the vanity. Going to the closet, he put on a pair of Calvin Klein khakis, a light blue dress shirt, a striped tie, and a sport jacket. His brown loafers were sitting on a shelf in the garage, although he thought it was probably not the best choice for footwear given the weather forecast. He walked downstairs into the kitchen where Diana sat with Christina, discussing a Disney movie that was coming out soon. She promised to take her next week, qualifying it with her standard, "As long as you're good for Papa."

The TV morning news was on, the CNBC host and guests were discussing the economy and the emerging banking crisis, which Michael paid little attention to.

It was 7:05 a.m. and Diana was anxious to get to work. She had a ten or eleven-hour day ahead of her before picking up Christina at Michael's dad's house in the early evening. With Michael now ready, Diana said her goodbyes with hugs and kisses, leaving for work and arriving at the office twenty minutes later. She would call Michael around 8:00 a.m. to confirm Christina's drop off at school, undoubtedly asking, as always, about Ms. Gina, the owner of Tiny Tikes Preschool. Diana would also check in with her father-in-law, Edwin Dolan, later in the afternoon to look in on her daughter, having made the decision almost two years earlier to keep her in preschool for half a day and have Eddy take care of her the rest of the time, until either she or Michael could pick up Christina after work.

Sitting at her desk, Diana briefly looked back on the morning and thought about what Michael had said about Bender Capital Lending but put it aside as her mind drifted to the more pleasant moment. *Had things gone a little further, I would have been late to work, well maybe not late, but later than usual.* Diana was never late for work. She giggled, saying to herself, "Well there are worse things, I suppose," as she typed in her computer's password, logging in for the day.

She smiled, still thinking about Michael and how deeply she loved him. She also thought about having another baby, thinking that it was time. She would mention it to Michael soon. Before she could give it more thought, Kelly Updike walked past her office, and abruptly stopping, he poked his head in the door and said, "Good morning Diana. Here already I see."

"Yes Kelly, just want to get an early start on the day," she said smiling.

He smiled back, "Well good, let's get together at eight and talk about the Biometrics audit."

"Absolutely, I've already sent you an email with the audit results." She thought there was no way he would have seen it yet. Diana worked on the email late and didn't send it out until just before midnight.

"Yes, I saw that last night," he said.

"Oh, ok. Did you get a chance to review the yearly and cumulative statements, the statement of sources, applications of funds?"

Politely interrupting, Kelly said, "Sorry . . . but yes, I skimmed through it all. But I want to look at everything in greater detail with you."

Diana was surprised that he had already reviewed the email and was that eager to discuss it. She assumed he wouldn't be ready until late morning or early afternoon. There would be no time now to set up the day's work schedule or speak with Michael following Christina's drop off. She also had two other audits her team was working on that needed attention. Diana would have to juggle her time and meet with Laura later, after her meeting with Kelly. She reluctantly shook her head yes, waiting for a reaction.

"Well good then, let's speak later," said Kelly. As he turned to leave he stopped, and twisting at the waist back in Diana's direction he asked, "By the way how is Michael?"

Diana again smiled and said, "He's good, really good. Thanks for asking."

CHAPTER THREE

AFTER Diana left the house, Michael finished cleaning the kitchen, swiftly putting the dishes into the dishwasher, and wiping down the counters with a damp dish towel.

All the while Christina sat patiently at the kitchen table, wondering, "Daddy why do you love mommy . . . do you like trees . . . why are they green . . . how is old is papa . . . can I have a puppy . . . why aren't you wearing shoes?"

Michael happily answered every question, avoiding only the subject of the puppy, while feverishly moving around the kitchen to quickly get out the door and on with the day. He took one last look around the house to ensure that everything was in its place and headed for the garage with Christina. She jumped into her car seat and Michael attempted to strap her in, but she insisted on doing it herself. Now driving away, he glanced in the rearview mirror, looking back at Christina and then the house. It was a small French colonial cape with grey shutters, wood-paned windows, and aged-copper accents above the white window and door trim. He thought Diana was right—this was the perfect home for them. It was quaint and full of character, a little different from most of the other homes in the neighborhood that consisted of a mixture of ranches, small colonials, and a few capes.

———◆———

The home was situated in a mature part of town, the houses older but well kept. It was the first and only house Michael and Diana saw, simply because Diana fell in love with it six weeks before the wedding. For her, there was no need to look at other houses, and with a promise of help from Eddy Dolan a day later, they put in an offer to buy it.

Forgoing a honeymoon, the young couple moved in three weeks after the wedding, living with Michael's father in his childhood home, temporarily sleeping in the tight and uncomfortable twin-sized bed of his youth. Despite making a few repairs and renovations to the house, the twenty-three hundred square-foot home had been in remarkable condition for its age. It was warm and inviting from the stone paver walkway leading to the light grey front door, into the small foyer, through the kitchen and family room, then through the French doors opening onto the New York style blue-slate stone patio. Michael thought Diana and their friend Karen, an interior designer, had done a fantastic job renovating and decorating the home, every detail thought out tastefully. He could not imagine it any other way now. He felt good, as he looked back on all the memories forged in the home over the past few years.

——————◆——————

Michael's trip down memory lane, as brief as it was, caused him to chuckle and lose focus. His drifting mind was suddenly jolted back to reality by Christina, who began squealing and waving her arms in excitement as they approached Tiny Tikes Preschool. It appeared that the thought of seeing Ms. Gina and her friends was a bit too much for her.

Laughing out loud, Michael cautioned, "Honey settle down we'll be there in a minute. I'm sure everyone will be happy to see you too."

Despite being startled, he smiled at the thought that Christina really enjoyed school that much, while also thinking it seemed only yesterday she had been born. The years had gone by quickly. Pulling into the small parking lot, he could see parents and children making their way into the school building that was constructed to give the appearance of a nineteenth century one room school house, complete with a steeple and bell atop a pitched roof. Standing at the school's front door were Ms. Gina and Mrs. Lena, who were diligently checking a list of student names, as each one entered. The school was small, no more than thirty-five students, and with a staff of five, including Ms. Gina, who lovingly cared for each of her students as if they were her own, Michael and Diana felt lucky to have found such an inviting and fostering environment for their daughter. Walking toward the school door, Michael noticed Ms. Gina smiling at them as they approached. Christina frantically waved her arms again, this time to say hello.

"Good Morning Christina," said Ms. Gina, as she scurried inside.

"Morning Gina, Morning Lena," said Michael.

"Good morning Michael," the two ladies said as they smiled at him.

It was almost eight, and Michael knew Diana would be calling soon. He hurried to the car and before he could drive away, his cell phone rang. As he expected, it was Diana. The call was a little earlier than usual. Picking up the phone and saying hello, she asked, "How's Christina? Did you drop her off yet?"

"She is fine, and she is already in class, probably involved in some sort of art project or something," he said.

Before he could say another word, Diana said, "Ok, good. Got to go."

Her abruptness was unusual as she normally would go on for a little while, but the brevity of the call was fine with him as he enjoyed this time alone in his car.

Michael pulled out of the parking lot into the morning traffic and drove the twenty-five minutes to his office in Greenwich, arriving there just before 8:30 a.m. Main Street was already busy that morning, and Tommy Williston was directing traffic, as big fluffy wet snow-flakes now began to swirl around him. The air was dank cold, not a good day to be outside of the patrol car for any amount of time. Even though Tommy was a respected twenty-three-year veteran of the police department, he was still occasionally assigned to traffic duty. A bitter cold and snowy February day like today made no difference.

Tommy, unfortunately, never rose within the ranks of the department like Eddy Dolan, who had retired as a detective, more than two years earlier. As a result, he was still occasionally assigned to duties that were normally reserved for younger officers. A good thing for Tommy, though, was he would soon get a promotion to patrol sergeant. He was ranked number one on the sergeant's list after scoring an eighty-eight on the civil servant exam. It looked like Sergeant Morris Wicker was going to retire in June, suddenly making a sergeant's position available. After many years of disappointments, it looked like it was now going to happen for Tommy, and both Eddy and Michael could not be happier.

Blowing his horn, Michael stuck his hand out of the car window in a wave as he slowly drove by Tommy, who acknowledged him with a tip of his head and flick of his hat. A longtime friend, Michael always remembered how he had been there for them when his mother had died and continued to be the many years since. He made his way to the office just around the next corner and parked his car in a designated space.

Walking into the lobby, he made a quick turn before the elevators and stopped in the first-floor cafeteria to grab a cup of coffee.

The Bender Capital Lending offices were located on the top floor of the Strauss Building, named for the family that owned the complex. With almost thirty employees in the Greenwich office and another sixty-five staff and loan originators in small offices throughout Connecticut, New York, and New Jersey, the company was a force in the subprime home mortgage lending industry, at least in the tri-state area. Bender Capital Lending was not in the same league as the big banks like Bank of America, Wells Fargo Home Loans, or Nationwide Mortgage Services. It was, however, very relevant in many urban areas, especially with lower to middle income consumers who were identified as subprime borrowers. This market segment consisted of people who could not obtain traditional home mortgage loans from their local community banks. As a result, they needed alternative sources for their home loan needs. Thanks to federal deregulation and the expansion of investment banking's reach into the consumer lending and finance markets, the subprime home loan business flourished. Bender Capital Lending quickly thrived as the market segment grew and took on new significance over the last dozen years.

Wallace Bender, CEO and Chairman of the Board, had started the company a little more than twelve years ago, after spending nearly twenty-six years with Chase Bank. "Wall," as he was known to his friends and family, had accepted an early retirement package from the company during a period of corporate downsizing and then used a portion of that money to open the first Bender Home Mortgage Broker office in Stamford, CT. Shortly after, Bender had opened a second and then a third office in Connecticut, later expanding into New York and New Jersey. Somewhere in the process, Bender had transitioned from a broker to direct lender, and now with eleven offices in three states, Bender Capital Lending accounted for a small but significant percentage of the local subprime loan market.

As Michael walked through the Bender offices, only a dozen people were already at work; Wallace Bender was one of them. Michael saw him leaning over his desk through the open door. *They're going to have to take him out in a stretcher one day. God, he's always here.* Wallace Bender was an imposing figure at six-foot-three, two hundred seventy pounds, and when he saw Michael, he straightened up and waved him over.

Michael corrected his path and nearly high-stepped into the office while taking a sip of coffee, almost spilling on himself.

"Michael, come on in. Shut the door and take a seat," he said, extending his large body and fat hand with some effort, while fading back into his chair. Michael leaned forward to grab it before sitting down himself.

"Good morning Wall. How are you today?"

"Fine . . . fine," he said with a gravelly voice that was getting lost in the layers of neck fat bulging outward from under his shirt collar. A yellow and green striped tie was working hard to keep the top shirt button from exploding and shooting across the room.

Directly to the point, he declared, "Gerald tells me that you're somewhat concerned about our internal audit process. What's the issue?"

Wallace peered at Michael and folded his arms in front of his large barrel chest waiting for a response. Michael thought, *Thanks Gerry, nothing like running to the old man, buddy*. He wondered if Gerry mentioned all the concerns they spoke about recently.

He started slowly, "Well it's not so much about the 'audit process' itself but the small number of audits conducted over the last three years. Originally, I looked back over this period to check the number and frequency, simply to use as a guide for myself going forward, and what I discovered was that Bill Tesler undertook only thirty-one audits in that time frame." Michael looked directly at Wallace and stopped, thinking there might be a reaction. There was none, so now picking up steam he continued. "That was less than two percent of the loans originated over the three-year period. And I was struck by that number because I believe it's much too low to be an effective due diligence tool. It should be around fifteen percent to be impactful or at least helpful." Michael paused. Wallace did not flinch, no response at all.

He went on, "I'm sure that I'm not telling you anything you don't already know but internal audits are designed to ensure the integrity of the process—from loan origination, underwriting, to loan closings, and the eventual sale of loans to our investors. Audits help to correct deficiencies in the way we do things, helps us avoid potential investor complaints and limit compliance issues down the line."

Michael hesitated, and looked to Wallace one more time for a reaction. Failing again to receive one, he said, "And while I'm on the subject of compliance, it appears that several red flagged banking department audits from all three state agencies were never completed.

Requests by examiners for additional information were not fully complied with or ignored entirely. It appears that no follow up occurred on our end or by any of the state agencies, and this —"

Wallace Bender put up his hand and cut him off. He was now about to speak, thought Michael. *Finally, he is going to say something.*

"Michael, the files you reviewed . . . did any of them exhibit any sign of fraud, any indication that someone did something wrong or that we failed to meet underwriting or regulatory standards? Anything that we should be concerned about?"

Michael was struck by the question. Clearing his throat, he responded, "Well no I can't determine the accuracy of the information at this point without a real investigation or complete audit with third party verification. It does appear that the few files we gave a cursory review to are in order, but only a small percentage of the loan files reviewed are fully documented loans. We have that supporting data, but the remainder are no document or no verification type loans that have no supporting or backup information, for the—"

Wallace again cut him off, anticipating the remainder of Michael's response. He retorted, "I know, I know, the reason being that our loan investors and banking regulations did not require it. But, if they don't require us to do something you would agree, wouldn't you, that we had no obligation to do it."

"Well yes, but it's the loose underwriting and regulatory standards, not to mention the real lack of regulatory oversight, that necessitates the audit process and begs for us to do more then what is expected or required," Michael exclaimed.

Wallace sat listening, seemingly interested now in what was being said. Michael, sensing that he had his attention, continued. "Although it looks like no one else cares about due diligence we, meaning the company, should care for our own sake." Wallace shifted in his chair again. Silent, but listening intently. "And as you know I've taken it upon myself to not only run compliance but to take on an almost General Counsel role to protect this company, the officers, board of directors, and even its employees from civil and potential criminal liability. I mean, I know you have Austin handling all the legal work for the company, but I feel an obligation. After all, Gerry hired me with my legal background in mind." He looked at Wallace, again no reaction. "And, I can only accomplish that by providing sound legal advice to ensure that we are in full compliance with all the regulatory requirements and obligations of the law," he said confidently. "Also, I need to make sure that we are not involved in any unethical, improper, or illegal business practices," Michael said dutifully.

Wallace thought for a moment, and said slowly, "Michael thank you for your concern and passion. I appreciate it, I really do. You have taken on more than what was expected of you, but this company has never received a serious consumer complaint." He paused, looking down as if deep in thought. Returning his gaze to Michael, he said, "As you know there have been no claims of any regulatory violations, nor have we been subject to any disciplinary action. I think Bill Tesler, although not a lawyer like yourself, did a very good job with compliance here. That is why Nationwide Mortgage grabbed him away from us. He was simply good at his job. Now you worked for him one or two months and I am sure he taught you some things, right?"

Michael wanted to say more like three or four months, but now unsure himself, he simply nodded his head in agreement as Wallace continued to talk. "So, let's forget about the past and concentrate on the present and our investor obligations. Let's also work to ensure our continued compliance with federal and state laws, ok?" He was now directing more than asking.

Staring at Michael he said, "Let's avoid allocating our somewhat limited resources to matters that are not relevant to our business moving forward and those things that are not expected or required of us by our loan investors and the regulatory agencies, because as far as I am concerned, it is not necessary. If regulators or the investors want it any other way, I am sure they will direct us to do otherwise, agreed?" Before Michael could answer Wallace noted, "Listen Michael you're doing a fantastic job in compliance, really, keep it up, and your legal analysis and advice is always welcomed."

Michael sat quietly for a moment, contemplating what he was being told and what was implied in the discussion. Then nodding his head in agreement, he said, "I will certainly focus our resources on what is relevant and appropriate, but I intend to speak my mind."

He was now in full lawyer mode, trying to be as noncommittal and vague as most attorneys are, but only because he did not fully agree with Wallace Bender's assessment of how he should run the compliance department. Michael preferred to be proactive not reactive, as Wallace was more than suggesting he should be.

"Ok good, well is there anything else?" Wallace gazed at Michael, trying to gauge his reaction.

Seizing on the opportunity to get a few things off his chest, Michael straightened and said, "Well yes, I am concerned about the percentage of high-risk loans that are in our loan portfolio."

Wallace, who now appeared genuinely surprised, looked at him and asked, "Ok, so what are you thinking?"

"Our loan portfolio is about eighty percent 'no documentation' and 'limited documentation' type loans, putting this company at a higher risk for fraud, loan defaults, investor loan buy-backs, and violations of predatory lending laws, as well as federal and state banking laws." Taking a breath, he added, "And I'm sure we could run into a multitude of other issues that I haven't even thought of yet. All of which, subjects the company, at the very least, to loan repurchases, like I said before, or even worse, civil and criminal liability."

Wallace shifted in his seat now looking concerned, "Ok, what are you suggesting Michael?"

"We need to rethink the types of loans the company is willing to make and the type of borrowers the loans are being made to. We need to better balance our loan portfolio . . . and we need to better consider the type and extent of risk the company is willing to take on—maybe, before it's too late and the company's bottom line is hurt or worse."

Looking at his boss, who had shifted uncomfortably in his chair, Michael went on, "Listen, I just think we might be taking on more risk than the company can handle, that's all I'm saying. It's a risk assessment analysis that we need to make, and when I say *we*, I mean me, you, and Gerry. It may be something that you get the Bender Board of Directors involved in for guidance, or at the very least to prevent any criticism of you down the line."

Wallace said nothing and continued to stare at Michael.

"I mean didn't Bill ever discuss this with you?"

Wallace sat pondering what he was just told, and avoiding the last question said, "Michael you're making some very good points, but isn't this what Bender Capital Lending does, take on high-risk borrowers and loans? It's the market segment we chose to be in. Right?" He asked this rhetorically and looked at Michael very curiously as if to say, *No kidding, you idiot.*

Before Michael could react, Wallace said, "Listen I need to consider all of this, as you suggested. I will talk to Gerald about maybe tightening underwriting standards and practices as well as reassessing our loan programs."

He stared at Michael looking for a reaction, who now remained silent. Wallace reluctantly continued, "And I think you're right; you need to be a part of any discussion. Your legal counsel and input would be invaluable. Maybe I will raise it with the Board at our next meeting. Thank you for bringing this to my attention, Michael."

"You're welcome," said Michael, uncertain where Wallace was heading with this.

"Now if there isn't anything else?"

"No," said Michael, as he got up to leave.

"Michael, hold on for a second."

"Yes sir," he said snapping to attention.

Hesitating, Wallace said, "Keep me in the loop on what you're doing in compliance, and don't discuss this with anyone." Picking up the phone he then turned his attention to the computer monitor on his desk, failing to say another word.

Michael was left standing there not knowing what to say or do. It took a few moments for him to refocus. Walking out of the office, he took an unusually large gulp from his coffee cup, throwing the empty container in a basket near one of the desks in the area known as the bullpen. The office was now busy with most of the staff beginning to settle into their routines for the day. Michael made his way through the heart of the work area passing underwriters, processors, and support staff, hurrying to his office to shake off the uncomfortable start of the day.

His secretary, Gillian, was also just arriving at her desk as Michael walked toward his office. "Good morning, Gilly. What a day," he decreed sarcastically.

She responded, "Good morning. Can I get you anything?" She wondered what he meant by the comment. She asked again, "Something from the cafeteria?"

Michael thought about another cup of coffee. He already had three this morning and was feeling a little jittery. He wasn't sure if it was the coffee doing it or the discussion he just had with Wallace Bender. "Thanks Gilly, no nothing," he said as he walked around her and went into his office, closing the door behind him.

Sitting at his desk, Michael played the conversation over again in his mind asking himself, *Was Wallace Bender telling him to back off? Was he reading him correctly, or was he just paying him lip service?* He wasn't sure. He sat for a few more minutes before putting the thought aside, for now anyway—too much work to do. Gerry would be stopping by his office later, like he did every morning, to unintentionally annoy him. It could wait, Michael thought, but he knew that sooner or later he would have to deal with these issues and Wallace. Sitting at his desk, he began working on the day's tasks, checking his computer for emails, and looking over the calendar. He was looking at the loans in progress and closed file reports and began to wonder again about audits moving forward, thinking he needed to do something. Just then Gerry burst into the office, startling him.

"Jesus, what the fuck Gerry."

"What's the matter did I catch you with your pants down?" Gerry said with a smile on his face.

"Grow up, you idiot," he said laughing.

"Hey, what are we doing for lunch today?"

"Not sure. Call me later," said Michael. "Now get out of here. I got work to do."

Gerry left the room as abruptly as he entered it. Michael glanced at his watch, it was now 9:10 a.m. He thought about what he needed to accomplish for the day and found himself thinking about lunch with Gerry and maybe Wallace. He was not looking forward to it. The notion was causing his head to spin. Turning his thoughts to Diana, he wondered how her day was turning out. He wasn't quite sure if he should speak to her about this morning's conversation with Wallace. He quickly decided not to, simply because it would only get her worried, and probably over nothing.

The discussion now still fresh in his mind, Michael began to type an email to his staff. Once finished, he read it several times before adding Wallace and Gerry to the recipients list. Hesitating to send it, he moved the email to his draft folder. He then called out to Gillian who was standing just outside his office door, speaking with Gerry's assistant, Joan.

"Gilly if you don't mind can you grab me that cup of coffee?"

Gazing at the door, somewhat startled and unsure what he had said, she opened his door and asked, "Michael did you want something?"

"Coffee, please," he sighed.

"Right away."

Michael pushed back in his seat, again weighing in his mind the conversation with Wallace, especially what he said about Bill Tesler. *Did he really leave on his own or was he forced out?* Michael wasn't sure, but his departure seemed odd and calculated. *Is Wallace hiding something?* Just then Gillian came in with his coffee. *Good that was quick.*

"Oh great, thank you," he exclaimed. Michael grabbed the container and took a drink, taking the coffee down as slowly as possible to savor every drop. The cafeteria's blended roast was not as tasteful as the coffee at home, but it was darker and served the purpose. He took another sip and felt his adrenaline kick back in. *Ok, that was just what I needed.*

CHAPTER FOUR

C ARTER Atkins walked out of his small office, closing the door behind him. His name was painted in stark white letters along with his title, semicircle style on the door's frosted glass. He had with him a handful of complaints received in the Office of the Attorney General, consumer affairs division, about Bender Capital Lending, all within the past two months. He was on his way upstairs to see the New Jersey attorney general, Richard Banks, when his secretary, who, in her twenty years in the AG office thought she never had a better boss, called out to him.

"Carter your wife is on the line, should I tell her you're out?"

Annoyed he said, "No tell her to hold on." This was the third time she called this morning. Turning back, he asked, "Kim what line?"

"Line 103," she said amused, as Carter ran into his office, slamming the door behind him, the glass rattling slightly.

Picking up the phone he said, "Yea babe. What's up?"

"Well hello to you too," responded Stephanie Atkins.

"Sorry, but I'm in a bit of a rush, on my way upstairs to speak with Richard."

"That's ok. How is the day otherwise?" she asked.

The same as before when we talked an hour earlier, dear Lord. "It's good, usual stuff," he said exasperated.

Almost before Carter spoke the last word, Stephanie began talking as if she was shot out of a cannon, "Well, let me just tell you that CJ mixed it up with another little boy at preschool today and got a 'timeout' for refusing to share, and more than that shoving the other child." Before Carter could respond, she continued, "The school called to let me know. So, we need to talk to CJ when you get home and explain to him that he needs to play nice and share with the other children, and no pushing."

"Ok, so we will talk to him," said Carter, somewhat annoyed with his wife for calling him with this when it could just have waited until he got home tonight.

"Anything else?" he asked, as he finally sat down at his desk, expecting more.

"No, I just thought you should know. Babe, any idea what you want for dinner?"

"Not sure, anything you want to make will be fine. What are you up to now?"

"I just had coffee with Wendy and Savanna, and I'm heading to the mall to do a little shopping. I'll pick up CJ in a couple of hours, give him a snack, and put him down for a nap . . . ."

My God, Carter thought, tuning her out as she continued talking. *She really needs a part time job or something.* Young Carter was now almost four and Stephanie hadn't gone back to work after his birth, not one day. He thought it was now time. They had no plans to have another child and CJ spent more than half the day in preschool, getting out at 3:00 p.m. She could at the very least work part time. His mother lived with them, so between the two of them CJ would be well taken care of. He would talk to her tonight he said to himself, as he began to listen to her again. He tried to pick up on what she was going on about, but Stephanie abruptly said, "Love you, bye." Before he could respond she hung up. *Why does she call me with this stuff?* She had a habit of calling four to five times a day, and sometimes more. Occasionally, Kim would deflect Stephanie's calls and tell her that Carter was in a meeting. She had a lot of practice at deflecting, although she would always ask if it was urgent or whether she should interrupt. Stephanie would always say no. Hanging up the phone, Carter was now back on track and, once again, heading for the Attorney General's office.

———◆———

Carter Atkins, a deputy assistant attorney general in the Office of the New Jersey Attorney General, started life in one of the toughest neighborhoods of Philadelphia, the seedy west side of the city that led many down a path to self-destruction. Mabel Atkins knew that staying was not an option. She didn't want her son to become another statistic that would leave him dead and her heartbroken. So, when Carter was nine, he and his mother packed their belongings into the back of a pickup truck and moved to Trenton New Jersey, to live with Mabel's sister. Carter, a bright boy and always a good student, received a scholarship to St. Peter's University in Jersey City. Mabel, a long time municipal employee for the City of Trenton, saved enough money to help send Carter to Rutgers Law in Newark to fulfill not only his dream but her own. With a lot of hard work, some luck, and student loans, Carter got his law degree. With the help of his pastor and a state representative, he quickly landed a position as an assistant AG with the New Jersey Attorney General's Office, and now thirteen years later he was about to take on the most challenging, and maybe the most important, case of his career. Although, he didn't know it at the time. Arriving shortly before noon at the office of the Attorney General, he sat waiting to be announced for a brief audience.

————◆————

Richard Banks, like most men in his position, was smart, educated, politically connected, and overly ambitious. He had been the New Jersey State attorney general for five years when his friend, Thomas Reeves, was elected governor and took office a few months earlier. Banks and Reeves attended Princeton University together more than thirty years ago, remaining not only friends but strong political allies. Both were stout Republicans serving in the state legislature together for many years, holding very similar political beliefs. They were tough on crime, believed in smaller government, wanted fiscal responsibility, and both were for more military spending. They each had their eye on bigger and better things, maybe even the presidency of the United States, yet each had a different plan on getting there. While Reeves was concerned about serving the public good, Banks was more concerned about serving his own good, mainly focused on his image and what was best for his political career, instead of what was good for the people of the state of New Jersey. His own self-interest is what drove him. Surprisingly, he was not motivated by money simply because he had plenty of it, having married Beatrice Goodwin, the only child of Frank and Doris Goodwin. The Goodwins were an old and wealthy New Jersey family whose roots went back to the early 1900's. They enjoyed generations of good fortune and, as a result, Bea was the heir to a small fortune. The Goodwins had old money, the best kind as far as Banks was concerned, because it came with social status and privileges. The inherited money afforded Banks many luxuries in life, the best of which was the luxury to be extraordinarily smug. He was now considering a run for the United States Senate and needed something to thrust him into the national spotlight. Little did he know that the perfect opportunity was about to present itself.

————◆————

As Richard Banks began to get up from his very large and worn desk, the phone rang. His secretary, Judith, announced that Deputy Assistant Attorney General Carter Atkins was there to see him.

"Tell him to come in," said Banks. A few moments later, Carter Atkins, one of the office's six deputies and thirty-eight assistant AGs walked into the room.

"Richard, how are you?" he asked, in a way that said he really didn't care. He knew Banks was a political animal only here to fulfill his own agenda and satisfy his aspirations. *Thank goodness for the staff of assistant AGs and investigators that did all the grunt work and really cared,* thought Carter.

"I am great, how are you?" he said smugly. "What you got," he asked, getting right to the point. Banks, full of his own self-importance, had no time to waste. Looking down on his desk, his thinning hair was exposed and apparent to Carter. Waiting, Banks began adjusting a few papers sitting atop his computer keyboard, almost ignoring Carter. He wanted to get through this quickly, whatever *this* was, so he could be on his way to his lunch appointment with the governor.

Carter excitedly blurted out, "I think we have something significant developing. I have with me nine complaints received over the last, maybe two months, in our division. The complaints have a common thread in that they are from residents in the Jersey City area. They involve a minority class of people, Hispanic and Afro-American mostly. All the complaints are related to home mortgages, most of the complainants' homes are in foreclosure, and, get this, all the loans originated from Bender Capital Lending." Banks looked up. Carter now had his attention.

Pausing a moment for effect, he continued. "I also cross referenced with the banking department and it received three complaints, and then I called a friend in the New York Attorney General's Office, who told me they have four similar complaints against Bender. The company has eleven offices in New York, Connecticut and New Jersey, it mainly deals with subprime loans, and most of them are for minority borrowers who are living in or near urban areas." He looked at Banks who was now looking directly at him. He had the entirety of his attention.

"Now we haven't moved on this and it sounds like the New York AG hasn't either, but with what is going on, you know, in the banking and financial services industry these days, this could be really significant." Hesitating again, he asked, "So, what do you think?"

Banks was thinking long and hard, as the wheels in his head were spinning. He realized this had the potential for an investigation on a very timely and developing matter, one that could result in substantial press exposure. It would give Banks the media recognition he craved. If he moved fast, he would have a jump on the New York and Connecticut AGs and every other attorney general in the country who might be facing similar issues. If he struck first, the other state attorney generals would have to fall in line behind him, if only to appear to be working toward a common goal. Banks thought they would have no choice but to defer to him as the lead to avoid looking petty. He was now getting excited at the prospect.

Carter asked again with even more conviction, "Richard, so what do you think?"

Banks, who had returned his gaze down at his desk as he thought about what Carter had delivered to him, picked up his head and turned to him saying, "Let's get moving on this immediately. Make this the office priority. We need to use all the resources we have and get the investigators out interviewing people today. Get the assistants working on the potential legal claims and thinking about a complaint. Coordinate with the banking department and advise the commissioner that this office will take the lead."

He stopped, "Wait don't call; I'll call the commissioner after my lunch date today with the governor so hold off there. As soon as I speak with him you should speak with the auditors in the banking department about auditing the Bender loan files . . . wait, delay that order too. Let me think on how to best handle their role. By the way, how many Bender offices are there in Jersey?" he asked.

Carter shot back, "Three offices—Jersey City, Trenton, and one in Newark."

"Ok, Carter take the lead on this and I want this to happen fast so let's meet tomorrow morning at 8:30 a.m. with the assistants and investigators to discuss progress and a game plan to move forward. I want this in suit no later than three days. You got it?" Banks was now more than excited. His mind was racing trying to take in all the possibilities this opportunity might create for his career.

Carter responded, "I'm on it." He then questioned, "You said three days?"

"Maybe sooner," Banks replied.

In a soft even tone Banks said, "Excellent work Carter. We need to kick ass on this, and quickly. Don't let me down." He walked out of the office heading toward the elevators.

Carter, walking behind him, was pleasantly surprised by the newly found passion Banks was displaying. He enthusiastically said, "Don't worry I won't."

"Good I'm counting on you," said Banks, as he got on the elevator.

Carter watched as the doors closed and Banks disappeared behind them. *Maybe he does really care*, thought Carter, suddenly realizing he should have gotten on the elevator with him. Carter pressed the button and waited. He needed to call Stephanie and let her know he wouldn't be home at 5:30 p.m., as usual. No doubt, they were going to be at the office late. Just then the elevator doors opened and as he stepped in, he instinctively began assessing, pondering first steps and next moves in the case that he knew would soon propel the Office of the New Jersey Attorney General into the national spotlight.

CHAPTER FIVE

I T was 8:00 a.m. and Richard Banks was in the office unusually early. He sat at the antique desk inherited by his wife, inquisitively peering through the bifocal lenses atop his crooked nose at Carter's preliminary report of the Bender Capital Lending investigation. He leaned back in the worn leather rocker, stretching his lanky frame, his balding head down, chin tucked into his chest as he continued to stare at the memorandum in his lap. He looked unkempt in an ill-fitting, shabby suit, too self-absorbed to worry about his physical appearance or to take notice of what others said about him. He paid attention, instead, to the army of pollsters he retained to tell him whether he would be the next senator for the state of New Jersey. Based on the data they had been collecting for months, the numbers thus far had him close, the best they could say was maybe. This investigation and what he did with it, he thought, should change that and ensure a victory. He was eager to move on this quickly, and he instinctively knew how to work the press to his every advantage and further his personal objective of making his way to the United States Senate. Banks would do what was best for Banks. There would be no doubt about that.

He finished reading the confidential memorandum and thought Carter did a decent job. The investigators had been out all day and into the early evening interviewing all the complainants. The assistants met with them the night before to review their notes, discuss the claims, prepare written witness statements, and consider the common elements of each individual complaint. Carter Atkins and a few others remained until after midnight to consider the civil claims and injunctive action the office might take on behalf of each complainant, and for the benefit of all the state's consumers, the AG's office existed to protect.

Banks put down the memo saying out loud to himself, "After all it's the attorney general who is entrusted with the cause of the public good and the protection of the state's citizens." He chuckled.

He said it aloud only because he wanted to hear how it sounded. *That's what I'll be saying at the press conference tomorrow, anyway. They'll eat it up, no doubt believing my selfless altruistic bullshit for sure.* Banks smiled and uncharacteristically did a fist pump in the air above his head.

Carter Atkins strolled into the office at 8:10 a.m., a bit earlier than usual. He was exhausted but eager to start the day. He had reserved the *William Livingston conference room*, named after the state's first governor, for the morning's assembly. Carter had twenty minutes before his meeting with Banks, thinking he had plenty of time to stop at his office, gather paperwork, and pour himself a cup coffee before the morning's scheduled event. Doing so, he headed for the conference room. Arriving five minutes later, he was surprised to see that Banks was already seated at the head of the very large mahogany conference table. There were sixteen black leather chairs around it, waiting to be filled by the staff. They would soon filter in as 8:30 a.m. approached. *Sweet Jesus*, Carter thought, *what's he doing here so early?* He was obviously caught off-guard by Banks' presence and early arrival. Seeing the look on Carter's face, Banks sensed his surprise and was amused. Now wanting to goad Carter a little, Banks said jovially, "Good morning Carter. How are you this fine morning?"

He is unusually chipper. What has gotten into him? Carter immediately responded, "I am good, how are you, sir?"

"I'm doing great, just great," Banks gleefully replied, maintaining his cheerful tone. "Looking forward to seeing what you put together for me this morning. I read the memo, good stuff, really good stuff," he continued excitedly.

Carter walked around Banks and sat to his right, his back against the windows, facing the conference room door. Both men quietly sat there and watched as the staff began to filter into the room. Once the table was full, the unlucky few who came in just before 8:30 a.m., stood against the wall facing Banks and Carter.

Richard Banks began to speak, as his secretary dashed into the room with a cup of coffee, leaning down low at an attempt to remain invisible. As she placed the cup in front of him, Banks turned to her and said, "Thank you Judith." She smiled and hurried out, shutting the conference room door behind her.

He started again, "I want to thank you for being here this morning and for what looks like a fair amount of hard work that was put in all day yesterday and into the late hours of the night. I also want to thank

Carter Atkins for calling this matter to my attention and for taking a lead role in this investigation and the civil action to come." He now turned his attention to his deputy and noted, "I have read your memorandum Carter . . . and so let's just get started. Why don't you summarize what we have so far?"

Carter nodded and began, "Well, as you all know this office and the banking department have recently received a dozen complaints concerning Bender Capital Lending. A source in the New York AG office tells me that it received several complaints against Bender as well. I have not confirmed whether any complaints have been filed with the New York Banking Department. I have not had any contact with the Connecticut AG office, and I am unaware if it received similar complaints. We know that Bender operates eleven offices throughout the three states, and its corporate office is in Greenwich CT. Bender is a licensed broker and lender in each state, dealing mainly in the subprime-lending market. As you know this market segment is now experiencing an unusual and extremely high loan default rate that is trending toward what could be epic property foreclosure numbers. If this market segment collapses as it is now being reported and industry insiders are now predicting the economic impact could be devastating."

"Wow," shrieked one of the younger assistants loudly. Realizing the inappropriateness of the outburst she quickly recoiled saying, "Oh sorry. Didn't mean to interrupt."

Ignoring the apology, Carter glared at her as she put her head down unable to manage the stare. He picked up where he left off, saying, "Bender is a small player in comparison to some of the larger banks and financial institutions. However, it has a significant presence in our area. Bender it seems has received an unusually high number of complaints and most of them stem from its Jersey City office. They appear to also involve one particular loan officer named, Carlos Perron. It is not to say that we don't have complaints from the other Jersey offices, but the complaints coming out of Hoboken seem to have a commonality and distinctive fact pattern completely different than the complaints emanating from other offices."

He paused to take a sip of coffee and then continued, "It seems that most of the complainants are Hispanic and Afro-American. They received what is known as 'no documentation' type loans that require no supporting documents or verification of information contained on the loan applications. These loans are typically adjustable rate mortgages that start with an artificially low interest rate of usually three, four or five percent, which is extremely good for these type of borrowers, who usually have poor credit, no or little down payment money . . . someone the banks typically consider a real risk." He looked at the staff for a reaction or questions. *Nothing yet. Good.* It seemed they were all with him, including Banks who sat and listened intently.

Carter continued, "The rate then adjusts anywhere from two to four percent every year after an initial one or two-year fixed-rate period. Now the borrowers in these cases report that the new mortgage payments are so high, it's impossible to pay. It's also reported that the income, employment, or other information on the loan applications are not accurate. The false reporting of income in some instances exceed the borrower's real income by more than fifty percent and sometimes as high as one hundred percent. It seems that the combination of the false information on the loan applications and the predatory loan products, Perron steered borrowers into was a recipe for disaster."

He again hesitated to allow what was said to sink in with the staff and Banks. The room was silent for a few moments when suddenly the door opened and in came Ralph Lagnese, the Banking Department Commissioner.

He looked at Banks and said, "Richard sorry I'm late."

"No worry come on in. Someone make way for the commissioner," Banks ordered.

One of the assistants, Janet Sung, seated directly across from Carter and next to Banks stood up and said, "Commissioner please have a seat." Immediately one of the investigators offered her his seat and he moved to the wall as she sat down in his place.

Banks announced, "Ralph, Carter Atkins from the consumer affairs division was just discussing the claims made against Bender. Carter, please continue."

He paused, shuffled through the papers in front of him, and then started speaking again.

"As I was saying, the complainants' income is falsified on the application and in almost every instance, thus far anyway, it appears at the insistence of this loan officer, Perron. The only excuse they offered was that Perron told them it would be alright and not to worry. It seems that they had such great trust in him, that a reassuring word was enough for them to lie on the application and to take out a loan that they should have known would be impossible to repay over time."

He paused and then said, "I'd like to add that Frank, Will, Tony, and Mike went out and spoke with all the current complainants and other witnesses, spending hours with them to develop this picture. So, guys, thanks for that hard work."

As Carter was about to begin speaking again. Richard Banks interjected. "Yes, gentlemen thank you. Excellent work, really." Carter, making another attempt to speak, was interrupted again by Banks, "Carter why don't we speed things up, so we can discuss our next steps." He was now becoming impatient and wanted to get to what was most important—the action the office was about to take that would make him look good.

Carter said, "Right. Well it also seems that most of the complainants know of others who have had similar experiences but who haven't filed any type of claim. We are going to follow up with those individuals today. It also seems that in many of the cases, Perron is somehow involved in acquiring the property, securing a release of the loan, and in some instances stopping a foreclosure. Then he manages to sell the property, presumably for a profit. We are still looking into that part and will be checking the County Clerk's Office. We need to go through the land records over the past three or four years in more detail to figure out exactly what Perron's role or interest was in acquiring the properties from these individuals. Tony and Will I think you are going to be handling that, right?"

Tony acknowledged Carter by nodding his head and raising a finger in the air, saying simply, "Absolutely."

"Ok, great let me know how that goes," said Carter.

Tony responded, "Will do, I'll have that information in about a week or so."

Banks jumped in and said, "Tony thanks that would be great, but let's get that done sooner rather than later. How about three days." He was not asking; he was telling. "I think we should also check court records for foreclosure claims involving Bender loans. Tony handle that too, ok."

Tony said, "I will get on it and have more answers in a couple of days."

"That's great Tony thank you," said Banks. He then added, "Remember no more than three days. Ok Tony?"

"Yes sir, will do," he said shooting a glance at Will Sumpter.

Carter looked at Banks and thought, *Richard is really engaging, nice to see for a change.* Normally, he is not this involved and usually gives no or very little input at this stage of an investigation.

Carter turned to Banks and asked, "Ok, but how do we treat the individuals who knew the information on the loan applications was false? Discussing this last night, we concluded that these people are co-conspirators in all of this and need to be held accountable to some degree for their actions. Richard what do think?"

Banks thought for a moment and said, "No." Pausing, he thought about it a little more and then continued. "Carter, we can't do that. These people are victims in all of this. They were seduced by a fast-talking con artist. They placed their misguided trust in him and were simply taken advantage of by this person. It seems most, if not all, of these people have a limited education, are lower income blue collar working stiffs and to vilify them would be wrong."

Carter shifted in his seat uncomfortably and looked at Banks wide eyed. He was pleasantly surprised by his display of empathy, although not completely in agreement with his assessment. Carter believed some of these people knew exactly what they were doing and, as such, should be held accountable. Despite his feelings, he sat there quietly and shook his head in agreement. He believed there was no other option at this point, otherwise he ran the risk of looking cold hearted.

Banks was not stupid, he instinctively knew that it was important for him to have a victim in all of this. The people of New Jersey needed to see him championing their worthy cause. Thy needed to believe that he was protecting them from the fraudulent and predatory lending practices taking place in their state for this to work to his benefit. He knew, most importantly for him, that without a victim he would not get the press coverage he craved and the public sentiment he would need to launch his campaign for the United States Senate.

Growing more impatient Banks thought, *This is just moving too slow*, and now returning to the "old Banks," he took control of the meeting saying, "People listen up this is what we need to do . . . and, oh thank you Carter, I'll take over from here . . . listen we need to get moving on a complaint . . . I want it on my desk by five o'clock and I want it served on defendants first thing tomorrow morning. By the way, who are the Bender Capital Lending officers?" Banks asked abruptly.

Carter sifted through the paperwork in front of him and pulling a page from the pile said, "Wallace Bender, CEO, Gerald Bender, VP of Underwriting and Operations, and Michael Dolan, CCO, as per the Connecticut and New Jersey Secretary of State filings, anyway."

"Ok, confirm that and name them individually along with the company in the complaint and don't forget that loan officer," said Banks, moving quickly now. "Obviously, I will be named as the plaintiff on behalf of the State, but on this one we are also naming Ralph Lagnese as co-plaintiff on behalf of the banking department. Let's allege all the usual, civil fraud, civil conspiracy to defraud, violations of state consumer protection laws and the applicable banking laws . . . regulations. Ralph your office will provide support on that one . . . and let's ask for declaratory and injunctive relief . . . Carter am I missing anything?"

Carter caught off guard fumbled for a moment and said, "No, I don't think so. But Richard this is moving fast don't you think we need to do a little more work on this before filing a complaint."

"Carter, I know you would like more time on this one, but we need to get ahead of it before more of our citizens fall victim to what Bender is doing. Anyway, we can always amend the complaint later as we gain more clarity. The important thing now is to put an end to this, don't you agree?" Looking him dead in the eyes Banks knew he had him. Carter had no choice but to agree.

Banks continued, "You are going to get support from the banking department auditors who will be going through the Bender files once the complaint is served, from there you can make amendments based on their findings. This is an important matter that needs our highest priority and I want this served on all defendants first thing in the morning . . . and by the way I am holding a press conference at noon tomorrow. Carter, I want you and the other deputy assistant there with the commissioner and myself."

Carter nodded his head in agreement and looked over to Janet Sung. She acknowledged the look with a nod of her own and began thinking about what to wear for the cameras. Banks was thinking the same thing. He was now ahead of everyone and moving fast, already speaking to his press secretary, Lanny Nardone, who was working on story and image for tomorrow. She was preparing to line up all the local coverage she could get during the noon time news cycle and would reach out to the network and cable stations early this evening to arrange for more news coverage there, as well. Banks wanted maximum exposure and with the type of attention he was expecting tomorrow, Banks would be widely recognized as the first government official to have acted on the now looming financial crisis.

He would beat even the federal government to the punch, so to speak, which, to this point, had failed to act all together, despite all the signs pointing toward a systemic breakdown of the banking and financial services sectors, not to mention a complete failure of governmental regulation and oversight. As such, Banks was confident that he would also make it into the evening news cycle and the nightly cable coverage. He relied on Lanny to make it happen. She was good, and that is why he personally paid her more money, above and beyond her state press liaison salary. *A good press secretary was worth his or her weight in gold*, Banks thought, and he had the best.

Following the noon press conference, he planned to reach out to his friend, Jim Harrison, United States senator from Pennsylvania and chairman of the Senate Banking Committee, to ask his opinion on how to best spin this. He knew that Harrison would give him good advice; he always did. They had been friends for many years and had moved in the same social circles thanks, in part, to their wives who were even closer. For now, Banks was feeling good about how things were progressing. He was looking forward to reading the complaint later today.

Carter headed to his office when the meeting broke with a few assistants and investigators to discuss drafting the complaint and the best way to effectuate service on the defendants. Banks returned to his office and realized he forgot one thing, calling Carter with one last instruction.

Carter Atkins hung up the phone and wondered, *Sensational, ok. How the hell do I do that?*

CHAPTER SIX

STARING at the screen, Janet Sung sat hunched at her computer reading the complaint again, this time making only minor changes as she scrolled through the pages. It looked good, and it was substantial. It contained forty-eight counts, and it was sensational, just like Banks ordered. Janet thought not only was it compelling, it was sexy and salacious, and Carter really outdid himself on this one. She printed a copy, saying to herself *It's always best to edit from a hard copy.* The fifty-five-page complaint rolled out of the printer slowly. Janet grabbed the pages one at a time and began to make more edits before the last pages printed. It was now 4:00 p.m., and Carter had been in the office with her when he decided to take a draft to Banks early. They were both proud of the work product and Carter wanted to get his opinion on the preliminary complaint as soon as possible. This way they could finalize it and have Banks sign the complaint before he left for the night. Carter, as lead attorney, would also sign it just below the attorney general's signature. Once finalized, the staff was left only to make copies. Janet and Carter would double check each one, ensuring that each copy of the complaint was complete.

Carter would then arrange for service of process upon the defendants. His plan was for Mike Wilson, a senior investigator in the office, to meet Connecticut State Marshal, Wilbert Hanson, in Greenwich with an original and numerous copies of the complaint at 8:00 a.m. The marshal would certify the copies and make an in-hand service on the Connecticut defendants as each one arrived at the Bender Capital Lending office that morning. He arranged for personal service to be made on Perron at his house at the same time. By 9:01 a.m., the company itself will have been served through the Office of the New Jersey Secretary of State, pursuant to state law. Service on the individual defendants was the most important and difficult part of the process, and Carter knew this had to be done right. Timing was everything, the AG had said. Service needed to be complete before the noontime press conference. He told Carter that he did not want to find himself in a position where one or more of the parties hadn't been served when he announced the lawsuit. Carter assured Banks that this would not happen. He prayed they could pull it off without a glitch.

Banks sat with the complaint in one hand and pen in the other, at times nervously biting on the cap as he thought about changes. He flipped through the pages as Carter anxiously waited for feedback. Twenty minutes later Banks was done reading and marking up the document. He looked up at Carter, past the glasses sitting on the tip of his nose and said, "This is good, very well done."

Carter, who had been sitting erect, leaned forward and let out a sigh of relief, saying, "Thank you. I did get a lot of help with it from the other assistants, Janet especially."

"I made some minor changes so look them over and incorporate the edits into the final draft. When you're done bring it back up to me for my signature and let's get it ready to go."

Carter took the complaint back to Janet's office where she was waiting to incorporate Bank's revisions. Reading his comments, she realized that most of his suggestions had already been taken care of by her during the last edit. The few remaining changes were made and with the complaint's edits now complete, it was ready for signatures. After going back upstairs to Banks to be signed, it was then copied and stapled. It was all set to go. Mike Wilson took one original and eight copies home with him. He planned on leaving his house at 5:00 a.m. for the drive out to Connecticut. Carter and Janet were the last to leave the office that night at 11:00 p.m., exhausted but satisfied in their accomplishment. Bender Capital Lending would soon feel the wrath of the New Jersey Attorney General's Office.

Arriving home that night the first thing Carter did was to grab a bottle of bourbon from the bar cart in the living room. He poured the whiskey into a tumbler glass filled with ice and began to relax while sitting in the dark. He thought about tomorrow's press conference and wondered whether the complaint was the best it could be. He believed it was and everyone had said so, but maybe there was more he could have done. He shook off the doubts he was suddenly having. Stephanie Atkins, seeing her husband sitting in the dark, announced she would go in and speak to him, when Mabel stopped her. His mom knew it was better not to disturb Carter with the day's trivial news. She would put a dish in the oven for her son, so he could eat later, after he was done unwinding.

It was almost 8:00 a.m., the next morning as Mike Wilson sat in the Greenwich Diner waiting for Marshal Hanson. He was getting worried when at 8:15 a.m., the marshal hadn't arrived yet. Wilson said to himself, "I hope this guy is going to show." He thought about calling Carter Atkins but decided to wait a little longer. Just then a burly and bearded Hanson walked into the diner and sat next to Mike, introducing himself. A waitress shuffled over with a cup of coffee and placed it in front of him, who turning to her said, "Thank you, darling."

Wilson looked at Hanson and without a word slid a manila envelope across the table, containing the original and eight copies of the complaint. Wilson then said, "Look it over, but we should be all set. I went through the documents last night and everything appears to be in order."

"Well then, here we go, here we go," said Hanson, as he sipped his coffee. He pulled out all the documents in the envelope and began to examine them, comparing the copies to the original. When Hanson was finished, he pulled from his jacket a stamper that read *True Certified Copy of the Original*. Stamping the copies of the complaint, he signed his name to each one. He turned to Wilson and asked, "All ready to go?"

Wilson nodded his head and said, "Let's do it."

———◆———

Wallace Bender got to the office at 7:30 a.m., his usual arrival time. The place was completely empty, as he was almost always the first to arrive in the morning, and one of the last to leave at night. He now walked around the open work space in the center of the office, relishing the moment to reflect on what he had built. Wallace's office was located at the far corner of the space, along the perimeter with the other private offices. Its tinted-glass walls and doors enabled him and the offices' other occupants to overlook the *bullpen* area in the center, as it was affectionately referred to, while the glass tinting shielded those who might attempt to look in from the outside.

He walked to his office and went straight to his computer to check the day's schedule and the eleven sales offices' daily reports. He first looked at the Hoboken office numbers from yesterday and saw that Perron had taken five new loan applications.

That made twenty-three thus far this month, and Wallace thought he might crack thirty. He knew that not all of them would survive underwriting, but most would. Wallace believed that he might just do over one hundred thousand in gross revenues this month. No other loan originator approached his volume of business, either in terms of number of loans or sales revenue. He was the most prolific loan officer Bender had ever worked with. Perron made Bender a lot of money on so many levels. Wallace would speak with him later today, like he did almost every day, to discuss their business dealings, pending loans, and the projected gross earnings expected from him and the Hoboken office. Perron ran that office, although technically he was not the person in charge. He did what he wanted, from directing the office manager and support staff to overseeing the other loan originators. He was an egocentric, money hungry, driven individual who believed Bender Capital Lending needed him more than he needed Bender. He truly enjoyed the thought that he was indispensable, whether it was true or not.

———————◆———————

It was almost 9:00 a.m., and Flavia Perron was preparing breakfast for her husband, when Carlos came down the stairs wearing only his boxers and a white tank top that barely fit over his considerable midsection. He planned to eat his breakfast, go to the club for coffee with his friends, and then maybe by 11:30 a.m. or 12:00 p.m., he would make his way to the office. As he was about to sit at the table, scrambled eggs steaming on the plate before him, the doorbell rang. Carlos walked to the front door, indifferent to the fact that he was in his underwear, and asked, "Yea, who there." The voice on the other side simply said, "Carlos Perron?" He opened the door to find an older, grey-haired man standing there who asked again, "Carlos Perron?" Carlos replied, "Yea." The man handed him a document saying, "Consider yourself served, buddy." He then turned and walked away. Carlos, who was at a loss for words, looked at the papers, flipped through a few pages and froze. After several minutes, he turned around dropped the complaint on the floor near the front door and walked upstairs. Flavia was washing a pan at the kitchen sink when she noticed the wide-open door, and wiping her hands, she walked over to close it.

She called, "Carlos . . . Carlito, dónde estás?"

There was no response. Seeing the complaint on the floor she bent down to pick it up, not knowing what it was. She walked to the stairs leading to the second floor and called his name a second time, but again there was no answer. Flavia Perron was left to wonder where her husband had gone and what the document in her hand meant. She would soon find out.

———◆———

The bullpen was beginning to fill with Bender Capital Lending employees, some who were settling in at their desks while others made their way to the kitchen for coffee or tea. Wallace watched from his office as his people filled their cubicles. It was now 8:45 a.m. and he looked to see if Gerald had come in yet. He noticed two men near the reception desk when his phone buzzed. It was Allison the receptionist.

"Mr. Bender, there are two gentlemen here who are asking to see you," she said nervously.

"OK, can you tell me who they are?"

"Yes, sir one is a state marshal and the other is an investigator from the New Jersey Attorney General's Office." The line was silent, no response. "Sir, are you there?"

"Yes, yes. Show them to my office if you would please."

Allison got up from her desk and escorted the two men to Wallace Bender's office. As they entered, he got up from his chair and walked around his desk to greet them near the sitting area within the office. Wallace turned to Alison saying, "Thank you for showing them in." Allison, who had turned and was rushing to get out, stopped and turned back to face Wallace. Staring at him vacantly, she said, "You're welcome?" She spun around again and pulled the door shut.

Wallace still standing, but feeling light headed and tugging at his collar, now asked, "Gentlemen what can I do for you?"

The two men looked at each other and smiled at the nervous Wallace Bender standing before them. As Marshal Hanson pulled a copy of the complaint from his briefcase and handed it to Wallace, he asked, "Where are Gerald Bender and Michael Dolan?"

CHAPTER SEVEN

THE recital went longer than Michael expected. He did not plan on being there as late as he was. It was now almost 10:30 a.m. and he wanted to get to the office, but there was a reception with tea and cookies afterward. He contemplated leaving and wondered if Diana even mentioned this part to him; he was sure she didn't. She had a pressing matter at work and had to leave, now almost forcing Michael to remain. Diana told Christina that she was sorry, and giving her a hug and a kiss, said, "Goodbye honey. You did an excellent job." Leaving she gave Michael a peck on the lips, telling him, "Ok, see you tonight." On the way out, Diana ran into Elizabeth Duffy, who lived in the neighborhood with her husband, Sean, and their daughter, Regina. They talked for a few minutes about getting the girls together next Saturday morning and embracing one another, they said goodbye. Liz walked over to Michael, who was sitting with Christina and her daughter and said hello, giving him a hug and kiss. She then said hi to the girls bending at the knee, and then sat down next to Michael to join them for tea and cookies.

Liz Duffy, a very cute blonde, often flirtatious, scatter brained, and somewhat naïve, was a good friend and always a fun time. Turning to Michael she asked, "So when are we getting together again? You know it's been awhile since we've been out and had some fun."

Michael and Diana had met Liz and Sean almost immediately after moving into the neighborhood, and they had quickly become friends. He was a contractor and she was a nurse at Norwalk Hospital. The couples had spent a lot of time going out together, especially lately, since their best friends, Marco and Lisa D'Angelo, often seemed unavailable. They were always very entertaining, as Liz Duffy was the type who was usually up for anything, particularly when it involved a night of hard drinking. Liz loved her wine, but then again, she loved just about anything that gave her a buzz.

"Liz, I'll mention it to Diana, we'll do it soon," he said putting his arm around her.

She laughed and said, "Can't wait. I'll call Diana. We'll set something up for next week, we can do dinner and lots and lots of wine." Michael shook his head in agreement saying nothing in response, his thoughts elsewhere.

Abruptly he said, "Liz, I really need to get to work. How much longer do we have to hang out here?"

She shrugged her shoulders and said, "Go ahead I'll stay with the girls."

It was a little past 11:00 a.m. and although he was anxious to leave, Michael stayed another twenty minutes, not wanting to disappoint his daughter. He sat and drank the lukewarm tea she offered, while the girls ate the cookies Ms. Gina had baked for the event. Michael and Liz continued talking as they watched the two little ones play and giggle. The reception finally over, Michael said his goodbyes to Liz, Christina, and Regina quickly making his way toward the car and offering his congratulations on a job well done to Ms. Gina, who smiled and thanked him. Sitting in the driver seat and pulling the cell phone from the cup holder, he saw six missed calls from the office. *Gerry must have been calling to arrange a lunch time for today.* He wasn't too concerned but thought to call as he pulled out of the parking lot.

He dialed the office and Allison answered the phone on the first ring, "Bender Capital Lending."

"Hey Allison, it's Michael." Before he could finish she asked him to hold.

Michael waited a few minutes when an unfamiliar voice came on the line asking, "Michael Dolan?"

"Yes," he responded.

"This is State Marshal Wilbert Hanson and I have a summons and complaint that I need to put in your hands immediately."

"Okay," Michael said slowly. *What is this about*, he thought.

Hanson asked, "Where can we meet?"

"Well I'll be in the office in about twenty or twenty-five," said Michael.

"No good," Hanson quickly retorted.

"Okay," Michael said again. He then asked, "What is this about?"

Hanson, ignoring the question, asked, "Where are you?"

"I'm just driving to get on I-95 in Norwalk, what should I do?"

Hanson shot back, "Ok get on and then get off exit seven. Meet me at the end of the ramp. By the way what type of car do you drive?"

"Grey, BMW 3 Series," he said.

"Figures," said Hanson.

The line went dead, and looking at his phone, Michael shouted, "Fuck you, asshole."

He drove to the exit as instructed and met Hanson, along with another man who remained in the car. Michael got out of his car and met the marshal between the two parked and idling vehicles on the side of the road. Hanson handed him the paperwork telling him about the noontime news conference. Michael returned to the car and began to read the complaint. After a few minutes, what *this* was about became very clear. *Jesus, what the fuck.* He called Gerry as he drove to the office but there was no answer. He knew this would have to wait until he got to Greenwich. He hoped Wallace would have some answers for him. Arriving at the office, he pulled into his designated parking space, and as he got out of his car and walked toward the building, he began to feel a sense of doom that he could not explain or shake.

CHAPTER EIGHT

IT was 11:44 a.m. when Carter Atkins got off the phone with Mike Wilson, who reported to him that all defendants had now been served. He hustled from the back of the auditorium over to Richard Banks, who was standing at the podium in the middle of a sound check. Carter, waved his hand and tried to get his attention among the group of technicians and cameramen surrounding him. After a few minutes, Banks raised his gaze and looked over at Carter who hastily shot him two thumbs-up. Banks smiled and returned his attention to the TV cameras pointed in his direction. The room at the State Capital Building was beginning to fill with reporters, and Banks began to get ready for the show that he spent all night rehearsing. Banks called Commissioner Lagnese, Carter, and Janet to the stage, who now took positions on the podium, standing to the left and behind him. Eight minutes into the noon-hour broadcast, following the anchor introductions, headline news and a set of commercials, the local and network stations would go live to Trenton New Jersey for breaking news on the financial crisis story. First the anchors would lay the groundwork by reminding viewers that the housing market was in swift decline, foreclosure rates were rising, and stock prices in the financial and banking sectors have been trending down. Viewers would also be told that just days ago, New Century Mortgage Corp., one of the nation's largest subprime mortgage lenders, closed its doors filing for Chapter 11 bankruptcy protection, sending shockwaves throughout the subprime home loan-mortgage industry. Putting this all in prospective, the news anchors will point out again the recent downward turn of the Dow and NASDAQ, all of which were very troubling for the U.S. economy, homeowners, and investors on Wall Street. With that backdrop, the Banks news conference would begin.

———◆———

Michael walked into Bender Capital Lending and headed directly to Wallace Bender's office where he and Gerry were waiting for him. Passing through the bullpen, it felt like all eyes were on him as people stopped what they were doing and peered at him from their cubicles. It was unusually quiet—no one dared to utter a word to him. He briskly walked across the center of the office space toward the far end where the private offices were located. As he entered the corner office, he could see that Wallace was seated behind his desk, the phone against his ear. Gerry was standing nearby, leaning against the wall as if it was the only thing keeping him up, vacantly staring at the television. The news conference hadn't begun, but when he walked into the office, a commercial about adult diapers was playing on the TV. Glancing at it he thought, *I might need a pair of those in about five minutes.*

Closing the door behind him, he stood there momentarily without saying a word. He then walked toward Gerry, dropped the complaint on the desk in front of Wallace, and angrily asked, "What the fuck is this all about?"

Gerry, choked out harshly, his voice cracking as if he was revisiting puberty, "Michael my dad is on the phone with the lawyers now. Sit down, please." His head slumped forward, no longer able to look at Michael, trying to avoid his gaze.

Michael turned back toward Wallace and heard him say, "Yes Austin we'll be there within the hour . . . yes, yes all three of us. See you then."

Wallace Bender put down the phone and without acknowledging Michael, turned his head and attention to the TV. The press conference they were forewarned about had just begun. The anchor was now saying, "Live to Trenton New Jersey for breaking news on the story of the looming financial crisis."

Michael stared at the TV, standing the entire time, as the New Jersey attorney general spoke. The televised portion of the press conference was only two or three minutes long, but it was enough to completely drain him. Michael stumbled back two steps and slowly lowered himself onto the leather couch near Wallace Bender's desk. Gerry was already seated, staring blankly at the TV, although the news program had moved onto a commercial. He sat with his elbows resting on his knees, arms raised, and the palms of his hands the only thing keeping his head from falling onto his lap.

Wallace, whose blood had drained from his face, was the first to speak. "I should go out to the bullpen and address everyone," he said more to himself than anyone in particular. Turning his head, he ordered, "Michael, you and Gerry need to come with me and talk to the attorneys. We'll leave for Westport in about ten minutes." Slowly getting up from his chair, he threw back his shoulders and stood erect. He stretched his considerable frame, and with a look of sheer determination on his face, loosened his tie. Without saying a word, he opened the door and defiantly marched out of the office. Michael, who had remained seated on the couch, looked out to the bullpen, watching the staff gather around Wallace. He realized that it was now dead silent.

The car ride to Wainwright, Berger & Miceli, PC was less than thirty minutes, although it felt longer to Michael Dolan. As he sat in the backseat with Gerry, his mind drifted back to the press conference. He tried to put aside the many different emotions he was experiencing and started reasoning like a lawyer. For the first time that day he began to analyze the claims laid out in the news conference by the attorney general. He couldn't remember every detail of the allegations but vividly recalled they were being accused of playing roles in a vast predatory lending scheme in New Jersey, which was also being conducted in New York and Connecticut. The attorney general used language like fraud, conspiracy to defraud, violations of consumers' rights, banking laws, and regulations.

At the time the words stung hard, as news station after station reported the allegations to the public, repeatedly naming Michael as a defendant and one of the conspirators in the scam. But as he applied legal analysis to the claims, Michael concluded the allegations sounded contrived and generic. Although the New Jersey attorney general described them as public enemy number one and painted a picture of them as being scumbags that had to be stopped at all costs before more people fell victim to the scheme, Michael thought, maybe somewhat naively, that in a court of law these allegations could be disproved—especially since he knew that all of it was untrue and the claims were completely ridiculous. He believed that they could probably prove it all to be wrong, given the chance. He also realized that in the court of public opinion, almost everybody would believe the allegations to be true, regardless of what he might say. The damage may have already been done. He also deliberated whether Bender Capital Lending was now finished. He could only wonder if Wallace Bender was making the same assessment.

The black Lincoln slowly turned onto Birch Street, near the center of Westport. Looking out from the backseat window, Michael took notice of all the houses that had one time, or another been converted to professional offices. The Wainwright, Berger & Miceli office was located on the corner of Birch and Main. It was a 1930's mansion style colonial with large Roman columns in the front of the house supporting a large portico that protruded outward at least twenty feet. Pulling into the driveway leading to the rear parking lot, Michael was struck by the home's splendor and size. The house had been completely renovated to its original grandeur and updated to suit the needs of a modern-day law office. Entering the grand foyer, turned reception area, Michael was struck by the ornate moldings and the shiny black and white marble floor that reflected the diverse contemporary artwork hanging on the walls. To the left was a majestic stairway leading to the private offices upstairs, straight ahead was a small caged elevator that lead to the second-floor landing, while to the right was a reception area with a modern glass desk where the receptionist sat. An attractive woman with long blonde hair pulled back away from her face smiled at the men as they walked toward her. Despite her obvious youth, she seemed very mature. Smartly dressed and seated with perfect posture, she watched the men as they came near her, before reacting. Michael's attention was still drawn to the splendor of the office, a tasteful blend of modern and historic. He also believed that given the décor and the level of sophistication, the attorneys were not going to be cheap, easily four hundred fifty to five hundred dollars per hour.

The men walked to the reception desk and standing momentarily before the young lady, she looked to Wallace and said, "Good afternoon, Mr. Bender."

Wallace simply responded, "Good afternoon."

"We've been expecting you sir," she said, pressing a button on the phone.

Austin Wainwright, impeccably dressed in a dark grey Brooks Brothers suit, white shirt, and light grey paisley tie, came out to meet the three of them at the desk. Before he could take them to the first-floor conference room, where Daniel Berger and Frances Miceli were already pouring over the complaint, the receptionist asked if anyone would care for a beverage. Michael impulsively thought vodka and tonic. Putting aside the urge to get totally blasted, he politely said, "Bottled water, thank you," and she responded right away.

Once in the conference room, the door closed behind them. The three attorneys, after some small talk, sat and listened to their clients deny the allegations and protest the "false" claims now being made against them, calling them absurd.

Finally, Austin Wainwright asked, "Wall, what about this loan officer in Jersey. Have you spoken to him?"

"No, not yet. I did call his cellphone, but I got his voicemail. I also called the Hoboken office, but no one has seen him today." He added, "Everyone's pretty nervous."

Frances Miceli jumped in and said, "Wall, the game plan right now is to resist and delay this lawsuit and any additional action taken by the New Jersey Attorney General's Office. We can also expect New York and Connecticut to jump in and when they do, we do the same there as well. Delay the filing of pleadings, delay responding to discovery, delay court proceedings—I mean everything, delay and deflect. Basically, anything they do we oppose. The reason being, number one, we delay the suspension or prevent the revocation of one or more of the Bender Capital Lending licenses. This allows you to continue to stay in business and earn a living. Second, it also slows this whole thing down and the slower it proceeds the better chance we have of this . . . this thing burning itself out. Most of the time, after the initial sensation and headlines, these matters end in some type of acceptable resolution that doesn't go any further. And, third, along the same thinking, the longer this drags on the more the public loses interest and then hopefully forgets this whole thing completely."

Wallace Bender and the others sat silently listening, unable to voice support for, or an objection to, what they were now being told.

Miceli continued, "At this point we are faced with a civil and regulatory matter, and we want to keep it that way."

"Meaning what," said Wallace.

"Meaning, we do everything we can to keep it under the radar and prevent a prosecutor from taking an interest in this, and starting a criminal investigation," said Daniel Berger, the only other attorney in the firm, along with Austin Wainwright, who practiced criminal law. Wallace looked blankly at Berger, as Gerry turned white as a ghost at the mention of the word criminal.

Berger continued, "We do everything we can to prevent that, so we keep an eye on the local prosecutor's office but more importantly the feds. If we can't deflect this, then at some point you will need to retain separate criminal defense counsel. Right now, we can defend all of you in the civil action, but if this takes a turn for the worse our continued representation of you may present a conflict of interest. But for now, we circle the wagons and hunker down."

Michael anticipated having this discussion but apparently, Gerry and Wallace did not. He began to formulate the next steps in his head when suddenly and unexpectedly his cell phone rang. He pulled it out of his pocket and saw that it was Diana calling. *Oh, shit I forgot to call her.* He contemplated not answering but tapped the talk button to take the call. All he could think to say was, "Hi, hon."

CHAPTER NINE

THE Connecticut attorney general sat in his office watching the live coverage of the Banks news conference. He picked up the phone and barked orders to his secretary, "Nancy get Dave in here right away." Frank Smith continued to watch the TV from his desk as he waited for Dave Harper, his number one, to come into the office.

In less than a minute Harper burst through the door saying, "I know I know, I was watching out there."

Frank Smith, the seven term Connecticut AG, waited until the coverage ended to ask, "How the hell did 'Richie Rich' get the jump on this?" He then added, "That bastard." Smith was a man who rarely used profanity. He, however, disliked Richard Banks very much, who he believed to be an egotistical, self-absorbed jackass.

Harper responded, "I don't know, but I will check to see if we have anything,"—implying he was going to determine whether any complaints against Bender Capital Lending had been filed with the office.

Smith angrily retorted, "I don't give a shit if we do or not, get a complaint drafted. I don't care if you have to copy Jersey boy," referring to Banks again. "Just get it done and out. We need to do something, got it?"

Most importantly for Frank Smith was the notion that something was going on in his state, like what was now happening in New Jersey. He was worried that people were getting hurt. If so, that he had to stop. Unlike Banks, he was genuinely concerned. He also worried that the New Jersey AG was going to make him look bad, and he certainly did not want to look foolish. He knew that Banks would get all the glory on this one, but at this moment Smith would settle for looking like a flunky for Banks. It was probably the best he could do at this point.

————◆————

Banks ended the news conference ten minutes after the live TV coverage was over. Reporters remained to compare notes and ask clarifying questions from the attorney general and commissioner. Network and cable news producers were in the back of the press room and on the telephone speaking to Lanny Nardone about doing recorded interviews and booking live appearances for Banks on evening and late-night news segments.

Returning to his office Banks was euphoric and Carter Atkins sensed it. The men sat together replaying the news conference in their heads, as they had done amongst some of the other assistants earlier, focusing on the highlights and the points that got the biggest reaction from reporters. Janet Sung joined them in the discussion to report that the office received two more complaints following the noontime broadcast. She told them that teams of two investigators were being dispatched and would soon meet with the new complainants to take statements. She would get details later in the day and report back.

Banks leaned back in his chair and smiled, saying to them, "Fantastic job guys. Let's move on that quickly. Also, follow up with the rest of the staff and the banking department to see if there are any other complaints."

It doesn't get any better than this. At that moment, Banks was thoughtfully focusing on his next move for the upcoming senate run. He also pondered when, where, and how to announce his candidacy. The idea was making him light headed. He had just leaned back and put his hands behind his head, when suddenly Judith buzzed in through his phone. The sound jolted him back to the present moment, eviscerating the pleasant day dream he was having about being in the Oval Office. From over the intercom he heard her say, "Attorney General Banks . . . Senator James Harrison holding on line 110." *That didn't take long, now did it.*

Banks pressed a button on the phone saying, "Thank you Judith." He then turned and said, "Carter, Janet . . . thank you very much for all the hard work and the support at the press conference. You guys were great. Now let's keep this moving in the right direction."

Carter replied, "Will do," as he began to get up from his chair, knowing that Banks would now take this call and in doing so would want privacy.

Banks motioned them to the office door, and as they shuffled out he quietly watched them leave. Once they were gone, he picked up the telephone and with a broad smile on his face bellowed, "Jim, how the hell are you?"

CHAPTER TEN

JAMES Benjamin Harrison II, known to most as Jim, was a four-term United States senator from Pennsylvania and presently the senate majority leader and chairman of the U.S. Senate Banking Committee. He started his political career thirty-two years earlier as many politically powerful men do—through the love, support, and money of an overly ambitious father. Jim's father like his father before him was the United States congressman from U.S. District 2, representing constituents in and around Philadelphia. At one time, Jim Harrison and his father, served in congress together. Their simultaneous service to the nation was brief, only a few years, tragically cut short as the older Harrison suffered a debilitating stroke that required him to step down. As his state of mind progressively deteriorated and his overall health got worse, James Frederick Harrison could no longer carry out his obligations as a member of congress. He resigned within the year, dying almost six years after that. It was a heavy burden to bear for the Harrison family, especially for Jim, and his mother, Natalie, who carried the brunt of the load caring for her husband during his illness. So, like many Harrisons before him, James Frederick Harrison was laid to rest in Philadelphia's Laurel Hill Cemetery. It was home to the Harrison family mausoleum, and generations of ancestors, going as far back to before the turn of the twentieth century.

At the funeral, he was eulogized by his son and two of his closest friends, also congressmen. Representative Harold Skelton of Pennsylvania talked about the long, rich history of the Harrison family's commitment to public service, going as far back as to the birth of our constitutional, modern-day government. He went on to point out how his friend exemplified the ideals of honesty, selflessness, and compassion for others. He described a life dedicated to the common good, painting a vivid picture of James Frederick Harrison as a great humanitarian. As Jim Harrison listened to his father being eulogized, he tearfully vowed to himself to continue the tradition of the Harrison men before him. He hoped that what was being said about young James' grandfather was not lost on him that day. As Jim Harrison sat in the pew of St. Paul's Episcopal Church, he prayed that his youngest child would also one day carry on the proud family tradition of public service, and he hoped that someday his grandchildren would do the same.

———◆———

The Harrison family came to Philadelphia at a time when it served as the young nation's capital. Benjamin Harrison, who was a young man studying the law, served as chief aid and clerk to William Bradford as he sat on the Pennsylvania Supreme Court. Later as Bradford was appointed attorney general under President George Washington, he followed as his chief of staff. The Harrison family continued to rise to social prominence as Benjamin and his brother, Isaiah, built a textile importing business that flourished, thanks to Benjamin's friends in the newly formed government. Political connections, the power that came with it, and the money that followed was the lethal combination that put and kept the Harrison family near the top of Philadelphia's social elite for generations. It also helped that a Harrison fought at Gettysburg and was later honored as a favored son of Philadelphia high society at the end of the war.

Jim Harrison's family prominence, political power and good fortune did not stop him, however, from wanting more for himself and his family. After all, he had three children and four grandchildren to think about now. He was especially focused on his youngest, James, who he believed had enormous potential and would go far in honoring the Harrison family. He thought that someday his son would do remarkable things for this nation. Jim Harrison foresaw it and was prepared to do whatever it would take to see that vision become a reality.

———◆———

The phone call with his friend was not long, but it was fruitful. Jim Harrison had been in Philadelphia, away from Washington D.C. for three days to rest and meet with a few constituents at his office. He watched the news coverage on the local CBS affiliate, after it was brought to his attention by an assistant. Jim Harrison was happy for his friend,

Richard, and called him with the intention of offering some advice on how to generate the most political hay from the gift that was laid on both their doorsteps. Harrison considered how he would also use this to his political advantage. He believed this lawsuit and the others undoubtedly to follow would soon begin to shift the trending national discussion about health care to the growing financial crisis. Harrison understood that the economy and the housing market would soon be severely impacted by the inevitable financial meltdown to come. He knew he needed to do something.

Harrison and his colleagues in the senate and their counterparts in the House of Representatives worked hard to pass legislation, making it easier for many Americans to realize the dream of homeownership. The Graham-Leach, Bliley Act repealed banking regulations that had been put in place by the Glass-Steagall Act, shortly after the Great Depression, which had been designed to prevent future systemic bank failures. Although the repeal of Glass-Steagall was lauded by many, the newly substituted legislation may have inadvertently stoked the embers of a fire that would result in the largest financial crisis since the Great Depression. Harrison worried that the public focus and blame would be diverted back at him and his Congressional colleagues. He vowed not to let that happen, and as he waited for his friend to pick up the line, he thought about how he could best use this Bender Capital Lending fiasco to his advantage. Suddenly, on the other end of the line, he heard an elated Banks say, "Jim, how the hell are you?"

"Richard, I am good. Of course, not as good as you. I just saw the press conference. Nice work, congratulations."

"I was going to give you a call to get perspective," said Banks.

"Well, Richard my perspective, um . . . this should pave your way to join me here in the senate, my good friend."

Banks smiled and reflected on what Jim Harrison just said. It was confirmation that his instincts were correct and that he had made all the right moves. He now said with false modesty, "It was really all about the protection of the constituents I serve more than anything else, Jim."

Ignoring the self-serving statement, Harrison continued, "Richard this is going to get worse, and it appears that you are the first government official to have taken action on what is now being discussed in the treasury, the Federal Reserve, and my committee. Very intensely I might add. This seems to be developing into what could be a crisis of epic proportion."

"Really," exclaimed Banks.

"The tip of the iceberg, at this point," said Harrison drearily. *My God, and we're the Titanic heading right for it.*

Banks momentarily wondered how bad it was going to get, but didn't give it a second thought, simply because he didn't care about the bigger picture. His only concern was for himself. He refocused, "Jim, any advice for me?"

"Certainly, keep doing what you're doing. But, why don't you send me everything you have on the case this far. I will look it over and give you my full assessment. I will then be in a better position to advise you on how to best spin this to your advantage," said Harrison.

"Excellent idea, Jim. I'll have my staff put something together for you and send it immediately. Thank you, my friend."

"Richard, I look forward to it. We will talk soon."

"Jim, thanks again for the call," Banks said, smiling as he hung up the phone.

Harrison reasoned that the information his friend was sending would come in handy and, at the very least, help his son, James. This lawsuit, he believed, would lay the groundwork to place blame where it belonged. It just might save Congress from the harsh criticism it would otherwise receive from the American public. He believed Bender Capital Lending was the perfect political foil, diverting attention away from him and his colleagues. Congress could soon put the focus back onto the banking industry and Wall Street, where it belonged. He could easily sell the idea that it was corporate greed, not the easing of regulations on the financial industry or the lack of proper oversight that created this crisis. But again, he did have a lot of friends in the financial services sector—good friends, who he did not want to see get hurt. Harrison easily and quickly convinced himself that Bender Capital Lending and the men involved were insignificant and powerless to prevent this public persecution and discussion. Without any reluctance, he thought they did this to themselves. As he sat in front of his computer surfing the Bender website and reading the bio of its CEO, Wallace Bender, and other corporate officers, Harrison concluded that in the end they would get what they deserved.

He was feeling good about this when the thought struck him— *What kind of resistance will congress get from the financial services and banking industry lobbyists?* These guys were certainly not easy pushovers or helpless like Bender Capital Lending, unable to push back.

On second thought, it might not be so simple to put the blame on some of the Wall Street types. The big boys will be hard to take down. *There had to be another way. Who else could they shift the blame to?* He didn't come up with an idea right at that moment, but Jim Harrison was certain he would figure it out. He put it aside for now, picking up the telephone again, noting to himself, whatever does happen, the federal government would not be blamed, and the American taxpayer will not be left holding the bag, of that he was sure.

CHAPTER ELEVEN

JIM Harrison dialed the telephone and called his son in New York to inform him of what he witnessed on TV and discussed with his friend. He wanted to fill him in on his plan to somehow spin this to their advantage.

The phone rang five times before a woman's voice answered and said, "United States Department of Justice, U.S. Attorney's Office, southern district of New York. How may I direct your call?"

"Yes, Assistant U.S. Attorney James Harrison please," said the elder Harrison.

"Hold please" was the response, and a moment later the phone began to ring again. After several more rings, the phone was answered by another woman who Harrison knew to be his son's secretary.

"Hi Angie, it's Senator Harrison. How are you?" Without pausing he asked, "I need to speak with James. Is he there?" He asked himself why he didn't just call his son's cell phone. *That was dumb.*

"Oh, yes. Senator, I am fine, thank you for asking. How are you sir? He is here, I will get him for you right away."

The line went silent, and as he waited, Jim Harrison mumbled to himself, "I hope James is not getting too attached to this one." *She was pretty and nice but not marriage material.* He knew everything his son did, who his friends were, the women he dated, and who he was fucking. Angie, a striking, tall brunette with ample breasts and long luscious legs, seemed to be James' most frequent and passionate lover. At least that was what his man in New York reported back to him. James Benjamin Harrison III had no idea that his father was keeping such close tabs on him, but after all, Jim Harrison needed to make sure his son did not screw up the plans he had made for him. He managed his son's life like he did everything else—by making calculated and gainful decisions. He had to admit that so far, so good; everything that he had hoped for was going according to plan.

Jim Harrison, however, could not anticipate what his friend, Richard Banks, had just dropped on their doorstep. *This bit of good fortune,* he thought. This would speed things up on the James Harrison timeline and would move his son toward the next career milestone sooner than expected.

Just then AUSA James Harrison came on the line. "Hey Dad. How are you? What's going on?"

"I've got something really important to discuss with you."

———◆———

Undeniably James Benjamin Harrison III was born with a silver spoon in his mouth; the stick up his ass, however, was something he acquired more recently in life. Unlike his father, Harrison was arrogant, egotistical, a self-righteous bastard who thought he was smarter and better than everyone else. Like his father, he was bright, hard-working, ambitious, and savvy. He was thirty-two years old, six-foot tall, athletically built, and strikingly handsome. He was the most eligible bachelor in Philadelphia society, and number twenty-eight on the Forbes *Top 50 Most Eligible Bachelors in Manhattan* list for 2007—all of which served to stroke his ego.

Harrison and his father discussed on many occasions a plan for his life. It began with his enrollment at Choate Preparatory School. After graduating as class Valedictorian, he attended Columbia University next, receiving an undergraduate degree in business and finance. He then returned to his father's beloved Philadelphia to attend his alma mater, the University of Pennsylvania, for his Juris Doctorate and an MBA from the Wharton School. There was no question, James Benjamin Harrison III was very bright. But, even more so he was very ambitious. The next step in the grand Harrison plan landed him at the U.S. Attorney's Office. Soon enough there would be a stop along the way for marriage to a daughter of one of Philadelphia's prominent families, and then onto state representative, if necessary, but most likely directly to the United States Congress. Jim Harrison believed that his son could even garner a cabinet position, such as attorney general, or maybe a vice presidential nod someday. Unbeknownst to his father, however, James Benjamin Harrison III thought in even bigger terms, believing there was no limit to what he could achieve. Nothing was out of reach.

The younger Harrison was not only ambitious, but incredibly ruthless. He would do whatever it took to get whatever he wanted, stopping at nothing along the way. His thirst for power was unquenchable, as his selfish desires led him to always want more. For James Benjamin Harrison III enough was never enough.

----◆----

The elder Harrison began to explain what Richard Banks had done and described to his son how this could best serve them. Jim Harrison pointed out that, as the AUSA in charge of the Complex Fraud and Cybercrime Unit, the Bender Capital Lending mortgage fraud claim was ripe for his prosecution team. He believed that James would receive national recognition as the first prosecutor to take on the greedy banks and maybe even corrupt Wall Street. Jim Harrison would help his son and do his part at the appropriate time, by calling for senate hearings on the causes behind the financial crisis. The hearings would hopefully then further expose what James will have undeniably already uncovered, that the root of this looming crisis is grounded in the greed of the banking and financial services industry, not the favorable legislation and federal deregulation of the sector.

Harrison thought about what his father had just said, and asked, "Well how does this office have jurisdiction over Bender and this mess?"

The elder Harrison having already anticipated the concern said, "James, Bender Capital Lending has an office in Mount Vernon, which is, as you know, within the jurisdiction of the southern district."

"Well the White Plains office typically handles matters in Westchester County, although given the broader implications I am sure I can convince the U.S. Attorney to turn this one over to me," said Harrison. Thinking on it, he directed his father. "Make a call to the DOJ in Washington to make sure it happens and that it does not get fucked up somehow."

The elder Harrison anxiously replied, "I will. I'll call the attorney general himself and make sure it is not an issue." He failed to realize that the power dynamic between himself and his son had just shifted.

----◆----

Jim Harrison knew Attorney General Bowler Erkens very well and did not anticipate any problem there. They had both served in the senate together as Democratic members of the Banking, Housing and Urban Affairs Committee before Erkens was tapped by the current administration to head the Department of Justice, when Alexander Crenshaw unexpectedly stepped down. During their years in the senate, Harrison and Erkens co-sponsored and passed important legislation that enabled many Americans to qualify for mortgages and buy homes. In the process, they also became good friends, and Erkens, who at the time was a three-term senator from South Carolina, spent many nights at the Harrison home in Philadelphia and got to know the younger James well. When the call came requesting an appointment to the U.S. Attorney's Office, Erkens was more than willing to do whatever he was asked. And when the elder Harrison wanted the southern district for his son, one of the most prestigious and highest profile offices in the Department of Justice, he was happy to give it to him. Three plus years into the job, James Harrison proved himself to be a very capable prosecutor, and Attorney General Erkens was more than pleased. Jim Harrison would call Erkens and explain to his friend the benefits of taking on this prosecution and the need for James to do so, no doubt understanding its broader political implications.

Wanting now to get off the phone, James Harrison said, "Ok sounds good, Dad. Take care of it like I said and let me know when it's done."

"I'll call Bo in the morning. Oh, by the way who are the named defendants in Richard's complaint?"

Jim Harrison said, "Wallace Bender, CEO, his son Gerald, Michael Dolan, and some loan officer out in Jersey."

"Michael Dolan?"

"Yes, do you know him, James?"

"No . . . well maybe. If it's the same guy from the Franklin Family Fund case, then yes."

"I don't recall your involvement in a Franklin Fund case."

"It was the first case I worked on when I got to the U.S. Attorney's Office, but it went nowhere, and the investigation was dropped after two months," he said. "This guy, Dolan, if it's the same guy, was in their legal department. It's nothing. Forget I mentioned it."

James Harrison said goodbye and hung up the phone. Sitting back in his chair, he buzzed his secretary, Angie, and directed her to come into the office. He was thinking back to the Franklin Family Fund case when she walked in, closing and locking the door behind her.

This was not lost on Harrison, and walking to him she asked with a smile, "James what can I do for you?"

Angie came around the desk, and he grabbed her right arm, gently placing her hand on the outside of his trousers along the outline of his aroused penis. Harrison wasn't sure if it was Angie that was making him hard or the thought of taking down Bender Capital Lending and attorney, Michael Dolan. His mind, now somewhat reluctantly, continued to drift further back to the Franklin Family Fund case.

———◆———

Bernard Franklin ran a small investment firm in Manhattan with his twin sons Bernard Jr., and William. They managed almost four hundred million dollars in investor money, mainly on behalf of Bernard Franklin's many friends and family members. One hundred million was Franklin's own money. The fund came under suspicion as part of a larger investigation that was underway when James had first arrived in the office. He was given the task of looking into the fund, which at the time was considered by the other assistants and FBI agents a waste of time and resources. He wanted to prove them wrong and make a good first impression, if only to immediately make a name for himself. Harrison thought the Franklin twins were spoiled rich kids who cared only about having a good time and spending their daddy's money. He was right. He met with them several times. Bernard junior, who was first to emerge from his mother's womb by three minutes, introduced himself as BJ, seemingly unaware of the connotation. He talked incessantly while William said very little. On each of the occasions they met, Michael Dolan was present as their counsel. At the meetings, the twins were more concerned about their prematurely receding hairlines rather than the potential problem the Department of Justice might pose. Dolan, on the other hand, was more than ready and capable of addressing all of Harrison's questions. It was Dolan who demonstrated that the fund was in full compliance with all the laws and regulations governing its operation. As such, it was quickly decided that no further action was necessary, and the Franklin Family Fund was spared the fate of the other larger funds that were ultimately criminally charged. Harrison, much to his displeasure, was unable to make the grand entrance he had hoped for, and he believed Dolan was in large part responsible for that.

———◆———

If the Michael Dolan in the Bender Capital Lending matter is the same Michael Dolan from the Franklin Family Fund case, I would like nothing more than to get another crack at him. This time around, Michael Dolan would not be so lucky.

His attention was now redirected back to Angie as she quickly wiggled out of her tight skirt and shed her white, silken blouse, leaving only her sheer undergarments on her tight and flawless body. She immediately lowered herself before him, and he dropped his pants. What Harrison couldn't sense or didn't care to know was that Angie Estrada was in love with him. She would do anything he asked, including dropping to her knees, anytime and anywhere. She unsheathed James Harrison's member from his Calvin Klein boxer-briefs as he thought, *God almighty she is good, really fucking good.* Angie went down on him, expertly swirling her tongue around his head while slowly working her way up and down his shaft. She took a deep breath, filling her nostrils with his scent, moaning deeply as her arousal became more intense. Angie looked up at her lover and placed her hands on his chest as her body went rigid. He tightened up and became stiffer as well—very close now, as she let out another moan. At that point, it didn't take long before he exploded in her mouth with a spastic force that caused her to momentarily jolt her head backward. James Harrison shuddered from the intensity of his orgasm and fell back into his chair, while Angie continued to hold him, swallowing the entirety of his offering.

When she finally pulled away, he reached out and gently cradled her chin with one hand, as she lovingly looked up at him. Content, he coldly told her, "Get dressed. We got work to do."

Angie, somewhat satisfied but emotionally frustrated, complied without a word of protest. Getting off her knees, she slowly got dressed, as Harrison pulled up his trousers. Standing near his desk, he put himself back together. Glancing backward through the drawn blinds of his office window, he noticed a woman looking in his direction from the building directly across his own. He poked his head through the white plastic blinds and waved to her. He wondered if she saw what was just going on in his office. There was no reaction from her. He quickly concluded she likely didn't see anything, but then again, he really didn't care. He looked at Angie as she continued to get dressed and said, "Babe come here."

She immediately complied, walking over to him, buttoning her blouse at the same time. He touched her chin again, and this time tenderly kissed her deeply. She swooned and eagerly submitted as a wave of sheer joy overcame her. He then spun her around and playfully slapped her ass. There was no question about the power dynamic between James Benjamin Harrison III and Angie Estrada. She willingly did everything he commanded.

CHAPTER TWELVE

MICHAEL and Marco D'Angelo had become good friends in their first year of law school together. Marco was born and raised in Brooklyn, where he and his new wife, Lisa, lived in the basement apartment of his parent's home. Marcello and Palma D'Angelo, came to this country in 1970, and settled in New York where after years of saving and working long, hard hours at the Brooklyn Creamery, they purchased a home in Brooklyn Heights, next door to Marcello's brother and sister-in-law, Mario and Donatella. *The boys*, as they were sometimes referred to by Palma, would often come back to the apartment following classes in order to study and outline the day's lessons together. Pam D'Angelo, as she was known to her American friends, would cook a hearty meal for them that always included a pasta dish with meat sauce. She had enough food in the house to feed an army, and in a moment's notice could go to the freezer and take out a tray of lasagna or manicotti that she kept there, just in case of a food emergency. She never asked Michael if he liked what he was eating; it was assumed that he did. There was no doubt that he enjoyed her cooking; it was evident by the way in which he devoured his food while he was there. Michael's mother had been gone a long time and although he was the first to admit his father's cooking was not bad, it could not compare to the meals he received at the D'Angelo household. Pam would always fill his plate and continue to refill it until he begged her to stop. When she attempted to overstuff the boys, Marcello would sometimes get angry and say in an unsettling tone, "Palma enough."

Marcello D'Angelo's homemade wine was always on the table with dinner, and the meals often ended with espresso coffee and sambuca. Michael's love of red wine took root at the D'Angelo home, and he eventually lost his taste, almost entirely, for beer, the beverage of choice in the Dolan home growing up. Although, Michael still enjoyed a stout Guinness, especially with a thick, rare rib eye every now and then, red wine was now his preferred drink, California Cabernets more than anything else.

When Michael and Diana began to date, he took her to meet Marco, Lisa, and his parents. Palma D'Angelo liked Diana right away for many reasons, but mostly because she was a "nice Italian girl" as Pam would often say. Diana enjoyed her cooking very much, and as taught by her mom, Maryann, she always helped in the kitchen while there. Pam loved that about Diana and would often say, "Eat, eat Diana . . . I no know. Lisa she no eat too much."

They would all laugh, and Mr. D'Angelo would tell his wife, "Stop-a Palma, enough." Diana and Lisa liked each other the moment they met and got along extremely well, despite the fact they had very little in common initially inasmuch as they both came from entirely divergent backgrounds. One grew up in the backdrop of the entertainment industry, parents who were talent agents, seeming to never have time for their child. The other came from a loving but strict Italian middleclass family, growing up in the suburbs of Boston. Despite their differences, they became fast friends.

One evening as the four of them were leaving Brooklyn for the drive to Westchester and Connecticut, Marco and Lisa having moved out of the basement apartment by then, Pam pulled Michael aside and wrapped her arm around his waist. "Listen me, you marry this girl." She looked him straight in the eyes, patiently waiting for a response.

Michael stood there silently for a moment and smiled, then giving her a kiss on the cheek he said, "Don't worry. I will."

Pam smiled back and said in her endearing Italian accent, "Good. Come on I make you a plate. You bring you father."

Michael knew that with Palma D'Angelo, he had no choice in the matter. He followed her into the kitchen like an obedient puppy dog. Diana, who was saying good night to Marcello D'Angelo, watched as Michael emerged from the kitchen with several plates in hand. Smiling at him she thought, *I'm going to marry this man for certain.*

CHAPTER THIRTEEN

MARCELLO D'Angelo, Jr. graduated at the top of his law school class and, although Michael Dolan wasn't too far behind, no one was more sought after by New York's top firms than Marco. He was the first person in his family to attend law school, let alone college, and his parents and wife could not be prouder of him, as was Eddy Dolan of his own son. Following the graduation day ceremony, the two families made their way over to Brooklyn where Palma D'Angelo had a meal waiting that was fit for a king. She wouldn't think of going to a restaurant to celebrate this once in a lifetime achievement. She was very proud of both the boys and wanted to express it the best way she knew how, through her cooking. Marcello D'Angelo was also proud of both Marco and Michael, but especially proud of his son, although he never actually came out and said so. His pride was plastered all over his face, manifested by his loud boisterous laughing and the vast amounts of wine consumed throughout the day. He could not understand why Eddy did not join them in a celebratory drink, having gone out to purchase a case of beer for the Irish, as he put it. Marco's uncle, aunt, and three cousins from next door were also there to celebrate with them.

Palma D'Angelo would fill their plates before they were empty, and Eddy Dolan asked, "Pam this is so good. What do you call this?"

Palma replied, "You like? This chicken cacciatore, sausage, gnocchi, broccoli rabe," pointing at each dish.

"No, this here," Eddy said, pointing to his dish.

"Trippa. Good no?"

"Yes, very good, I never had it before. What exactly is it?"

When told, Eddy was taken aback a little, but he kept eating, enjoying it nonetheless.

Mario laughed and said in Italian, "Eddy manga," which meant eat up. He raised his hand in the air toward him waving. "Good, no?

You eat, eat." Eddy shrugged his head and Mario laughed again, while Donatella, without being asked, put more food on his plate.

At the end of the meal, they all continued to sit at the table stuffed and satisfied. Pam and Donatella then brought out the fruit, cookies, pastries, and a graduation cake that had been waiting in the downstairs apartment refrigerator because there was no room in their own. Marcello D'Angelo made the espresso, although he needed his wife's help at that point, the wine getting the better of both him and Mario. Lisa brought out the sambuca, the men pouring generous amounts into their coffee. Eddy took his with three teaspoons of sugar instead of liquor.

Driving back to Connecticut, Eddy Dolan thought about how Maggie would have really enjoyed this day, and would have really liked Marco, Lisa, and the whole D'Angelo family. His wife would have been proud of Michael's accomplishment, but not surprised. Maggie Dolan always had good instincts and had known that her son would go far in life. She had said it so many times to Eddy and Michael alike. It had been what encouraged him to want to do more, be better, work harder and to achieve greater. His mother was an inspiration to him, and he missed her dearly, especially today. As Michael sat in the car with his father, he also wished that she had been there to celebrate with them. He thought about her often, even now. The one irony that resulted from his mother's tragic death was the relationship Michael now enjoyed with his father. Her death had not only been the sobering event that may have saved Eddy Dolan's life, but it also had become the source of healing for father and son, who had been divided for years over Eddy Dolan's alcoholism.

Michael, looking out the car window, watched the city lights reflecting off the East River and thought that he would never know another woman as good, loving and caring as his mother. He would soon prove himself wrong.

CHAPTER FOURTEEN

MARCO D'Angelo immediately landed a position with a very prestigious intellectual property litigation firm following graduation. Even before taking the bar exam, he was working with clients such as Google, Intel, E-Corp., and Microsoft. Three months later, he and Lisa purchased a small home in Rye, New York, even smaller than the house Michael and Diana would eventually purchase, although much more expensive. The new home was situated in the southern end of Westchester County, just north of New York City. Pam D'Angelo protested and did not understand why they needed to move out of the basement apartment or move so far away from Brooklyn, even though it was less than an hour by car or train. Marco and Lisa enjoyed their new home and loved the town in which they settled. The house, a split-level ranch, was quaint, tasteful, and perfect for raising a family. The city was close enough for dinners, shows and nightlife, while the drive into Brooklyn was not much farther. Marco's commute to New York was relatively short, less than thirty minutes by train, his office in midtown making it that much easier.

Lisa D'Angelo held a position as a brand consultant at the Ralph Lauren Fashion House in White Plains, also less than thirty minutes from home. Her modeling days behind her, Lisa offered valuable insight on fashion, style, and makeup. She was well renowned, her advice now much sought after by many of the buyers at several of the larger clothing retailers, such as Nieman Marcus, Saks 5th Avenue, and Bloomingdales. It was her job to anticipate fashion trends, and she was good at it. Still very much in tune to what women found desirable and fashionable, Lisa was beginning to enjoy a new success, separate from her previous accomplishments on the fashion runway. She and Marco were very happy and in a good place in their lives. Now married three years, they were ready for children. They both set their sights on three or four.

Michael, who was still living at home with his father, waited to search for a job, opting to put all his efforts in passing three bar exams at the first go around, his thinking being, why not take them all? Following his admission to the New York, Connecticut, and New Jersey Bars, he accepted a position in the legal department at the Franklin Family Fund, a small investment firm in New York City.

Calling his friend's cellphone that day Michael was excited to tell him the news. Marco looked at his new iPhone and excused himself from a meeting in which he had been discussing with several other associates the starting lineup for the firm's softball team. He answered the call saying, "Hey bud. What's up?"

Michael said, "Not much." The excitement getting the better of him, he blurted out, "Just landed a job mother fucker." He exaggerated the last word in the same way as the Hank Moody character in the popular HBO show, *Californication*, which Michael religiously watched every week.

"Oh yea, great. Where at?"

"Franklin Family Fund, a boutique investment firm," said Michael.

"Never heard of it. Where?"

"It's a small firm right here in New York . . . hence the term 'boutique.' That's why you haven't heard about it."

"Ok, got it. Well I'm happy for you man, that's great. When do you start?"

"Next week—making a cool seventy-five thousand," Michael boosted. In comparison Marco was earning more than twice that at Cooper, Williams, McBride and Gold, LLP, although he would never bring it up to Michael.

"Awesome, we got to go out and celebrate," Marco said enthusiastically.

"Well I'm thinking of getting some people together tonight. Are you in?"

"No can do tonight. I'm working through dinner till about nine or ten but more importantly Lisa is ovulating, so I have to be home tonight to take care of some business. You know what I mean?"

"Yea I get it, you need to do what makes your wife happy, go home, bang the snot out of her, make a kid."

"What the hell, Michael. No need to be so crude. Asshole." The two of them laughed. "You know what? We'll get together, just you and I next week," declared Marco.

"Ok, another time. I get it," said Michael.

"Speak soon," said Marco as he ended the call.

Michael next dialed Gerald Bender, his old college roommate from New York University, where they both studied finance. He hadn't talked to him in a couple of months, losing touch during the lengthy period leading to the bar exam and beyond, to the subsequent job search. So, it came as a real surprise when Gerry picked up on the first ring.

"Michael, hi. How are you? Heard you passed the bar. Congrats. Everything good?"

"Yea everything's great Gerry. Sorry I haven't been in touch the last few months, but just jammed up with all that I had going on. Wondering if you're available tonight, just got a job and wanted to get a few people together to celebrate. Thinking of going to Ryan's in Stamford. You in?"

"Yea, wouldn't miss it. I'll give Steve and Brian a call and we'll celebrate like the old days. How does that sound buddy?"

"Good. Really good."

"Ok. See you later then. You can tell me all about the job tonight."

Michael interjected, "Thinking seven, you know . . . early, more like a happy hour than a late night. Don't want to be out too late, got to check in early with human resources at the new job. Ok?"

"Yea we're good. Seven it is."

"Ok then, it'll be good to see you and the guys. See you then . . . I guess."

Ryan's Pub was not very crowded when Michael arrived, so it wasn't difficult to find his friends, who were waiting for him at the far end of the bar. He had not seen them since his four-month disappearance to study for the Bar exam, taking on the rigorous task twelve hours a day, seven days a week. When they saw him approaching they walked away from the dart board. Letting out a roar, they converged on him like a rock star, giving him hugs and back slaps. Smiling, Michael thanked them for coming and shouted to the bartender to serve up another round and to add a Guinness for himself. No wine for him tonight, at least not here.

As Michael leaned on the bar, after getting his beer and doing a shot of tequila courtesy of Gerry, he noticed a group of women beyond the bar well. He focused on the most attractive of the three. She was about twenty-five years old, brown-reddish shoulder length hair, full lips, blue almond shaped eyes, long muscular legs, and tall, but not too tall, maybe five-eight. On a second glance, he noticed her lean body, tight ass, and great tits. She was standing with two other women, one close to her age and the other older, all professionally dressed. They appeared to be drinking martinis, as best as he could tell. Staring at her, he now noticed that she carried herself in a way that was generally reserved for a more worldly and sophisticated woman, one clearly beyond her years. He couldn't put his finger on it, but he sensed that she appeared very dignified and refined, even somewhat sophisticated— maybe out of his league. He smiled as he watched her laughing, tossing her hair, and sipping from her glass. As he stared at her, she turned and caught his eye. Michael a bit startled, smiled and could only think to raise his glass of beer and nod his head. She immediately turned to the older blonde standing next to her, and in doing so seemed to blush.

Diana felt her face go flush and wondered if the handsome dark-haired guy across the bar was staring at her. She did not want to be presumptuous, but the thought gave her butterflies. She refused to look back, feeling like a teenager with a crush on the captain of the high school football team. She began to make nervous idle chatter with Nancy and Laura, talking about the upcoming Krandle Packing audit, when the man from across the bar approached. Staring she thought, *Nice hair, big brown eyes and very kissable lips.* The stranger was now standing in front of her, and she noticed he was tall. That was good. She didn't really fall for guys who were short. She unexpectedly got nervous as she stood and faced him. A sensual thought crossed her mind, making her blush again. She felt warm, almost overheated. She blamed it on the martini but knew better.

"I'm sorry to interrupt, but my friends and I are wondering if you would like to join us for a drink? By the way I'm Michael," directing his comments to Diana. He extended his hand and she took it eagerly, refusing to let go. The greeting pleasantly turned into unintentional handholding.

She softly replied, "Diana Caruso, nice to meet you."

Michael said, "Nice to meet you too. So how about that drink?"

"Ok, but I have a two-martini limit, and then beyond that I get crazy," said Diana smiling, still hanging onto his hand.

As she talked, Michael couldn't help but think how very cute she was. Flirting with her now he said, "Don't worry. I'll make sure to stop you . . . before you get too crazy, that is."

Diana laughed nervously as the butterflies began to flutter faster. Laura and Nancy instantly sensed the chemistry between the two and gave each other a knowing smile as if to say they approved.

At second glance and thought, they most certainly approved. He escorted them to the other side of the bar where he introduced Diana to Gerry, inadvertently forgetting to introduce Nancy and Laura, leaving them to do so on their own. Gerry, jumping right in like he used to do in college, said, "Hi, I'm Gerry and that's Brian and the ugly one there is Steve." They guys turned saying hello to the women who now reintroduced themselves, explaining they were all co-workers out for a few drinks after work. Gerry interrupted and asked, "Can we buy you a drink?"

Laura and Nancy looked at each other as if to say, *We're really not sure that's a good idea.* They immediately turned back to Gerry, and affirmed their willingness by saying, almost simultaneously, "Absolutely." They quickly ordered two more dirty vodka martinis as Gerry waved the bartender over. He then yelled for everyone to do a shot and ordered a round of tequila shooters. A few minutes later, they noticed that Michael and Diana had moved off from the rest of the group. Gerry nudged Laura, and said, "Look at these two." She and Nancy smiled back at him as if to say they were all on the same page. They were clearly witnessing the development of a romance between the two. It was obvious that the two of them had gotten lost in one another, and it was occurring right before their friends' eyes. Gerry, shaking his head whispered, "Oh boy. Buddy, you're so done."

CHAPTER FIFTEEN

OPENING her eyes slowly, Diana could barely make out the figure lying beside her. It was her husband. She shut them again in an attempt to fall back to sleep but the alarm clock on the nightstand began to ring, preventing her from dozing off. Despite the extreme state of drunkenness from the night before, she was somehow able to set it. She reached over to shut off the buzzer but missed the button on her first attempt. She took another swipe and got it on the second try. Diana had passed her two-vodka martini limit early in the night, having two at dinner and then another two at the bar before leaving the restaurant. She, no doubt, had too much to drink and was still feeling the effects of the alcohol as she lay in bed. Reaching over with her right hand, she felt for Michael beside her. He was naked; they both were. The memory of the night's love making was now coming back to her. The thought of it stirred her once again. She began to cuddle up against Michael's backside. He was still asleep laying on his left side, facing the bedroom windows, the morning light now pouring in on them. Diana wrapped an arm around his waist, pulling herself tightly to him. She felt a warmth between her legs, as her hand wandered downward onto Michael's flat stomach, into his pelvic area, and back up to his chest. Her hand resting there, left to feel his beating heart. Feeding her growing desire, she kissed his shoulder. Diana attempted to move herself closer to him, as if she could get any closer, her body now completely against his.

He moaned, saying, "Good morning, tiger," without fully waking or turning to her.

She asked, "What happened last night?"

"You were an animal," he said, now coming to life.

"Really, what happened? The night is a blur."

"You got blasted. We came home. We fucked. You wore me out. That's what happened."

He rolled over to face her, now fully awake. He wrapped his arms around her, kissing her deeply. She surrendered to him, suddenly recalling fully the impassioned and rough sex of a few hours earlier. Diana had been the aggressor. Her desire was insatiable—the martinis, no doubt, helping. The thought of their lovemaking was causing her to squirm, her arousal now peaking again as they continued to fervently kiss.

Suddenly their lips parted, her tongue darting out of his mouth. She pulled her head back and her eyes were now wide open and staring blankly. She asked, "Oh my God, what about Liz and Sean, what did they have to say?"

"Not much, they were pretty wasted too. They walked home at about midnight. Left their car here. You were passed-out on the sofa. I was somewhat good, maybe the only sober one," he said, now bragging. Shifting the conversation, almost forgetting about the kiss just a moment ago, Michael asked, "Should I go down and make the coffee?"

"Can you? My head hurts a little. Are you going into work today?" He simply shook his head up and down, in reply. "It is Saturday," she protested with a pout.

"I have to hon. I am meeting with Bernard and the boys about the audit. I'll only be gone for a few hours. I will drive in and be back before five."

Michael refused to tell Diana that the government "audit" was not a regulatory matter but a criminal investigation. He didn't see any reason to do so. Not now anyway when she was so excited at the thought of having a baby. Today, he was going to recommend to Bernard that the company lay all its cards on the table with the feds. They had not broken the law, he was sure of it. He had to meet with the Franklins to discuss his strategy, to put an end to this scrutiny, and avoid a criminal prosecution for Bernard and maybe even the boys. The fund had done nothing wrong, and Michael had been all over it, certain he was right. He only had to convince that new prosecutor, James Harrison.

"All right let me go downstairs. I could use a cup of coffee. God knows you need it more than I do," he said.

Michael attempted to extricate himself from the bed sheets and comforter, but before he could Diana stopped him. She grabbed his ass and thrust her pelvis onto his groin, "Wait, Michael make love to me again." This time his penis reacted to the words before he could. Taking the lead as she had done earlier, Diana kissed him, putting her tongue deep into his mouth while pressing hard against him. They began to make love for a second time since going to bed a few hours earlier. Diana twisted her body so that she was on top of Michael. Pushing herself down on him, he entered her. Diana arched her body, quickly throwing her head backward and upward toward the bedroom ceiling, as she experienced her first orgasm. They continued the lovemaking until both were sweating and exhausted. The sex, although not as rough and lustful as before, was still just as pleasant and satisfying. When done, Michael and Diana lay in bed for a few minutes before he got up to go downstairs. He slipped on his sweat pants, without putting on a shirt or underwear. His bare chest was still heaving as he leaned over to kiss Diana one more time. As he began to walk out of the bedroom, she threw off the bed covers, and contorted her body, projecting her hips upward and raising her legs above her in an apparent effort to help Michael's sperm swim up her fallopian tubes toward her eggs as they anxiously waited to be fertilized.

Michael laughed, "You really think that's going to work?"

"I think it will help. You know we've been trying awhile without any luck. I will consider anything at this point."

"Listen hon, we haven't been trying that long; it's only been a few months. Some people wait years before something happens, and with others nothing happens at all." He was now thinking about their friends, Marco and Lisa, who wanted a baby desperately and weren't having any luck.

"Well, I'm worried we're not working hard enough then. Maybe we should try harder."

"Listen, I think we are both working at this real hard but you— you're putting out a real effort. I mean you're fucking like a champ, really. Believe me, I'm working as hard as I can. I've only got so much sperm to go around. Just—you know what, just give it some time. I'm sure it'll happen soon. I don't think you should worry, but you go ahead and do what you think you need to do. Whatever works for you, ok?" he said, trying not to discourage her.

"Well, ok. Thanks for putting up with me. I know I've been acting a little crazy lately," she countered. "Anyway, if you're going to work today I'm going shopping with Karen. We need to pick out some things for the house, but tomorrow I want to spend the day together, ok?"

"You got it. We'll spend all day together."

She continued talking as if he had not even responded. "In the morning, after church, I want to go to the flea market. We'll have brunch somewhere along the shoreline, and then I want to come home to spend the rest of the day in bed together, making love."

Michael reacted with a smile and said, "Sounds good; can't argue with that."

As he walked out of the room he left Diana in bed with her legs in the air, unable to convince her that trying to force his sperm up her would simply not work. She, however, wasn't giving up that easy. Diana was a very determined woman. When he returned with coffee, she was now settled back down in bed. As she sat sipping her coffee, Diana swore she could feel Michael's sperm making its way toward her waiting eggs. He laughed and said, "You're nuts. It wouldn't be something that you could actually feel." To her credit, however, their daughter, Christina, was born at Norwalk Community Hospital, exactly nine months later.

CHAPTER SIXTEEN

THE christening was Saturday morning. Maryann Caruso, and Diana's sisters, Linda and Maria Caruso Fanning came down Friday night from Boston for the weekend. Jason, Maria's husband, also made the four-hour trip. They were all staying with Diana and Michael at the house. After all, it was convenient; there were two spare bedrooms, comfortable enough for everyone. At least for now. The baby would sleep in Michael and Diana's room until she was a little older, her crib next to the bed on the side Diana slept. Eddy Dolan was running late. He called Michael and told him that he would just meet them at St. Anthony's Catholic Church. He still had a few stops to make. Father Paul Corvento was performing the ceremony, and Diana reminded Michael, for the third time that morning, to make sure he slipped father a fifty at the end of the christening. After all, he was doing this special for them because Diana was such a good parishioner, attending church every Sunday morning with or without Michael. As a member of the parish's executive board, she also attended every church function. Diana was very involved. How she found time to do it all was a mystery to Michael. Even the breakfast spread she intended to put out this morning was a lot of work, and with everything ready and in place, Diana was still running around the kitchen attending to her guests. Hopefully, Marco and Lisa, Christina's Godparents, would soon arrive at the house and then she could put out the food. It was just before 8:00 a.m., and Diana thought they would likely arrive anytime now.

A few minutes later, Marco and Lisa pulled up in front of the house. As soon as they walked in, Diana announced, "Right on time." Walking over to her friends, she hugged and kissed them both saying, "Come on in. Do you want a Bloody Mary, mimosa, coffee, or juice? Tell me what can I get you?" Diana hurriedly moved about the room, and before they could even answer, she ran to the refrigerator and placed fruit on the table.

She then went over to the oven to remove a quiche. Michael grabbed two Bloody Mary glasses for his friends, and everyone began to pick at the food.

Maryann walked over to the island and asked, "Diana what kind of quiche is this?"

"Vegetable quiche, Ma," replied Diana, as she cut the quiche into twelve pieces.

"Why didn't you just make a frittata . . . you know, a nice frittata?"

"I don't know, Ma. I made a quiche; it's like a frittata."

"Not really," mumbled Maryann as she helped herself to a piece.

Michael jumped in, "Mom, why don't you have some more coffee. Do you want me to refill that cup for you, or maybe you want a Bloody Mary?" He knew that Diana was easily annoyed with her mother and he was now trying to divert her attention. She was on a short fuse and had been ever since the baby's birth. Michael did not want the exchange to erupt into something that they would all regret later.

"Yes Michael, fill it up," as she extended her cup. "Bloody Mary? What? No thank you . . . I can't drink that. Are you crazy?"

Turning to his friend Michael said, "Marco grab something to eat. Come on, try the eggs," referring to the quiche.

Maryann interjected before Marco could respond and asked, "Marcello what part of Italy is your family from?" She took a fork full of quiche into her mouth and sipped from her coffee cup, waiting for a reply.

"They are from Sicily," he said.

"Oh, Sicily," exclaimed Maryann, as if to say that's not a part of Italy. "We are from Calabria. My husband Vincenzo was born there, you know," she offered.

Marco nodded his head, "Oh that's nice."

"Are your parents still alive?"

"Yes, they are both still alive," Marco said. "They will be here shortly, I'm sure."

"Oh, are they coming?" asked Maryann.

Marco nodded his head yes. He looked over at Lisa, who was standing near the kitchen island with Diana's sisters and brother-in-law. His gaze was fixed on them, as if to say get me out of here. Michael picked up on the furtive glances and came over to rescue him.

The monitor in the kitchen made a sound—it was the baby. She was now beginning to fuss. Michael, standing with Marco and his mother-in-law said, "Diana the baby."

Diana put down the box of pastries that Marco and Lisa brought with them and asked, "Oh, is she getting up?" Glancing around the kitchen to make sure everything was in order, she said, "Let me go check." She headed upstairs with Lisa right behind her.

"Marco let's go upstairs with Diana. I think she is going to get the baby ready," said Michael. "Why don't we go see?"

"Great idea. I'm right behind you."

Overhearing their discussion, Maryann put down her plate and cup and said, "I'll come up too. Diana may need my help."

The two friends looked at each other and rolled their eyes as she walked ahead of them shouting, "Diana, it's your mum, I'm coming up to help," as if Diana didn't know who it was calling out to her.

———◆———

Eddy Dolan was just putting on his tie when he realized that he forgot to buy a christening card. It had always been his wife who had remembered the birthdays and anniversaries, had bought the cards and presents, and had attended the wakes and funerals, all because Eddy never remembered to do so. His heavy drinking had been a real problem at the time. Margaret Dolan had been gone for more than eleven years now from a heart attack at the age of forty-six while Michael was still in high school. Eddy had not gotten used to the idea that he needed to do these types of things for himself. Sometimes Michael would remember and help him. Other times, it was his daughter-in-law. When no one was around, it would some-times not get done at all. This was one of those times, although through the years, Eddy had gotten much better, ever since his sobering moment.

He once again unknotted the tie and began to loop it through for the third time. Eddy looked at himself in the mirror and wished Maggie was still with him. He had asked her to stop smoking, but she hadn't. She had said, "I'll stop when you stop drinking." Neither one had listened to the other, and the two packs a day tragically had a deadly effect on her heart, a blocked artery, the doctors had told him. Nothing they could have done.

The heart attack had been massive, and just like that, she was gone. The Friday evening Maggie Dolan had died was the day she had stopped smoking; it was also the day Eddy Dolan took his last drink.

He continued knotting the tie. *Maybe next year I'll retire and spend time with my granddaughter. Maggie would have liked that.* She also would have loved this little girl. His eyes filled with tears, and a familiar sadness overcame him. He tried to refocus and shake off the feeling of despair he still occasionally felt when he thought about his wife. He looked at himself in the mirror, the grey hairs now outnumbering the black. He refocused on his tie. He tried to shake off the sadness and thought that this was a time to celebrate his granddaughter, not to lament over the past. As he straightened himself up, Eddy knotted the tie tightly to his collar, combed his hair, and brushed his clothes with both his hands, as if to ensure there were no wrinkles anywhere. It was a habit. He looked good. *Not bad for a guy who had no fashion sense.* Now he was getting excited to get to the church and see everyone. He would first run to the CVS and get a card, then make another stop at the bank to get cash. He would take one thousand dollars from his savings account and stuff it into the card and head over to the church. He grabbed his keys and slipped on his new shoes, quickly running out the door.

CHAPTER SEVENTEEN

NATIONWIDE Mortgage Services was one of the largest mortgage-lending companies in the country, with offices in thirty-two states. Bill Tesler was one of five compliance officers in the company and at age sixty-one, the oldest. His department had thirty-four employees, and he was responsible for overseeing compliance for the northeast region. Nationwide's corporate headquarters was located on Water Street in New York City, on the thirty-third floor of a building overlooking the Brooklyn Bridge and the South Street Seaport, almost directly below Tesler's office window. His office had an unobstructed view of the East River, from the banks of lower Manhattan to the shores of Brooklyn. It was one of the things that impressed Tesler and visitors alike. The company office could be found in the shadows of the banking and financial industry giants—Wall Street and the New York Stock Exchange only a few blocks away.

When the news about Bender Capital Lending broke, Tesler was in his office gazing out the window with several files laid out on his desk. He was dealing with a dozen issues involving loan irregularities—regulatory and statutory violations that required his immediate attention. The auditors were not so friendly these days and were up his ass over the issues that he was now working on to clear quickly. It wasn't until day's end, when Bill Tesler learned of the New Jersey attorney general's lawsuit and the allegations being made against Bender and its officers, including his replacement there, Michael Dolan. He was watching CNN in his New Canaan Connecticut home just before 8:00 p.m. when a recorded interview of Richard Banks with Wolf Blitzer aired. He stared blankly at the TV until Emily, his wife, called him to the kitchen table. He wasn't sure whether to call Gerald Bender or not. He then thought maybe he should call Wall but realized that made no sense.

He decided to wait and see what if anything else unfolded. He got up from the couch in the family room and went to the freezer, pulling out a bottle of Beefeaters gin and opening a bottle of tonic he poured both over some ice into a tall glass. Emily looked at him in bewilderment but said nothing as she placed the roast and potatoes on the table. Bill Tesler calmly sat down, took a large mouthful of the cold drink, and then asked his wife to pass the chicken, oblivious to what she was serving. As he took the plate from her he then asked, "Any lime for my drink?"

———————◆———————

Kelly Updike sat in his office and watched the reporter on the Bloomberg Financial News recount the allegations of a lawsuit brought by the New Jersey attorney general against Bender Capital Lending. Listening intently, Kelly, was more importantly focused on one of the named defendants, Michael Dolan. He could not believe what he was hearing, immediately thinking of Diana, and how this would affect her. He wondered if she even knew. If she did, he was sure she would have called him and asked to leave to be with her husband. He concluded she didn't. It was 2:00 p.m., and Diana was just finishing an audit, a short distance away, in New Rochelle, New York. He spoke to her earlier and guessed she was probably now in her car on her way back to the office. He buzzed his assistant Nancy, asking her to come into his office. He greeted her at the door, closing it behind them. He instructed Nancy to have Diana come see him as soon as she returned. He began to fill her in on what was going on.

———————◆———————

Diana was a surrogate daughter to Kelly Updike, in some sense making up for the two daughters that no longer spoke to him. His divorce, after twenty-three years of marriage, had come as a shock to the girls, although it had been inevitable after years of not getting along with his wife, Lorna. They'd been living separate lives and had hardly spoken to one another at the end. The split had been mutual, but when Kelly foolishly and prematurely had announced he'd been seeing Nancy, his assistant,

Lorna had become vengeful and had turned the girls against him, telling them it had been an affair with a younger woman that had driven them apart. Kelly was fifty-six and Nancy forty-three. It wasn't like Kelly had fallen for some twenty-year-old gold digger. But Kelly's twenty-one and nineteen-year-old daughters had naturally believed their mother. The girls had completely abandoned him and had recited over and over the mantra, *How could dad have done such a thing to mom?* As much as he'd tried to explain, they wouldn't listen. Kelly had felt helpless and betrayed after the divorce, deciding to leave Boston to head the new office in Connecticut, a move the partners had contemplated for a long while. Nancy and Diana were the only company employees to leave Boston and join him. He would never forget what Diana had done and the sacrifices she had made to help him open that office. He really respected her for it and was now deeply concerned for her.

———————◆———————

Kelly asked Nancy not to tell anyone in the office about what he just saw on the TV. He was worried about what others might say to Diana before he could speak to her and break the news. Nancy, of course, agreed as Diana was a dear friend who she liked very much and would do anything for. She was now visibly shaken and worried about her and Michael, wondering how Diana would take the news. Not good, she supposed. Nancy's voice trembled as she spoke, and Kelly put a comforting arm around her, telling her everything would be ok. Nancy looked up at him saying, "Kelly, do you really think so?"

Nancy stood near the window talking to Patty, the receptionist, and seeing Diana she ran outside to meet her, as she was bustling toward the building from the parking lot. Approaching her with a smile on her face Nancy said, "Diana honey, Kelly wants to see you right away."

"Ok, do you know what about?"

"No honey. He just said he wanted to see you as soon as you got back to the office."

"Thanks Nancy. I'll go see him in a few. I have to stop at the ladies' room first."

"He said immediately. I'll walk with you to the office. Come on," she said.

Wondering what he could possibly want, Diana hurried to his office as ordered. Nancy bounded beside her, making small talk along the way.

When the two of them arrived at the office, Kelly was standing at Nancy's desk. Diana asked, "Kelly hi. You wanted to see me?"

"Yes, step into my office," he directed, gently putting his hand around the small of her back as he guided her through the door.

Turning, she looked at Nancy who was now standing stiffly at her desk, looking very stoic, her arms folded in front of her. At second glance, Diana saw tears in the corners of Nancy's eyes, as she dabbed them with a small tissue she was holding in her hand.

The look on her face was initially one of confusion and disbelief. She was trying to absorb what Kelly delicately told her about the story he just saw on the cable news, almost an hour ago. Kelly had no other information other than what was in the news report and what he could read on the internet, which was more of the same. He had even checked YouTube to see if the press conference was posted there yet, but it was not. Diana sat silently as Kelly assured her that this would likely pass, and truth be told, no one would believe Michael could ever have been involved in such a scam. He assured her that there was nothing to worry about, that it had to be a mistake. Kelly knew that Diana would not be so easily persuaded, and he was not surprised when she slumped in her chair and began to shake and sob very reservedly. Diana was not one to show her emotions publicly, but she was comfortable doing so in front of Kelly, her mentor and good friend. He put a hand on her shoulder, offering comfort and support. He again reassured her that this had to be a big mistake.

She wiped the tears from her eyes, smudging her makeup, saying, "I need to call Michael and see if he's ok." She sat silently reflecting. After a few moments, she said, "I can't believe this is happening."

Kelly nodded his head and said, "Stay here. Use my office to call Michael. Take all the time you need and use my bathroom to freshen up before you come out."

Kneeling before her, Kelly gently took her hands in his and said, "Everything will be ok." He then got up, gave her a kiss on the forehead, and walked out of the room saying, "If you need me I'll be outside with Nancy. She's worried about you. Are you ok? Do you need anything?"

She shook her head and whispered, "Thank you, Kelly. You're a good friend. Tell Nancy I'm fine. Thanks."

Diana got up from the chair and walked into Kelly's bathroom. Standing at the sink, she looked at herself in the mirror. She was pale, and her makeup had run down her face. She frowned. *I look horrible.* Diana washed her face, hoping it would lift her mood. It seemed to help a little. She next took eyeliner and lipstick from her purse and began to apply it. *That's better, much better.*

She was now ready to call Michael and face whatever he had to tell her, unsure of what to expect, but hopeful it wasn't as bad as she understood it to be.

CHAPTER EIGHTEEN

THE lawyers continued talking, and all the while the three of them sat silently listening to their game plan for moving forward. All Michael heard was; do nothing, monitor, ignore, avoid, and hope to hell it all goes away. *Was this really the best they could come up with?* Suddenly his cell phone rang. He instinctively knew it was his wife. *Fuck it's her. Forgot to call, big mistake.* Answering he said, "Hi hon."

Diana did not respond but breathed a sigh of relief upon hearing his voice. Her own voice now quivering, she whispered, "Michael are you ok?"

Immediately he knew that she knew, and without any attempt to explain he answered, "I'm fine, we are at the lawyers' office right now."

Unable to maintain her composure, she began to sob. Holding the cellphone to her ear with both her hands she asked, "Michael what is going on?"

"Well it's complicated but nothing to worry about . . . the lawyers say they are very optimistic, they think it may turn out to be nothing."

Overhearing the conversation, everyone in the room, who already had stopped talking, looked at each other and then back at Michael in bewilderment. Ignoring them he said to Diana, "Hon don't worry. But can we talk at home? I'll be leaving here shortly, I just want to finish up and I can fill you in then, ok?"

"What does that mean, is everything going to be ok?" she asked hopefully.

Ignoring her question, he said, "You know that this is bullshit, right?"

Diana paused for a moment and said, "Of course. I know you wouldn't be involved in such a thing, but I'm not so sure about Gerry and Wallace." Hearing herself say those words suddenly made her feel better. "I am leaving work, see you at home," she said with a little more confidence. She hung up before he could respond.

Michael held the phone to his ear, her words resonating with him. Putting the phone down, he looked at Gerry and Wallace. He now didn't know what to make of the two of them, Diana having planted a seed of doubt.

Almost immediately Wallace asked, "How is Diana?"

Michael said, "A little shaken but ok. I better get home. Do you still need me?"

Austin stood up and said, "Michael no. No, of course not. Go home to your wife and tend to her. I imagine she is upset."

Of course, she is upset wouldn't you be? "Yea, ok thanks," replied Michael.

"But just keep a few things in mind," said Austin. "It's going to get worse before it gets better. There will be more media coverage on this and it may—no, it will get ugly."

Michael grimaced at the thought, causing Austin to mercifully end it there, although he could have gone on about the severe pounding they would all likely get from the press. Changing the subject, he warned, "Any calls you get about this matter, please no comment. Refer any inquiries to this office. We will issue a press release to try and get ahead of some of this. Minimize the impact, so to speak. Please don't talk to anyone about the lawsuit, friends, family, no one. We don't want the press, or more significantly a government agency, to twist and use your words against you, no matter how innocently spoken. And most importantly you don't meet with anyone concerning this matter without our approval and our being present. If anyone approaches you from law enforcement, tell them you want to speak with your lawyer. You got it?"

Michael shook Austin's hand and said, "Thanks, will do." He then said goodbye to Francis Mecili and Daniel Berger, shaking their hands goodbye as well.

Wallace stood and grabbed Michael's hand with both of his own, saying, "Thanks Michael. We'll get through this. You're a real team player. Thanks again."

Michael smiled, not sure what he meant. He turned to say goodbye to Gerry who absently waved his hand, turned his head, and remained seated looking very distressed. Michael pivoted toward the door. *Let me just get home and give my wife and daughter a hug and kiss and try to put this day behind me. Tomorrow is another day. Let's hope it's better.* He wasn't too optimistic. He then realized his car was at the office, and he had no way of getting back there.

Wallace, sensing Michael's confusion, pulled the keys from his pocket and said, "Take the car. We'll get a ride from Austin."

Michael nodded in agreement and said, "Thanks."

When he got home, Diana was already there. The moment he walked into the kitchen from the back hall, she ran toward him crying. Wrapping her arms around him, she buried her face into his chest. As he held her, she began to shake, sobbing uncontrollably. He quickly moved one hand from around her waist and raising it to her face gently caressed her left cheek.

He then kissed her on the lips, saying, "It'll be ok. I love you."

She looked in his eyes and the tension drained from her body. "I love you too," she said.

He smiled and said, "Good."

She then asked, "Are you sure everything is going to be ok?"

Taking a step back and turning his head away to avoid her gaze, he now said, "I'm not really sure. Let's hope so."

CHAPTER NINETEEN

IT was 7:40 a.m. and looking at the clock one more time, Karen reluctantly got out of bed. Half asleep, she walked down the hall to the kitchen and began to brew the coffee. Diana, in the guest bedroom, was still asleep, or so Karen thought anyway. She did not want to disturb her. Not yet, not after last night. Looking out the window, it appeared to her that Greenwich Avenue was coming to life. Joggers and early morning strollers were now picking up coffees, bagels, and pastries, as they filled the sidewalk below Karen's second floor apartment. There were only a few cars on the street, not like the busy weekday traffic that typically flooded the roadway. She turned as the coffee maker began to beep, signaling that it was done brewing. Karen poured herself a cup of coffee, adding cream and one sugar. She walked past the sink filled with martini glasses, sipping the hot coffee slowly and holding the cup with two hands. She always started Saturday mornings slowly, especially after a Friday night of drinking. Usually, by midday she was ready to take on the world. Today, however, would not be one of those days. Karen was wiped out from drinking way too many martinis, and she could only imagine how Diana felt.

She looked at the cell phone on the kitchen table, picked it up, and thought about calling Michael, but set it back down. She wanted to tell him Diana was fine and still sleeping but decided to wait. It was early, and Diana told her last night that she would probably sleep in late this morning. Karen was sure that the martinis had something to do with it, but she also knew that Diana was likely also physically and emotionally drained from the events of the past couple of months, let alone last night.

Karen sat at the kitchen table, thinking about how the press reported one story after another regarding the growing financial crisis, and the toll it was taking on the economy, hard-working families, and the real-estate market. It was a theme repeated throughout the various news cycles on TV, internet, and print. The lawsuits from the Connecticut and New York attorney generals that quickly followed the New Jersey suit, brought the matter home that much harder. The local press made it appear that Bender Capital Lending was at the center of the emerging mortgage mess, and the news focused on the individual defendants, especially Michael Dolan who was characterized as the company attorney. This unwanted and, in Karen's opinion, undeserved attention only added to the indignity Michael and Diana had been feeling since this all began. As Karen sat thinking and sipping hot coffee, her phone rang. She picked it up on the first ring.

"Michael, hi," she whispered.

"Hey Karen. Good morning. Can you talk?"

Karen said, "Yes, she is still asleep. I'm in the kitchen having coffee."

Concerned for his wife, he asked, "How is she?"

"I think she is ok." Continuing she said, "Last night was very fruitful, in the sense that our time together alone loosened her up a little. We had a few drinks, we prayed together, we laughed, we cried, we talked late into the night. It did her good to be here. She needed some time away from you, Michael."

That last part stung a little, and he was hurt by the comment but brushed it aside, knowing she was probably right. He also believed that in some sense, he just may have deserved it. In any event, he was only concerned at this moment with Diana's well-being and was glad to hear that the overnight with Karen had a somewhat therapeutic effect on her.

Michael said, "Ok, that's good, I'm glad to hear your time together was helpful. I just hope she is truly feeling better."

"I think she is, and it was really good for her. Michael, I think she is doing a lot better and will be able to deal with this a little easier moving forward. Keep in mind that her world has been turned upside down. As you know Diana is a very private person and she now feels that her life is not her own . . . and with all this playing out in the news in a very public way, she feels helpless and out of control as if her life is now on display for all the world to see—completely out of whack, so to speak, and Diana needs to stay in control of her life. It is the accountant in her; it's who she is. You know?" Karen paused and then chuckling said, "And by the way she insisted that we clean the apartment first thing last night."

Michael laughed and said, "Not surprised, I don't mean that your apartment was a mess or anything, it just sounds like her."

"I know what you meant. Don't worry, no offense taken," she said still smiling.

Clearly Diana was a neat freak, a part of her need for order and control. Michael was accustomed to it, as was Karen.

"Well that is Diana for you," Michael said. Getting serious he said, "Karen, I know this is really hard on her and I am trying to do the best I can to make this easier. But there just doesn't seem to be an easy when it comes to this . . . this big lousy mess."

Karen, sensing his frustration said, "Michael I am sure this is hard on both of you. How are you holding up?" she asked, shifting the conversation in another direction, trying to alleviate some of the tension she suspected Michael was feeling.

"I'm ok. I may be a little more resilient," he said.

"Both of you are strong people. You will get through it . . . and this too shall pass."

"Thanks Karen for your support . . . you know . . . just for everything. I agree with you. I think we are both very resilient, and I also think it will fade away, somehow. One thing though, is I will not allow this to define me in anyway."

Karen then said confidently, "You'll come out of this stronger for having gone through it, believe me. I know you, this will not break you . . . the both of you, I firmly believe that." She paused and then said reassuringly, "Michael you have to know that you will not be defined by this. You're bigger and better than that."

Before Karen could say anything more, Diana walked into the kitchen, rubbing her forehead, complaining about a headache. Without revealing who was on the phone Karen said, "Got to go, talk to you later," and hung up.

Looking at Diana, as she sat down at the kitchen table, Karen said, "I'll get you a couple of Advil."

Diana said, "Thanks." She went to the cupboard, grabbed a mug, and filled it with coffee. She then went to the refrigerator for cream, pouring a slight amount into the coffee, barely changing the color or texture.

Karen put the tablets on the table in front of Diana and asked, "Are you ok?"

"Yes, I am better. Last night—talking with you—was a tremendous help. Thanks."

"How are things between you and Michael? We didn't talk much about the two of you, as a couple," asked Karen, as she put two fingers together signifying unity. "Everything ok?"

Diana paused, saying, "We are good. There is some tension, but we are good." Then hesitating once more she said, "After all, I can't blame Michael for this."

Karen said, "No. No, you can't. This was not his fault, and certainly all of this was beyond his control. And, Diana you shouldn't think that it was. Got it?"

Diana sat at the table quietly, she then smiled slightly and said, "I know. You're right." But as she took another sip of coffee, Diana wondered if he was to blame for what was happening to them. For the very first time since this began, she was not sure what to think. She immediately tried to push the thought from her mind, feeling remorseful and ashamed for having entertained the idea in the first instance. *No, of course Michael wasn't to blame for this.*

Karen asked, "What are you thinking about?"

"Oh nothing. Michael and I are good, really," Diana repeated, still having doubts about whether or not it was his fault, and if they were truly good.

CHAPTER TWENTY

THE Federal Building, located at One St. Andrews Plaza in lower Manhattan, was a large and imposing structure that impressed visitors and federal employees alike. With the U.S. Marshals at the entranceway, no one got in without a thorough screening. Security was tight, and rightly so as terrorist threats were on the minds of everyone, especially those involved in federal law enforcement. FBI Agent John Anderson strolled into the building, flashed his credentials at the U.S. Marshal closest to him, who he knew well, and walked past the metal detectors, avoiding the line of people waiting to gain entry. Agent Anderson was one law enforcement officer who was not assigned to investigating terrorism. He was one of the few who focused on financial crimes. As cool and collected as Agent John Anderson may have appeared to the visitors, and maybe even a few of the federal employees waiting on line, truly he was a bundle of nerves. To some he was not only a nervous person but a very nerdy one, as well. Anderson was the only agent in the Federal Bureau of Investigation to carry a gun and a pocket calculator inside his suit jacket. Likewise, a pocket protector, pencils and pens were always tucked in his white button-down shirt. He was usually the first agent requested by Assistant U.S. Attorney James Benjamin Harrison III for his complex financial crimes cases because as nerdy and smart as Anderson was, he was also often easily manipulated into doing exactly what Harrison wanted. That, more than any other reason, was why he demanded Anderson work with him on the Bender Capital Lending investigation.

John Anderson was always good with numbers growing up as a child. Not surprisingly, math had been his favorite subject in high school. He was generally a shy person who had very few friends.

He was socially awkward and unable to relate to people. He could, however, manage numbers, mathematical formulas, and equations. He enjoyed the order and sense math brought to his world. It satisfied a need to achieve perfection. A PhD in mathematics and an MBA with a concentration in accounting from the University of Chicago, John Anderson had been destined to accept a position as a professor of mathematics at some small New England college. That is until the FBI came knocking on his door. He had liked the idea of becoming a federal law enforcement agent. It had been, in his mind, much *cooler* than taking a position as a nerdy professor. John Anderson also had believed that this career opportunity would open the social doors his dull personality could not and introduce him to women he could never date, let alone approach. He had thought he would even enjoy the job, doing something that no one in his family had ever done before. The Anderson men had usually stuck to careers in education. His parents, both college professors at the University of Chicago, and his three brothers, also teachers, would just shit themselves to hear he was going to be an FBI agent. This thought alone had thrilled him.

So, it was almost thirteen years ago that John Anderson had picked the bureau over academia, much to the dismay of his family. Naturally, the math and accounting background had landed him in the financial crimes unit, the perfect place for an intellect who was good with numbers. Suffice to say, the badge and gun did nothing to improve his social life and at the age of forty, John Anderson was still single. He was awkwardly tall at six-foot-seven, skinny, had short, cropped brown hair and wore reading glasses. He certainly wasn't the cutest puppy in the litter but not the ugliest. He did, however, lack the physical appeal, social skills, and grace that would have imparted a very active social life. Because of his awkwardness, he was uncomfortable in large groups of people, although, he did work well with others, if it was one on one. He liked working with Assistant U.S. Attorney James Harrison. The crush he had on AUSA Harrison's secretary also helped make their relationship easier. It wasn't a real friendship, but it was as close to one as one could get. The two men were what could only be dubbed as work friends and Anderson supposed it would be the best it would ever get. He did hope for more when it came to Angie Estrada.

Now coming off the elevator, Agent Anderson made his way into the secure area of the U.S. Attorney's Office and immediately noticed Angie Estrada sitting at her desk, located near Harrison's office. As he walked toward her, Angie looked up from her computer screen and noticed him approaching. She instinctively smiled, and John Anderson's nervousness went into overdrive. All he could think about was that pretty smile and the look she had just given him. Angie had short brown hair just passed her shoulders, big brown eyes and full lips that now shone with glossy pink lipstick. She was tall and pretty. *Perfect for a man like me,* he thought. *Maybe today is the day.*

"Hi John," she said.

"Hi Angie. How—how are you doing?" He was now stuttering.

Before she could answer he asked, as he had done numerous times before, "Hey why—why don't you let me take you out for a drink or something after work today?"

No, sorry. I can't today. I'm getting the shit fucked out of me by James later, but thanks for asking anyway big fella. "John you're so sweet but you know I don't date anyone from work; it's not just my rule, you know." This was her standard answer, and John Anderson never thought to question or ask what she meant by it.

"Well if anything changes and you want to get together let me know," Anderson said, as he had done at least a dozen times before.

"John you're so sweet," she said again. "Go on in. He is expecting you," motioning him toward Harrison's office door.

"Bye, bye Angie," he said shyly as he walked into the office where he was immediately confronted with the soles of Harrison's shoes. He was sitting behind his desk with his feet on top, reading a newspaper.

"Look at this asshole. Look at what he says here. Doesn't he know he is only incriminating himself?" Harrison asked, to no one in particular. "This Perron guy is talking to the newspapers and just digging himself into a hole that we can bury him in. Fucking idiot."

Now noticing Agent Anderson, he asked, "John you see this shit?"

"No, no James. I didn't," said Anderson nervously, as if he was unsure of the right answer.

"Stupid fuck," Harrison said, as he tossed the paper down on the desk. "But good for me, or us, I guess."

Now focusing on Anderson sitting before him, Harrison asked, "John what have you come up with since we talked last?"

FBI Agent John Anderson now did what he does best, he started to tell Harrison about the forensic accounting work underway on the subpoenaed bank account statements and records in his possession.

Anderson said, "James I now have not only the Bender Capital Lending operating account and the credit line that it uses to initially fund all their loans, but I also have Wallace Bender's personal accounts, Gerald Bender's, Michael Dolan's, and Carlos Perron's personal accounts. I have an account out of Jersey for a company called New Frontier Properties, Inc., and get this, the signers on that account are Gerald Bender and William Tesler. Or should I say Tesler was on the account until about seven months ago. Now it's just Bender." He paused and continued. "Now this account is really interesting because there is a lot of money flowing in and out of it, payments to real estate companies, attorneys, construction companies, checks to both Wallace and Gerald Bender, Tesler, Perron and others. Big checks—millions in and out over the last several years."

Harrison sat taking it all in, allowing Anderson to talk on.

"And I should have Tesler's accounts shortly," Anderson added.

"John show me the money," said Harrison, in a sarcastic almost playful manner.

"Fucking show me the money," he now said louder, reminiscent of the Jerry Maguire character in the movie of the same name. He got more excited at the prospects this information brought to the table. It was significant, and he liked the direction this was heading. It was the beginning of a good case, something he thought would result in an indictment with multiple convictions, but maybe he was now getting a little ahead of himself. Anderson sat looking at him, waiting to see what was next, as Harrison slapped the desk with the palm of his hand, now anxious to learn more.

"I assume you can trace deposits and withdrawals related to Bender Capital loans and customer transactions, real estate transactions involving this company New Frontier, monies in and out of personal accounts, and to Bender customer property foreclosures and shit like that," asked Harrison. "By the way anything to Dolan?"

"Yes, tying all that in now. I can trace deposits, tie in withdrawals from out of the account to deposits into the personal accounts. I can trace it all and I'm talking millions. And it all flows to tell a beautiful story of fraud and deception," said Anderson melodramatically. "And to answer your last question, no nothing to Dolan, not yet anyway."

Harrison stared at him silently taking it all in. He then looked away. *That's a problem. We need to show a connection between Dolan and the money.* Turning his attention back to Anderson he said, "Ok, keep looking for a connection between Dolan and the doe-re-me. Let's do this. Get out there and start rattling cages now. Let's see who we can flip. Start with Tesler and that idiot Perron. It looks like Tesler was involved and may have bailed for some reason. Once we lock these two down, they give up Gerald Bender for sure and then they give up Wallace Bender too. Maybe the kid gives up his college buddy, Dolan. We can then start picking apart the rest of the players after that, the borrowers, underwriters, processors, loan originators, office managers, attorneys, real estate agents, appraisers, and even the banks, the lenders buying the Bender Capital paper, if we can do that . . . . Shit this could be huge," Harrison said excitedly.

Anderson asked, "What are you thinking, how do we implicate the banks in all of this?"

"Well we simply get one of these guys to say that they knew and that they directed them to lie—you know something like that. If all else fails, we point out that the information on loan applications is so out of whack . . . so unbelievable . . . we assert willful blindness. They turned a blind eye to what should have been obvious . . . or maybe we claim both. As we dig deeper I'm sure we'll be able to discern a pattern from the way they're interacting with one another and with some of the financial institutions they're doing business with. I'm not sure yet on that point . . . . You just gather the information. Once we take a better look at it I'll figure it out," said Harrison confidently. He added, "We'll shape the narrative to make it work. Leave it to me."

Anderson, without saying a word, nodded his head in agreement.

He continued, "John, the income reported on some of the applications are just so out of whack, not reasonable at all, and for that reason we easily get a willful blindness charge to a jury at trial." Harrison paused, and while picking at his ear said, "I mean construction workers don't normally make one hundred twenty . . . twenty-five thousand a year, nor do kitchen workers make fifty or sixty like some of the asshole Perron customers claimed. Take another look at the loan files."

"Good point. No need. I saw them and I'm with you on that," said Anderson.

"You got W-2s and tax returns, I assume, on some of these borrowers."

"Got them. On most of the applicants anyway. IRS is always happy to help."

"Well, match, no match?"

"No, some don't match the loan applications. Not at all."

"Good," exclaimed Harrison.

He got up from behind his desk and started to pace the office. "Now if we can demonstrate that the banks knowingly and purposefully failed in their underwriting process—ignored the obvious, and then tie this into the Wall Street firms, demonstrate that they knew this was shit, that they at least ignored that things didn't pass the smell test, or they willfully and intentionally failed in their due diligence . . . then we've really got something," he said, as he now stood staring out of the office window, his back to Anderson.

"How are the transcriptions coming on the interviews?" asked Harrison, turning around.

"You should have the 302s of a dozen people next week—several Bender employees from the Hoboken and Greenwich offices, borrowers who are now complaining about Perron, a few real estate agents, and an attorney," said Anderson. "Some of them were in this up to their necks, including some of the so-called victims," he exclaimed.

"Ok, let's work on turning some of them too, once I review the 302s, I will let you know who the most likely candidates are. No immunity for anyone. They get one shot at this; I'll make that clear to them. Guilty pleas to criminal information in lieu of indictment, one count of conspiracy at a minimum, then and only then cooperation deals with our assurance of a 5-K.1 letter to the judge recommending a downward guidelines departure, but that's it. Once I figure it out, we'll get potential cooperators in here and I will lay it out for them. Anyone represented yet?" asked Harrison.

"Other than the Benders and Dolan in the civil cases, no. I don't think so," said Anderson.

Harrison said nothing and turned again to look out the window. He looked at his reflection in the glass and straightened his tie. *I look good, fuck me.* His mind wandered back to the Franklin Family Fund case, thinking that he could finally forget about the missed grand entrance. He now had a case that might provide him with a grand exit, instead.

He snickered and checked his reflection again. "Michael Dolan, this time you're going down," Harrison whispered to himself.

Anderson asked, "What—what was that James?"

Harrison turned around and said, "Nothing, just talking to myself. John let's finish up the analysis on the bank accounts. I want a clear money trail on this one so there is no room for doubt. I want the cooperators in here soon, the target letters out in six months, and four or five weeks after that we get back in front of the grand jury and we indict; we indict them all."

Anderson was surprised by how quickly Harrison wanted to act. "Sure you want to move that fast? I could use a little more time."

Harrison asked, "Why, what else you got?"

"It seems that an investor on the secondary market is buying a lot of the failed Bender paper, loans that have been sold and bundled into those securitized investment products . . . ."

"You mean the mortgage-backed securities," interjected Harrison, referring to an investment vehicle utilized by Wall Street financiers wherein numerous home loan mortgages are bundled into one investment product and then sold to investors, such as hedge funds.

"Yes, that's it. Some of the loans are defaulted upon, and the properties go into foreclosure. This company comes in, and seems to strategically buy certain loans, substituting themselves in the foreclosure actions, in the process. I just want to see if there is a connection. It may be nothing, but I want check it anyway," said Anderson.

"Ok, follow up on that. I don't want it to slow us down. I'm sure we'll have what we need in a few months to get an indictment at the very least," Harrison said. "Let's also get these guys on the watch list. We don't want anyone skipping the country before we are ready to bring in people or indict," said Harrison.

"You got it," said Anderson. "Don't worry I'll keep an eye on them. No one will be going anywhere."

"Ok John thanks. Now get going and tell Angie to come in here."

"You got it," said Anderson again.

As he opened the door and began to walk out of the office, Harrison called out to him, with undetected sarcasm, "John tell her I have some dick-tation for her."

"Dictation?" questioned Anderson.

Yes, fucking dick-tation John. "That's right. Thank you John," said Harrison nicely.

CHAPTER TWENTY-ONE

INITIALLY the delay and deflect tactic undertaken by the attorneys had seemed to be an effective tool in slowing down the legal proceedings against Bender Capital Lending. Through a series of very smart maneuvers executed by Carter Atkins, having nothing to do with the lawsuit, the Bender Jersey offices were shut down within three months of the lawsuit's filing. Sensing trouble early in the extraordinarily slow legal process, Carter, with pressure applied by Banks himself, convinced North America Causality to cancel the insurance bond issued to Bender Capital Lending, which it needed to operate in the State of New Jersey. Without it the company's lending and broker licenses were immediately suspended by the New Jersey Banking Department, pending an administrative hearing. A proceeding that Bender could never win or even attend, as Austin Wainwright forbade Wallace and the others from testifying, fearing that it could be used against them later in a potential criminal prosecution. Bender Capital Lending had no choice but to permit the hearing to proceed uncontested and suffer the permanent revocation of its licenses within the state.

Banks, was impressed with Carter, telling him, "That was well played." He also told Carter about his plans to run and win the New Jersey senate seat, suggesting there would be a job for him once he arrived in the nation's capital. Banks, now getting to know Carter a little better, thought he could use someone like him, a person who could think on his feet and outside of the box. Carter did not know what to make of Bank's plans or the offer but thought either way it was a win-win for him. He could be rid of Richard Banks altogether and remain in the Office of the Attorney General or ride his coattails to a career in Washington politics. He was not sure which option he liked better, but the offer was tempting.

The Bender shut down also played well in the press, sending Richard Banks on another round of cable network news appearances that would now all but lock down the senate seat win for him come November, or so he thought. He used this opportunity to make his announcement to seek the Republican party nomination for the U.S. Senate. No one in his party would oppose him. The good fortune Banks was enjoying would likely lead him to victory in the Fall.

The New York attorney general, who was the last to file suit, followed Carter Atkin's lead and three weeks later also succeeded in shutting down the Bender New York offices. Austin Wainwright managed to keep the Connecticut attorney general and the state's banking department at bay for the time being, although he was running out of options.

Despite being put out of business in the two states, the lawsuits continued, if not only to humiliate the defendants and provide each attorney general with the constant nationwide exposure and press coverage all politicians craved. Wallace Bender, feeling the pressure of the bad press, the lawsuits, and the public's disdain, voluntarily shut down all but the Bridgeport, Stamford, and Greenwich offices, trimming the staff to less than a dozen employees. As Michael now walked into the Bender corporate office one late morning, only a handful of people were at their desks. It was a mystery to him why he was still employed. Business was almost nonexistent and Michael's job at this point was limited to assisting the attorneys with reviewing loan files that would be eventually turned over in discovery to the AG offices in the pending lawsuits. *Is that the only reason I am still valuable to Wallace Bender? Why am I still here?*

Seeing him now Wallace called out, "Michael come on in here. I need to speak with you."

Turning toward Bender's office, Michael muttered to himself, "What now?" Arriving at his door Michael asked, "What can I do for you Wall?"

"Michael take a seat. I got word from Austin just a little while ago and his sources tell him there is an active criminal investigation underway at the U.S. Attorney's Office in New York, the southern district I believe. He is going to call you, but I thought I should mention it." Wallace paused giving him a moment, allowing it to sink in. Michael was shaken and sat down as Wallace continued. "Also, I'm shutting it down. Chase canceled our credit lines. We can't do business without them and I have no fight left in me at this point . . . you know, given this news," Wallace said dejectedly. He now slumped slightly in his chair. "Gerald is taking this hard and is a mess.

I am going to tell the remaining staff to wrap things up. I figured it would just be a matter of time before we were forced by the Connecticut attorney general to close our operations here, anyway. It makes no sense to wait for the inevitable, even though there are no complaints against us in this state."

Michael got up and said, "Wall I am sorry . . . for all of us." He did not really know what else to say.

Wallace stood and said, "I've prepared a severance check for you," as he handed it to Michael. "Austin has made clear that the errors and omissions insurance carrier will continue to provide for your defense in the civil cases . . . but a criminal case . . . well, that's something entirely different."

The words *criminal case* stung hard. Michael felt lightheaded and sick to his stomach. "Understood," was all he could think to say, as he stuffed the check in his shirt pocket without looking at it or saying thank you. Both men stood facing one another silently. Michael was the first to speak.

"Ok, well I'm sure we'll be talking," he finally said, as he extended his hand to Wallace.

"Of course we will," said Wallace.

"Goodbye Wall," he said without moving.

"Goodbye Michael."

The two men stood in the office for a moment, staring at one another, again, like two fighters getting ready to exchange blows. They both knew that it was very unlikely the two of them would ever speak again. Michael and Wallace understood that it was now every man for himself, the distrust between them becoming evident as they parted ways. As Michael slowly walked through the office he said nothing, avoiding glances from others, now unsure who was friend or foe. Walking out the door, he heard Wallace shouting to his skeleton crew, "Guys gather round please . . . can I have your attention . . . I have something to tell you."

Driving home, Michael felt sick to his stomach again. He now realized that it had been days since he spoke to Gerry, thinking it wasn't like him to go almost a week without calling. He wondered what his friend was up to. He dialed his number now suspicious. No response . . . only voicemail. He did not leave a message. Michael next called Austin Wainwright. The receptionist asked him to hold while she transferred the call.

"Michael, how are you?" asked Wainwright.

"Austin, you tell me," he said.

"Well, I've been meaning to call you."

Yeah, no shit. Michael asked, "Really, what about?"

"There is no way to say this but there is a criminal investigation underway, the U.S. Attorney's Office in the southern district of New York. And I believe the three of you are targets. I am not sure who else, but it has to be you, Gerry, and Wall . . . oh yea, I'm sure Perron too."

Michael remained silent, unable to react.

"You still there? Michael did you hear me?"

"Does Wall know?"

"Yes, I spoke with him a couple of days ago. I wanted to confirm the information before calling you," said Austin.

Bullshit, you wanted to strategize with Wallace first before talking to me, you lying-mother-fucker. "I guess it makes sense," said Michael.

"I will be representing Wall in this should it develop further, which means you need to seek other counsel at this point. I can suggest a few good attorneys, if you like."

No thanks, fuck-head. "That would be great thank you Austin," said Michael.

"I will email you some names in the morning," he said.

Michael disingenuously thanked him again and hung up. He next called Marco, who picked up on the first ring.

"Michael, hey what's up buddy?"

He hesitated and then said with trepidation in his voice, "Marco, you got time for lunch today? I'll come down to meet you."

Marco, sensing Michael's nervousness, said, "Sure, how about Peter Luger's? We grab a couple of steaks and a few beers."

Michael said, "That sounds great I should be there in about an hour or so. See you about one."

Marco asked, "Everything ok?"

"Yea, everything's fucking great," Michael said sarcastically. "We can talk when I see you," he added.

Michael hung up the phone, while making a U-turn to get himself onto the I-95 southbound. He was nervous, so he turned on a CD and began to listen to Sinatra. "All or Nothing at All," a Sinatra standard, began to fill the air around him. He thought the music would soothe him. It did. It always did.

———◆———

Michael had not always been a Sinatra fan, but his mother had been; she would play his albums at home incessantly. He had no choice at times but to listen, if not only to make her happy. Eddy Dolan had surprised Michael with tickets to see him at Radio City Music Hall one snowy night in February about a year after his mother's death. Although Michael had resisted initially, he realized it was the first time his dad had invited him anywhere. So, the two of them took the train into the city, hurried into the theatre, found their seats, and sat down, waiting for the show to start. First out was the opening act, comedian Don Rickles. Eddy Dolan really liked him and his style of insult humor. Sinatra joined him on stage before the end of the routine for a few minutes, laughing and joking with a drink in hand. Rickles then exited the stage, and the chairman of the board was left alone, with the orchestra down in the pit before him. After the third song, Michael, despite his youth, began to appreciate the genius of Sinatra. And when "Old Blue Eyes" stumbled on the lyrics slightly, as he sometimes did at that point in his career, Michael impulsively stood up in the silence of the auditorium and shouted toward the stage, "We love you Frank." It set off a roar of laughter and applause from the audience, and Sinatra, in a way only he could do, raised a pointed finger to the balcony toward Michael, with Jack Daniels and water-rocks in hand, saying, "I love you too kid," to everyone's delight. Eddy Dolan threw his arm around his son, doing so tearfully, but full of laughter. Michael cherished the memory of that evening not only as a tribute to his mother but also as the start of a long overdue father-son healing process. It's now what he thought of as he drove to Brooklyn and listened to the music playing in his car all those years later.

Marco looked at his phone and wondered sullenly what was up with Michael, sensing it had to be something significant. He just did not sound right, and Marco was worried. Whatever it was, he would know shortly. He called out to his secretary and asked her to clear his schedule the rest of the day. He told her that he had a personal matter to attend to and that it was likely he would not be back to the office before five, if at all. Walking down the hall to his friend and supervising senior partner's office, he poked his head in and asked Jeffrey Gold if he knew any good criminal defense attorneys.

Looking puzzled, but not asking any questions, he offered up one name. Walking down the hall to the elevators, Marco called for a car service, one way to Brooklyn, no waiting necessary, one passenger, pickup midtown, departure immediately. He jumped through the first elevator door that slid open, not knowing if it was going up or down. It was down. Marco waited in the lobby a few minutes then walked out to meet the black sedan as it slowly pulled up in front of the building. He got in and left to meet Michael, still wondering what was going on.

CHAPTER TWENTY-TWO

PHILLIP Richardson impatiently stood in line at the Federal Building with his court-issued attorney ID in one hand and a briefcase in the other. The line of people in the separate attorney and employee entrance was much shorter than the one reserved for the public. Despite this, the renowned criminal defense attorney was annoyed by the short wait nonetheless. Richardson was not very patient. A very good-looking man, he was only about five-foot-seven and weighed around one hundred ninety-five pounds. Although some considered him fat, he and most others thought him only a little plump, while some would even say pleasantly plump. Despite his diminutive stature, in a courtroom he appeared a giant. He was smart, articulate, flamboyant, and smooth talking. He was charming and disarming to judges, prosecutors, and jurors alike. Richardson was a very talented trial lawyer not unlike a Clarence Darrow or an Alan Dershowitz, the latter to whom he was most often compared. As impressive as he was in the courtroom, he was equally talented at the negotiation table, able to strike lucrative bargains for his corporate and business minded clients, and favorable plea deals for his mostly white-collar, criminal clientele.

Today he was on his way to see James Harrison about the Stuart Vogel insider trading case, a prosecution that already resulted in three guilty pleas but that in the end was obstinately going nowhere. He knew it, Harrison knew it, and FBI agent Carl Bronson knew it. But the attorney and agent insisted they had something, still refusing to let go—and rightly so.

⸻

Vogel was as high profile as they come. He ran a nine-billion-dollar hedge fund known as the Vogel Fund out on the Gold Coast of Long Island. It was by invitation only. If your cash net worth was one hundred million or more, consider yourself invited, Vogel would often jokingly say to his South Hampton beach house party guests. But there was no joking about what he was doing for his clients. Vogel was all business and his return on investment was significantly better than any other. He surrounded himself with the brightest and best in the industry. He knew and befriended everyone from doormen to CEO's, and politicians to celebrities, some of whom were clients and others who were not. Despite the nature of the relationship, they all played a role and served a specific purpose; there was a use for everyone. Vogel extracted every bit he could from every resource he had—that's what made him more than successful.

So, it wasn't unusual when a young analyst, looking to curry favor with the boss, came to him with information on Pharma Sales Corp., which could make Vogel and the fund a very large sum of money. The information was highly sensitive and, of course, acquired in a manner that violated multiple SEC rules and federal criminal statutes. Pharma was in the middle of negotiating the extension of an exclusive distribution agreement for several branded and lucrative prescription drugs that was set to expire soon. It seemed that the contract would not be extended. The failure to do so would open the door for other pharmaceutical distributors to make the drugs available to retailers, leaving Pharma Sales without an exclusivity arrangement and a long-term lockdown on the marketplace. The announcement, if made, was to be made shortly, and with Pharma's stock at an all-time high, the news would be devastating to its share price. Vogel and his people checked and confirmed quickly that the analyst's information was solid—the vetting completed in only three days. The intelligence was now corroborated, and Stuart Vogel knew just what to do with it.

Vogel, who held a rather large position in Pharma, slowly began to dump shares while shorting the stock—a practice of selling a borrowed security at a higher price only to be purchased later at a lower price—knowing that the company's share price would plummet shortly before the announcement. He did this quietly through the fund and various other entities surreptitiously owned or managed by him, so as not to panic the market or alert the SEC and other government agencies to his activities. The well-timed trades worked like a charm, and the Vogel Fund made one hundred twenty-one million dollars on the sale and three hundred forty million on the short. Stuart Vogel cautioned the analyst to say nothing, and his security people made certain he remained silent. They watched his every movement, scrutinized his every association, and monitored all his communications.

If the analyst so much as farted in church, Vogel's people would smell and air it out before the stench hit the choir. There was nothing he did that they didn't know about.

When the young attorney, who passed on the information to a friend, came under suspicion and a lone text message containing the confidential information was discovered, an SEC investigation was started. In that moment, Vogel was aware, mobilized, and tightening the reins. The DOJ was alerted, and the attorney gave up his friend as part of a plea deal, and the friend gave up the analyst. At this point, Vogel was already insulated and speaking to Richardson, who he met years earlier through an exclusive S&M club frequented by the two of them. So, what started out as a small, no-nothing insider trading case involving three nobodies, turned into arguably one of the biggest insider trading cases in recent memory including a high-profile target like Stuart Vogel—and AUSA James Harrison had it.

———◆———

Now as Richardson rode the elevator up to Harrison's office, all he could think about was how effective the ten million dropped into an offshore account worked to insulate his client from criminal prosecution. The Vogel Fund analyst's recent guilty plea was the last. Ultimately, he admitted to his own trades from the illegally acquired information and nothing else, Stuart Vogel made sure of that. He would likely receive a sentence of a year and a day, and serve seven or eight months in a federal minimum-security prison, a camp, as it is more often referred to, and afterward out to some Caribbean island where he would day-trade under an assumed identity and live large.

Richardson could almost feel how tight Harrison was over the fact that he could not turn the analyst. He just needed to convince Harrison that he now had nothing. Richardson believed that he could do so without a problem, and as he approached James Harrison's office, Richardson sensed he had the upper hand.

CHAPTER TWENTY-THREE

MARCO was the first to arrive at the restaurant, and seeing the crowd at the door, he made his way into the bar before the maître d' could even think to say hello to him. *It's unusually busy*, thought Marco, not knowing that a bus full of tourists just offloaded at the famous eatery. It seemed that a group of thirty or so New York Sights & Eateries passengers, snapping pictures with cameras and cellphones, were noisily interfering with a few regulars who come for Luger-Burgers and beers this time almost every day. Paul Nuzzo, with his head down and cutting lemons, saw Marco approaching the moment he walked in the front door. Grabbing a towel, Paul quickly wiped his hands clean and came out from behind the bottle-lined mahogany altar where so many came to worship through the years, including Brooklyn native Marco D'Angelo.

"Marco fucking D'Angelo, where the fuck ya been?" Paul asked from the end of the bar.

"Paulie," Marco shouted as the two men approached and embraced one another.

Paul asked, "How you doing?" Then, before Marco could utter a response, he asked again, "How you fucking doing?"

Before Marco could explain where he had been the past several months, or how he was doing, Paul continued, "Look at that hair, perfect, just fucking perfect. Nobody got better hair than you."

Marco laughed and throwing his arm around Paul's neck kissed him on the cheek, still speechless.

"I saw your mom the other day. She's still crying, ya know, about you and Lisa moving away . . . how's that beautiful lady? You never thanked me for that, ya know. You . . . you, lucky son of a bitch. Tell her I said hi. You, lucky son of a bitch," he repeated. "Me I got no fucking luck. If pussies were falling outta the sky, my luck I'd get hit in the head with a dick. You . . . you, lucky bastard."

Marco laughed and nodded his head repeatedly, finally saying, "You're right I'm lucky. Very lucky. You're right." He then asked, "How are Debbie and the kids, everything good? We got to get together, have Debbie call Lisa and . . . ."

The two friends continued to talk for a few more minutes, knowing that they would not be getting together anytime soon, Marco and Lisa having moved on from the old neighborhood and, as a result, from most of those friendships too, including Paul and Debbie Nuzzo. The couple now moved in a different social circle and the men knew it. As Paul returned to cutting lemons behind the bar, Marco made his way to a corner table to wait for Michael to arrive. Twenty minutes later, he walked in, sat down, waved to Paul, and ordered a Guinness.

"Thanks for meeting me. I know you probably don't have time for this," said Michael.

"Yea, no problem buddy. It's been too long since we did lunch. Steak for two?" Marco was now trying to keep the conversation light. Paul arrived with the beer and took both of their orders.

"Michael how ya doing?"

"Hey, Paul. Good. How you been?" Paul nodded his head saying, "Good, good, good . . . really good," replying uncomfortably.

As Paul walked away from the table toward the kitchen, Michael leaned in and asked Marco, "Paul knows, right?"

"Michael everyone knows," Marco said callously as he leaned forward, staring directly at his friend.

Following a brief pause and without lifting his gaze, he added gently, "You can't worry about what people know or don't know."

Michael looked away and muttered, "Guess not."

Leaning in again and looking him directly in the eyes once more, Marco asked in a firm even tone, "Michael what's going on?"

He was caught off guard by the directness of the question and pulled away. "Nothing. What . . . what do you mean?"

"I know you. Something is wrong. Has it gone criminal?"

Michael paused and then nodded yes. He looked down at the table, tears filling his eyes.

"Are you sure?"

Michael nodded his head again, struggling to hold back the tears.

Marco closed his eyes and leaning back in his chair, waited a minute before opening them. Looking back at Michael he said, "Shit, I thought so. You tell Diana yet?"

Michael looked up, and this time nodded no.

Marco stared at his empty glass, and after a few minutes yelled over to Paul at the bar for two more beers. The friends sat there quietly until the beers arrived at the table. "Thanks, Paulie," said Marco.

"Yea, no problem Marco." Turning his head from side to side and looking at the two of them, Paul could sense the tension. He walked away wondering what was going on.

There was a few more minutes of stillness, as the men sat staring into their beer glasses. Michael, breaking the silence, finally said, "It's the feds, southern district. Not sure how far along. Don't know much. Is there any way to find out?"

"Michael, your guess is as good as mine. At this point you need a criminal defense lawyer, someone who does this type of shit . . . white collar. Someone good, really good," said Marco.

Michael nodded his head once again.

"I have a guy. We'll go see him together. His name is Phillip Richardson. One of the partners recommended him; he is pretty high profile," said Marco.

Michael thought the name sounded familiar. Paul returned to the table with their medium rare steak for two, a side of fries, and creamed spinach. They both looked at the food for a moment, and then without saying another word began eating.

Marco was the first to break the silence between them and asked, "Michael is there anything you want to tell me? I mean as your counsel it would be confidential . . . attorney-client privilege, you know."

Michael turned his head and looked out the window.

Are you asking me to confess my sins, padre? Is that what you're asking? How many Hail Mary's and Our Father's do I get for fraud and conspiracy anyway?

"What, we're not here talking . . . just as two friends? Now you're my attorney, Marco? What the fuck," exclaimed Michael, now looking back at his friend sitting across from him.

Marco stared at Michael for a few moments and abruptly said, "I'm sorry. I don't know why I said that . . . forget I said it. I wasn't thinking. I'm just worried about you."

That's it. That's your explanation? "It's forgotten," said Michael, who was now very uncomfortable—a feeling he never experienced with his best friend before.

"Ok, I'll call Richardson. I'll set up a day to go see him, just you and me. Why don't you take some time and think about how you're going to break this news to Diana? Go on now, get out of here. I got the check," said Marco, now trying to redeem himself.

CHAPTER TWENTY-FOUR

AS usual, all roads leading from the city lead out to nowhere. Today was not any different. The FDR was backed up with afternoon bumper to bumper traffic. The Brooklyn Bridge traffic was also heavy, always a clear indication of things to come. There was no going anywhere anytime soon, although Michael did attempt to weave his way through the east side gridlock, moving from one lane to another, hoping to make it onto I-95 and home before 5:00 p.m. It was slow going. It was now 3:40 p.m., and it appeared that he had no chance of making it home quickly. He hit the play button and the CD picked up where it left off. Sinatra began to sing "The Way You Look Tonight" reminding him of Diana and tonight's taunting task. He hit the shuffle button. *I like New York in June how about you, I like a Gershwin tune how about you . . .* spilled out, and Michael shaking his head said, "No, no, no." It was the twenty-third of June, a day Michael would like to forget, leading him to think June was now his least favorite month. Sinatra's lament ceasing to soothe, Michael turned off the CD player and heading in another direction, tuned in to the radio—WPLR, the Beatles, "Hey Jude." Michael shouted, "Fuck yea," turning up the volume. Much better. Just what he needed. He was now wired.

It was almost 4:30 p.m. when he called Diana from the car. Her cell phone rang twice before she nervously answered, whispering, "Michael hi, everything ok?"

Avoiding a direct response to her question he said, "Just wanted to let you know that I was on my way home and will pick up the baby at my dad's. Ok?"

"Oh, that's fine . . . can you give her a bath when you get home. This way when I get there all I need to do is start dinner," said Diana.

"Sure," he replied. "See you later."

"Michael, I love you," she responded, hanging up the phone before he could tell her that he loved her too.

I love you too, Jesus. Fuck. He turned the radio louder. Fifteen minutes later he called his father, "Hi Dad. What are you doing?"

"Hey Michael. I'm just cleaning up a little." Now anticipating his next question, he said, "Christina is watching TV, I took her to the park earlier, I made a little snack, and she finished that about an hour ago."

"Ok, well I'm going be stopping by in a little bit to pick her up."

"I'll start packing things up and get her ready then."

"No rush Dad," said Michael. "I was actually going to sit and talk with you a little anyway, if that's good?" he asked hesitantly, his voice cracking nervously.

"That's fine. See you then." Eddy briefly considered asking if everything was alright but decided not to.

Michael arrived forty minutes later at the home of his youth, 22 Elm Lane. It was a sixteen-hundred square-foot red brick ranch that was well maintained and neatly manicured. Eddy Dolan took care of everything in and out, from cutting the lawn, trimming the shrubs, and cleaning the gutters to painting walls, repairing light fixtures, and fixing leaks. He was not only a very handy person, capable of doing many things, but he was also a very smart man and in the opinion of most, a very good detective. The years on the police department taught him how to focus his mind, analyze information, reason, react appropriately, and read into people's words and actions. From the earlier conversation, he instinctively sensed something was not right, and now seeing Michael walk toward the house with his hands in his pockets and head slung low, he knew something was wrong.

He entered through the unlocked front door that opened into the living room where Christina and his father were watching the History channel. She was sitting on his lap, with her head leaning on his shoulder, looking bored. Seeing her father, Christina reacted first and shouted, "Daddy," running to him. He knelt on the carpeted floor to give his daughter a hug and kiss. Eddy Dolan got up from the couch slowly and stood, smiling at the father-daughter reunion.

Michael said, "Hi honey." Looking over at the TV he then asked, "What are you watching?"

"A show Papa wanted, Attila-hum," Christina said.

Eddy Dolan smiled and said, "A show about Attila the Hun." Adding, "Never too young for a little history."

"Well dad that might be a little too advanced for the baby. Don't you think?"

"I'm not a baby," quipped Christina.

"You may be right Michael," he said laughing. "But I stand by my decision to help educate my granddaughter as I see fit." Turning to Christina he now said, "So how about some cartoons honey?" He walked over to the TV and changed the channel to Nickelodeon.

Christina screeched, "Yes," and this time sat down on the floor right in front of the television. Michael and Eddy moved into the kitchen and sat at the table nearby, so they could keep an eye on her.

"Son, you want a drink? I can make coffee."

Michael began to shake his head no. Eddy persisted, "Let me see what I have in the fridge." Now moving quickly across the floor to the yellow Kitchen-aid refrigerator that had been there twenty years or more, he put his hand on the handle ready to open it.

"No, I'm good dad. Just sit. Let's talk for a minute." Eddy Dolan took his hand off the refrigerator door handle and slowly walked the few feet to the kitchen table where Michael sat waiting. Eddy thought his son's demeanor appeared unusual, and he knew Michael had something to tell him, sensing it wasn't good. The two men sat quietly and stared at each other momentarily as Michael searched for the words to tell his father what he came there to say.

Before he could utter a word, Eddy said, "Michael I know all of this is weighing on you heavily. I know it's killing Diana," he paused, swallowed hard, and then continued. "It's killing me to see the both of you this way. I know this is easy for me to say and you might not believe it . . . but this problem will work itself out and you will be ok. It doesn't matter what they write or say about you; I know it's not true, your friends do too, and I think . . . ."

Michael cut him off, his eyes moist and red. "Dad," he said, taking a deep breath, exhaling even deeper, and leaning forward toward his father so he could speak softly, "I'm a target in a federal criminal investigation. It's likely that I will be indicted soon."

Eddy Dolan was taken aback and now leaning in he gently grabbed the back of Michael's neck to draw him near, their cheeks almost touching. He whispered, "Son, I love you, I'm am here for you, Diana, and the baby. I'll do whatever I can and what has to be done. Don't worry about a thing. God knows your mother is watching over you from heaven above us. It'll be alright."

He released his grip and Michael's head sank forward as he began to silently weep. With that, Eddy Dolan quickly got up, ambled to the hallway bathroom, closed the door behind him, and looking at himself in the mirror began to vomit into the toilet.

He was in there for a little more than five minutes before Michael thought to check on him. Lightly knocking on the door, he asked, "Dad . . . Dad you ok?"

Eddy Dolan quickly responded, "Yea, I'm fine. I'll be out in a minute." Holding on tightly to the vanity he said, "I'm ok, just washing my hands." Michael waited by the door and hearing the water run, he returned to the kitchen. Glancing at the living room, he saw that Christina had not moved, obviously unaware what was happening. Michael then pulled a napkin from a kitchen drawer and wiped the drying tears from his cheeks.

Looking in the mirror, Eddy paused a moment before washing his face. Seeing himself, he suddenly noticed that his skin was pale—no color whatsoever. He slapped his face, trying to bring back the rosiness to his cheeks. He next rinsed his mouth and checked his clothes before turning to walk out. Michael, now back at the table, heard his father open the bathroom door. He watched as he came down the hallway, studying his face as he slowly walked toward him. *My God, his pain is so apparent.* Eddy Dolan suddenly looked his age, a little worn and tired, almost beaten. Michael wondered if what was happening to them was now doing this to him or if it was more so the death of his mother and the years of living without her. The last few months were hard on everyone, but he always thought his father was the strongest of them all. Now, he wasn't so sure. For the first time since his mother's death, Michael thought his father seemed weak and vulnerable.

After packing Christina's belongings into her backpack, Eddy Dolan lifted her into his arms and kissed her face, while holding her tight. It prompted Christina to declare, "Papa you're squishing me."

Putting his granddaughter down, he turned and embraced his son, kissing him for the first time in a long time. Handing the backpack to Michael, he held the door and wished them a good night. Closing the door, he walked over to the window, watching as Michael backed the car out of the driveway, and drove away.

Eddy Dolan then went to the kitchen table and began to cry, not unlike the night Maggie Dolan died. He was now feeling that same despair.

After a few minutes, he walked to the counter and pulled a paper towel from under the cabinet, using it to wipe his face and blow his nose. Eddy Dolan looked anxiously toward the basement door and thought about a bottle of Johnnie Walker Black Label scotch hidden inside a storage trunk full of Maggie Dolan's clothes that he sentimentally clung to all these years. He didn't move, afraid of what might happen if he did.

CHAPTER TWENTY-FIVE

MICHAEL arrived home before Diana and immediately went upstairs with Christina to give her a bath, as instructed. When Diana got home, she began to prepare for dinner, and going to the freezer, removed a Tupperware full of spaghetti sauce and meatballs that she had made the Sunday before. She defrosted it in the microwave and emptied the container into a small pot, filling another with water putting both pots on the stove. She went upstairs, straight to the hall bathroom to check on Michael and Christina. Michael was beginning to towel dry her hair when Diana got there. "I'll finish up here," she said. "Why don't you open a bottle of wine and check the stove," now taking over for him.

"Good idea," he declared. Michael went down to the kitchen, stirred the sauce, and walking over to the wine chiller, picked out a Coppola red blend. He uncorked the bottle and poured the wine into a decanter. Michael next took two Riedel glasses from the cabinet and waited for Diana before taking a drink, allowing the wine to breathe. He stirred the sauce again and checked the pot of water, as it began to boil. Several minutes later, Diana came downstairs with Christina. She walked past him, without a word, and checked the pot on the stove, putting pasta in the now furiously boiling water. Michael poured wine from the decanter and walked over to her with a glass. *A few of these will really dull the pain of the news she's about to receive. Although, another bottle might be needed*, he speculated.

"How was your day?" he asked.

"Uneventful for a change. No questions from Kelly, Nancy, or anyone else about how I, you, or we are doing—no sorrowful remarks about how ridiculous or unfair this all is—no reassuring comments about how this is going to go away and not to worry. Almost normal for a change, thank God," she remarked. "It was normal . . . just normal," she said looking at him, drinking her wine and stirring the pasta, so it wouldn't stick to the bottom of the pot. Taking another sip of wine, she added, "The sympathy I don't mind. It's the pity I hate."

Michael took a gulp of wine and allowed it to sit on his tongue for a moment before swallowing, and in a manner like the very affable character, Forrest Gump, he said glibly, "Well that's good, your day was good, I guess." He immediately turned away from her, realizing how silly he sounded. It didn't matter, however, because she barely noticed what he said, now focused on the spattering water from the pasta pot.

Looking toward Christina, trying to redirect the discussion, he asked his daughter, "How was school? Did you have fun with Papa today?" Christina, looking bored, said, "Good," and "Yes." Then turning her back to him, she abruptly announced that she was going to color and marched herself into the family room looking for her crayons and coloring book. Michael followed, giving her a hand, and once she was settled, he returned to the kitchen.

"Do you want salad tonight?" asked Diana.

"No, I'm not that hungry," Michael said, as he took another swallow of wine, the fruitfulness of the blend now dancing on his tongue. It tasted good, sweet with a hint of oak, and a bit dry, just the way he liked it and probably as Francis Ford Coppola intended, he imagined.

Pulling the pot off the stove and draining the water into a colander, Diana announced, "Dinner is served."

They continued their conversation throughout the meal, avoiding the subject matter that was most on his mind. Christina ate two meatballs with her spaghetti, which was very impressive, Diana thought. After dinner, Michael, who did not eat much, cleared the table while Diana made espresso. They had finished the bottle of wine quickly and Michael was tempted to open another, but Diana stopped him.

Now sitting down to his coffee Michael said, "Wall shut down Bender today."

Diana looked at him as she cleaned the stove and moved around the kitchen, wiping the table and counters. Stopping she then turned to him and said, "Well you knew that it was just going to be a matter of time. What will you do now?"

"Not sure, I guess I can call Bernard and see if he is interested in hiring me back. It's been less than a year since I've been gone."

Diana nodded her head in agreement. "Well you know Bernard always liked you. Call him. He may be happy to have you back."

Michael shook his head saying, "Oh, almost forgot Wall gave me a severance check." He pulled the check from his pocket, saying, "I'm not even sure how much." He unfolded it and almost fell off his seat. "Holy shit," he cried out.

Diana turned quickly toward him and excitedly asked, "How much?"

Michael, without responding, flipped the check around exposing the amount to Diana. She looked at him and said, "Oh my God, fifty thousand dollars!"

Michael nodded his head in agreement and with wide-eyed wonder said, "I didn't expect that."

"That was very generous of Wallace," Diana added. "You should call and thank him." Turning away from Michael she then called out, "Christina it's time for bed. Honey come on over here and pick out a book for Daddy, so he can read to you. Ok?"

As Michael and Christina went upstairs, Diana finished cleaning the kitchen, now packing everything into the dishwasher. Once finished, she headed to the bedroom with her laptop to do a little more work. The water was running in the bathroom, and Diana knew that Michael was done reading. Dropping the computer on the bed, she went to check on her daughter, who she hoped was fast asleep. She was. It was almost 8:20 p.m. and still light, prompting her to want to take a run before settling down for the night. She thought it would help clear the wine from her head. Returning to the bedroom, Diana went to the closet and threw on a pair of jogging shorts and a t-shirt. She left Michael a note and ran out of the house. He had no choice but to wait and talk to her.

Back from her run, Diana found Michael asleep atop the bed with the TV still on. He had been watching the O'Reilly Factor on Fox News. The program was addressing the developing financial crisis and for that reason alone, Diana shut it off. She walked over to Michael and bent down to kiss him on the lips. He did not move. When she emerged from the shower, Michael was awake and sitting up in bed. He sat Diana down and told her. He explained, as best as he could, what probably would happen. She cried, wailing at times. He cried, cursing the day he accepted Gerry's job offer. She held her rosary beads and prayed. They asked for God's help and grace. They hugged, cried some more, and fell asleep in each other's arms.

In the morning, Diana phoned the office and for the first time in a long time called out sick, stomach problems. She told them that it was likely something she ate. Her eyes were puffy and bloodshot. Feeling drained, she lay in bed not wanting to move.

She turned to Michael and with what little strength she had left asked, "What are you going to do about this?"

He did not have an answer, and with despair in his voice said, "I don't know, I just don't fucking know." He began to cry again, this time doing it alone as Diana had no more tears to give.

When he was done feeling sorry for himself, she asked, "Did you speak to Marco?"

"Yes, I saw him yesterday. He has an attorney he wants to go and see."

"Well, go and see him today. Don't wait. Do it now," she demanded.

Diana, now giving Michael the strength he needed, stared at him until he said, "I will. I'll call Marco right now."

He then looked at the clock. It was 6:50 a.m. "What are you going to do today?

Diana, getting out of bed, said, "I'm going to go see Father Paul this morning, and Christina will stay home with me today while you and Marco go and meet with the attorney."

As she walked toward the bedroom door Michael asked, "Where you going?"

"To make the coffee like I always do," she replied.

CHAPTER TWENTY-SIX

MICHAEL called Marco, who next called the attorney, unbelievably getting an appointment for 11:45 a.m. that same day. Michael, rushing out of the house, took the train into the city and met Marco in midtown. They then walked the six blocks to Phillip Richardson's office. Arriving early, they were met by an associate who was younger than the two of them. He introduced himself as Odell Brown. He was lean, just over six foot, muscular with a shaved bald head, a strong jawline, and green eyes. He was handsome and well dressed in an Armani suit. He was sharp, very sharp. He offered the men a drink and told them that Attorney Richardson would be out soon. They sat and waited almost thirty minutes.

Phillip Richardson strode down the hall toward the reception area with a cellphone to his ear. He put it in his suit jacket pocket upon seeing the two men, who were patiently waiting for him. Walking toward them he extended his hand and said, "Phillip Richardson, sorry to keep you. Did anyone offer you a drink?"

Michael said yes, then introduced himself and Marco as the three men exchanged handshakes. Odell Brown reappeared and asked Michael to follow him, directing Marco to wait there, leaving Richardson to explain, "We are going to meet with Michael alone to maintain the confidentiality of our discussion and the attorney-client privilege." He added, "I'm sure you understand."

"Completely," said Marco, who sat down again pulling out his phone to check in with his secretary.

Walking into Richardson's office, Michael was struck by its size and shape. It was big and round, and windowless. The one side of the room was completely open to the hallway from which they just came. It reminded Michael in some sense of the President's Oval Office, except without the pomp and circumstance.

The office was sparsely furnished with a large desk in the center of the room. To the left was a long sofa flanked by two leather chairs, between them a rectangular glass coffee table. In the middle of the table was a silver tray filled with water bottles, and on one end a pad and pen. Oddly to the right of the desk was an expensive looking and what could only be described as a massage chair. On the same side of the room was a door that led to a bathroom and small walk-in closet, which was filled with suits, shirts, ties, and other things.

Phillip Richardson motioned for Michael to take a seat on the sofa and offered him a water. He sat on one of the leather chairs and Odell Brown on the other. He reached for a small remote control within his suit jacket pocket, and pushing a button, the wall began to move, closing the entranceway and sealing the room.

Richardson said, "Michael this room is soundproof, as you can see there are no windows and we check the entire office daily for electronic surveillance devices."

Michael shook his head and said nothing.

"As you probably already know I have many high-profile clients and part of the reason why they come to me is because they feel safe here. The security of this office is the first step in helping a client embrace that comfort level, making it easier for them to speak freely. Michael, I want you to feel safe with me and this place, so that you can speak freely. Because the only way I can help you is if you are open and honest with me. Ok?"

Michael, still speechless, nodded once again.

"Now we've done a little background on you, thanks to Odell, and we're aware of the civil cases pending against Bender Capital Lending, you, and the others. We know there are multiple fraud allegations. I know you previously worked with the Franklin Fund and had a brief run-in there with the DOJ. I know you are an attorney and that you're a smart guy, but other than that not much more. You want to tell me why you came here today?" he asked.

Michael, choking up slightly, said, "The Bender matter is going criminal and I need representation. You were recommended. I know you are a very good lawyer. I saw you on the news . . . the recent representation of Stuart Vogel, that's as high profile as they come, and you must have done a good job because it appears the U.S. Attorney's Office is not filing charges."

Richardson smiled saying nothing, as his associate Odell Brown picked up the legal pad and pen from the coffee table and got ready to write.

Michael continued, "I saw you defend mob killer Frank Daytona a couple of years ago, and get him off . . . ."

Richardson, now interrupting Michael, said, "Alleged."

Furrowing his brow and looking puzzled Michael said, "I'm sorry?"

"Alleged mob killer," Richardson said as he began to smile. "Frank has never been convicted of murder or any other crime."

———————◆———————

Phillip Richardson and Frank Daytona were friends growing up in Jamaica Queens, then living in the same neighborhood. In those days, Frank's Uncle Vinny was a bookie for the Colombo crime family, and he talked his nephew into taking bets for him from the kids in high school. Frank would take bets on everything, including high school sports. When one of the kids couldn't or didn't pay, he was his own enforcer, although he did not enjoy it. At six-foot-three and two hundred and forty-five pounds of pure muscle, he could certainly take care of his own business. But when Frank needed help with his operation, he asked the smartest kid in school, his friend from the neighborhood, Philly Richardson. Together they organized and expanded the bookie operation to the point where everyone was making bets with them. Soon, they were taking in more than fifteen thousand a week, and suddenly Frank caught the attention of capo Salvatore Canaletto. After graduating high school, the friends, however, walked two different paths. Phillip went to college, St. John's University, undergrad, and on to the law school afterward, all the while still in Jamaica, his hometown. Frank went into a life of organized crime, still in Queens, his home turf. Frank Daytona, the "Kid Bookie" became Frankie the mob enforcer.

———————◆———————

Frank Daytona did not like killing people, but he had done it because that's who he was—it was his job. It had earned him the nickname, or more appropriately the alias of "Frankie Feelings." Before pulling the trigger on every one of his fourteen murder victims, he had uttered the words, "This is gonna hurt me more than it's gonna hurt you." Thinking back on this, Phillip Richardson realized that his friend, Frank Daytona, had disclosed all of his indiscretions to him in this very office—the room where men bared their souls, confessed their sins, and spoke the truth. It was their sanctuary. It made him laugh to think that Frank Daytona had been so comfortable in his presence and in the "oval office" that he hadn't thought twice about revealing all his murderous deeds to him. Michael and Odell Brown, watching him laugh, joined in, not really knowing what he was laughing about.

Richardson stopped laughing and said, "Michael remember you're innocent until proven guilty," still thinking about Frank Daytona, "which brings me to a very pointed question: Are you innocent?"

"Of course. That's why I'm here," said Michael calmly.

Richardson said nothing for a few moments as he looked up and stared at the ceiling. Looking back down he bellowed, "Don't give me that bullshit. Guilty or innocent, it wouldn't matter, would it? Either way you'd still be here." Richardson, leaning back in his chair, coldly glared at Michael, waiting for a reaction. Unknown to Michael the associate, Odell Brown, leaning forward in his seat, also waited for his response.

Michael, without hesitation but with anger and conviction in his voice, said, "I'm fucking innocent. None of it's true, not one fucking bit. So, go fuck yourself." He was clearly disturbed by Richardson's comments.

Phillip Richardson waited a minute, thinking, *Good, he might be telling the truth*. He then responded by saying simply, "Ok, then." Odell Brown pushed back in his chair and jotted something down on his legal pad.

Richardson continued, "Michael it was important to have gotten that out of the way because it makes a difference in the way I defend you, believe it or not. It is easier to defend a guilty man because his expectations are different . . . lower, than those of an innocent man."

Michael, uninterested in an explanation, nodded his head and asked, "So where do we go from here?"

"First, you need to know that I am expensive. I require a retainer of one hundred thousand dollars, right up front. That is good to trial, and in the event of a plea deal, then through sentencing . . . ."

Michael interrupted saying, "No plea deal."

Richardson nodded his head and continued, "If this goes to trial then I need an additional twenty-grand for trial preparation, and then five-thousand for every day of trial, plus expenses. Can you afford that?"

"No," said Michael. "But I have a cashier's check with me for fifty-thousand dollars," he said, having gone to Chase Bank that morning with his severance check. "I will get you the rest by the end of the week," Michael said confidently, thinking his father would certainly help.

"Ok good. My secretary will draft the retainer agreement and it will be ready for you to sign before you leave. You're going to sit with Odell and tell him everything you can think of. Don't skip any detail. It doesn't matter what you think—significant or insignificant, I'll be the judge of what's important or not, got it?"

Michael said, "Got it."

"Any questions?"

"Yes, how many of these cases have you handled?"

"Maybe four dozen or so, primarily on behalf of Wall Street execs, bankers, lawyers, loan originators, and other licensed professionals . . . or just big shots who got caught up in shit. Never really a big deal in the past, a slap on the wrist, usually probation." He paused, "Sometimes house arrest, others got jail time, depending on the gravity, but rarely. I have had more acquittals than convictions, obviously." Pausing again, he then said, "But this . . . this is different. This time I have a feeling they're going to be coming after everyone, and it looks like to me, anyway, they will be coming hard."

Michael was dumbfounded by the comments and reflected momentarily on what Richardson had just said. Odell Brown also uneasily shifted in his chair.

"Not to scare you, but this time it just might be a big shit show. That's why we need to get ahead of this thing."

Michael, now even more astounded thought to ask, "Am I fucked?"

"Don't know yet. Now where's the check?" Richardson asked smoothly.

Pulling the check from out of his pocket, Michael showed it to him, and asking for a pen, endorsed it over.

"Ok, I have a meeting at the U.S. Attorney's Office. I'll speak to Harrison and take his temperature on this in a way that doesn't let him know I'm interested or why. But we can expect he will be ready to indict in a few months given the high-profile nature of this case.

I'm not sure if he will but we need to be prepared if he does."

Michael, surprised by what he just said, asked, "James Harrison?" Richardson nodded his head.

"How did you know he was handling this . . . this investigation?"

Phillip Richardson stood up and said, "Because Michael I'm good, very good. Isn't that why you hired me?"

CHAPTER TWENTY-SEVEN

"**O**K Michael, relax a minute and we'll get started," said Odell Brown as Phillip Richardson excused himself and exited the room. The young associate walked over to the desk and activated a switch that began moving the wall again, sealing them in.

As Odell sat back down in the leather chair Michael asked, "Where do I start?"

"Well why don't we just start from the beginning, when and why you came to work at Bender Capital Lending," said Odell as he crossed his legs, and brushed nonexistent lint from his pants, before laying the note pad on his knee.

———◆———

Odell Brown came from Beverly Hills California to study law at Yale University, the school attended by his father, Federal District Court Judge Malcolm Brown, thirty-six years earlier. Odell was a legacy. He was near the top of his class, a very bright man, with an even brighter future. Upon his graduation, Odell Brown had an associate's position waiting for him with one of the biggest and most prestigious law firms in California, the office of Cooper, Brown & Stern, Counselors and Attorneys at Law, the firm that still bore his father's name. He was set to join his older sister there, Tonya Brown, who had married Mark Stern, son of Malcolm Brown's dearest friend and law partner for many years. Odell was destined to carry on his father's legacy, a new generation of lawyers to continue the vision of the firm's founding partners. Cooper, Brown & Stern represented the biggest, richest and most powerful in all of California. In doing so it earned millions for its partners. At one point, Odell thought that this is what he wanted too, but somewhere along the way, his view of life changed, and money and power were no longer his guiding force.

While working as a volunteer at a Yale Law School fundraiser for needy inner-city children living in New Haven, Hartford, and Bridgeport he met Phillip Richardson. After talking that evening, he discovered they shared the same principles, passions, and outlooks in life. He believed Phillip to be a loving and decent man who cared only about helping others. Although Richardson was seventeen years his senior, Odell Brown was smitten. As his proud family gathered in New Haven Connecticut for graduation day, Odell announced that he would not be returning home but would remain on the east coast to work with renowned trial lawyer, Phillip Richardson. Needless to say, Judge Malcolm Brown was not happy. After all, he had a plan for his son, and this was not what he had in mind, nor what he intended for the long term. He was unable to convince Odell otherwise, no matter how hard he tried. So, all he could do was to set his son up in a Soho village apartment and hope that he would soon come to his senses and change his mind. What Odell's salary failed to pay, Judge Malcolm Brown provided. Two plus years later, Odell Brown still had not changed his mind, as he was extremely happy with his personal and career choices, believing he was doing incredibly good work.

———————◆———————

Sitting with Michael Dolan in the oval office Odell wondered, *is this guy as genuine as he seems?* He wanted to believe in him. "Go ahead Michael," he said, waiting for a response to his question.

Michael began, "I guess it started when Gerry—that's Gerald Bender, I'm sorry—called and asked to meet for lunch a little less than a year ago. He offered me a job in the company's compliance department. It was an offer that was difficult to resist. Gerry offered about sixty thousand more than what I was earning at the time, which was a ton of money. He said the company could use me and benefit from my experience. He said that my finance and law background would be a big plus, and that they could use my professionalism in compliance, claiming that Bill Tesler, the CCO at the time, did not have the credentials I had. I was not sure about that, so I took his words with a grain of salt."

Odell said, "Ok got it."

Pausing and looking at Odell, Michael added, "You know, I thought maybe he was just blowing smoke up my ass."

Odell Brown chuckled to himself. *Been there, done that.*

Michael continued, "He also mentioned that if things worked out well I might just be the CCO soon. He thought that maybe Bill Tesler was thinking of leaving after eight years with the company, but he wasn't sure. Gerry thought it would be a good opportunity for me if he did and there would be even more money at some point. We were friends, I thought he was just trying to look out for me and so I said yes after thinking about it and speaking with my wife."

"You mentioned Tesler. What happened? Why did he leave?"

"I don't know. A few months after I got there, it seemed that Gerry's intuition paid off and he abruptly left, but it felt more like something went bad, something was wrong between him and Wallace, maybe even Gerry . . . like they were fighting over something. I was told he was recruited by Nationwide Mortgage, but now I'm not so sure, but anyway that's how it went down. Honestly, he could have been the one to seek out Nationwide instead of the other way around. But I didn't think much of it, until recently."

Odell continued to sit cross-legged, taking notes and nodding his head as Michael spoke. Failing to receive any further cue from him, he continued the narrative.

"I then became the company's CCO after a few months. And so, as I began to wrap my head around managing the six remaining employees and running the department, it really proved to be a difficult task. Peter Li, who knew everything about compliance, went with Tesler to Nationwide, following him less than a month later. He was close with him and did everything in the department. You know a real work horse. But as I settled in I quickly realized that things had not been run all that well. There was a lot of catchup and cleanup that needed to be done. I thought maybe that was the reason for the falling out, but again Wall made it seem like Tesler was doing a bang-up job and had a real handle on things. I disagreed, but I really did not get a chance to put a finger on what the problem was because all of this happened."

"Michael what can you can tell me about the fraud claims in the attorney general lawsuits? Do you know this loan officer, Perron? What is your interaction with him? What about the claim that he and others at Bender, yourself included, were involved in a scheme to defraud people and take their homes? And what about the claim that in doing so you made a considerable sum of money reselling those homes that you and the others essentially stole away from these people?"

"First, let me say again, I was not involved." He wanted to make that very clear. "That claim is false. Pure fucking fantasy. As it relates to me that is. The others though, I'm not so sure. I mean I just don't know what was going or who could have been involved—I certainly wasn't. I don't know if it wasn't just Perron himself. I do know that Gerry once told me that he and—I think his dad were buying foreclosed or dilapidated houses, but again didn't think much of it." Now trying to reason it out, Michael said, "Listen, if I was involved wouldn't I be living large at this point? Look at it this way, all the problems seem to stem from that Jersey office and a few complaints out of the New York offices. It seems the Connecticut offices did not have any issues. I have been to the Bender offices outside of Connecticut only a couple times with Gerry. I went with him one time to Jersey where he met with Perron in the Hoboken office. Being in operations and underwriting he was out of the office more than anyone, checking on the processing and the loan officers at all the local offices. Wall would visit the offices too. But I really did not go out there much. Everything that we needed to do in compliance could be done in Greenwich. I really don't know if Wall or Gerry were up to something, I don't know what they were doing, again I just don't know," he said somewhat deflated.

"Did any of the staff come in on the weekends? What about you?"

"No, I didn't at all and I don't think any of the staff did unless Gerry or Wall asked someone to work overtime, but I don't think they were doing that."

"Ok, did you notice if anyone was having money problems. Did anyone seem to have an extravagant lifestyle, excess spending, Wallace, Gerry, Tesler, anyone?"

"I don't know. I wasn't thinking about it that way then. I guess they all did ok. I just didn't give it much thought," said Michael.

"Ok, let's talk about what was going on in the industry, the different loan programs used at Bender, the bank representatives who came into the offices, who were they, how often did they come in, who talked to them?" asked Odell.

Here comes the real interrogation. He sensed this was going to be an all-day affair. He thought about Marco sitting in the waiting room as he answered Odell Brown's questions, but then quickly forgot about him as he got lost in the discussion. After about an hour, they took a break. Michael remembered that Marco was still waiting and went out to speak with him.

"Marco, no need to wait; I think it's going to be awhile, at least a few more hours. There is not much you can do sitting out here. Thanks for everything. I'll call you tomorrow."

"Yea, no problem. Call me in the morning. Give Diana my love."

"Thanks again. Tell Lisa I said hi. I'll call first thing in the morning and let you know how this went. Take care."

The two friends shook hands and embraced. Marco wished him luck on the way out and walked the six blocks back to his office. It was 2:15 p.m., realizing that he could still fit in about eight hours of work, and twelve or more billable hours before heading home at 10:00 p.m., or so.

Heading back to the oval office, Michael wondered how long this was really going to take. Sitting down again, after the sanctimonious sealing of the room, Odell continued his questioning. "Michael who interviewed the applicants? Were the loan applications handwritten or typed? Who ran the applicant credit reports, reviewed and made underwriting decisions on the loan applications? Who had a role in loan approvals, underwriting, processing? Who decided what loan programs to use? What about audits? Did you notice anything, patterns, things out of sort? Who else worked in compliance? Give me the names of all the other employees, you know, involved in the processing and underwriting of loan applications. What were their titles and job descriptions?" Odell was relentless in his questioning. He had a penchant for the cross exam, or interrogation as some saw it. In Richardson's opinion, it was the only way to the truth, and he instilled this into Odell's DNA during the last two years. As they both saw it, the truth was always consistent and exacting.

Michael answered every question as best he could. After every answer came another question. At some point, Odell got personal, asking, "What was your relationship with your secretary, this individual and that one, Gerry, Wallace, your wife, who was sleeping with who . . . what about you, screwing anyone? Do you have any enemies? Tell me about Gerry. Tell me about Wallace. Are they fucking anyone? Do you think the two of them did any of the things they are accused of? Do you think they did anything wrong? Do you have any dirt or gossip that can be helpful to you, and us?"

On and on it went until Michael was so lightheaded he couldn't think, couldn't process, reacted more than thought, and started to answer with the first thing that came to mind. This rapid-fire questioning was done intentionally as it was designed to catch inconsistencies and lies.

In the end, Michael was exhausted, having answered all of Odell's questions, some of which were purposefully asked multiple times to test him and the veracity of his answers. If there were any doubts in the beginning, Odell had no doubts now. He was satisfied that Michael had not lied to him, as his answers met the criteria for truthfulness. Almost five hours later, Odell Brown knew everything there was to know about Michael Dolan, Bender Capital Lending, its operations and employees. One thing he didn't know yet was who were the bad guys, but he did know that Michael Dolan wasn't one of them.

It was just after 6:00 p.m. when Michael finally left. Odell Brown told Michael that they would be in touch. He then returned to his own office and next prepared a confidential memorandum to Phillip Richardson that outlined the meeting and offered insight on the matter. Odell Brown believed Michael Dolan was innocent, and he said so in the memo. He would be certain to also tell Phillip in person tonight, before going to bed. It was 7:20 p.m. when the day's work was finally done, and Odell left the office to meet his boss for a late supper at Angelo's Restaurant with client, Frank Daytona.

Mob enforcer and hitman, "Frankie Feelings" Daytona, did not know about the two of them and had no idea his friend, Philly Richardson, was gay. If he did he would have probably killed them both, thought Odell. Richardson told him discretion was necessary, no public displays of affection or declarations of love, for now anyway. Daytona's type didn't like their type even though, oddly enough, his type didn't really know why. But Frank Daytona did like his longtime friend and attorney. He even liked the young associate who he got to know over the past two years, understanding why Phillip Richardson had hired him in the first place. He was smart and a good attorney, not like his friend, but good nonetheless. As the men left Angelo's on Mulberry Street in famed Little Italy that evening, Frank Daytona stumbled out of the door, having drunk a little too much wine with his linguini and clam sauce. Now standing on the curb he kissed "Philly" on the cheek and embraced them both, saying, "Good night fellas . . . . Let's do this again real soon and next time I'm fucking paying, ok?"

If he only knew, thought Odell Brown.

CHAPTER TWENTY-EIGHT

THE Lilian August store was located in Norwalk, less than fifteen minutes from the house, and Diana wondered why she never thought to go there before. She had spent hours at Ethan Allen in Milford, looking to fill their new home, and in all that time could only find a kitchen set she liked, a square, high-gloss cherry table with four high-back sandstone-colored tufted chairs. Diana had hoped to find a large sectional sofa and accent chairs for the family room but was having no luck. More importantly, Michael wanted something big and comfortable enough to throw himself on while watching football on Sunday afternoons. He also needed a large TV, nothing smaller than forty-eight inches, to watch his New York Giants play.

The house had an oversized kitchen with large eat-in area, but a small formal dining room. This was fine with Diana and Michael because they saw no need for formality in the home, wanting to keep things more contemporary and casual. They had purchased a small dining set complete with a round table, six chairs, and a buffet server. It was not a very formal set but was perfectly suited for their needs. The living room off the front foyer, with glass sliding pocket doors, was converted into a home office. It was nicely decorated with a large writing desk, chairs, and a small chocolate brown leather sofa. The family room, however, was proving to be the problem and remained unfurnished.

Walking through the Lilian August showroom, Diana was looking at everything, wanting desperately to find something. Coming across a micro-fiber taupe sectional with rolled arms, square legs, and modern lines, Diana sat down. She rubbed her hands across the fabric. *Ok, this is nice. It's big, soft, and comfortable.* She believed that Michael would like it too. Just then, a tall, striking, impeccably dressed blonde in what looked to be her early-to-mid-forties was walking toward Diana carrying fabrics and a note pad. She sat down next to her and asked, "What do you think?"

Diana hesitated a moment, trying to decide what she thought of it, unsure still. She then responded, "I like it."

"Me too." The woman smiled.

"I'm not so sure it will work in my house though," Diana said with a frown.

"Tell me about your home. By the way, I'm Karen. Karen Bennett," she said smiling again.

"Oh hi. Diana Caruso—I mean Dolan. Sorry, just got married," Diana said, glancing at her wedding ring as she blushed.

"Congratulations, that's nice," Karen said, with a slight disdain. She was happily single and had no plans of ever getting married herself. Sitting there, Diana told Karen about the house and her efforts to furnish and decorate it. Karen informed her that she was an interior designer shopping for a client who wanted to redecorate her home in Greenwich—wall colors, window treatments, and furnishings, the whole shooting match as she described it. As they talked, the two of them really hit it off. The conversation flowed. It was comfortable and natural, like they knew each other a lifetime. Diana thought, *I really like her.* Karen thought the same. Diana invited her back to the house for a look.

They had opened a bottle of red wine and were sitting at the kitchen table, laughing and enjoying themselves when Michael walked in. He could see that they were more than half way through an expensive bottle of Robert Mondavi Cabernet, and feeling no pain. Michael, who had a few beers with Gerry at the Patterson Country Club Tap Room after eighteen, was also feeling good—the Saturday morning round and drink ticket signed for by Gerry but paid for by Wallace Bender's member account. Diana introduced Karen and after an exchange of pleasantries, Michael poured himself a glass and joined them. The three, now hitting it off, decided to go to dinner after killing a second bottle. Although no one was really in a condition to drive, they attempted to head over to a restaurant in South Norwalk, a recently rejuvenated part of town consisting of a few city blocks of restaurants, bars, and nightlife that made it a popular spot for many, young and old alike. They, however, soon realized it was not a good idea. They went back into the house and Diana threw together a chicken penne pasta dish, al-dente. She could cook, taught well by her mother, Maryann. Another bottle of wine, some espresso with sambuca, and two shots each of Mr. D'Angelo's chilled homemade limoncello and they were down for the night.

Karen slept in the spare bedroom, and in the morning their new friend had an entire design plan worked out in her head that included a kitchen renovation, new interior and exterior paint colors, furniture, accent pieces, and window treatments. Diana quickly agreed to all of it. Even Michael liked everything Karen suggested. She told them no charge, but Diana insisted on paying something, pulling out the checkbook. The trust and friendship was now forged in stone.

Within three weeks of their meeting, the kitchen was gutted. Michael, Eddy, and Sean, the new neighbor from a few houses down the street, taking care of the demolition and makeover. Diana and Karen spent weeks together running around picking out paint colors, shades, curtains, furnishings, rugs, and accents. Eddy took care of the plumbing, redoing the first-floor half bath and upstairs hall bathroom, while his buddies from the police department knocked out the painting. Eddy was relieved that the master bath was renovated by the previous owner a year earlier. Diana and Karen both agreed it could stay with some minor changes, as the house was now almost completely transformed—more contemporary and pleasantly casual. The four-inch-wide golden-honey hardwood floor planks throughout the house maintained both the original charm of the home while complimenting the more modern look and feel. Stainless steel appliances, an apron sink, and black granite countertops all worked well with the new white kitchen cabinetry. The stainless wine chiller in the kitchen was the only contribution by Michael in the overall design scheme. The family room, just off the kitchen, now complete with the Lilian August sectional sofa, large screen TV, and the Ralph Lauren brown leather accent chairs, recommended by Lisa DeAngelo, were exactly what the house needed in the end. Michael and Diana were very happy with the transformation.

Once done, the furniture now in place, the accents thoughtfully scattered, paintings hung on the wall, and a tweed rug laid upon the floor, Diana looked around and said, "I love it."

"I do too," said Karen. She then declared, "I told you the wall colors would work."

"You were right." The two women embraced, throwing their arms around each other's waists. They walked around the house laughing and talking about the design elements that now made the home look so beautiful.

Michael, watching as they left the family room, thought to himself, *Look at the two of them, as if they did this all themselves. I hope they realize I had a lot to do with it. I better get some recognition. After all, I didn't do all this work for nothing,* eyeing the wine chiller as if it was the most important design element in the overall renovation.

CHAPTER TWENTY-NINE

*T*HIRTY-TWO *years on the police department is long enough,* thought Eddy Dolan, remembering his twenty years in patrol and another twelve in the detective division; he could leave on a lieutenant's pension. The baby was now two years old, and he wanted to spend as much time as possible with his granddaughter. He was only fifty-nine years old and would retire at the end of the month, although he suspected it would be bittersweet. He told the guys, no retirement party. Tommy Williston, although sad to see his friend go, hoped that with Eddy leaving he would get that promotion he had been waiting for and rightly deserved. It wasn't too often that a member of the department unexpectedly retired, opening the ranks for a patrolman to make his way to patrol sergeant. It only happened once every few years, and Tommy was number three on the promotion list; he was the most qualified, and the officer with the most seniority. This was Tommy's chance. He had taken the test four times, and it was his highest ranking so far. Seven weeks after the surprise retirement party, Eddy was disappointed to hear that Tommy did not make sergeant.

Eddy thought he would miss the department, but soon realized he did not. He was now enjoying his retirement, although still not spending as much time as he would have liked with his granddaughter. It was six months later when Eddy suggested that he take care of Christina and pick her up at daycare in the afternoons, instead of having her remain there late until Diana could get her after work. He reasoned this way she wasn't stuck there until five or six and maybe even later like so many other children whose parents had no choice but to leave them. He argued that it would be a good thing for her, good for all of them. At first Diana resisted, afraid Eddy was not up to the task of caring for a little two-year-old girl, but Michael disagreed. He talked to her and she eventually succumbed to Eddy's request, which surprised everyone including himself.

Not only was he capable, but it turned out to be a very good thing for Christina, who adored her grandfather and enjoyed being with him. It was a good thing for Eddy too, now making up for the fact that he had rarely been there for Michael growing up, whose early childhood rearing had been mostly left to Maggie Dolan.

Diana was very pleased by the arrangement, realizing the benefits of Christina spending time with her grandfather and less time in daycare. She knew that it would have been difficult to pick up Christina at Tiny Tikes before 6:00 p.m. nightly. Christina was now with Eddy all afternoon, and it was good for her—more relaxed and less stressful for Diana too. Eddy would take her to the park, give her an afternoon nap, feed her a snack, and when necessary give her dinner too. He wasn't a bad cook, learning to adapt over the years.

Michael and Diana both had jobs making good money. They had a charming home and a beautiful child. What more could they ask for? Hopefully Diana would soon get the promotion that was promised to her and then things would be even better. She was looking forward to the coming new year and the pay raise that came with the senior auditor's position.

It was Christmas Eve and Diana was getting ready for her family, who were coming down from Boston later in the afternoon. They were spending the holiday in Connecticut. Michael was out at the package store picking up bottles of wine for gifts, but even more importantly for him, their consumption over the next few days. Eddy would also join them tonight and tomorrow, and Diana was looking forward to having all of them.

Eddy called Michael to ask what he could bring. Of course, Michael told him, "Nothing Dad. We're good." Eddy Dolan insisted that he bring a couple bottles of wine. Michael had no choice but to say, "Ok, fine Dad," and left it at that.

Diana was making a traditional Italian Christmas Eve dinner, serving only fish—linguini with shrimp and clams, grilled tuna with a side of vegetables and potatoes. Maryann Caruso was bringing smelts, and codfish—*Merluzzo*, as it is known to the Italians. Diana told her not to bother, but she insisted. Diana was also preparing a roast for Christmas day.

She was in the kitchen cleaning the shrimp and clams for the night's dinner when Michael walked in with a case of assorted wines. She asked, "What did you get?"

"All my favorites, I was selfish," he said, putting the case down on the counter and rubbing his hands together. Diana said nothing, knowing that he had good taste when it came to wine and she was sure it was all good. "Are Sean and Liz stopping by after dinner?"

"Yes, around eight thirty, but only for a little while. The girls need to get to bed early."

"What about Karen?"

"She wasn't sure. She said she would let me know. Going to her brother's in White Plains, maybe after that," said Diana, distracted by the task at hand, now proving to be more work than she expected.

"Ok, well I have bottles for them. They even wrapped them at the liquor store," he said, pulling a bottle out of the case with gaudy gold cellophane wrapping.

Diana looked at the wrapped bottle and said, "Oh Michael, that's no good. You can't give a gift of wine with that cheap-looking wrapping to anyone. I got nice gift bags for the wine, use that."

Michael shook his head and said, "Ok, I'll change them out later." Then seeing Christina watching TV in the family room, Michael shouted, "Hey, honey. What are you doing?" He walked over and sat next to her on the sofa. She turned and climbed up on his lap, saying nothing, eyes still glued to the Mr. Magoo Christmas Carol cartoon she had been watching.

"Hon, you need help?"

"No, I'm good. You relax. You're going to be up late tonight," Diana said smiling at him.

"Yea baby," Michael said with a burst of enthusiasm, thinking he was going to get laid later, thrusting his arms into the air.

"Not that, you horn dog. Remember, assembly required?"

"Oh that. Forgot," he said disappointed, now putting down his arms.

"Never mind, I'm just going to get your dad to handle it. You're useless," she said laughing.

Michael got up from the sofa and came up behind Diana and wrapped his arms around her waist, kissing her neck. She shrugged her shoulders. Giggling, she said, "Michael stop, my hands smell like fish."

"Ok, what does that mean?"

"It means stop, not now. I'm trying to get dinner ready and my mum will be here soon."

Walking back to the family room Michael shouted, "I love Christmas. I just love it." He glanced back at his wife and then over to Christina, both ignoring him. Looking out the window, Michael noticed a flurry of snowflakes falling to the ground. *A white Christmas. Shit, it doesn't get any better than that.*

CHAPTER THIRTY

THE commute into New York City was less than an hour by Metro North Railroad, the drive to the station less than ten minutes. As the commuter train pulled away from the elevated platform in the Bronx, the last stop before Grand Central Terminal, Michael's cell phone rang. It was Gerry Bender.

"Gerry, hey what's going on?"

"Not much. You on the way to work?"

"Yea," answered Michael.

"Got time for lunch today? I'll be in the city."

"Sure, how about noon? Come by my office and we'll go around the corner to Moe's Deli for some corn beef."

"You got it. See you then," said Gerry.

He hung up the phone and didn't give the conversation a second thought. Michael, who was looking out the window critiquing graffiti on the stone walls lining both sides of the tracks, put his head back and closed his eyes. The train made its way into the terminal tunnel causing the walls and car to fade to black. Michael knew instinctively that it would pull into the lower level terminal in less than fifteen minutes. He would then have to quickly work his way through the commuter shuffle to get to his midtown office before 8:30 a.m. Doing this everyday was no small feat. At night, he would usually leave the office around 6:00 p.m., running to make the 6:20 p.m. express to Stamford. Michael was getting a little tired of the commute. He had been doing it for a few years now, night after night watching the veteran Wall Street traders crowd into the bar car and stand elbow to elbow working their way back to suburbia while getting drunk on twenty-ounce Foster Lagers. Most of them were commuting from Fairfield, Darien, Cos Cob, or Green Farms, some for twenty or thirty years. Others came from affluent towns far beyond the City of New Haven. They traveled back and forth to provide their significant others with the quality of life they had become accustomed to and now could not live without.

The bar car was always crowded, and Michael would usually end up there when he was running late and could not find a seat in any of the passenger cars. It was better than standing in the aisle leaning over someone who constantly looked up at you as if to say, *Really, dude?* The crowded bar car was not any better but at least there no one seemed to mind the tight quarters. Sometimes it was so tight, or the patrons were so intoxicated they would miss their station, ultimately having to get out at the next stop only to grab a taxi back to the last stop. They would then search for their car in a sea of BMW and Mercedes Benz SUVs, sometimes in vain due to their extreme state of drunkenness. The Wall Street types, he thought, seemed like a shallow and unhappy bunch, and he dreaded the idea of perhaps someday becoming one of them.

Michael arrived at his office just shy of 8:30 a.m. and ran into Bernard Franklin at the coffee machine, who was pouring himself a cup. He knew that the twins would not get to the office for at least two hours, no earlier than 10:00 a.m., as they did almost every day. Michael mentioned to Bernard that he had a lunch date with his old college roommate and he would be out of the office from around noon to 1:00 p.m., maybe 1:30 p.m. Bernard said, "Go ahead," as they did not have anything pressing going on and didn't really seem to mind. Gerry walked into the office just before noon and asked the receptionist for Michael, who once contacted, came running out of his office putting his coat on at the same time. He told Miriam, a shapely and flirtatious twenty-two-year-old redhead, that he would be gone for an hour or so but could be reached on his cellphone. "Enjoy your lunch," she said, smiling at Gerry as the two made their way to the elevator.

"She's hot. What's up with that?" Gerry asked, jerking his thumb back in the direction of the office.

"Shut up," said Michael. "Anna would kill you . . . jerk."

Gerry smiled and gave Michael a shove. "So, where we going? Moe's, right?"

"Yea. You ok with that?"

"Absolutely. I love that place. I think you took me there the last time I was in the city. Anyway, it's quick and easy and I don't have a lot of time today."

The two left the building, and while walking on the crowded sidewalk Michael asked, "Almost forgot. How was Aspen?"

"Oh shit. It was great. My dad and mom flew out for a couple of days, you know for the holiday. We had a really good time. Aspen is sweet. You should try it sometime," said Gerry.

"Can't afford that," said Michael.

"Well . . . that's what I want to talk to you about," Gerry said cautiously.

Michael looked at Gerry a little puzzled as he held the door open to the restaurant. Moe's Deli was already busy—it always was. They made their way to a table for two, each quickly ordering Moe's famous overstuffed corn beef sandwiches, coleslaw, fries, and cokes.

"So, what's up?" asked Michael.

Gerry now got right to the point. "Listen my dad and I want you to come and work for us. Bender needs someone with your skill set, the finance background, the legal knowledge . . . you know, someone we can count on and trust Michael."

"What type of position? What are you thinking?" He was caught a little off guard.

"To start, working in our compliance department. I think we have half a dozen employees doing compliance now. It's busy and we can use a lawyer there. Our chief compliance officer, Bill Tesler, may be leaving and if he does then that job's yours. But for now, you would work under him. This would be a good opportunity for you. We are working in the subprime market segment, which is really hot right now. We're doing direct lending, funding our own loans, and the company is making a ton of money."

Michael looked at Gerry and asked, "Why is your CCO leaving?"

Gerry looked away and shrugged his shoulder. "I don't know. I think he is considering a better offer, anyway he may be gone soon. The position pays a hundred and thirty-five grand, and if he does leave it would mean another twenty to twenty-five thousand a year, as you move into his spot. Now that's more than anyone is getting in compliance, but then again nobody has the credentials you have either. I also pushed my dad to offer top dollar," Gerry added, gloating a little.

The waitress arrived with their food, and they started eating. "So, what do you think?" asked Gerry with a mouthful of sandwich and coleslaw. He put the back of his hand to his lips to keep food from spilling out of his mouth onto his shirt as he talked.

"Sounds great. Let me to talk with Diana tonight and I'll get back to you tomorrow."

"Ok." Gerry hesitated and then said, "Also, my dad and I have been involved in buying some properties mainly in New York and Jersey. If you're interested I can talk to him and my other partners—you know to see if they would be willing to bring you in. It's an opportunity for you to invest and make a lot more money," said Gerry, now carefully trying to gauge his reaction. "It's a good investment; we're mainly buying foreclosures and properties that need repair. We go in, fix what needs fixing, and resell them." Staring at him for a few moments, he asked again, "What do you think?"

Michael swallowed the french fries in his mouth and took a sip of his coke. "One thing at a time Gerry. Let me think about it, talk to Diana, and get back to you. But it sounds great, really, and thanks for thinking of me. Tell your dad thanks too. I appreciate the opportunity."

"What are friends for?" exclaimed Gerry.

The two of them walked back to the office building, where they said goodbye to one another in the lobby. Michael said, "I'll get back to you shortly. Say hi to your mom and dad for me." Gerry left for an appointment he and Carlos Perron had with a group of investors who were interested in purchasing properties they owned in New Jersey. Michael returned to his office and thought about the offer. The idea of a new job and getting out of the city intrigued him. He would have to give it more thought, but for now he had work to do, as he settled in behind his desk.

Just then BJ and William Franklin walked into his office. The two of them sat down and BJ asked, "Michael you busy?"

"Yea of course. Why wouldn't I be?"

BJ and William looked at each other. Michael looking at the two of them asked, "What? What are you up to?"

BJ then asked, "Want to go come to Scores with us? I'm paying for lap dances. What do you say?"

He grinned and said, "You're kidding, right?"

Michael missed the 6:20 express out of Grand Central. He called Diana to let her know, explaining he had to work a little late. Making the 7:10 instead, Michael arrived in Norwalk just after 8:00 p.m. He pondered Gerry's offer again while on the train and the car ride home. When Michael walked into the house, Diana was in the kitchen standing in front of the stove, as she prepared dinner and drank a glass of red wine. Without a word, Michael came up behind her. He put his arms around her and kissed her on the cheek. She turned and gave him a quick peck on the lips and asked, "Have you been drinking?" Diana did not wait for an answer but turned back to the stove, taking another sip of wine.

He responded, mumbling, "Ah, had a Fosters on the train," as he quickly walked into the family room. He lied, but what could he do? There was no way he was going to tell her that he spent the afternoon at a gentlemen's club with the Franklin twins getting lap dances from hot twenty-one-year-old strippers.

He strolled over to Christina, who was sitting on the floor with crayons and a coloring book and began to tickle her. She squirmed and laughed saying, "Daddy, stop." He bent down and gave her a big wet kiss that she wiped with the back of her hand, saying, "Daddy, you smell pretty." Walking back into the kitchen, he poured himself a glass of wine. *Shit I smell like perfume.* Before he could think what to do or even take a drink of wine, Diana asked him to put the baby to bed. Carrying her upstairs, he could see that she was tired. Laying her down in bed, Christina fell asleep almost immediately. Michael went to the master bedroom where he changed his clothes, washed his face, and brushed his teeth. After dinner, Michael and Diana sat in the kitchen and discussed Gerry's job offer.

"So, what do you think I should do?"

"It sounds good. It's more money, closer to home, less travel, less hours. It sounds good," Diana said, as she busily cleared the table.

"So, I take it, right?"

"I guess so. But you like working at Franklin. Bernard has been good to you. Are you sure?"

"Look at all the benefits. You just said it. It makes sense. I'll call Gerry in the morning and after that let Bernard know. I'll have to give him at least two weeks."

Diana said, "That would be the right thing to do."

The next morning Michael called Gerry from the train. He told him that he was taking the job but that he needed to give notice and could not start for at least two weeks.

Gerry said, "That's great, just great. Take all the time you need to transition out of there."

"Ok, thanks. I just don't want to leave them high and dry. Gerry thanks again, and tell your dad thank you too."

"Michael."

"Yea?"

"Trust me. You're not going to regret this," said Gerry.

CHAPTER THIRTY-ONE

As much as John Anderson epitomized the intellect of the FBI, agent Carl Bronson represented the brawn. At six-feet-five inches tall, weighing two hundred sixty-five pounds, and sporting a shaved bald head, tattoos, and a goatee, he was nothing less than menacing. It was the reason why AUSA Harrison always had John Anderson and Carl Bronson work as a team to interrogate a witness or subject of his investigations. Anderson would do all the talking while Bronson would hover over the individual being probed, occasionally and forcefully interjecting with a few queries of his own. It was this combination of properly phrased questions and the fear of bodily harm that usually elicited a prompt and truthful response from the subject of the FBI probe. If not for this reason alone, the two agents went to see Mr. William Tesler, former Bender Capital Lending CCO, at his downtown Manhattan office, not too far from the United States Federal Building.

Anderson and Bronson pulled their government issued Chevy Tahoe to the curb along 2 Water Street, parking right in front of a fire hydrant with knowing disregard for the obvious violation of city ordinance. Bronson leaned over and pulled from the glove box a lanyard that read *Official FBI Business* and placed it on the driver-side dashboard so that it was visible through the front windshield. As the agents got out of the car, Bronson set the alarm and locked the doors with a touch of the electronic key fob.

The two men walked into the lobby and stopped at the security desk, identifying themselves and their destination. The security guard waved them on without issuing a guest pass or calling up to Nationwide Mortgage Services to announce them as he would normally do. As the two men got off the elevator and walked into the reception area, the receptionist, Andrew, wondered why building security did not inform him of the visitors now approaching his desk. Anderson and Bronson, standing in front of the large raised semicircle reception platform, asked to see William Tesler. Andrew, who would have typically been looking down, now looked across at the two of them and asked, "Who should I say is here to see Mr. Tesler?"

Bronson, pulling his ID and shield from his jacket pocket, intentionally exposing his weapon, said, "Just tell him the FBI."

After receiving the call from reception, Tesler rushed out of his office into the hallway at a very brisk pace, his heart racing. *No, can this be happening? What do I do? What the hell do I do?* Almost before he knew it, he was bursting through the double doors leading into reception. Out of breath he asked, in between heavy sighs, "Gentlemen, how can I help you?"

Looking at one another, the two agents were slightly caught off guard by the stumbling Tesler. "Catch your breath, old timer. Sit down before you have a heart attack," said Bronson.

Tesler leaned forward and put his hands on his knees as he attempted to fill his lungs and gather his composure. Anderson and Bronson looked at one another. Turning to his subject, Anderson asked, "Mr. Tesler where can we go to talk?" Without a word, he pointed to the doors behind him and gestured with his hand for the agents to follow. The receptionist watched as he disappeared with the FBI agents beyond the doors, and immediately called Claudia, Jamie Preston's secretary, to report what he just witnessed. A very colorful and quick summary by Andrew of what happened about ten seconds ago was all that was needed, and without so much as a thank you or a goodbye, Claudia abruptly hung up the phone. She briskly walked the twenty feet to Preston's office, knocked on the door, and entered, without waiting for a response. He was startled but not surprised by Claudia's sudden appearance. He also knew that her unannounced presence meant something urgently needed his attention.

Jamie Preston, Nationwide Mortgage's CEO, chairman of the board, and largest shareholder, listened intently, got up from behind his desk, grabbed his suit jacket, and began to bark instructions to Claudia. "Get on the phone with Wiley's office. He needs to find me immediately. I'll be wherever Tesler went with these agents . . . also get in touch with security. I need two men with me and another two sent to Tesler's office. I want it locked down. Nobody in or out—and have them get another two over to compliance. Nobody leaves—and get the kid from tech support over there too," Preston ordered, as he ran down the hallway toward reception.

Claudia returned to her desk and made the calls as instructed. Robert Wiley, the company's General Counsel, at first was confused by the directive until Claudia mentioned that two FBI agents had come for Tesler. "Oh shit," said Wiley, immediately bolting for his door and running in the same direction as Preston.

Bill Tesler had taken the agents to an infrequently used conference room near reception, hoping that this would go unnoticed. Finally calming down, he asked, "What's this about?"

"I think you know what this is about. Don't you?" Bronson asked pretentiously, almost mockingly.

Anderson looked at Tesler. "William, may I call you that? Or do you prefer Bill?" Without waiting for a response, he said, "Well, Bill as you may have guessed, this is not good. Not good at all." And before Anderson could say anything else, he began to squirm in his seat, saying, "Oh God. Oh God—I'm going be sick. I need to go to the bathroom."

Bronson, without an ounce of sympathy for the older distressed man sitting in front of him, said, "Don't shit yourself. I'm not cleaning up that mess. Hell no."

Before Tesler could register Bronson's crass remark, Jamie Preston burst into the room with Robert Wiley directly behind him. Preston, a banker and self-made millionaire who didn't take crap from anybody, shouted, "Ok, what the fuck is going on?"

Carl Bronson stood up and walked over to Preston. In an obvious attempt to intimidate, he hovered over him and said, "FBI Agent Carl Bronson and Agent John Anderson," jerking a finger at his partner. "This is a private matter that does not concern you or your company. So back off."

"Well Agent Bronson, what *is* this all about?"

"It's about Mr. Tesler, and that's all you need to know. It does not involve Nationwide Mortgage at all."

Preston was slightly relieved to hear it did not involve the company but wasn't entirely sure if he believed it. Just then, two security personnel walked into the room, taking positions near the door.

"Gentlemen, I am attorney Robert Wiley, general counsel for the company and Mr. Tesler's attorney as well. I am sure he wants me present during your discussion with him. Don't you Bill?"

He nodded his head yes. Before Wiley could say another word, Preston put up his hand, shutting him down. "Fuck that. There will be no interrogation. Do you have a warrant?" Without waiting for an answer, he said, "If not, then you're just trespassing, and I will have to ask you to leave.

My security officers will escort you out." Gazing at the agents, Preston added, "Without a warrant I insist that you leave. Have a good day, gentlemen."

Everyone in the room was astounded by Preston's abrasiveness, including the agents. Wiley now following Preston's lead and suddenly feeling empowered himself, said, "Tyrone and Julio, can you please escort Agents Bronson and Anderson out?" Now speaking to the agents directly Wiley spit out, with extreme contempt, "Thank you, gentlemen."

Anderson looked at Bronson, who was now fuming. He was not used to being talked to this way. Usually a flip of his badge worked to subdue most people, but not this time. John Anderson simply said, "Ok, we will be back when we secure either an arrest or search warrant."

Bronson added mockingly, "And I'll make sure it allows me to look up your ass with a fine-tooth comb."

Preston was not backing down. "I look forward to it. It's been awhile since I had something shoved up my ass." He grimaced almost immediately knowing the tough talk did not come out the way he had intended.

Seizing on his misstep, Bronson, who felt a need to ridicule him, said, "Somehow, I doubt it," getting in the last word as the two agents began to walk out of the conference room.

Security was now right behind them. Out in the hallway, Bronson put up his hand and the two guards froze, left only to watch the agents walk through the doors into reception. They waited a few minutes and then went to see if they got into the elevator. Andrew seeing the men and sensing exactly what they were doing, shook his head yes.

"My God. Jamie you were wonderful," began Tesler.

"Shut the fuck up Bill. What the hell is this all about?"

Startled by Preston's reaction, Tesler began twisting his head back and forth in short, swift little turns like a bobble-head figurine. He then lied and said nervously, "I'm not sure."

"Don't fuck with me Bill. Is this going to be a problem? Is it—is it?" Preston asked unrelentingly, as he glared at Tesler.

"No. No problem for you or the company," he hesitantly responded.

Jamie Preston stared at him for a minute or more when Robert Wiley finally said, "Jamie why don't I talk to Bill for a moment as general counsel to this company. His discussion with me as an employee is privileged and confidential." Then turning to Tesler he said,

"Bill our discussion is not subject to scrutiny by the FBI or any other government agency. Do you understand that?"

"Yes, I understand."

Wiley, was now thinking like a lawyer. He did not represent Tesler and the assertion earlier could have been a problem for him if the agents succeeded in their efforts to question him. Wiley realized he had to be more careful. He could end up in a conflict of interest that would preclude him from representing the company when needed most. Wanting to clarify, he said, "Also, please know that I am not representing you, despite what I said earlier, so I will not ask you any questions other than those that relate to the company because my goal is to protect my client, Nationwide Mortgage. You understand that?"

Tesler again said he understood. Wiley walked over to the credenza on the far end of the room and pulled a legal pad and pen from the top drawer. He turned to Preston and said, "Jamie give me a few minutes alone with Bill."

Complying with Wiley's request, Preston turned and began to walk out of the room saying, "I'll be in my office."

As soon as the door closed, Tesler blurted out, "It's all about Bender, nothing to do with Nationwide I swear." Pausing, he then said, "I hope this won't affect my job."

"I'm sure it won't," repeated Wiley, trying to relax him, hoping to extract as much information as possible before he understood the trouble he was in. What Bill Tesler didn't realize, and what Wiley already knew, was that he had been fired the moment those two FBI agents walked into the office. The trick now was to determine whether Nationwide was at risk before Tesler perceived the mess he was in. *Stupid bastard*, thought Wiley as he said, "Bill relax we are all friends here. Let's just get started. I have only a few questions. Everything is going to be fine. Just fine, I'm sure."

CHAPTER THIRTY-TWO

BACK at the Federal Building, Bronson was now fuming over the exchange he just had with Preston. He paced back and forth around the office, saying absolutely nothing. He was mad, much more so than he had been in a long while.

Breaking his silence, he turned to Anderson and said, "That motherfucker. Who does he think he is? Who did he think he was talking to like that? That fucking cocksucker."

John Anderson sat silently listening to an onslaught of colorful expletives from Bronson, who clearly needed to vent. Anderson occasionally shook his head in agreement when prompted by one of Bronson's particularly descriptive outbursts that warranted acknowledgement. Five minutes into a very colorful tribute to Jamie Preston's mother—that fucking slut who should have kept her legs closed so dickhead was never conceived—the intercom on his telephone beeped and a male voice echoed, "Anderson, line 102." Picking up the phone, and in his most official FBI tone he said, "Agent John Anderson."

"John, it's Tony Russo. How are you doing?"

"Good, good, Anthony. How are you? What can I do for you?"

"Wanted to let you know we got a hit on your boy, Carlos Perron. He booked a round trip flight on United Airlines, out of Newark, to Ft. Lauderdale about an hour ago. Then about twenty minutes ago, he booked a one-way ticket on a flight with Copa Airline out of Miami for tonight at ten to Mariscal Sucre International Airport in Quito, Ecuador."

"Oh, boy," Anderson reacted. "Anthony, please email me the particulars. I am going to need an affidavit with certified copies of the flight information. I'm sure Harrison is going to want to stop him." He said this without thinking how stupid it sounded.

Anthony Russo burst out laughing, saying, "You think?" Still chuckling he then said sedately, "I'll get that info to you shortly."

Anderson thanked him and hung up the phone. *That was dumb. Why did I say that? Of course James wants him stopped. I better get in touch with him right away.* Bronson continued to pace, as he listened to the conversation. When Anderson ended the call he asked, "Someone making a run?"

"Yes, Perron." Anderson did not volunteer any further information, as Bronson failed to ask for any of the specifics. He next called James Harrison and filled him in on what he was just told about Perron's efforts to leave the country.

Assessing the information calmly, Harrison asked, "How much time do we have?"

"The Newark flight is scheduled to leave at four," said Anderson, now looking over the email sent to him by Russo. "So, we have a little more than four hours to get it together."

Harrison asked, "TSA on board, right?"

"Yes, no problem there. They will hold the gate for any flight he's on."

"Ok, get your paperwork together. I will get working on the warrant application and affidavits for you and Carl to sign. I'll get it over to a magistrate, get the arrest warrant signed, and you guys serve it. Coordinate with Newark PD and Port Authority Police as soon as possible. I want them on board—and take a couple of other agents with you when serving the warrant. Let Perron board, and once he's bottled in on the plane, go and pull him out—unless he tries to make some sort of run before that."

"Exactly what I was thinking James. By the way, Carl is here with me now and we will get working on it. See you in about an hour."

"Right," said Harrison, forgetting to ask how the interview with Tesler went earlier that morning.

CHAPTER THIRTY-THREE

ORTY minutes later, Robert Wiley was done asking his quetions, satisfied that he extracted as much information as he could from Bill Tesler. He was still unsure whether any of this presented a risk to Nationwide, but Wiley didn't think so. He knew that Tesler would not be any help in answering the question that mattered most. Robert Wiley got up from his chair and snatched the pad from the table that contained his notes of their conversation. "Bill, why don't you sit and relax for a moment. I will be right back . . . can I get you something?"

"No, no just need to get back to work."

"Relax for a moment and if you need anything Julio will be right outside," Wiley said, as he began to walk out of the room.

Tesler immediately realized that not only was he prevented from leaving the room, but that he was also in some very serious trouble. Jamie Preston was now heading back to his office, after having spent a significant amount of time going through Tesler's office and his computer, when Wiley turned the corner and approached him. The two men converged near Claudia's desk.

Preston asked, "Anything?"

"No. What about you?"

Jamie Preston shook his head and said, "No."

Both men knew exactly what the other had been doing the last forty minutes or so. It was a real concerted effort on their part to try and piece together what this FBI investigation was about and whether it concerned Nationwide. From what they could tell, there was no indication the company was a subject of the FBI inquiry or that anyone other than Tesler was on their radar. Preston informed Wiley that the kid, Conner, a computer genius, or geek, depending on who you talked to, was still working on Tesler's computer, combing through it to see if there was anything that should concern them. So far everything appeared to be in order, although, he still had a way to go.

As they stood near Claudia's desk, the men realized they needed more privacy and went into Preston's office to speak further.

Preston wondered, "So, what did he have to say?"

"That it was all related to the Bender civil proceedings in the three state court actions and nothing else. He claims he was not involved in any of the things alleged in those cases. He also claimed no knowledge."

"Do you believe him?"

"No, no way. If it's all true—all that going on and he doesn't know about it? Especially if he's doing his job in compliance . . . and we know he does a pretty good job. At the very least he has been doing a decent job here, so I don't think there is any reason to believe he didn't do a decent job there. There is no way he doesn't know something."

"Well we do know this is a criminal investigation. Otherwise the FBI would not be involved . . . and that it's not small-time bullshit civil state court lawsuits. This is the real deal."

"Agreed, but it doesn't appear the feds are looking at us, or that Tesler did anything here in his present position to warrant scrutiny," said Wiley.

"That doesn't mean they won't start sniffing around. We have to make sure that doesn't happen."

"Ok, what are you worried about? I know things have been a little loose around here—the whole damn industry really. But, we're good, right?"

Ignoring his last question, Preston picked up where he left off and said, "If the feds look at us—I mean all of us—we just might be fucked. The whole fucking banking and financial services sector. Shit, this whole business—it's been a real mess for a while now."

Jamie Preston momentarily looked away from Wiley. *If things go south, I may have to cash in my get out jail free card with my good friend who can literally make anything happen.*

Very few people knew just how connected Preston was. He could make a call and any amount of trouble he had would just disappear. He decided to hold off doing anything for now. He would just wait to see what develops. No need to call in any favors—not yet anyway.

Now looking at Preston nervously, Wiley asked, "So what do you want to do?"

Preston thought for a moment. "Tell Bill to take a few days off. We continue to go through everything and speak to the compliance staff, especially that guy who came with him from Bender. And when we are certain he didn't expose us to anything and we don't need him for anything else, we cut him loose. Come to think of it, maybe we fire everyone in compliance."

Wiley shook his head in agreement. "Well, I don't think we can fire *everyone* in compliance, but I'll tell Bill to take the rest of the week off and that we are working through how to best deal with the FBI. Basically, that we will circle back on Monday."

"Sounds good," he said. As Wiley began to leave, Preston stopped him. "Maybe I should come with you to give the appearance that everything is ok. I don't want him to overthink this or do something stupid."

"Good idea. Just lull him into a false sense of security and then *bam*—get the fuck out. You're fired," said Wiley with a smile on his face.

Preston looked at Wiley and began to laugh, the seriousness of the earlier conversation now beginning to fade. "You're cold, stone cold, but my thoughts exactly. Let's go see our friend Mr. Tesler. He's probably wondering what the hell happened to us."

The two men made their way down the hall to the conference room where they left him earlier. When they arrived, the two security guards, Julio and Tyrone, were there alone. Tesler was nowhere in sight.

Wiley asked, "Julio where's Bill Tesler?"

Julio hesitated and said, "He told me he was not feeling well, like he was going to throw up or something, so I took him to the bathroom and when we got there he passed out on the floor. I ran out to get help and when I got back with Tyrone he was gone."

Preston looked at Julio. He got in his face and screamed, "Jesus Christ, are you kidding me? Are you fucking kidding me?"

Julio looked at Preston and then Wiley. "I'm sorry, I didn't think the old dude was going to run out like that, man. It's crazy, just crazy."

CHAPTER THIRTY-FOUR

HUSTLING through the Newark International Airport terminal, Carlos Perron looked toward the United Airlines baggage
check-in counter about fifty feet away. Out of shape, over-
weight and sweating, it was a labored effort. As he approached, Perron,
who was breathing heavy and wheezing from years of smoking, began
to relax. Now walking up to the counter with his boarding pass in
hand, he was completely calm and under control. The younger attractive female agent accepted his boarding pass with a smile and began
typing on her computer keyboard, while eyeing the screen before her.
Perron looked at her name tag pinned just above her right breast—
Venessa. Then moving his eyes downward and back up, he looked her
over. *Pretty face, but ass and tits too small, too damn old.* He liked them
young, much younger.

"Just the one bag sir?" she asked, snapping him back to the present.
He looked at her without responding. She asked again, "One bag?"

"Si—yes, yes, one bag," Perron stuttered.

Without looking at him, eyes still glued on her computer screen,
she instructed him to place the bag on the scale in front of him. Perron
complied and lifted the suitcase onto the stainless-steel gauge, the LED
dial quickly turning from triple zero to forty-eight. Perron sighed. *Just
under the weight limit.*

"Just made it. Must be your lucky day," Venessa said smiling. "May
I see your driver's license Mr. Perron?"

Again, he complied as she finished processing him for his flight,
confirming his new seat assignment. Printing out a new boarding
pass, she took the suitcase, tagged it, and placed it on the conveyer
belt behind her. She next turned to Perron and explained that his seat
assignment had changed. "Mr. Perron you've been assigned a new seat,"
showing him the new boarding pass. "You are now seated in row four,
Seat A. That is an aisle seat." She handed the pass to him with a smile.

He was curious about the sudden seat change but concluded that it really must be his lucky day. His first seat assignment had him near the back of the plane between an aisle and window seat. The new seat location was much more convenient. It would make it easier for him to get on and off the plane. *Perfect.* The FBI agents who directed the seat reassignment thought the same thing.

———◆———

AUSA James Harrison prepared the application for the arrest warrant quickly and arrived at the chambers of Federal District Court Judge Lois Cooley precisely at 1:15 p.m., twenty minutes before her return from lunch. He sat outside chambers and waited for her arrival. He had already given the paperwork to her clerk, Lawrence Tobin.

"Assistant U.S. Attorney Harrison, what do you have for me today?" Judge Cooley asked, walking into the office, as Tobin, a Harvard Law School graduate, handed her the application papers. He had looked them over earlier, providing the judge with his notes on a coversheet attached to the set of papers before her. She walked from the outer office into her private chambers as Harrison waited.

Sitting down to read her clerk's typed notes, the warrant application, the criminal complaint, and accompanying affidavits with exhibits, Cooley considered Harrison's request as he stood by patiently waiting. The application set forth the details of the overt acts—the criminal conduct that is committed as part of a crime, or conspiracy to commit a crime. The paperwork depicted Perron as a leader and a major participant in an overarching scheme to defraud. It also outlined his plan to flee the country to escape the government's prosecution and avoid the court's jurisdiction. The application more than adequately pointed out the exigency of the circumstances needed for the court to take immediate action without the benefit of a federal grand jury finding of probable cause and the issuance of an indictment. Putting down the paperwork, Cooley said, "Mr. Harrison come on in here . . . please sit down. I have read your application and the supporting documentation, and I think we need to do this on the record in my courtroom." Hearing this, Harrison and Tobin knew that she was going to grant the application and issue the arrest warrant. Tobin instinctively went to the phone to summon Cooley's court reporter.

Ten minutes later, and on the record in open court, Judge Cooley ceremoniously stated, "We are here today on the United States Government's application. Present, on behalf of the U.S. Attorney's Office, is Assistant U.S. Attorney, James Benjamin Harrison III. The application before me seeks the arrest of an individual identified as one, Carlos Perron. The Complaint before me details a criminal conspiracy involving Mr. Perron and others to defraud mortgage lenders, and borrowers alike, by providing false and misleading information to these individuals and numerous lending institutions to induce the borrowers into taking loans and facilitate these lenders into making home loans. These loans were later sometimes defaulted upon, and Perron and his co-conspirators would next fraudulently induce homeowners to transfer the homes without consideration, later selling them at a profit, again all as part of and in furtherance of this scheme. The application goes on to state that Mr. Perron has made plans and is presently carrying out those plans, in an attempt to flee the country and evade criminal prosecution. Now, Mr. Harrison, is that it in a nutshell?"

"Yes, Your Honor. I would only add that this criminal conspiracy is ongoing and has been active, as best as our investigative efforts can tell, for approximately six years or more. It involves numerous, not yet named, co-conspirators and a multitude of victims. The arrest of Mr. Perron as a leader of this conspiracy would, in all likelihood, prevent further victimization of lending institutions and individuals. I would also add that Mr. Perron has taken substantial steps to evade prosecution and is very near to leaving the country, again as detailed in the application. Thank you, Your Honor."

"Thank you, Mr. Harrison. On the basis of the complaint, the affidavits and documentary evidence attached to this application, I will find that there is probable cause to believe that the defendant has committed the crimes, as more fully set forth in the government's criminal complaint. More particularly, it alleges violations of eighteen United States Code sections 1341, 1343, and 1349, that the application has been filed in compliance with Rule 3 of the Federal Rules of Criminal Procedure, and that the defendant has and is taking substantial steps to evade prosecution. On that basis, I will grant the application and issue a warrant, which I find to be in compliance with Rule 4(a) and (b) of the Federal Rules of Criminal Procedure, for the immediate arrest of Carlos Perron. I am signing that order now.

Please see my clerk at the end of these proceedings. And if there isn't anything else, I believe we are done. Mr. Harrison?"

"No, Your Honor. I believe that is it. Thank you, Your Honor."

"So, then I believe we are adjourned. Thank you everyone."

"Thank you, Your Honor," said Harrison again.

AUSA Harrison was pleased with the court's swift response to his request and thought it was a job well done given the short amount of time they had to prepare the criminal complaint, warrant application, affidavits, and to piece the operation together. Harrison, returning to his office, had Angie make copies of the signed original order. The agents, who had been waiting, now took the arrest warrant and headed for the airport.

FBI Agents Anderson, Bronson, Hernandez, and Stone were in the Newark Airport Port Authority Police command center when the call came from the TSA, informing them that Perron just passed through the security checkpoint on his way to gate twenty-two. The four agents and the two assigned Port Authority uniformed police officers walked into the terminal, making their way toward their subject.

When the agents arrived in the terminal, Perron was sitting alone. Agent Anderson watched him as he fidgeted and checked, with a pat of his hands, the money belt wrapped around his waist and tucked inside his shirt. *Still there*, Perron thought, knowing it hadn't moved despite the security check. He would have Flavia come with the rest of their cash later, when things cooled down. Gerry told him there was a criminal investigation underway and he was nervous. He would also call Gerry in a couple of weeks to get his share of the partnership money. They already discussed selling everything and shutting down New Frontiers Properties. He now had no choice but to trust that his partners would take care of everything in his absence. In the next few days he would open an account at Banco Ecuador and tell the gringo to wire his money. Right now, he could only think about his eighty-six-year-old grand-mother, Carmen, Uncle Victor, Aunt Julia and his cousins, Mariana and Bridget, who were waiting for him in Riobamba. As he sat there thinking about the long overdue reunion, he failed to notice the two agents board the plane ahead of everyone. Entering the airliner through the main galley, they were met by Captain Jennifer Marsh, who had been alerted by the Port Authority Police, TSA, and FAA to the FBI's presence and plan to arrest Perron.

"Gentlemen, I am Captain Marsh. Welcome aboard the aircraft," she said. Marsh had been a captain in the Air Force twenty years prior to beginning her current career. In her three years as a commercial pilot, this was the first time an arrest was to take place on one of her flights.

"Captain Marsh. Nice to meet you," Stone said, shaking her hand. "I'm Agent Walter Stone and this is Agent Eduardo Hernandez. I assume you've been filled in on what is about to go down here."

"Yes, Agent Stone. A little. But why don't we meet with my cabin crew who are in the rear galley. I think we should speak to them together to ensure they are prepared for what is about to happen. I don't want anything to go wrong here."

Walking to the rear of the plane, the agents met the five crew-members who were prepared to cooperate with them in facilitating the arrest. The crew's job was to ensure that Perron and all the passengers were secured in their seats to avoid any problems or interference in the process. Hernandez and Stone would position themselves in the back galley until it was time to take Perron into custody. Anderson and Bronson would board right after the announcement from Captain Marsh directing the crew to lock the plane doors. The agents would then converge on Perron to arrest and remove him from the plane, quickly, and, hopefully, without incident.

The passengers began to board as the crew somewhat nervously greeted them, unsure of how the arrest would all go down. Despite their concerns, they kept up appearances. When the arrest took place, the crew worked with the agents to keep everyone calm and as a result, it went off smoothly. Agents Hernandez and Stone approached Perron from the rear of the plane and Anderson and Bronson from the front. He was quickly boxed in before he knew what was happening. He did not resist. They handcuffed him right there on the plane, before he could even get out of his seat. Although passengers were stunned and those sitting next to him recoiled, not wanting to be near him or get caught up in the events now unfolding, nobody freaked out. Captain Marsh checked from the cockpit with her senior steward, via the aircraft's audio system, and was pleased to learn it was over without incident. As the agents walked Perron off the plane, he began to blubber like a baby. It was embarrassing.

CHAPTER THIRTY-FIVE

TWO of the four investigating FBI agents walked the hand-cuffed Perron into the federal courthouse through an entrance-way in the underground garage, accessible only to federal law enforcement and court personnel. Hernandez and Stone each held an arm tightly on either side of him, as if he could suddenly get away from them before he could be contained. Perron was clearly under wraps and going nowhere. Anderson and Bronson had gone ahead to the Federal Building, going directly to Harrison's office where he was waiting for them. The two agents and Perron got into a large freight type elevator that was commonly used for prisoner transports, taking him straight upstairs to a processing and holding center. On the ride up, he nervously wondered where they were taking him and what was going to happen next. He was not encouraged by the somewhat dirty and musty smelling elevator, thinking he was probably heading for some urine-infested shit-hole of a prison cell, equipped with a room-mate named *Killer* or *Bubba*. His eyes now nervously darted back and forth as he profusely sweated from his brow and armpits. They made their way to the secure area and all the while, Perron couldn't help but think, did he really deserve this treatment. This type of persecu-tion was reserved for real criminals, and after all, he had done nothing wrong. He helped people get homes—that's what he did. So what if he made a little money along the way. There was no crime in that.

Perron turned to Stone and asked, "Why you doing this?" Stone stood there stunned and during the pause, he asserted, "I do nothing wrong. Nothing wrong."

Stone didn't answer right away but looked at him with a scowl on his face and shook his head. "Mr. Perron, you can't possibly be serious."

Arriving at the holding center, he was placed into a cell that appeared to be clean and sterile. The combination toilet-sink, which was interconnected as if the two had been melded together, and the five-foot bench along one side of the unit, had a polished stainless-steel look. Despite the cell's shiny and sparkling clean appearance, there was nothing pleasant about it. Perron was going to spend the night, and it would not be comfortable. He was in the cage for more than twenty minutes before the agents returned and took him to the processing center for fingerprints, photos, and a DNA sample. The modern-day procedure was now much more streamlined and less messy. Fingerprints were scanned into a computer without the use of ink, DNA was taken from a swab of the cheek, then placed into a sterile vile for entry into an FBI national registry, and photos were taken with a digital camera that instantly appeared on a computer screen. Perron's personal information, case number, and date of arrest were previously input into a database and popped up automatically under his mug shot photo. The entire process took less than ten minutes. Once done, the detainee-arrestee was returned to his cell. Perron was now very quiet, did what he was told, and did not ask questions, knowing he would not receive any answers.

Once back in his cage, he was left alone. Fifteen minutes later, Hernandez returned and asked, "You want to make a call?" He pointed to a phone on the wall behind him that appeared to have a cord long enough to reach the cell.

Perron uneasily answered, "Yes, I call my wife, ok?" He wanted to let her know what happened as his family was anxiously awaiting his arrival in Ecuador, and to tell her to call an attorney immediately.

Hernandez said, "Ok, give me a few minutes. You can make that call when I get back." He walked down the short hallway and leaving the holding area, closed the door behind him. Perron was alone again. Hernandez did not return immediately, as he purposefully kept his prisoner waiting and wondering. It was a simple psychological tactic the FBI used to break down a subject. It was often very effective, and it would be in this case, as Perron nervously paced his cell wondering when he would get to make that call.

—————◆—————

Harrison sat at his desk with Anderson and Bronson, who were sitting in the chairs in front of him. They waited for instructions on what to do next, knowing that Harrison liked to control every aspect of his investigations. Harrison now looked at the gold, white-faced Rolex, given to him by his father as a law school graduation present, hastily taking note of the time. It was 7:40 p.m., and he believed they were the only people left in the U.S. Attorney's Office. Even Angie Estrada was gone for the night, unable to stay. *A family commitment or something. One thing about civil servants*, he cynically thought, *they rarely have the desire or ambition to work overtime.* Looking at the agents he asked, "Has he said anything yet?"

Bronson responded, "Nothing, but Hernandez and Stone are still with him in lockup. He'll be making a call to his wife in a little bit. I just got a text. They should be here shortly."

"Ok, let's get ready for tomorrow morning's arraignment," said Harrison.

Anderson asked, "James, who's the judge and what time?"

"It's scheduled for 10:00 a.m., before Judge Cooley."

Bronson interrupted and exclaimed, "Oh God, Cooley."

Ignoring him Harrison continued, "Guys, listen up. I want Perron thinking about the trouble he's in. Let's put a bug in his ear. Then let him stew on it all night long in that cell. Carl, you go down there in a little while and ride him hard. Paint the picture."

Bronson nodded. Harrison looked at him and acknowledged him with a sharp nod of his own. "I want him thinking about the twenty or thirty years he is facing in a federal prison, then enlighten him about the benefits of cooperation. Perron needs to know that the more help he is, the more people he gives us and the more assistance we get from him prosecuting others, the better chance he has for a substantial reduction in his sentence. But I don't have to tell you this, right?"

Again, Bronson nodded. "Don't worry. I'll work on it. His head will be spinning when I'm done with him. He'll cooperate."

"Good. Alright, I'm going to prepare a press release. I'll run it by the U.S. Attorney, and get it out tonight so it makes the morning news." Now looking at Anderson he said, "By the way how did your little talk with Tesler go today?"

John Anderson fidgeted and looked at Bronson. "We had a little interference from Jamie Preston. He prevented us from talking to him. He was very adamant that we had no right to interview his employee in the company's office without a warrant. I can't say he was wrong. We were not welcomed and technically we were trespassing, leaving us no choice but to get out of there without our interview."

Harrison frowned and looked at Bronson who appeared irritated. He sat silent for a moment, absorbing what was just said. Eyes closed, he wondered why Preston would care about Tesler and Bender Capital? A few moments had gone by before Harrison opened his eyes again. Turning to Anderson, he asked, "Well ok. Anyway, what are we doing about Tesler. Do you think he is going to lawyer up now?"

Bronson red in the face, hands clenched, and looking as if he was going to blow his stack, blurted out, "That little motherfucker."

Harrison turned to him, "Who, Tesler?"

"No, that motherfucker, Preston. Something is up with him. I can sense it. He's worried. He's hiding something."

Anderson jumped back into the conversation. "Tesler is in this deep. The money trail bears that out. I'm not too worried there. Once we confront Tesler with the financial evidence against him and the others, he will have no choice but to cooperate. If he knows what's good for him. He's a smart guy. He'll know it's the right move." Fidgeting in his chair and crossing his right leg over his left he added, "The guilty ones always cooperate."

Harrison, quickly shifting his thoughts from Tesler to Preston, was now focusing on the reaction, or more likely the overreaction, of the Nationwide Mortgage Services CEO. He began to wonder what prompted it. He continued to be introspective, staring down at his manicured hands, turning them around slowly time and time again, ignoring the agents as he sat there thinking. *What is going on with Preston? What is it? Is there something more to this? Maybe he's worried about getting pulled into this mess? Could it be that Nationwide is already involved? That must be it. He's worried that this investigation is about him and Nationwide Mortgage.* He turned back to Anderson, "John, who are some of the banks buying the Bender Capital paper?"

John Anderson thought for a moment and looked up with a smile. "James, there are a few of them, including the ones I already talked to you about, but I think—and I will have to check this—the bank buying most of Bender's loans is Nationwide."

Suddenly Harrison's face lit up. He was silent again, immersed in his thoughts and blocking everything else out. *Ok, what does this mean? Does Preston know something? He must, why else the pushback?* With the wheels now turning, he began to connect the dots—his financing background and his training and knowledge of Wall Street now taking over for the attorney in him. *Ok, so Bender sells bad paper to Nationwide, and then Preston goes to Wall Street with an unending supply of financial instruments to be securitized. Everything is bundled up, probably labeled as triple "A" securities by the rating agencies, and then pushed out in the mortgage-backed securities onto unsuspecting investors, together with those CDOs I've been reading up on for a while now. That's it—they think they're buying quality triple A loans but really, they're getting shit. This motherfucker is part of it. It's a vicious cycle. It explains why Tesler left Bender Capital and went to Nationwide. Preston needed someone who could keep the supply chain open and continue to do business this way. Shit, we need to expand this investigation. This could be the break I've been waiting for. Next stop Congress. After that, who the fuck knows.*

"James, what are you thinking? Do you think Nationwide is somehow involved?"

"Um?" Lifting his head, Harrison stared at Anderson, knowing that he had asked a question although he was unsure what it was. It took a moment to register. He quickly refocused, "Yea, right. Let's get to Tesler as soon as possible. Both of you go see him at his home in Connecticut and set him straight. He's a smart guy. He'll know that it only makes sense to cooperate. Once we have him and Perron wrapped up, this is going to move fast. Also, Preston knows something. I'm sure of it. I got to believe he is a player here. Nationwide is somehow involved, so expand this investigation beyond Bender Capital Lending. Let's grab the low hanging fruit now and get them out of the way. Let's flip them and use them as best as we can, then we go after the rest. Guys, let's double down on Nationwide and Preston—particularly that Jamie Preston. You're likely to find significant financial evidence leading from Bender to Nationwide and then out to Wall Street, ending with the sale of really bad securitized instruments. Preston had to know what he was peddling was shit. Wall Street too. Let's focus on these players next." Looking at the agents he cheerfully declared, "Fellas, I have a feeling this is about to blow up."

"Jamie Preston and Nationwide Mortgage Services, targets of a Department of Justice–FBI investigation," repeated Bronson in his best Don Pardo, TV announcer voice. Without waiting for a reaction, he said, "Good, I can't wait to shove this shit right back up Preston's ass." He was now giddy, like a small child who was high on a sugar rush.

Anderson nodded in agreement and was about to say something when Hernandez and Stone walked into the room. Immediately Harrison asked, "Is our boy tucked in for the night?" The remark resonated with everyone, releasing some of the tension in the room. Bronson burst out laughing, his euphoria over Preston now uncontrollable.

Harrison ignored him. "Did he make his call?"

Hernandez knowing exactly where he was going with the question, said, "Yea, called his wife, talked to her in Spanish, and asked if she heard from Gerry Bender. He then tells her to call him and to get the rest of his money. He also wants her to let Bender know what happened tonight. He tells her to hire an attorney. He doesn't even think to wonder if I speak or understand Spanish. Worst yet, doesn't realize the line is recorded and we have the entire conversation on tape. Then get this, he asks me for a cigarette."

Harrison smiled and said, "Funny shit." He wanted to get the agents out of his office, so he barked, "Bronson and Hernandez go back to lock up and start planting the seed. I want him in here as soon as possible, singing like a little fucking canary." Next, turning to Anderson he said, "Get me an outline of the financial breakdown for tomorrow. I want to sit with you and go over the records of deposits and withdrawals and look at the flow of money. Let's do it before the arraignment, so meet me here at eight. Now all of you get the fuck out. I need to work on this press release." He directed them to the office door with a dismissive wave of his hand. The agents silently and quickly left the room as Bronson and Hernandez headed to lockup to speak with Perron, while the others returned to the FBI offices located on the floor below.

As soon as everyone shuffled out, Harrison began to write the press release. He planned to distribute it tonight to the Associated Press, knowing that from there most of the other news agencies would pick up the story for the morning papers and news programs. Harrison knew that the U.S. Attorney would have to be called to offer up his blessing on the statement before it could be distributed. It would, of course, outline the lead role of the Honorable Caleb Moore, U.S. Attorney for the southern district, the important but supporting role of Assistant U.S. Attorney, James Benjamin Harrison III, and the role of the FBI in quickly shutting down an ongoing multistate conspiracy to defraud, which was being carried out by Perron and his yet unnamed co-conspirators. It would also highlight his attempt to flee the country to escape prosecution, and ultimately justice.

As he wrote, he liked the sound of it more and more. Twenty minutes later he was finished, and as he began to proofread it, before he even had a chance to call the U.S. Attorney, his cellphone rang. Picking up the call on the third ring and without looking at the caller ID that read *unknown,* he knew it was his father calling, no doubt fully briefed and aware of what happened tonight. He answered the phone, "Hi Dad. What took you so long to call?"

CHAPTER THIRTY-SIX

THE morning papers, local and national, ran the Associated Press article that had been sent out on the wire just before midnight. The network and cable stations also provided coverage that next morning, dedicating thirty seconds or more to the story and outlining its ties to the growing financial crisis. Once again, the news reports took the opportunity to summarize the Bender Capital Lending civil cases, to vilify not only Perron, but also Wallace, Gerry, Michael, and now, for the first time, the banking and financial services industries. Catching an early morning segment on CNN, Harrison was pleased with the coverage the story was receiving, especially the part focusing on him. The CNN reporter detailed Harrison's pedigreed upbringing, academic background, and some of the high-profile cases he had prosecuted in the past. He referred to the Stuart Vogel matter, asserting that the "Hedge fund mogul proved to be an allusive big fish that Harrison could not reel in . . ." but that, "good fortune may have laid another opportunity on this young prosecutor's lap, which might change all that . . . providing him with another chance to net a few of Wall Street's most greedy." He shut off the TV, believing the reporter, Dylan Shepard, had put a nice spin on the story. He liked what he had to say, although really didn't care for the fishing clichés. He wondered if he should call him after the arraignment and offer some exclusive insight. Rushing out of his small one-bedroom apartment on John Street in the heart of the financial district, he pondered if and how he could still nail Vogel. The CNN report opened the wound he suffered at Phillip Richardson's and Stuart Vogel's hands. The inability to successfully prosecute him was a bitter pill to swallow, and he still wasn't over it. He put it aside for now, as he exited the building and walked out onto the sidewalk. James Benjamin Harrison III had more important things to think about this morning.

He walked to the corner and took a cab the short distance to the United States Federal Building. He needed to focus on Perron for now and prepare for the arraignment. He had already made up his mind—he was going to ask Cooley to deny bail based on Perron's attempt to leave the country. Obviously a flight risk. That alone would normally be sufficient. Alternatively, he could ask Cooley to set bail so high that it would require the posting of a bond impossible to meet. After all, what bail bondsman would take a risk on a lowlife scumbag like Perron? He was fucked either way. Keeping him in custody would make it easier to turn the former Bender loan officer into a confidential informant or as some would say, a "fucking rat."

———◆———

Looking at himself in the large bathroom mirror, Austin Wainwright scrutinized and adjusted his tie slightly—the Windsor knot was flawless. His full head of mostly grey hair was slicked straight back with a small amount of gel to help keep it all in place. His white shirt, lightly starched, was perfectly pressed, and his suit jacket now hung on the back of a kitchen chair. The newspaper and a poached egg waited for the attorney on the kitchen table, as they did every weekday morning. Each day, Austin would promptly leave the house at 7:10 a.m., always arriving at the office before 7:30 a.m., without failure. He had been doing this longer than he could remember, and at age sixty-seven, he wasn't going to change his routine now. He was a creature of habit—meticulous and focused. It's what made him a good, highly sought-after lawyer despite the five-hundred-dollar per hour price tag that came with every consultation or representation.

"Señor Wainwright, you breakfast ready," called Cassandra, the live-in help, as she took the lightly toasted multi-grain bread from the toaster and placed it on a small dish for her employer. Cassandra had been with him the last seven years, ever since his wife, Evelyn, had passed. In that time, the two had become very close and had grown to care for one another, but the relationship between them remained platonic. This was simply because Austin would never think to soil the memory of his wife and the image of a blissful thirty-four-year marriage, despite the fond feelings he had for his companion and friend. If not anything else, he was proper and restrained.

"Coming down now. Gracias Cassandra," he said graciously as he descended the rear stairwell that led to the kitchen of his large Wilton home. He should plan a trip for her birthday in November, maybe to her beloved Dominican Republic. She hadn't been back home since her work engagement began almost eight years ago, and he sensed she was a little homesick. He should accompany her; it's the least he could do. After all, she took very good care of him. He considered this for a moment, wondering what people would think. It had been at almost ten years since he'd gone on a vacation. He had been consumed with only work after his wife's death. It had been much too long, and he now thought some rest and relaxation was in order. The girls and his grandchildren were no longer nearby—Katherine, Doug, and the kids had moved to Houston almost three years ago. Olivia was also gone, having accepted the assistant dean's position at Moore University Law School in Tennessee just over a year ago. No one was left at home. He would do it. His secretary could make all the arrangements, and he would surprise Cassandra with the trip soon enough; her birthday was only a few months away.

It was Friday morning just before 7:00 a.m., as Wallace Bender's attorney sat down to butter his toast. Flipping open the Connecticut Post, he viewed the article that boldly announced: *Federal prosecutors arrest Bender Capital Lending loan officer as he attempts to flee the country. Caleb Moore, U.S. Attorney for the southern district of New York, announced the arrest of Carlos Perron, a former Bender Capital Lending loan origina-tor, charging him with wire fraud, mail fraud, and conspiracy to commit mail and wire fraud, relating to a far-reaching mortgage fraud scheme taking place across multiple states. Assistant U.S. Attorney James Benjamin Harrison III, prosecuting the case on behalf of the U.S. Attorney's Office, alleged in a criminal complaint filed yesterday in the Federal District Court, southern district of New York, that Perron, and numerous unnamed and yet to be charged co-conspirators conducted and conspired . . .* Now skimming the rest of it, knowing where this was going, Austin went to the very end of the article to see when the next court proceeding was scheduled to take place. *Perron is to be arraigned today before Federal District Court Judge Lois Cooley.* Meticulously folding and putting down the paper, Austin mumbled under his breath, "Here it comes." He got up from the table to call his longtime friend and client, who he knew would be very unhappy to hear the news, if he didn't know already. He also thought the vacation would have to wait.

———————◆———————

Unable to shake the habit of getting out of bed early, Wallace Bender was downstairs brewing the coffee before 7:00 a.m. Although he didn't have anywhere in particular to be today, or any day for that matter, he was still an early riser. Noisily rummaging around the kitchen, wrapped only in his robe, he patiently waited for the coffee to finish brewing, inadvertently rousing his wife from their bed as he opened and closed cabinets. Strolling into the kitchen of their fourteen-hundred square-foot Fairfield beach cape, Amanda asked, "Wall, what are you looking for down here? My God, you're making a racket."

"I'm looking for my NYU coffee mug," he answered. "Do you know where it is?"

"Check the dishwasher," Amanda responded, as she took a mug from the cabinet, waiting to fill it with the Maxwell House roast still percolating in the electric coffee maker.

Wallace could smell the coffee now as the aroma filled the kitchen. He was not one of those fancy coffee drinkers like his son who drank only Starbucks at eight dollars a cup. Wallace couldn't recall the concoction he preferred, but it was something like a frappe-crappy cappuccino, don't forget the cream on top. It just wasn't for him. Recalling the one time he had been, he remembered he couldn't even get a regular cup of coffee from that darn counter person, the *barista*, as they are called, or something like that.

Amanda, watching her husband search for his favorite ten-year-old mug, walked to the slider and pulled it open, allowing the sound of the ocean waves to crash into the room. As the fresh morning ocean air also made its way into the house, Wallace announced, "Here it is," triumphantly holding the mug above his head, while shutting the dishwasher. He put it down on the counter and walked to the small TV, perched atop a shelf, turning it on and tuning in to CNN. He was floored by what he saw and heard, unable to react. Amanda simply said, "Oh my God." Wallace stood there unable to move. The telephone on the counter began to ring.

After the initial shock of the news story and discussion with Austin, who he was going to see later in the morning, Wallace called his son.

Anna answered the phone, "Oh, hi Dad. How are you?"

"Fine, just fine. Is Gerald up yet?"

"No Dad. Gerry is still asleep. I'm just getting Erica ready for school. Erica come here and say hi to your grandfather."

Before she could hand over the phone to his six-year-old grand-daughter, Wallace interjected. "Anna, I really need to speak with Gerald. Can you wake him?"

Surprised by his unusually harsh tone she said, "Sure Dad, sure. Hold on a minute. I'm in the kitchen. Is everything ok?"

"Fine. Fine. Everything is just fine." He lied. Everything was not fine.

Anna, now walking down the hallway toward the bedrooms, shouted, "Gerry, you awake?" As she walked into the master bedroom at the end of the hall, Wallace heard her say, "Gerry, it's your father. He needs to speak with you."

———————◆———————

Marco arrived at his office shortly before 9:30 a.m. and with a full day ahead of him, began to make a few calls. He first called Lisa and checked in with her, reassuring himself that she made it to work ok. He next called Michael to check on him. His friend answered on the first ring.

"Marco how are you?"

"Good. How's it going? Anything happening, you know . . . with the job search?"

"No, nothing yet. Did I tell you I talked to BJ Franklin? Bernard wouldn't take my calls. BJ finally did, and when I asked for my job back he told me I was toxic. No one would touch me."

"Yea, you told me. That cold-hearted bastard."

"No, no he's right. He's only being honest with me. More than I can say for a lot of people. So-called friends."

Hey, why don't you fill out an application here with the firm? I'll put in a good word for you. Obviously, you can use me as a reference," he said jokingly.

"Come on Marco, what do I say to the application question: *Have you ever been convicted of a felony?* 'Not yet?'"

There was a brief silence, then the two of them simultaneously broke out laughing. Michael then said, "No Marco I wouldn't put you in that position. My dad's buddy, Tommy, said I can work with him and his crew, painting. I worked with them a couple of summers during college, so I'm not too bad with a brush. Worst comes to worst I go to work for Tommy."

"Michael, really why don't you consider it? I'm sure we can find something for you to do."

Did he really just say that? "No Marco thanks. I don't think it's a good idea."

"Ok, well—"

"Anyway, yesterday I was served with an order to show cause, to appear in New York Supreme for a temporary suspension-revocation proceeding of my New York license. I was going to call and tell you," announced Michael.

"Shit," was all Marco could think to say.

"So, as you can see, my license to practice law will be suspended in a little while anyway. No sense fighting it. I'm sure Connecticut and New Jersey will soon follow."

Marco did not respond immediately. "Listen, I'm sorry to hear it. Can we talk later? Got to get ready for a meeting." Before Michael could answer he said, "I'll call you later. OK? Hang in there."

"Will do," said Michael.

Twenty minutes later, Michael received an unexpected call from his attorney's office. It was Odell Brown.

"Michael hi. It's Odell. Are you busy?"

"Odell. Hi. how are you? No, no I'm good . . . I can talk."

"Ok, good. By the way, yes, I'm good thanks for asking," said Odell. Getting right to it, he asked, "Michael have you heard about Perron's arrest?"

He told him he had not, and as he continued to speak to the young lawyer, Michael went to his laptop and onto the internet to look for an article. He found the Department of Justice press release first and clicked on it. He began reading as Odell continued. "Well, Phillip is attending the arraignment right now to gather some intelligence. He'll call you in a couple of hours to discuss what took place and next steps, if any."

Michael was shaken, although he had the presence of mind to say, "Thank you for calling."

"No problem," said Odell. "I wish I had better news."

Michael hung up the phone and immediately called Marco, who did not answer his cellphone, rationalizing that if he wasn't busy he would've picked up. Clearly, Marco couldn't talk, and Michael didn't want to call his office number. He next called Karen but got only her voicemail. There was no one he could speak to, and Michael desperately wanted someone to assure him that everything was going to be ok.

He couldn't call Diana or his father, only because he knew it would upset them. He didn't think that they may already know or that they would find out on their own. He resigned himself to the idea that he had to wait a couple of hours for Phillip Richardson to call. Michael sensed that the wait would likely seem an eternity.

CHAPTER THIRTY-SEVEN

THE pathway leading to a Federal District Court judgeship for most is a long and arduous one, requiring, among other things, an appreciation for the rule of law, dedication to the ideals of justice, a keen intellect, an acute knowledge of legal principles, and years of service to the legal profession. For others, not so much— as political connections, influence, power or money can also often serve to clear the way to such a prestigious position. Federal Judge Lois Cooley, an African-American woman in her mid-forties, received a lifetime appointment to the federal bench only eighteen months ago. Despite possessing many of the qualities needed for consideration to such a position, she was one of those individuals whose path was paved through political influence and favor. Her recommendation for appointment to the federal bench originating from a strong and close ally, her father.

———◆———

For more than thirty-five years, Reverend Alvin Cooley shepherded the flock at the Church of Christ the Savior in Riverdale, New York. His parishioners came not only from the Bronx, where the church was founded, but the entirety of New York City. His appeal was far reaching within the Afro-American and Latin communities largely due to his weekly TV show, *Reverend Alvin Cooley's Gospel Hour* airing on the city-wide public-service station, channel 1-NYC, and the daily sixty-second radio spots, *Words of Inspiration with Reverend Alvin Cooley*, running several times a day on numerous R&B, hip hop, and Spanish-speaking stations throughout the tri-state area. The New York preacher not only served the community in which he lived and worked, but he also served as a civic leader and activist—an important fixture in the city's political scene. His advice and support were highly sought after by politicians throughout New York, and it came as no surprise when his friend, Rabbi David Greene, requested the reverend's assistance and endorsement of former city comptroller, Neil Stein, a democrat from Brooklyn, then running for congress.

Alvin Cooley, having mobilized and rallied his people behind what could only be described as a lukewarm candidate, somehow delivered a victory that fall for Stein and several times over ever since. He was now clearly indebted to Cooley, who patiently waited for the day Stein's political power was solidified on the Hill. At the time of Stein's victory, Cooley's only child was one of the youngest appointed Justices to the New York Supreme Court, thanks again to his political connections. Although she enjoyed a little more than six years in the Bronx County criminal courts, the reverend wanted more for his daughter. Ultimately, it was Stein's tenure in congress, his ranking membership in the House Judiciary Committee, and the power it wielded that served to repay Reverend Alvin Cooley for the work he had done in securing the congressional election wins. The reverend knew exactly what he needed from Stein the very first day he joined the campaign: a federal judgeship for his daughter – daddy's little girl, Lois.

———◆———

It was 8:45 a.m. when Judge Cooley arrived at her chambers. AUSA Harrison and attorney, Juan Cornado, out of Newark, New Jersey, would soon be waiting in her courtroom, prepared to argue at the morning's arraignment hearing. The defendant, Carlos Perron, was to be brought upstairs from lockup at exactly 10:00 a.m. by the FBI case agents, Anderson and Bronson, where he would, in all certainty, enter a *not guilty* plea. The request for reasonable bail conditions would then be made by his attorney to the judge. Harrison would argue against it. Cooley sat down in her oversized black leather chair as the file was placed on her desk. The office was large, and the walls were lined with bookcases, containing a set of the United States Codes and Federal Regulations. The shelves were also lined with countless books, fiction and non-fiction alike, all of which were read by the judge sometime or another during her lifetime. Lois Cooley was a prolific reader, especially of the classics. There were many favored books, but her ultimate favorite was the King James version of the Bible, which sat on a table against the window right behind her black leather chair. As she settled in, her secretary walked over with a mug of hot green tea and placed it on the desk in front of her.

"Thank you, Andrea," she said, then turning her attention to her law clerk. "Larry, so what are we going to do today?" she asked teasingly.

She had not yet decided on the action she would take on the Perron case and wouldn't until first speaking to her law clerk who had graduated at the top of his law school class. He had been with her this past year and a half, and she valued his opinion very much.

She picked up the mug and began to sip her tea as Tobin sat in front of her desk facing her. Now with the chamber's copy of the court file sitting on his lap, he began filling her in on the finer points of the case, offering suggestions on how to best proceed. Ultimately, he recommended that she deny bail, as Perron was, in his opinion, a bad actor and an extreme flight risk. Judge Cooley thoughtfully pondered Tobin's assessment, remembering what her father told her early in her legal career—*consider the law, act compassionately, and rule wisely, as the Lord alone judges righteously.* With that and what Tobin had said in mind, she considered her options, weighing the defendant's constitutional rights and his God given right to freedom, against the public's interest for protection and that justice be served.

Over the years, Judge Lois Cooley had proven herself to be not only a brilliant legal scholar, but also a very practical and judicious decision maker. She quickly decided to set Perron's conditions of bail, starting with a one-million-dollar surety bond. She would also require him to surrender his passport and restrict his movement with an electronic bracelet that enabled federal probation and parole to monitor his every move. He would be confined to his home as a condition of bail with only preauthorized travel from his residence. At the very least, she thought, it gave him a chance to keep himself out of federal pretrial lockup pending a jury trial that might take a while to appear on her trial calendar. She believed it to be a very fair compromise for all involved while considering the defendant and the public's interests. Cooley's heartfelt compassion and sense of justice were just two of the traits that made her a very good judge. It also earned her a reputation as an outspoken protector of criminal defendants' constitutional rights. It's what caused many prosecutors to lose sleep at night, and what gave Harrison pause, and cause to worry. Cooley finished her tea, put on her black robes, dismissed Tobin, and closed her office door for a moment of solitude, reflection, and a short prayer before starting the day.

CHAPTER THIRTY-EIGHT

TEN days had passed since the arrest and his release from federal custody. Having made bail and now wearing an electronic bracelet around his ankle, Carlos Perron and his wife sat at the kitchen table with his lawyer, who was found in the yellow pages under the section entitled, *abogado—se habla Española*. The attorney was now telling his client to plead guilty and most importantly to cooperate with the feds, emphasizing that doing so was a good thing, for him.

"Carlos, look in my opinion the first cooperator in wins," he said in a tone that suggested this was not a novel idea. "You are looking at twenty years or maybe more in a federal prison. I talked to the prosecutor and agent, and they have a money trail leading to you— hundreds of thousands over the years. They have borrowers saying you told them to lie on the loan applications and some at least saying that you changed the information they gave you. From what I'm being told and what they've shown me in the form of records, documents, and 302 witness statements, you're in deep, and there is no doubt you're going to prison," he repeated. Flavia sighed loudly, causing Cornado to abruptly stop talking.

Perron looked at her and without a word, only a stare from him, she quieted down. He turned back to his lawyer and said, "Go, go," while gesturing with his hand.

Cornado continued. "And soon they will have someone else cooperating against you, and then you have a big problem. But if you're in there first, who knows ten years or maybe less . . . instead of twenty or maybe more." He finished off heavy-handedly. "It depends on how helpful you are to them. The more people you implicate . . . the more convictions as a result . . . the better for you." He paused looking for a reaction. Perron continued to stare at him silently. *Ok, nothing yet. Is he getting it?* He continued. "There is no way you're not going to jail.

It's now just a question of how long." Rubbing his moustache with the first two fingers of his left hand, he stopped speaking completely and again waited for a reaction. *Well, come on Carlos. What are you going to do?*

Flavia Perron began to cry as her husband momentarily put his face into the palms of his hands. He quickly looked up and coldly said, "Ok." She began to cry louder and violently, even shaking as she got up, kicking out the chair in which she was seated. Now stumbling away from the table, she left the room. Going upstairs to the bedroom, she threw herself onto the bed, leaving her to wonder what would happen to her, the children, and the house. Flavia grabbed one of the pillows and placed it over her head, wishing this would all just disappear.

Cornado stared at Perron for a moment, as if to say, *You sure?* He then said, "Ok, I will get in touch with the U.S. Attorney's Office to let them know. We need to prepare for your cooperation. You'll need to come to my office next week. Remember, the more you give them, the better. I should have the cooperation and plea agreements in a few days. Once I get them, I'll call you."

"Ok Juan. Ok. More is better. Ok," Perron repeated.

"By the way, I need another twenty thousand. Right away," Cornado said.

"Si, Juan," he said robotically. Perron now thought incoherently about everything, his mind a jumbled mess. *Forty thousand to lawyer . . . that's almost all the money—the house, the bond, Flavia, the kids. Gerry has my money. Gringo, give me my money.*

Moving in a hundred different directions, Perron's head was now about to explode.

CHAPTER THIRTY-NINE

THE ride to the attorney's office was a short one, only fifteen minutes, but Gerald Bender nonetheless could not restrain himself, almost hyperventilating on the way. Joel Goddard, who had been an Assistant U.S. Attorney for the district of Connecticut for three years, in private practice ever since, called his client to tell him that there had been a new development. He needed to see him right away, certain that Austin Wainwright was making the same call to his client's father. After all, it was his longtime friend who referred Gerry to him, and now it was Goddard returning the favor by sharing this latest information about Bill Tesler's cooperation deal with the feds.

Gerry drove into the crowded parking lot of the office complex, located on the Post Road near downtown Fairfield. The building in which the law firm was located was only five stories high and the offices of Goddard, Epstein, Frazier & Ryan, LLP occupied more than half of the top floor. With eighteen attorneys and almost double that in support staff, the firm's criminal practice was just one of the many areas of law in which it was engaged.

Joel Goddard learned quickly, after nine years in the public sector—first as an FBI agent and then as a prosecutor—that defending criminal clients was more rewarding than prosecuting them. His defection to the criminal defense bar occurred more out of necessity than anything else. At the time, his daughter had needed extraordinary medical treatment and care that had not been completely covered by insurance. On a government salary, he couldn't afford to keep her well. So, it had come to pass that the rising star of the U.S. Attorney's Office defected to head the criminal defense practice of a large firm that he had subsequently left four years later to start his own. Following the death of his only child, Sarah, and the subsequent breakup of his marriage, Joel Goddard had poured himself into his work and into the bottle. In a few short years, he had built a large and prestigious firm.

It had been a very profitable business—all the money he had needed or could've ever wanted, although it had done him no good. It had not been enough to restore his daughter's health or keep her alive. In the end, it could not bring him happiness. Joel Goddard, for all that he had, was a very unhappy man. Even though he was recognized as one of the state's premier criminal defense lawyers, he was also known to his colleagues as a prolific boozer. Hardly a day went by where he did not have a drink, and most nights he drowned his sorrows in just about any bottle he could get his hands on.

"Mr. Goddard, Gerald Bender is here to see you sir," announced the receptionist. It was 11:00 a.m.

"Send him on back Rachel. Would you please?"

"Yes sir." Putting down the phone, she looked up and asked, "Mr. Bender you know where it is, don't you?"

"I do. Thank you," replied Gerry as she buzzed him in through the locked door.

Walking down the hallway, he passed six small offices occupied by first year associates, and the cubicles housing their legal assistants. He made his way toward an open area where he saw Joel standing and waiting for him. He waved. "Hi Gerry. Come on over. We'll meet in my office."

Settling in, they were joined by a young associate who introduced himself as Tucker Sheridan. He took a seat in one of the leather chairs at the small round conference table with pad and pen in hand. Gerry also took a seat there, while Joel stood at the cabinet behind his desk, pouring a scotch into a glass full of ice. He took the glass, held it up and shook it. "Here you go," he said to Gerry, offering the drink to him. Accepting it he took a sip. *A single malt*, he concluded.

Now turning his attention to his attorney, he asked, "Joel, what's going on?"

"Gerry," he said as he poured another drink. "Bill Tesler is cooperating. That makes two witnesses who now put you in the thick of things." He stopped talking, took a drink of scotch, and walked over to the conference table joining the two men.

"Besides that, you and I know that they have a money trail a mile long leading back to you. Substantial payments from Bender Capital, New Frontier Properties, and WGB Investments. It's now all being corroborated a couple of ways—all of it connected to a conspiracy that Perron and Tesler are happy to throw your way.

I spoke to Harrison extensively and he wants you to take a plea to one count of conspiracy." He stopped talking as Gerry turned white and began to shake.

"Take another drink. Finish it," he said without any emotion. Gerry complied and sucked down the remainder of the scotch. Taking the glass from his hand, Joel got up and walked over to the cabinet and poured another one. "Here. Drink," he said, handing the glass to his distressed client.

Gerry mumbled, "What the fuck. I'm not doing that." He then immediately asked nervously, "What should I do?"

"Hold on. Here's the rub to all of this. Harrison knows that Anna kept the books for New Frontier and WGB. Although, I don't think he figured out what her role in this was exactly, outside of bookkeeper, he's threatening to indict her if you don't cooperate and take a plea. If you cooperate, he leaves her out of it."

"What! Indict Anna? Fuck no, that can't happen. My daughter . . . Jesus." Gerry's voice trailed off as he slid down in his chair.

The associate, Sheridan, sat listening to the exchange without ever lifting pen to paper. Suddenly he began to feel sorry for their client, who now sat there shaking his head, staring into the scotch glass on the table in front of him.

Joel Goddard looked at the young attorney, and without missing a beat took down the remainder of the scotch in his own glass. Putting it on the table he said, "Gerry." No response. He then shouted, "Gerry," trying to get his attention.

He picked his head up slowly and looked at him with a glazed look in eyes. Goddard asked again, "Will you cooperate with the feds? I recommend you do."

It appeared that the question snapped Gerry back to the present. He sat up and looked at his attorney, saying, "Cooperate, they want me to cooperate." He then asked, "Against who?"

Joel Goddard looked him straight in the eyes and leaning closer to him, he declared, "Michael Dolan."

———————◆———————

"Wall have a seat. Can I can get you anything?

"Austin, no I'm good. Thanks. So, tell me. What's going on? What was so urgent?"

"Thanks for coming on short notice. I've got some news today that changes things. I am not going to sugarcoat this. Gerry's attorney, you know him, Joel Goddard, he still has plenty of contacts in the FBI and Department of Justice. Well anyway he tells me that Bill Tesler is cooperating and is implicating you and Gerry in all of this. He is pointing to the fact that you were funding the real estate company . . . ."

"Wait a minute. Wait a minute—what do you mean funding? I bought a few apartment buildings with Gerald, Carlos, and Bill that's all . . . but there was nothing illegal about that. I did help fund them with some purchases of houses they made on their own, if you want to use that term. But those were just loans. I'm not even sure what they were buying—I think fixer-uppers. I didn't want to get involved in buying those properties. It just wasn't my thing," he said with his hands in the air. "They paid me back quickly. Nothing wrong with that, right? I mean I just used my credit lines to help my son. That's ok, right?" Wallace now looked to Austin for confirmation of his perceived innocence.

"Wall, I agree with you. The building purchases seem legitimate and our investigation into those transactions support that, but Tesler is spinning this into something else." He paused and then said, "More sinister so to speak. He claims that your financing of the real estate company was part of an overarching scheme to defraud Bender Capital Lending borrowers, steal their property, and force them into one of your apartments. And—"

"That's ridiculous. Austin, that is just ridiculous."

"Wall, it gets worse. He claims that WGB Investments was strictly targeting Bender Capital loans, and that you and the others knew they would end up in default. He claims WGB would pick them up for fifty, maybe sixty cents on the dollar. He said it was all part of the plan and that it was all your idea."

Wallace sat motionless as Austin now stopped talking. Looking curiously at his friend he asked, "Wall are you alright? You're sweating and your face is flush. Are you feeling ok?"

Without answering, Wallace got up, loosened his tie and undid his collar. "No, Austin. I don't feel well," he said, almost defiantly.

"Sit back down. I'll get you some water." Austin now appeared flustered, saying, "Just . . . just sit and try to relax."

As Austin turned and began to walk out, Wallace clutched his left arm, saying to himself, now barely a whisper, "Oh God no." His body suddenly fell forward onto the conference room table with a loud, sickening thud.

Hearing what sounded like a bomb going off, Austin turned to see his friend spread out and face down on the conference table, motionless. He moved toward him shouting to anyone who might hear him, "Someone quick call 911. I think Wallace Bender is dead."

CHAPTER FORTY

SITTING at the kitchen table and playing with her doll, Christina asked, "Mommy, is Daddy bad?"

Diana turned around quickly, and almost dropping the wine-glass from her hand, instantly asked, "What honey? What did you say?"

"Is Daddy a bad man? Regina said Daddy is bad," Christina repeated as she continued playing with her American Girl doll, eyes down, refusing to look up at her mother.

"Who told Regina that?"

"Her mommy. She said Daddy stole from people," explained Christina.

Oh my God, Liz. Diana was frozen at the counter. After several moments of panic that caused her to feel faint and got her heart racing, she gently responded, "No, Daddy is not a bad man. Daddy is a good . . . a very good man." She barely choked out, "Ok?" The words had slowly fallen from her mouth as she moved to the table and sat with her daughter who continued to play with her doll. Trying to maintain her composure, Diana stared at her daughter. "Look at me honey," she softly demanded. Christina now stopped playing and turned to her mother. Diana lightly touched her daughter's shoulder and repeated, "Your daddy is a good man. You understand, don't you?" Christina slowly nodded yes.

Staring at her twisted doll now lying on the table, she said with enthusiasm, "Yea, I know. I told Regina that Daddy was best not bad." Diana turned and got up from the table unable to hold back the tears, but certain that Christina understood what she had told her. She didn't want her daughter to see her crying, so she quickly walked to the sink, turned on the faucet, and splashed a handful of water onto her face followed by another handful. She grabbed a dish towel to wipe off the droplets of water and tears. She almost forgot. *Shit, the chicken.* She could now smell it burning.

Michael came downstairs, having just gotten out of the shower. "Ladies," he cheerily said, entering the kitchen. Tilting his head upward and amusingly putting his nose in the air, he inhaled deeply, asking, "Is something burning?"

"Hi Daddy," interrupted Christina, as she continued to play with her doll. "Daddy do you want to play with me and Missy?" Michael, unintentionally ignoring her, turned to Diana for an answer to his question. Christina continued to amuse herself at the table, quickly forgetting she had invited him to play.

"Yup . . . the chicken," said Diana, now answering him, pulling the tray of cutlets from the oven, and gingerly tossing it on the counter. She threw the pot holder into the sink muttering, "Fuck" under her breath, but loud enough for Michael to hear.

"No big deal. It's not too bad," he said, now realizing that Diana appeared to be very distressed, too much it seemed for slightly burnt chicken. He leaned into her and whispered, "Everything alright?"

She said, "Fine, talk to you later about it." Diana was thinking of walking the few houses to Liz and Sean Duffy's home to give them a piece of her mind, maybe even to tell Liz or both to fuck off. That's how angry Diana was. Instead, she plated the chicken, took the rice from the pot, and dished the steamed broccoli into a bowl, placing all of it on the table. Sitting next to Christina, she fixed her a plate, cut the chicken and vegetables into small pieces, and watched her eat.

Michael helping himself asked, "Aren't you going to eat?"

"Not hungry," she said, as she poured more wine into her glass.

She sat there without saying a word as Michael tried to engage her in small talk. Diana was fixated on the small specks of white and grey paint spattered on Michael's hands and arms, not really listening, barely hearing what he was saying. *How did it come to this? Dear God, please help us. Give me the strength I need to—*

"So, what do you think?" Michael repeated, waiting for a response, her plea for help suddenly interrupted.

Diana looked at him blankly, trying to figure out what he had just said. "What?" Looking at him with more clarity she said, "Oh, this weekend? Yea fine."

"Ok, well, I'll call the Viking to make a reservation for Saturday and Sunday," said Michael.

"Go ahead. We could use a little get away," agreed Diana. Newport was quiet this time of year and would provide for a nice distraction.

It was still warm enough to go to the beach, shop during the day, and take in the sights. The Viking Hotel, their favorite place to stay, was near the center of town within walking distance to almost everything they would want to do there. "Yes, go ahead. It's a good idea. Let's get out of here for a couple of days," she repeated, as she took a sip of wine.

Christina putting the last piece of chicken in her mouth asked, "Mommy may I be excused from the table?" Diana looked at the plate in front of her and turning her attention to their daughter simply shook her head yes. Christina immediately jumped off her chair and bounced into the family room, turning on the TV to Nick at Night. Michael and Diana were left at the kitchen table, alone.

Michael grabbed Diana's hand and asked, "What's going on?"

Looking down at his hand now atop her own, Diana focused on the paint specks once again. She asked herself, *How did it come to this? My husband the attorney, now a God damn house painter. Lord forgive me.* They sat in silence for a few minutes as Diana searched for an answer to his question. "Christina asked me if you were a bad man," she finally said.

Michael looked at her and loudly blurted out, "What?" He looked at Christina, but she did not move, unaffected by his sudden outburst.

"Well, Liz must have said something about you to Regina or maybe she overheard them talking, but anyway, no matter how it happened, Regina said something to Christina." Staring at him silently, she added, "I guess this is what our friends now think of us."

He sat motionless for a minute and said, "Me, this is what they think of me— not you."

She immediately snapped. "Wrong Michael. This is what they think of us. Don't you see this affects me the same way it affects you? Whatever anyone thinks about you, they're also likely thinking the same about me . . . wondering if I knew, how could I not know, or if I was somehow involved in what is reported in the news or claimed in those fucking lawsuits." Diana drew her hands away from his and grimaced. Now with a contemptuous look on her face, she asked, "Don't you feel how uncomfortable people are when they're around you? Can't you see it in their faces, the doubt? Clearly, they're questioning your integrity . . . wondering about your character. Don't you feel uncomfortable too, sensing how they feel? I'm not just talking about acquaintances, people who barely know you, who have read something and now have the audacity to be critical of you, but I'm talking about our friends and family who know and supposedly love us. Because I do. I see it. I feel it. It's there—with very few exceptions."

Michael pondered what his wife had just said and in doing so acknowledged that she was right. He now said slowly, "I feel differently, I do. I also see how people are different with me. They're uncomfortable, I'm uncomfortable. You're absolutely right. Yea, no doubt about it. But, I had no idea you felt the same way." Diana nodded her head. Again, he said to her, "You're right. It's fucking uncomfortable. But I don't get that with Karen or Marco. They're different." *Well, on second thought, maybe Marco and I have had a few uncomfortable moments.*

"Oh, I agree," she said interrupting him. They're great, Kelly has been wonderful, and of course your dad too. But Lisa, Pam, and even Nancy sometimes, it's . . . it's different at times. Awkward, uneasy, and sometimes distant. Even my mum, but that could just be her, you know how she is," said Diana. Michael just nodded his head in agreement, now realizing that his pain was her pain too. She then asked, "When was the last time you heard from Jason?"

"It's been awhile."

"You two used to talk all the time," said Diana.

Michael wondered when he last spoke to his brother-in-law. He had called him about two weeks ago and left a message on his voicemail but did not hear back.

He declared, "Jesus, him too."

"So, you see it's different. Not just for you . . . but for me too. This is what they think of the both of us." Michael stared at her silently unable to respond, suddenly feeling guilty again for putting her through all of this.

Sitting at the table, not a word between them for several minutes, Diana whispered, "And my God if you get indicted, what are we going to do? I can't even think about that. I can't even imagine it right now."

"Let's not get ahead of ourselves," was all Michael could think to say, not wanting to reveal to her the ever-present fear he was living with. The fear of not just being indicted, but also the fear of what would happen to her and Christina if he did.

CHAPTER FORTY-ONE

THE voice message from Amanda Bender was short, emotional, and to the point. *"Michael, honey. It's Amanda Bender. Wall has had a heart attack."* A pause, then a sigh. *"He's ok, and he's at Norwalk Hospital. He wants to see you. Please come."* The voicemail ending as abruptly as it began.

Jesus fucking Christ, was Michael's initial reaction. *A heart attack, shit. I hope he's alright.* He next wondered, *What does Wallace want with me?* Putting the phone down on the bathroom vanity next to his coffee cup, he finished blow-drying his hair. *Better get there this morning . . . after dropping the baby off at school.* Instead of putting on work clothes, the old ratty pair of jeans, sweatshirt, and boots, he went to the closet and put on a nice pair of Chino's, a button-down shirt, and a pair of new loafers. *I'll call Tommy on the way and let him know I won't be in until later this morning.* Throwing on a jacket, he ran out of the house.

Walking into the hospital lobby, Michael made his way to the reception area and stood at the counter for a few moments wondering if Gerry was going to be here with his father. He hadn't seen or talked to his friend in months, although he reached out several times, again, without a call back. If he was here, it would be awkward, and Michael now questioned whether he should even go up to see Wallace.

"Sir, what's the name of the patient," asked the elderly grey-haired woman at the counter. Embroidered on her sweater were the words, *Norwalk Hospital Volunteer.* Michael blinked, and she said again, "Patient name," a little annoyed this time.

"Yea sorry. Wallace Bender," he said somewhat dumbfounded. "Heart attack," he added, pointing to his chest. She looked at him curiously and then back to her computer screen.

"Bender, Bender. Ah, here it is. Wallace T," she said. "Room seven o' four, down the hall, past urgent care services, to the set of elevators on your left, and then on up to the seventh floor. Once on the floor, follow the signs to your room. If that's all, have a nice visit," she said in a somewhat short tone. Turning away from Michael and looking to the next person waiting behind him she asked, "Patient name?"

He turned and began walking away mumbling to himself, "Ok, seventh floor got it, thank . . . thank you," he shouted over his shoulder now concerned about what to say or do if he ran into Gerry.

As Michael arrived at room 704, located toward the center of the corridor, the door was open. He heard the cable news. Peeking in, Michael could see that Amanda Bender was the only person in the room along with Wallace, who was lying in bed propped up on four pillows. An oxygen tube was tucked under his nostrils, the air hissing as it was being delivered, somewhat forcefully, up his nose and into his lungs. Wires were tucked inside his hospital gown attached to his left chest muscle, leading down to the floor and back up to a monitor beside him. The screen displayed heart rate, blood pressure, and oxygen levels. An IV line was attached to his arm and another monitor was clipped to his left forefinger to check his pulse. Wallace appeared pale and somewhat tired. He tapped on the door gently and they both looked up.

Amanda Bender was the first to say something, simply announcing, "Michael honey," as she got up from the chair, raising her arms into the air. Now quickly coming to him, she wrapped them around his neck and kissed him on the cheek, saying, "Thanks for coming so quickly."

"I didn't know," was all Michael could muster as he walked into the room heading toward the bed, acting like a deer in the headlights. He swallowed hard, not wanting to see Wallace or anyone in this condition. Gathering his composure, he asked, "Wall, how are you feeling?"

Wallace Bender smiled at him and said, "Michael thanks for coming. It's good to see you."

Amanda asked, "How are Diana and the baby?" Without waiting for an answer, she asked, "How old is she now?" The small talk and reminiscing continued for a few minutes until Wallace suggested that Amanda go and grab a coffee for herself, as she had been in that chair most of the night. She asked, "Michael do you want something?" She sensed that Wallace wanted some time alone with him.

"No, no I'm good," he answered. Once she left the room, Michael turned to Wallace and asked again, "So how are you doing, really?"

"Well, they tell me I had a massive heart attack, lucky to be alive. They want to operate and do a little repair work, a little damage, some swelling going on around the heart, but doctors want me to gather a little strength first. Typical stuff, I think. A couple more days of this and I'll have it all back, feeling a little weak right now. But, when I feel stronger that's when they go in I guess."

"So, everything is going to be good. That's good."

"Change my diet, lose weight, get some exercise. You know the usual, 'alter your lifestyle Mr. Bender.' That's what they said anyway."

"Well, good," Michael said again. "Good, good. That's good," he continued to say now somewhat awkwardly.

"I asked Amanda to make the call, wanted to talk with you," said Wallace as he tried to adjust himself in bed, moving a pillow. He stopped talking, grunting as he tried to get comfortable. He started again. "This thing is getting serious and heading in a direction that no one is going to like." The monitor beeped as the heart rate jumped up along with the systolic blood pressure number. Michael glanced at it and wanted to say, *It's ok Wall, take it easy*, but said nothing as Wallace continued talking. "It appears Gerald was up to something with Perron and Tesler that can only be described as no good, and I may have unwittingly helped them." Michael was shocked, but again said nothing. "I would tell you what little I know, lthough I think the less you know the better," said Wallace.

Michael, raising his hands out in front of him, shook his head saying, "I don't want to know, believe me."

Wallace continued, "As soon as I've recuperated a bit, I'll go see Austin and we'll both go in to talk with the federal prosecutor. I never thought the three of them were up to something like that. I'm going to make it clear that anything I may have done was unintentional. We'll see where that gets me, but anyway . . . ."

Michael stood there listening. All he could think to say was, "Ok."

"Listen Michael."

"Yes?"

"I'm going to let them know that you were not involved or aware of any of this. In fact, I will tell them you tried to warn me about what you perceived as 'loose business practices' at Bender that needed changing. I'll let them know that I spoke to you, but did nothing about it. I'll make sure to tell them that you were on top of things once Tesler left and you took over." Wallace looked at Michael, waiting for a reaction. Again, he was at a loss for words.

Several tense moments went by before Michael finally said, "My God, thank you Wall. Really thanks. I was afraid that I might get sucked into this mess even though I knew that people might not believe me . . .

you know, that the allegations in the civil cases were all wrong. Wait, were they all wrong?"

"No, afraid not. For the most part, they had it right. That is, with one exception—you and me. Anyway, I just wanted to let you know that I have your back. By the way Amanda has no idea about Gerald's involvement in all of this. Don't say anything to her. I'm going to have to break it to her gently after I go see the prosecutor," said Wallace.

"No, no of course not. Thank you again." *Jesus, Gerry what were you thinking?* "You have no idea how relieved I am Wall. Again, on behalf of me and my family, thank you so much." Michael couldn't say it enough.

Just then Amanda Bender returned to the room carrying a coffee and a bag. "I got us bagels from the cafeteria," she announced.

Michael said, "No thank you. I ought to be going."

The goodbyes were said quickly as Michael was feeling restrained excitement at the prospect that Wallace would soon be heading into Harrison's office to tell him to go fuck himself, and that Michael Dolan was an innocent man. He couldn't wait to tell Diana and his father.

On the way out, Amanda Bender walked him to the elevator and Michael said, "Please let me know when Wall goes in for surgery."

"I will. By the way what is going on with you and Gerry?"

"Not sure. What do you mean?" he asked.

Amanda Bender shook her head and said, "Remember the two of you are good friends." She stared at him for some sort of reaction and not getting one she said, "I better get back before Wall gets into that bag and eats a bagel, something he shouldn't do. Not good for him, you know. Take care Michael."

He said, "You too," and then got on the elevator.

Michael was excited, and as soon as he got to the car called Tommy Williston. He told him something came up and that he wouldn't be in today. Michael next called Marco and left a voicemail on his cell, "Call me. Need to talk to you. Have some good news." He next called his father, no answer. *He must be running some errands.* He then dialed Phillip Richardson's office number. The receptionist informed Michael that both he and Odell were in court and would not be returning until later in the day. She would leave a message that he called. He was almost home now and had no one to share this news with. He was still elated and didn't want to lose that feeling. Michael would wait until tonight to tell Diana the good news, in person, wanting to see the look on her face when he did.

CHAPTER FORTY-TWO

"WHERE the hell is Anderson?" asked FBI Agent Carl Bronson, annoyed that his partner was late.

Harrison replied, "Not here for this one. You know what a goody twoshoes he could be sometimes. Everything by the book. Well this one is not going to be that neat. Not if we want to take down all of the players."

Bronson shook his head and asked, "Got it. What time are they coming?"

"Any time now," he replied. The two men sat in the office discussing the case when twenty minutes later Angie called on the intercom, announcing that they had arrived.

"Ok, send them in," said Harrison. A few moments later, in walked the two men. Goddard was smiling, but Gerry Bender looked very serious. "Gentlemen good morning," said Harrison smartly.

"James, good morning," said Goddard. Seeing Carl Bronson, he emphatically said, "Carl, how the hell are you?" The two men knew each other, having worked together for years during the time Goddard was with the bureau.

"Joel, good. How the heck you been? It's been awhile," he said grabbing Goddard's hand with both of his. Bronson knew better to ask about *the family*, having attended his daughter's funeral. He also heard about his breakup with his wife, Jenny, who, as he understood it, had remarried an ATF agent and had another child. He knew his old friend had a rough go of it, and he felt sorry for him. *I should go have a drink with him after this. See how he is really doing*, Bronson considered for a moment, then thought better of it. The two men stood there with not much else to say, their once close friendship now a memory as they drifted apart and lost touch over the years. With pleasantries out of the way, the four men sat down and got to business.

Goddard asked, "James you got my changes to the plea deal, right? I want to make sure we are good on the offense conduct, limiting the number of victims, the loss amount, and that we agree on the sentencing guidelines range."

"Got it, and we are good. I can live with the changes we discussed. Now, let's get down to it. My secretary will be in with the criminal information, cooperation agreement, and plea deal shortly."

Right on cue, Angie walked in with the documents. Harrison took the them from her, keeping two sets for himself and handing another to Goddard. Looking them over carefully for the next ten minutes, Joel Goddard finally said, "Ok, looks good." He then handed them to his client, who looked at the documents. His attorney leaned into him saying, "The changes are all there, just like we discussed."

Gerry stopped flipping the pages and asked, "What about Anna?"

Harrison responded, "Like we said, can't put that in writing but you have my word, as long as you are helpful in this matter, and in the manner discussed . . . ."

Goddard jumped in, "Gerry that's the type of thing that doesn't make it into the agreements. It's an unwritten and more importantly, unspoken understanding. We discussed this, and as long as you give them what they want, be assured Anna will not be indicted." The attorney leaned in again to his client, this time closer, and whispered into his ear, "Remember the more helpful you are, the better for you and her." He paused. Displaying some anger, he said, "Just sign the fucking thing." The attorney pulled away from him and straightened, sitting firmly against the back of the chair, waiting for his client to react.

Gerry looked at the two of them and without another word signed three originals of both agreements; his attorney did the same. Harrison collected the papers, signed them, and handing two sets to Angie, asked her to make multiple copies. He then gave Goddard an original set.

Harrison spoke up first. "I'll file the criminal information, notify the court of the plea deal, and let you know of the arraignment date. You enter a guilty plea and we wait for sentencing. As simple as that Gerald—or do you prefer Gerry?"

He looked at Harrison with contempt and said, "Gerry," now obviously annoyed. He turned and glanced at his attorney, having second thoughts about all of this, feeling like he was misled and strong-armed into making the decision to cooperate. Goddard pulled back and smiled.

Harrison glared at them peculiarly but said nothing for about a minute and then asked, "Are we good?"

Goddard responded immediately saying, "Yea. We're good."

Both Bronson and Harrison took out note pads, ready to write down the exchange of questions and answers about to take place between them and Gerry Bender. The agent's notes would later be transcribed into what is known as an FBI-302 witness statement, the written account of the interview session. The document is then generally made available to all defendants and their lawyers, post indictment, during the discovery phase of a criminal case. Harrison's notes would be considered attorney work product—exempt from discovery as privileged material. He would not have to turn them over in any of the proceedings to follow as they might contain his thoughts and impressions as well as notes concerning strategy moving forward.

Harrison looked at Gerry again and said, "Here's how this works: We talk big picture, set the narrative, and you fill in the details to support it. Do that and we get what we need . . . you get what you want." He paused and then continued, saying firmly, "Don't fuck with me, understand. In other words, I say jump and you say how high. Got it?"

Gerry fidgeted in his seat and knowing that the government now owned him, he simply said, "Got it."

Harrison began, "Now let's talk about Michael Dolan."

CHAPTER FORTY-THREE

STUART Vogel stepped out of the black Cadillac Escalade with two of his most trusted people, the Vogel Fund CFO, Barry Livingston, and his bodyguard and driver, Ronnie. The fully loaded and modified eighty-five thousand-dollar SUV pulled up and parked in front of Twenty Central Park West, in a restricted loading zone area, as the doorman came running out of the lobby to question the men now walking to the front door. He immediately recognized the building's most affluent and, in his opinion, likable tenant, putting the brakes on the admonishment he had intended to hand out.

"Mr. Vogel, sir. Forget something, sir?" inquired Hector.

"Just a laptop that I needed for today." He paused and then said, "And oh yea, I forgot these, Yankee tickets for tonight's game," pulling out an envelope containing a set of tickets and two passes from his jacket pocket. Handing them to him, he said, "Here you go Hector. Right behind the Yankee dugout. You go enjoy the game."

"Mr. Vogel, I don't know what to say," he responded dumbstruck. A division league series game against the Indians—Hector couldn't believe he was going. "Sir, thank you," he said. The other two men looked at one another as they continued to walk into the large ostentatious lobby, past the concierge, heading toward the elevators, the doorman right beside them.

"It's nothing. You just go and have a good time. Those passes get you into the clubhouse too." In the envelope was a one hundred-dollar bill, as well. He added, "Get some dogs and beers on me. Why don't you take your daughter with you? I know what big fans the two of you are."

"Mr. Vogel sir, thank you. Again, I don't know what to say."

Stuart Vogel tapped Hector on the upper arm several times, and moving his other arm around his shoulders, he unintentionally led the doorman into the elevator with their conversation.

Inside he turned to Hector and said, "Should be just a minute." The doorman stepped out and said, "Thank you again sir," as the elevator doors closed on him.

As the men rode up to the top floor, which had a spectacular view of Central Park and Columbus Circle, Livingston asked, "What's with you and the doorman?" He looked at his longtime friend and commented, "You're always so chummy with him."

"Barry, you have no idea what I get from that guy. And for what, a few dollars here and there, no. Just friendship . . . some respect. A kind word and generosity. That's all. Those two tickets, for a game like this, for a guy like him, born and raised in the Bronx, still living just eight blocks from Yankee Stadium—shit, they are like winning lottery tickets." Livingston shook his head as Ronnie, the former Navy Seal, stared forward, tuning out the conversation, focusing on what might be on the other side as the doors opened, always ready for the unexpected. "And for that little bit I get all kinds of information," he concluded. "Things you just can't imagine."

Livingston looked at him and said, "Ok, if you say so. I mean what kind of information can you get from this guy? The date and location of the Puerto Rican Day Parade?"

Vogel looked at him and laughed, saying, "Barry, this is why you're a numbers guy. Don't get me wrong, the best one out there, but you'll never be a people's person—not until you see them for what they can be and not for who they are or what they appear to be. Take Hector for example, I unleashed his potential with a few questions about him and his family and, of course, a little kindness and friendship. That's it, and now I get some of the most important intelligence on all types of things. Shit that makes us a lot of money and has even saved my ass.

Livingston said, "Ok if you say so. Well, I'll be sure to thank him on the way out then."

Vogel laughed and shaking his head said, "Ok, asshole."

Quickly walking to get out of the building, Vogel was now in a hurry, but he did not forget to say goodbye to the doorman, telling him to enjoy the game and to keep on top of "that thing . . . that thing we talked about. You know that thing," suddenly sounding like a mafia don.

"No . . . of course I will. I'll stay on top of it and if anything changes I'll make sure to call you."

"Good man," he said walking out the door, held open for him by Hector, swiftly making his way back into the Escalade.

As the SUV pulled out, Hector, left standing at the curb, watched the vehicle speed away. He then returned to the lobby and pulled out the tickets, passes, and the hundred from the envelope. "What a guy."

CHAPTER FORTY-FOUR

THE two FBI agents, Anderson and Bronson, were in the elevator on their way up to see Jamie Preston, when building security called Andrew, the receptionist, telling him to expect them any minute. Leo Holtz did not want to be scolded like a child by Jamie Preston again, as he was the last time when the agents went up unannounced. Andrew said, "Leo thanks," and immediately called Claudia to let her know what was going on.

Before Andrew could do anything else, the elevator door slid open and Anderson and Bronson entered the reception area together with two loan processors, who were returning from lunch. "Agents Bronson and Anderson, so nice to see you again. Welcome back," said Andrew with a hint of sarcasm. "How can I help you today?" Andrew turned to the processors, who were now very curious, and buzzed them in through the main doors, leaving the agents to wait.

"Here to see Jamie Preston. Tell him we want to talk," Bronson demanded as Claudia now suddenly appeared through the doors.

"Andrew," she said, "I'll show them in. Thank you." He nodded his head in agreement and she then said, "Gentlemen, this way please."

Leading them to a small conference room, Preston was seated at one end of a rectangular table with Robert Wiley beside him.

Bronson commented, "Well, well. I see our arrival didn't go unannounced this time. Gentlemen."

Preston immediately asked, "Agents Anderson and Bronson, what can I do for you?" Before they could answer, he smiled and added, "Please have a seat."

Jamie Preston's tone and demeanor were now much different from their first visit. His mind was wandering, trying to focus on events taking place in the financial services industry and the recent seventy-five billion-dollar government superfund that was created by Treasury Secretary Lloyd Coulter. The fund's goal: to provide liquidity to banks and hedge funds that purchased asset-backed commercial paper and mortgage-backed securities that were now declining in value. It was an effort by Coulter to stave off further economic decline. Preston's Nationwide Mortgage was one of those banks feeling the effect of declining asset values and the tightening of the money supply. Preston was hoping the action would work to stabilize the markets and save his company from massive losses. He now needed to tread lightly with these agents so as not to cause further pain, financial or otherwise. There was no room for error if he was to keep the FBI's focus away from him and the company, which was experiencing its own problems due to unwise investments in subprime mortgages. He certainly did not want to invite any more trouble. Wiley had warned him to say nothing, urging him to just listen. Anything he might say could be construed as a crime—making a false statement to a federal agent. Any statement, if not entirely true, regardless of how innocently spoken, could be problematic. Preston needed to be careful.

"Please, please sit," he said again.

Anderson and Bronson looked at each other and thought the same thing: Preston was hiding something—they had him. Bronson was the first to speak. Seizing on the inviting demeanor and slight apprehension, he said aloofly, "Don't you want see our warrant?"

Wiley stepped in, nervously asking, "Do you have a warrant?"

Bronson smiled and tapping his jacket pocket he said, "No, no we don't. We have something much better. I have a Bill Tesler tucked away in my little right-hand pocket."

CHAPTER FORTY-FIVE

WASHINGTON D.C. was now abuzz with talk of a full-blown financial meltdown and the need for a call to action on how to avert a disaster. The Federal Reserve was already acting decisively to aggressively lower the federal funds rate, and the Treasury Department was doing its best to stabilize the financial markets. Fannie Mae and Freddie Mac were doing all they could with their *Homestay* and *HomePossible* programs—an effort on their part to allow homeowners with adjustable rate mortgages to get out from under the loans before a rate adjustment took place, making the monthly payment unaffordable. This, of course, did nothing for those people whose rates had already adjusted and were experiencing difficulties, and whose homes were overleveraged. Jim Harrison and his committee were working with both the Federal Reserve and the Treasury Department to come up with a plan to prevent the displacement of families and the deconstruction of the housing market and banking industry. It was proving to be a daunting task and people were now getting very nervous.

Jamie Preston sat waiting in a quiet corner of the Capital Grill Restaurant for his guest, who was now more than twenty minutes late. The African mahogany paneling, dark wood coiffured ceilings, and art deco chandeliers gave it an ambiance and allure unlike any other restaurant in the Washington D.C. area. Located on Pennsylvania Avenue, it was not at all inconspicuous or out of the way. A local favorite of the Washington elite, it was the perfect place to hold a meeting of this sort because no one would think twice to look at a celebrity diner or a power broker because everyone dining there usually was one or the other, or in some instances, both. Preston was now on his second vodka martini, and it was not quite noon yet. The minimal lighting made it possible for him to disappear into the background as he watched the entranceway from his table for two, located across the room near the kitchen entry. Suddenly, before him appeared two men. He was unsure where they came from. One he recognized, the other he did not.

"Senator Harrison. Jim, good to see you," said Preston half rising from his seat.

Harrison put a hand on his shoulder in a gesture to prevent him from going through the formality of getting up, while asking, "Jamie, how are you my friend?"

He sat down and his security detail from the Capital Police sat at the end of the bar, not more than thirty feet away from them. The ranking membership of the Hill were always assigned armed security. Harrison's man, Owen, had been with him for a little more than two years.

Harrison asked, "Jamie you sounded upset. What's going on?"

Before he could answer the waiter came to the table with a Tom Collins in a tall glass and placed it before Harrison saying, "Good afternoon, Senator."

"Toby, how the hell are you?"

"Fine sir, thank you for asking. And you, sir?"

"Grand, just grand. You look good my friend." He then asked, "Is everything alright at home?" Before the elderly grey-haired gentlemen in the white shirt and black bowtie could answer, Harrison next asked, "How are those granddaughters of yours?"

"Very good sir. Yes, very good."

"That is wonderful, Toby. Just wonderful," he said to the waiter, who had a forty-two-year familiarity with Washington's movers and shakers. He smiled politely and left the table, knowing that the brief exchange was all there was and that it was now over. He knew that Harrison would signal him when he was ready to order or in need of further service.

Turning his attention back to Preston, Harrison asked, "Jamie, how can I help you?"

"Jim, I had two FBI agents at my office a few days ago—at the direction of your son I might add—who are trying to drag me into that Bender investigation. Jim, I don't need this shit. I've got my own problems, some real problems as you know, and I don't need this shit," he repeated.

Harrison looked at him expressionless and said, "Jamie calm down. I will take care of it."

"You know I was there for you when you needed me, and half the boys on the Hill too. I don't need this fucking shit."

Harrison repeated, "I'll take care of it. Don't worry. I'll talk to Bo and, of course, James. We're driving the narrative on this thing. No one at the top is going to get hurt. And don't worry no one we care about is going to jail. Believe me."

Preston looked at him without saying a word, prompting Harrison to say, "We take care of our friends in the banking and financial services industry, don't we?"

"You always have; let's make sure it stays that way."

Harrison now getting angry said, "Jesus Christ, Jamie you and Lloyd Coulter came up together. How long have you known him? Thirty, thirty-five years? You were both at Goldman," referring to their tenure at the Wall Street investment brokerage firm of Goldman Sachs. "Do you think he is going to let anything happen to you?"

Ignoring the question, he said, "Well, I thought of going to him first, but I knew I should come and see you. By the way, I'm having dinner with him tonight. You can join us if you like."

"Damn right you needed to come and see me first. I'll take care of everything." Then abruptly shifting gears and looking away from Preston as if he was suddenly remembering something, he said, "Oh, tonight, no I can't make it— other plans." Turning his head and looking at him again, he reiterated, "Jamie our friends will not get hurt by this. Some heads will roll, unfortunately, that's for sure. This is a mess, a real mess," his voice tapering off until he stopped talking altogether.

Harrison then waved the waiter over to the table, who, within a minute, took their lunch order. Harrison, almost forgetting, said, "And Toby another round of drinks."

"Right away Senator Harrison, sir," said Tobias White, whose mortgage was also now in default like many others. His heavily mortgaged home, the proceeds of which were used to pay for his twin granddaughters to attend Georgetown University, was in foreclosure. He now considered approaching the senator about his problem, maybe after he was done with his lunch, but then decided better of it. After all, who was he to a man like Senator James Benjamin Harrison II, anyway?

CHAPTER FORTY-SIX

WALLACE Bender had been in the hospital for more than ten days now, and it didn't appear that he was getting any stronger or better. He was told that the surgery had been delayed as long as possible. The doctors did not like what they saw in the most recent echocardiogram, CT scan, and EKG tests, deciding it was best to move forward with the procedure rather than wait any longer. Wallace's cardiologist, Dr. Mitchell Howe, discussed with him and Amanda the inherent risks of having surgery soon after a debilitating and damaging heart attack. The inflammation and swelling of the tissue around the heart that happened within days of the occurrence was still present and getting worse. This condition, known as pericarditis, was not responding to the nonsteroidal anti-inflammatory treatment Howe prescribed. It was time to try something else. Dr. Howe warned that waiting any longer could risk further damage to the heart in a way that just might be irreversible. They agreed to schedule the surgery for the morning and address all medical issues then. Gerry, Anna, and Wallace's granddaughter left the hospital about 11:00 p.m., leaving Amanda to spend the night with her husband. As they began to leave the room, Wallace assured them he would be fine and not to bother coming back until later in the day tomorrow when he was awake and could actually visit with them. Amanda walked them down the hall to the elevators and wished them all a good night, saying, "See you tomorrow—and don't worry about a thing; your dad is going to be fine, just fine."

———◆———

The cellphone on the vanity began to ring, but Michael was brushing his teeth unable to answer it. Once he was done putting on a pair of pajama bottoms, he listened to the voice message. It was Amanda Bender.

Diana, despite the hour, was still up reading a book. It appeared to be a legal thriller, instead of a spread sheet or profit & loss statement, for a change. The bedroom was dimly lit, the light on her nightstand illuminating her book as she read. A*mbiance, how romantic*, Michael reflected as he walked out of the closet and approached the bed. Tossing the sheets aside, he uncovered Diana's shapely legs. He paused and stared. After getting in, he failed to flip the covers back onto her, and without looking up from the book, she asked, "Are you done?" Diana grabbed the sheets and yanked them upward, covering herself again, now annoyed.

He immediately stopped moving and said, "That was Amanda Bender. Wallace is going into surgery tomorrow morning. That's good. It must mean he is getting better."

She stopped reading and said, "Michael, he can't be getting better if he's going into surgery. He wouldn't be having the surgery if he was better."

He reconsidered the comment and said, "Well ok, stronger then."

"I guess they wouldn't be doing surgery if he wasn't up to it, and if it wasn't going to be helpful," reasoned Diana.

"That makes sense. He'll probably be in the hospital past Thanksgiving but hopefully out before Christmas," he said, now making small talk without stating the obvious. What he really wanted to say was more like, Fuck yea. As soon as Wall is better, he is going to tell the feds to fuck off. That's right, Michael Dolan had nothing to do with it. He's innocent. He didn't say it, however, for fear of sounding too self-absorbed. He was almost certain Diana was thinking the same thing, but also feeling reluctant to say it herself. Instead Michael asked, "What are you reading?"

"A legal thriller. Murder mystery."

"Not your usual," said Michael.

"It's interesting. An innocent man accused of murder, trying to defend himself and prove his innocence," she replied.

"Reminds me of someone I know," he said jokingly, with a smile on his face.

Diana giggled, "Me too."

Michael now cozied up to her throwing his arm around her waist, quickly moving his hand up to her chest, trying to undo one of the straps on her nightgown, hoping to arouse her. Without taking her eyes off the page or putting the book down, she said, "Michael stop. I'm not in the mood."

Without removing his hand, Michael said, "You haven't been in the mood for weeks."

Never mind that they made love only a few days earlier, the night Michael announced that Wallace was going to clear him with the feds. But to Michael the days now seemed like weeks, and for him what was like weeks bordered on eternity. His thinking on the subject now revealing the true essence of the male libido—there is no such thing as too much sex.

"Can you blame me," she said, swatting his hand away.

Diana was feeling added anxiety as she waited for Wallace to get well enough to finally put an end to all of this. Michael didn't answer her but rolled over wondering, *Are we ever going to make love again?* His erection slowly began to fade.

———◆———

Amanda Bender watched the elevator doors close and taking a cell-phone from her sweater, she called Michael and left a voice message when he did not answer. Returning to the room, she immediately went to Wallace's side, noticing he looked uncomfortable. She asked, "Wall are you feeling alright?"

"Yes, a little tightness and pain across the chest. It's nothing," he promptly said, rubbing the left side of his torso from under the hospital gown.

"Honey, be careful of the wires. Do you want me to get the nurse, so she can give you some pain medication?"

"No, I want a clear head. Let's talk," he said, beckoning her to sit. Amanda sat down on the oversized chair positioned near the bed, moving the pillow the hospital staff left for her, now trying to get comfortable.

Wallace held her hand, saying, "You've been a good wife. Thank you for all the years together. I know some of them, especially lately, have been tough ones. But know this, that I love—"

Amanda put up her hand and stopped him. "Wall you're going to be fine. Stop talking like you're saying goodbye," she said getting emotional, her lower lip quivering, and eyes misting.

Wallace sighed and said, "I'm just feeling my mortality Manda. But if something should happen . . . ."

Again, she stopped him, "Nothing is going to happen." Looking directly at him she now scolded, "You hear me . . . not a thing."

He shook his head in agreement and turned away still rubbing his chest. Looking back at her, Wallace stared at his wife intensely and said, "I have something I need to tell you."

———◆———

The morning seemed to come quickly. Michael got up exhausted. His sleep was restless no doubt due to the excitement that he would soon be cleared with the feds, but mainly because of the carnal desire he was feeling for his wife. It kept him up all night, literally. *A neglected hard-on could easily fuck up a good night's sleep—it might even kill you,* concluded Michael, as he took a cold shower. Coming out, he dried himself off. Wrapping the towel around his waist, he looked at himself in the mirror. *Um, not bad. Lost a few pounds I think.* He then called out to Diana, "Hon, is the baby up yet?"

"No, not yet," she replied from the walk-in closet where she was getting dressed.

Good, he thought. He would get himself ready and then make breakfast for his daughter, afterward taking her to school. He was home for a few days as Tommy did not have anything lined up for him or the crew, which was fine; it was near the end of a busy season, and he knew that it would eventually come to this. Work started to become scarce this time of year—it always did in the house painting industry. He could spend time with Christina and his dad today as he waited to hear from Amanda Bender on how Wallace was feeling after the surgery. She had said in her voice message that she would probably call late afternoon, when he was expected to be in recovery. He was heading into surgery at about 7:00 a.m. and was likely to be in there six to eight hours.

Dropping off Christina, he immediately drove to his father's house to have coffee with him. He had called earlier to let him know he was stopping by.

"Dad, Wallace Bender is in heart surgery this morning."

Taking a sip of coffee Eddy responded, "Gee, I hope all goes well."

"I'm sure it will. He's a bull." Pausing a moment, he said, "Always the first in and last to leave."

Eddy shook his head in agreement. "You think once Wallace goes into the feds your attorney can get some assurance from them that you're cleared and no longer a target of the investigation?"

"I hope so dad. I don't think Harrison would proceed with a case against me without any evidence or probable cause."

"Maybe not, but stranger things have happened," replied Eddie, failing to consider how the remark would resonate with his son.

Before he could respond to his father's comment, Michael's cellphone rang. It was Diana. "Yea hon."

"Hi, just checking in. What time did you bring Christina in this morning?"

"Not until nine. I'm at my dad's now, just having some coffee."

"Ok, remember I won't be home until about seven . . . trying to finish up a few audits here."

"Alright, no worries. I'll take care of things."

Diana and Michael exchanged goodbyes. "I love you." They hung up without saying another word. A moment later, Michael's phone rang. *Amanda Bender.* It was only 10:40 a.m., much earlier than expected. "Hello . . . Amanda."

Eddy saw that Michael answered the phone, doing so with what appeared to be grave apprehension. It was obvious he was not expecting a call this early. He heard him say hello and watched as he curiously cocked his head. The hello was followed by an ok, as he frowned and started to shake his head no. Abruptly he said, "Oh my God, Amanda. Oh my God. I'm sorry. I can't believe it. I'm sorry." The color ran from his face as he put his hand to his forehead, pushing back the hair from his brow. He then began to shake all over. It was right then and there that Eddy Dolan knew Wallace Bender had died on the operating table—along with Michael's chances of ever being exonerated.

CHAPTER FORTY-SEVEN

THE funeral was somber. Amanda Bender, usually an emotional woman, a *wear your heart on your sleeve* type of person, was now standing in the receiving line appearing very calm and collected. Gerry, however, was a mess. Michael and Diana approached the casket. They reflected and prayed, saying their goodbyes to Wallace Bender, and then, almost reluctantly, moved on to offer their condolences. Amanda saw them approaching and smiled, beckoning them to her as she opened her arms. The embrace between Michael and Amanda was warm and heartfelt as she held him tightly. Michael declared sympathetically, "I'm so very sorry, truly," as he was suddenly overcome with emotion, feeling a deep sorrow for her. Amanda was a caring and loving woman who was very good to Michael, always treating him like a second son, ever since he and Gerry became friends and roommates.

She said, "Michael thank you." Releasing him from her hold slightly, she whispered, "Wallace was very fond of you." Michael looked at her and could not speak as he struggled to hold back the tears. Turning to Diana, who began to weep, she commanded, "Come here honey. Don't cry, it's ok." Gently, Amanda wrapped her arms around Diana. They chatted a moment about Wallace. Diana assured her that he was a wonderful man and that he was with God, in a better place. The widow shook her head in agreement without letting on how she felt one way or another.

Amanda Bender was nothing short of stoic as she greeted, embraced, and kissed the mourners that day, refusing to allow them to see her true feelings over the loss of her husband, setting aside that grief and pain for a private moment of her own.

Michael and Diana made their way to Gerry, who appeared distraught, even more so when he saw his friend. Their eyes locked, and Gerry immediately looked away. *Jesus, poor guy, the grief has gotten the better of him.* Michael felt badly for his friend and quickly went to him, but their embrace was surprisingly cold and awkward. He said, "Gerry, I'm sorry. Really sorry."

He turned his head away and said to himself, "So am I," looking even more distraught than before. Gerry's comment wasn't about his father, but more directed to the fact that he was about to throw Michael under the bus to save himself with the feds. They quickly parted uncomfortably as Gerry avoided speaking to the two of them by saying, "The other mourners . . ." as he awkwardly pointed to the people behind them waiting to offer their condolences. Michael and Diana both quickly glanced behind their shoulders, somewhat mystified by the comment, and stood there motionless until Michael finally said, "Yea right, sorry." They moved on to greet and offer condolences to the rest of the family members. From the funeral home, the procession moved to the nearby cemetery, only a few miles away.

Wallace's daughter-in-law, Anna, offered a brief but stirring eulogy at the grave site, as there was no church service. Wallace was not the church going type and, as such, wanted only a quick graveside funeral. The family invited the many mourners to join them for lunch at a restaurant in Fairfield. Michael and Diana declined, sensing Gerry's uneasiness, unsure what exactly was causing it.

———————◆———————

Michael had called his attorney a couple of days before Wallace's funeral and informed them of his death. Wallace had another heart attack in the middle of the night while Amanda slept in the chair beside him. The hospital staff rushed in as soon as the monitoring alarms had gone off, but there was nothing they could do to save him. As Michael relayed the information, the attorneys who were both in the oval office and on the speakerphone, listened to the details of this unfortunate development. Phillip Richardson was the first to speak and without any emotion in his voice, analyzed it like a lawyer. He now offered his utmost expert legal opinion, saying, "This really hurts our chances of changing Harrison's mind about you. I'm not so sure where that leaves us but avoiding an indictment is going to be that much more difficult now. Damn, we really needed Wallace to set the record straight." Michael thought, *No shit.* Richardson added, "Maybe I need to feel out Harrison a little more. I'll set up a meeting after the new year."

Odell interrupted him and trying to be sensitive to the situation said, "I'm sorry for your friend and the loss." More discourse between them ensued for a few minutes, ending in Odell overstating the obvious, "You know, of course, this a huge problem." Again, Michael reflected, *No shit.* He was very much aware of the grave problems Wallace Bender's untimely death presented for him.

————————◆————————

The conversation on the ride home was nonexistent, which was fine with Michael, as it provided him an opportunity to reflect on the events of the last few days. Wallace's death had been heartbreaking and disappointing on so many levels. The adulation he was feeling after his last visit with Wallace now gave way to not only grief but also extreme frustration and worry. He wondered if there was no avoiding the inevitable. Holding onto a glimmer of hope, Michael believed, perhaps naively, that there still was a chance he would not be indicted—after all he didn't do anything wrong.

Michael made the decision not to discuss what he was thinking with Diana, keeping silent when asked, trying to shield her from it all. Instead of sparing her from what he perceived to be the unnecessary burden of knowing, his silence served to drive her further away. He failed to realize that not only was their relationship unsteady, it was in danger of falling apart. The "if she doesn't ask, I won't tell" routine did nothing to help.

As they remained still in their seats, quietly observing the roadway ahead of them, Diana asked, "Have you talked to Phillip and Odell?"

Startled, Michael replied, "Ah . . . yes I did. Couple of days ago as a matter of fact."

"Well, what did they say?"

"Phillip seemed to think that the next move should be to call Harrison and set up a meeting. But, he thinks it won't likely take place until after the holidays. He claims the government essentially shuts down this time of year. Nothing will get done until after January for sure is what he said."

"Ok, where is that going to get us?"

He turned and looked at her a little puzzled, which prompted her to say, "I mean how does that help . . . really Michael."

"Thinking about it," he quickly responded. Considering the question for only a moment, he blurted out, "I'm not fucking sure."

He suddenly appeared agitated. "Maybe it's just intelligence gathering, or he tries to persuade Harrison that I should not be indicted. I don't know."

"Get back in touch with them and find out," she said, ignoring his tone. Although she was exacerbated by his lack of clarity, she was even more so frustrated by his lack of interest in what his attorneys were doing.

Becoming agitated once more, he shot back, "I will. Jesus, give me a break. I'll talk to them again." The stress of Wallace's death was now beginning to get to him.

Diana looked at her husband and decided not to respond, opting to remain silent. She did not want to argue with him, especially since he seemed a little irrational. *Clearly,* she thought, *he doesn't have a grasp on this whole thing.* They both sat through several more minutes of silence, before Diana asked, "Do you want to grab some lunch?"

"Sure," he said indifferently, still reeling over the discussion and feeling overwhelmed by just about everything these days. "What are you thinking?"

"Something inexpensive," she said. And without thinking how it might be interpreted she quickly added, "With you not working we really need to watch our overhead," sounding like an accountant.

Michael paused and then reacted, "My God Diana, we can afford to go out for a nice lunch. It's not going to break the bank." His angry response, rightly or wrongly, was prompted by the "out of work" comment, which he considered an affront to his manhood.

Diana ignoring his tone calmly replied, "Michael we just don't know what the future is going to bring."

Holy shit. She is so fucking melodramatic. "Ok, pick a spot . . . anything," he said, extremely annoyed with her. Diana's detachment now agitated him, yet it wasn't so much her, but the constant fear of not knowing what might happen next that really bothered him.

CHAPTER FORTY-EIGHT

THE holidays came and went quickly. Although Thanksgiving and Christmas did serve as a pleasant distraction for everyone, including Michael and Diana who seemed to be getting along a little better. It was a welcomed break in the tension between them. Christina, as usual, enjoyed all the attention she was receiving, obviously unaware of the events taking place over the last several months. Karen joined them Christmas Eve, as did Eddy Dolan. Diana's family decided not to make the trip down to Connecticut due to the weather, so they claimed, and the Duffy family was not invited, no longer welcome. It was quiet for a change and nice—completely relaxing. Christina went to bed at about 9:30 p.m., and as usual Eddy began to assemble the Santa presents. As Michael tried to help his father, Diana and Karen sat on the sofa in the family room drinking wine and laughing at his inability to follow simple instructions on the doll house assembly. Eddy corrected a few of his missteps along the way. Frustrated, Michael gave up and went into the kitchen to retrieve a glass of wine for himself. Needless to say, Christmas morning was a hit for Christina, who woke up early to see what Santa had left under the tree for her.

———◆———

It wasn't until the end of January when Michael received a call from Odell informing him of a meeting that was going to take place with the U.S. Attorney's Office.

"Michael, listen," Odell said. "Phillip spoke to James Harrison yesterday. He called us and asked to meet. They are getting together next week."

He asked nervously, "Ok, how does this work? Do I go to the meeting? Do I say anything? What's the deal?"

"Hold it, slow down. No, you are not going. Phillip is going alone, and Harrison is intending to do this as a reverse proffer."

Michael asked, "What does that mean?"

"Essentially, it is an attempt to persuade. He is going to offer some or all of the evidence against you . . . ."

Interrupting, he asked, "What evidence?"

"Michael I'm not sure what the evidence is, or if there is any at all. So, don't get nervous. Not yet anyway."

Not yet, what the fuck does that mean? "I'm not nervous," he replied.

"This can be a good thing because it gives us an opportunity to assess what evidence they believe supports whatever prosecution theory they are pushing. It helps us make decisions moving forward." Odell paused, anticipating a question but there was only silence on the other end. He knew Michael was thinking, and so he waited. He then thought to himself, *Decisions like whether to accept a plea deal or go to trial.* He waited a few more seconds and then finally asked, "Michael, still there?"

"Yea, I'm here. Ok, but I want to hear from you immediately after that meeting."

"Of course. Phillip and I will call you next Friday at around 4:00 p.m. How does that sound?"

"Fine," Michael said absent mindedly, hanging up without saying goodbye.

The next several days seemed to move slowly as Michael anxiously waited for the meeting to take place and hear from his attorneys afterward. He had discussed this with Diana who could only say, "At least we'll have some clarity shortly." Michael agreed. It seemed this just might be a turning point for them. It could be good or bad, however, not knowing what the net result would be.

Eddy waited with his son, hoping that the call would bring good news, although he was not very optimistic. He knew, from his years on the police department and working with several federal joint task forces investigating a few of the Greenwich elite, that once the feds set their sights on you, it was extremely difficult to persuade them to look any other way.

The phone call came at 4:00 p.m., as promised. Phillip Richardson and Odell Brown were both on the speakerphone, waiting to talk to Michael about the meeting. Before the call, Richardson filled in Odell about the conversation with Harrison as he dialed the phone, explaining that he had a plea agreement all ready and waiting for him on the desk when he got there.

The phone was answered on the second ring. "Michael, hi. It's Odell, and Phillip is here with me. I have you on speaker, ok?"

"Sure, that's fine. How are you?"

Richardson got right to the point and began, "Michael listen, as you know I met with James Harrison and FBI Agent Carl Bronson just a little while ago. I spent about forty minutes with them and essentially they want you to take a plea."

"What?" exclaimed Michael, as he nervously got up from his father's kitchen table. Eddy Dolan remained seated, listening to one side of the phone conversation, trying to figure out what was being said on the other end. He glanced into the living room and saw that Christina was still asleep, napping on the couch. Looking back at Michael, he continued to listen.

"Hold on Michael. Take it easy," Richardson implored. "I told him that any discussion about a plea was way too premature. I didn't even look at it and left the agreement on the desk without ever touching it."

"Jesus, Phillip. I'm glad you did that. You, of course, told him that I would never agree to any type of plea deal, right?" Eddy Dolan nodded his head in agreement.

Richardson did not respond to the comment, but instead said, "I mainly listened. I wanted them to feed me information, not the other way around."

Odell interjected himself into the conversation by adding, "Michael remember this was a reverse proffer, so we were there, essentially, to gather intelligence from the government."

"Exactly," said Richardson.

Michael said, "Ok, so what did you learn?"

"Well, for one thing I now know several people are cooperating. The narrative they are spinning puts you in the middle of a broad conspiracy that extends beyond Bender Capital and the other companies controlled by them. It extends out to other lenders, they wouldn't say who, and to several Wall Street investment firms."

Michael thought, *what the fuck is he talking about.* He said, "Phillip I'm not sure I'm following you."

"Well, the government is claiming that fraudulent loans were sold into the secondary market purchased by companies like a Nationwide or a Bank of America for example, as part of the plan. Then they're bundled into securitized instruments to unsuspecting investors. When the loans went bad, certain ones were selectively purchased back for pennies on the dollar, let's say by companies, again, controlled by the

Benders and others. The properties are then foreclosed, resulting in huge profits for the conspirators."

Michael interrupted and asked, "What does that have to do with me?"

"Michael, they are claiming that you were brought in to help continue and facilitate this conspiracy. The government asserts that you were a trusted friend, who the Benders could count on to continue the scheme, and when Bill Tesler went to Nationwide, they claim you came in to take over Tesler's role at Bender, essentially to keep the regulatory agencies at bay and cover up the tracks from regulators and law enforcement."

"That's bullshit, complete crap. You know it and I know it. Fuck them," he shouted.

Eddy Dolan got up from his seat, looked to the living room and put his hand on his son's shoulder to try and calm him down, telling him, "Michael take it easy. Getting angry isn't going to help."

"Michael I'm just telling you what I know and think," said Richardson nonchalantly.

"Who the fuck is feeding them this bullshit about me anyway?"

"Michael, I'm pretty sure it's Gerry Bender."

CHAPTER FORTY-NINE

"SENATOR Banks, where would you like these?" asked young Charlie Brandt, the senate aid, who was completely focused on helping the newest member of the United States Senate.

"I think over there," said Banks, pointing to the far wall nearest the large mahogany desk and tan leather chair. Banks had already set up the furniture throughout the office and was now working on getting photographs, plaques, and awards on the walls. He was in a rush. He had been in Washington for several weeks now, but he still was a bit unsettled. He had been busy running back and forth to the Capitol tending to his new duties and the demands put upon him by his friend, Senator James Benjamin Harrison II.

Carter Atkins walked into the outer office placing a box of his personal belongings on his new desk, and turning to the maintenance worker asked, "Morris, can you come with me into the senator's office to see if he needs help with anything?"

Morris Biggs stopped what he was doing and looked over at the senator's chief of staff. The fourteen-year government staffer, who was assigned to the Dirksen Senate Office Building maintenance crew, said, "Yea sure. You got it Carter." Hiking up the work belt around his waist, he followed him toward the back office. To look at him, anyone would say he was a big man. At six-foot-four and two hundred twenty-eight pounds, Biggs was lean and solid. A former army infantry sergeant and Gulf War veteran, he was a fixture on the Hill and well-liked by all the staffers and congressmen. The two men met within days of Carter's arrival in Washington and immediately bonded. Biggs limped slightly as he walked behind Carter over to the senator's office, as the nine surgeries that took place at the Walter Reed VA Hospital over the years could not completely repair the damage done to his leg by a bullet delivered courtesy of a Saddam Hussein Republican Guard member. It was the wound that earned him a purple heart and brought an end to his army career.

In a deep throaty voice that was reminiscent of Barry White, Biggs said, "Carter, if you need a hand at home I'm happy to come over when we're done here."

"Sure, I could use some help. I'll let my mom know to set another plate for dinner," said Carter, as he smiled at his new friend, knowing exactly why he offered his services. He thought, *I better call my mother now to let her know that Morris is coming over, so she can get herself ready.* Mabel Atkins had her eye on him from the first day they met, seduced almost entirely by his good looks and the tone of his voice. Morris Biggs seemed to like her too, almost boyishly unable to contain his excitement in her presence. It was the first time Carter could ever recall seeing a spark of romance in his mother, and he was elated. Morris Biggs seemed to be a good man and his mother had never had a good man in her life, ever, including Carter's father, who had left Mabel Atkins before he was born.

"Ok, let's see what the illustrious senator from New Jersey needs a hand with," said Biggs, grinning, as he looked forward to seeing his new lady friend later this evening. He was sure Carter knew he had an eye on his mother, and it seemed as if he didn't mind. Morris thought that his unspoken approval was a good thing.

———◆———

Senator Harrison's office was located on the second floor of the Capitol Building. It was a large opulent office suite with frescoes painted by the Italian artist Constantino Brumidi, who was dubbed the Michelangelo of the Capitol, as he was most famously known for the painting of the fresco in the eye of the Capitol rotunda entitled the *Apotheosis of Washington.* Banks' office paled in comparison to Harrison's in both size and splendor. The Capitol and Dirksen buildings were connected by a series of underground tunnels that housed a monorail system used to shuttle people back and forth between them. The tunnels also linked the Capitol to the other buildings housing additional congressional offices and staff. The underground labyrinth was the quickest and easiest way for Banks to shuffle to the Capitol. This was significant for a few reasons, the most important being that it enabled him to respond promptly when summoned by Harrison, like the lapdog he was quickly becoming. After all it was Harrison who arranged for Banks' appointment to the prestigious Senate Committee on Banking, Housing, and Urban Affairs, an unheard of selection for a freshman senator. And it was also Harrison who directed Banks' assignment to the Financial Institutions and Consumer Protection Subcommittee, which was also unheard of. It was all a part of Harrison's plan to properly position another political ally right where he needed him, and Harrison had Banks right where he wanted him. He knew he could count on him to do whatever he commanded, despite their different party affiliations. He would use him to help insulate Nationwide from this mess, and Jamie Preston from the criminal investigation currently underway, or any other that might come his way. Thinking about it now reminded him that he should go and see Bo Erkens, again, over at Justice later today. He called his chief of staff, Samuel Brandt, whose son he had assigned to Banks' staff, and asked him to make the arrangements. Together, he and Bo, could call James in New York to tell him to back off Preston.

At this moment, however, Jim Harrison was focused on Bear Stearns, a large Wall Street investment firm, who was having monumental problems and would likely need to be bailed out. It appeared that J.P. Morgan Chase would be the one to do it, but Harrison believed that the Federal Reserve would need to guarantee the bailout to the tune of about thirty billion dollars. Hopefully it would end there, but Harrison wasn't too optimistic, thinking there might be more bailouts to come.

CHAPTER FIFTY

THE Target Letter from the Department of Justice, U.S. Attorney's Office, arrived on a Wednesday. It was signed by James Benjamin Harrison III, and it was meant to inform Michael Dolan that he was a target of a federal criminal investigation. He looked at it and asked himself, *What the hell is this?* Never having seen one, he was not sure what to make of it, and worse yet not being told about it. Reading further, the letter informed him that if he wished to testify before the grand jury he may do so, but anything said in the matter could and would be used against him in all other legal proceedings to follow. With that, Michael decided that he needed some clarity and, putting the letter down, he called his attorneys.

Speaking to Odell, he asked, "What is this all about? I've never heard of a Target Letter."

"Michael, it's called a 'Target Letter' for a reason. It's telling you are a target of a federal criminal investigation, and most, but not all, targets receive one just prior to a grand jury proceeding and the subsequent indictment to follow. It is the government's way of saying you can come in and testify to try and explain yourself, essentially to offer evidence of your innocence."

"That was the sense I got, but never heard of such a thing."

"Well, almost always no one goes in to offer himself up because, like the saying goes, 'even a bad prosecutor can indict a ham sandwich.' It almost never helps to go in and testify and, in most instances, it hurts you. So, these offers to come in are usually ignored for that reason and are a very disingenuous."

"Ok, so what should I do?"

"Michael, you do nothing," said Richardson, as he walked into the office, now interjecting himself into the conversation before Odell could respond. "It's complete fucking bullshit."

"Oh, Phillip I didn't know you were there," Michael said, surprised by his sudden input.

"Just walked into Odell's office and overheard a bit of the conversation. Wanted to give you my two cents. Again, you do nothing."

He allowed his advice to sink in and then asked, with a strain of questionable optimism in his voice, "Isn't there anything we can do?"

"Michael, let me put it this way—it is what it is. We do nothing because there is nothing we can do. Harrison is going to indict you. All we can do is wait for it. I'll talk to him about a self-surrender at the appropriate time, and hopefully he grants us that courtesy."

Michael, as always, was once again stunned by Richardson's bluntness who, unlike Odell's soft touch, pulled no punches. He considered the situation and not fully grasping the comment about self-surrendering, simply asked, "How long?"

"No way of telling. But once it goes down, we circle the wagons and hunker down for the fight of your life," said Odell in response, suddenly triggering the memory of similar words spoken to him by Austin Wainwright and his partners when this all began.

"Michael, that is when the real work begins. We will do everything we can to try and take control of the narrative and steer this into a direction that ends in an acceptable outcome," said Richardson. *The operative words being, "Acceptable outcome," and what is acceptable is different for everyone*, he reflected.

"So, if I'm not going in to testify, then I should prepare for the inevitable, the worst, right? But, I think I want to testify. I want to tell this grand jury that I'm innocent. I have a right to do that, don't I?"

"There is no way you're going in to speak with Harrison's grand jury, no fucking way. It's suicide," said Richardson. Waiting a moment, he softly added, "Michael, you have no right to be there, by the way— that invitation to testify was made only to bury you. Please understand that. Yes, prepare for the worst." He paused again for a reaction, but there was none. The phone was silent on the other end, except for heavy erratic breathing. Richardson tried to sound reassuring and said, "Michael, we will work hard to find out when this is going down because, as you know, the grand jury meets in secret. We get ready for it as best we can and try to minimize its impact for you and your family, again, as best we can. In fact, I will call Harrison in the next few days to see what I can uncover and try to soften him up a little," he said, in an attempt to prevent the complete demoralization of his client.

Michael pondered what he was being told and could only think to say, "Ok Phillip, I have no choice but to trust you. After all, I'm sure you're only doing what you think is best."

Richardson now said sadly, "Michael, I'm only telling you what I think is best for you and your family. Believe me, I'm here for you, Diana, and your daughter. I'll say it again. If you go in and testify, it would be suicide. But let me see what I can do with Harrison, ok?" He tried to be as sensible as he could, although he wasn't too optimistic that he could prevent what was about to happen from happening. AUSA James Benjamin Harrison III would do what he wanted, when he wanted, and was not the type that was easily swayed otherwise.

CHAPTER FIFTY-ONE

ALL twenty-three members of the grand jury were present and waiting for Harrison to make his way to the courtroom. They sat patiently and chatted amongst themselves, curious about the matter that would soon come before them. The grand jury had not been in session for several months and now having been called back into service, many of the jurors were looking forward to the next case for their consideration, while a few were more than annoyed by the sudden and unexpected call to return. The clerk was already in the courtroom and provided a brief explanation of the services that were required of them as they waited for the Assistant U.S. Attorney.

Harrison walked into the grand jury room, rolling in behind him a large square trial briefcase with wheels and an adjustable handle that was strikingly similar to a carry-on suitcase. It was filled with bank records, documents, 302 FBI witness statements, and his typed notes. Pulling it alongside the large desk, and without saying a word to anyone in the room, he began to unload the briefcase. Looking over to the court stenographer he said, "Why don't we get started."

He turned to the grand jury members that were sitting in the jury box to his right and began by reminding them who he was and that they had been reassembled to hear more evidence in a matter that they should be somewhat familiar with. It was this grand jury that issued subpoenas for bank records in the recent past at Harrison's request. "Remember," he said, "this process does not involve oversight by a judge. I, and I alone will present you with the law, evidence, and witnesses in this proceeding. The court reporter will create a record of what takes place here. Keep in mind you may also ask questions at the appropriate time, and as you may already know, this entire matter is undertaken in secrecy. No one other than the appropriate court personnel will know who you are so you may act and speak freely, ok?"

The jurors collectively nodded their heads affirmatively. "Anyway, if you determine there is probable cause to believe a crime has been committed at the end of this proceeding, this grand jury will return an indictment, or a true bill, as it is sometimes referred to. Got it?" Before they could react or respond, Harrison said again, "Let's get started. Oh, keep in mind there are no formal rules. This whole proceeding is very informal. Ok?" Again, Harrison said smiling, "Now let's really get started."

The first witness was waiting to come out from the small witness room just off the courtroom. FBI Agent Carl Bronson, called in by Harrison, took the stand and was sworn in by the Grand Jury Foreperson. He was first asked preliminary questions about his background, credentials, experience, training, and education. The jurors appeared very impressed with Bronson. It was exactly what Harrison wanted because it made him seem more credible and what he was about to say more believable.

"Agent, please describe in a very general sense the type of case you are currently investigating and the subject of this grand jury inquiry," Harrison stated.

"Well, it's what we refer to as a mortgage fraud case, which typically involves fraudulent loan applications and other misrepresentations made to lenders to induce them to provide a loan. It usually consists of a conspiracy by two or more to commit the fraud, and it can involve money laundering. It is what is commonly known as a white-collar criminal case, the reason being these types of cases take place in corporate America . . . you know, individuals in professional occupations such as lawyers, bankers, investment bankers, essentially the Wall Street types."

Shaking his head in agreement Harrison directed, "Ok, please describe for the jurors the particulars of the case and the individuals involved."

Bronson went on to discuss the events surrounding the Bender Capital Lending investigation. He detailed a scheme that was created and carried out by its owners, their lawyer, Michael Dolan, several company employees, licensed professionals, and numerous borrowers who falsified loan applications, all of whom, in one way or another, defrauded banks and other investors. He described a conspiracy that essentially induced financial institutions to purchase loans in instances where they would not have otherwise done so.

He went on to give numerous examples of mortgage loans containing falsified and inaccurate information from length or type of employment, income amounts, asset descriptions, and more.

"As you can see, it seemed that Perron and the others would direct borrowers to falsely report information on the applications or in many instances would just do it themselves," Bronson described.

"Ok, please explain further," asked Harrison.

"Sure. Bender Capital would then sell the mortgage loans to a secondary market investor. The financial institution takes a fraudulent loan and bundles it together with other loans into an investment product known as a mortgage-backed security and resells that to other investors, such as a pension fund." Bronson looked over at the jurors as he said it observing that many of them were older, who were retired or nearing retirement, hoping that his comments would resonate with them. "I might add the other banks did not do so knowingly."

"Ok, the banks on the secondary market didn't sell bad loans purposefully," Harrison tried to clarify.

"That's right, the banks or the financial institutions selling to pension funds."

"And this scheme not only hurt the banks, but also individual investors, such as the pensioners you mentioned."

"That's right." Bronson again looked over at the jurors, who were nodding their heads in agreement.

Harrison next called FBI Agent, John Anderson, who testified about the forensic accounting work he had done. Based upon a review of the individual accounts and company bank statements, Anderson found a clear money trail leading directly to the scheme participants, with one exception.

"Well, it is easy to explain," Anderson said in response to Harrison's question about why it appeared no money was going to Dolan. "According to Gerald Bender, one of the originators of the conspiracy, Michael Dolan, who came in toward the final months, insisted on taking his share of the scheme's proceeds in cash. It appears he was concerned about money being traced back to him. Clearly, he thought this out better than the others. Must have been the attorney in him," joked Anderson.

A few of the jurors chuckled while others shook their heads in agreement as they had done with Bronson. Harrison asked the Jury Foreman if he had any questions. "Yes, I think I do."

Getting right to it, the juror asked, "Agent Anderson, do you know how much money Michael Dolan netted from this conspiracy?"

"Well I'm not exactly sure. But according to Mr. Bender, that is Gerald Bender not Wallace, who is now deceased, Mr. Dolan received the same amount as the other co-conspirators commencing on the day he started working at Bender Capital Lending," reported Anderson. "So, it was months of payments in cash, and as best as I can tell it exceeded one hundred thousand dollars. He also received a check from the company that was labeled 'severance pay' as a ploy, but according to Mr. Bender, again, it was a final payment of the conspiracy proceeds. They all did pretty good, I might add."

"Thank you, Agent Anderson," said the foreman. Harrison asked if anyone else had any questions, and receiving no inquiries, he moved on.

"Ok," said Harrison. "Tell us about who else was involved at the company and what their positions were."

"Certainly, there were numerous individuals from several company departments involved. Mr. Bender's assistant, for instance, was aware of what was going on. Her name is Joan Archer. Brad, sorry, Bradley Wright, who was the underwriter on the Perron-originated loans was also involved. He was the person who, next to those already mentioned, was most responsible for manipulating the information on loan applications. A loan processor, Janice Hernandez, also falsified documents that were needed to support the claims on the applications, such as paystubs, bank statements, and tax returns. Also, Bill Tesler had a 'right-hand man' in compliance that went with him to Nationwide Mortgage who was deeply involved. His name was Peter Li. He essentially helped his boss hide the loan irregularities from regulators."

Anderson named eight other individuals who Bender, Tesler, and Perron claimed knew about the scheme or played a role in it. He identified more Bender employees, lawyers, real estate agents, and appraisers who he now asserted contributed one way or another to the overarching scheme.

"Agent Anderson, you also discovered that many of the Bender Capital borrowers knowingly falsified their own applications, didn't you?"

"Yes, in our investigation we uncovered numerous loans where the applicants themselves falsified the information on the applications with the aid of Bender employees. These borrowers knowingly and intentionally participated, or in some instances, were complicit in this scheme," said Anderson.

Harrison asked, now reemphasizing the point, "You're saying that these borrowers were co-conspirators in all of this."

"Yes, they were."

Anderson next went through the loan documents pointing out the falsities in each of the applications, such as the false employment claims, income amounts, and asset claims. He next went through the bank records demonstrating that deposits and withdrawals correlated with payments to the scheme's participants, the sale of homes by New Frontier Properties, the purchase of mortgage loans by WGB Investments, and rent deposits of now displaced borrowers into the Bender-owned and controlled rental properties. Anderson's testimony continued for almost two days. Harrison knew that once it was done, no other witnesses were necessary. The grand jury returned a sealed Indictment within the week. It indicted everyone, including Michael Dolan.

CHAPTER FIFTY-TWO

DIANA directed more than asked, "Michael, why don't you go and see Father Paul?" She waited for a reaction as he sat in the dark drinking wine. "This . . . this not knowing is really stressing you out," she said.

"No kidding," he said to himself. Michael sat silently, as if he didn't hear her. She was about to repeat herself when he abruptly said, "I'll call him in the morning." He remained seated, staring blankly at the TV screen, holding on tightly to his wineglass.

Diana continued, "His counseling has helped me to better deal with all of this." She stopped what she was doing and looked over at him. His back was to her still, as he refused to turn around and face her for what was turning out to be a one-sided discussion. She sighed and said, "You'll feel better once you talk to him. I think he'll help you make some sense of . . . well everything." Diana hesitated and wondered if she should offer any more pearls of wisdom. She reasoned that perhaps one more wouldn't hurt. "Michael, you really need to seek and get closer to God," she preached. Diana waited for a reaction.

"Yea. Maybe," he finally said. Michael had become what can only be described as very anxious, almost fearful, ever since the discussion with Phillip and Odell about the indictment they now perceived as a certainty.

Diana watched him as he continued to stare at the screen. She then asked a little exasperated, "Do you want me to turn on the TV?"

———◆———

"Come in Michael," said Father Paul. Michael suddenly appeared apprehensive, prompting the young priest to say, "It's ok, come on in. I know it's been awhile . . . don't worry no pressure here," as he motioned him to step inside.

The office in the rectory was large—at first glance, imposing. Once inside, it appeared very inviting and comforting. As Michael walked past the double doors, Mrs. Frazier, the parish secretary, closed them behind the two men who were now left alone facing one another. It was the first time Michael had come to see Father Paul at the rectory. He took in the room with a quick glance, noticing that two walls of the office consisted of large cherry wood bookcases that stood from floor to ceiling. The shelves were devoid of books and seemed to exist to only gather dust, as it appeared that they could use a good cleaning. A large desk was positioned near the row of oversized windows located opposite the room's entrance. The morning sun was now pouring through, as rays of light filled the entirety of the room that was once, long ago, the former owner's library. Father Paul motioned Michael to sit on one of two identical small leather sofas that were across from each other. Between them was a small octagon shaped table with a pot of coffee, cups and saucers, a sugar bowl, and a pitcher of cream. Both men stood momentarily facing one another before sitting on the sofas opposite each other. Michael now felt at ease in the room, notwithstanding his earlier nervousness.

The priest sat silently staring at Michael. He was not much older than him, maybe eight or nine years. Despite his boyish tousled brown hair and a childlike innocence, Father Paul had a deep understanding of the human condition. He possessed a profound wisdom and loving nature that became apparent by the relaxed and measured manner in which he spoke. In many instances he could communicate by a simple stare of his soft deep-blue eyes. These unique attributes served him well when connecting with and counseling his parishioners. He waited now for Michael to speak first as they sat facing one another, his eyes penetrating and tranquil.

"Sorry Father. I know it's been awhile since I've come to mass."

He smiled, "You're not here for that now are you Michael?" He sensed his nervousness and said, "Relax Michael, I'm here to help you make some sense of all of this." He then immediately asked, "Coffee?" Before Michael could respond, the priest poured him a cup. "Now Michael tell me what's really on your mind?"

"Well, I'm not sure what you know," he began.

"Diana and I have talked quite a bit. She was hoping you would come to see me." It was his way of letting Michael know he knew everything.

Michael shook his head and said nothing. Father Paul sipped from his cup and remained silent, waiting. He lit a cigarette and politely asked Michael, "Mind if I smoke?"

He stared intently at Michael, with a penetrating gaze, who after a few minutes of silence suddenly said, "Father I'm afraid. Help me." His head and body slumped as if he was completely drained by these words.

Putting down the cigarette, Father Paul simply said, "Michael take my hands. Let's pray together."

———————◆———————

Harrison got to the office early to meet with his agents. He wanted to make sure that tomorrow's predawn raids went off smoothly. Anderson and Bronson would arrive soon, and he would go over every detail with them. The indictment would be unsealed, the arrest warrants were ready to be served, and the agents and local police were prepared to act precisely and quickly. Still, he wanted to be certain everything was set for the morning. After all, it was Harrison who convinced Judge Cooley that he needed the predawn no-knock warrants, claiming that evidence would be destroyed and firearms were in the homes of many of the defendants, necessitating the element of surprise. This was, no doubt, a significant case not only for him but also the Department of Justice, requiring absolute precision. The planning was difficult enough, but the execution would likely be more difficult. Considering that there were twenty-two arrests to be made in three states, the operation needed to be coordinated and carried out simultaneously at the very least to avoid any one arrestee from receiving advanced notice of the police action heading their way.

Bronson and Anderson arrived sooner than expected. After a few minutes of small talk and an explanation of what was planned for tomorrow morning, Harrison firmly said, "Just make sure nothing goes wrong."

"We are good. John's been planning this for days," Bronson assured him.

"John did all the planning and coordinating. Ok, good," he replied. He then asked, "Now the two of you are taking out Dolan, right?"

"Yes, James that's right," said Anderson.

"Ok, good," he said again. "Now explain to me again how this is all going down. I want to make sure nothing gets fucked up."

———————◆———————

Father Paul closed his eyes and began to pray, "Our Father who art in heaven, hollowed be thy name . . . thy kingdom come, thy will be done on earth as it is in heaven . . . ."

Michael also closed his eyes and joined him in the Lord's prayer, feeling light headed as he prayed. It had been awhile since he had been to church or tried to communicate with the Lord. It was surreal, and he was feeling anxious as if he was about to explode. When they were finished he opened eyes to find that Father Paul's eyes were still tightly shut, his lips trembling slightly, as he softly continued to pray. He could not make out the words, but it sounded foreign. Father Paul was not speaking English. Unbeknownst to Michael, the priest was now speaking in tongues. He sat and listened for more than ten minutes and eventually concluded it was some sort of religious gibberish, not knowing any better, nor appreciating the power of the Holy Spirit now within the priest. Michael looked down and waited, for what he wasn't sure.

Father Paul opened his eyes and said, "Michael let's pray. Father, we pray to you today so that you can help Michael and his family . . . Protect him as he walks through the darkness and . . . ." They prayed together as Michael lost all sense of time, completely overcome by his emotions and feelings of exhaustion. He vaguely heard Father Paul praying for many things that never occurred to him. He gave praise and thanks to God, the Son, and the Holy Spirit. Michael was somehow able to do the same, saying tearfully, "God please hear our prayers . . . Jesus hear our prayers."

When they were done forty minutes later, in what can only be described as an intense prayer and reflection session, Father Paul released Michael and leaned back into the coolness of the sofa, now exhausted. Michael also fell backward into the supple leather of the cushion as he began to shake and cry uncontrollably. After a few minutes, he looked at the priest directly across from him as if he was a stranger and asked, "Why is God doing this to me?"

Father Paul leaned forward and softly said, "God is not doing this."

Michael quickly replied, somewhat agitated, "Then why is He allowing this to happen?"

The priest grabbed Michael's forearms and pulled him forward, almost dragging him onto the table between them. He looked at Michael, his face only inches away from his own, and said, "God didn't do this, nor did He cause this to happen. He does not substitute his will for your own or that of others. He did not put us here to suffer.

He desires a happy and full life for you." Pulling him closer Father Paul whispered in his ear, "Michael, remember He loves you and wants only the best for you." He then pulled back and said, "Now, what is done is done. But know this, God will bestow upon you the grace needed to face this problem, but only if you allow Him." Suddenly, he stopped talking and sighed. He looked down at the floor between his legs, still holding onto Michael's arms. A moment later he looked up and gazed into Michael's eyes, saying, "He will also give you the strength needed to get through this. All you need to do is ask. Michael ask Him with faith."

CHAPTER FIFTY-THREE

IT was 3:30 a.m. and the nine separate groups of law enforcement officers were gathered at their designated locations throughout New Jersey, New York, and Connecticut, waiting for instructions from Agent John Anderson, who was the lead FBI agent in the case. Each team consisted of four agents and two state police officers, who were set to start executing warrants at 4:00 a.m. Most teams were making two arrests that morning, while a few were making three, depending on the proximity of one defendant to another. The Anderson-Bronson team had only one arrest to make—Michael Dolan's.

The teams were on the move now that Anderson gave them the green light. Three cars, one police cruiser and two unmarked vehicles, pulled in front of the seven-story Hoboken apartment building. It was 3:54 a.m., and the street was empty. The four agents and two state troopers exited their vehicles as they quickly assessed their surroundings. It was all clear. At this hour, the law enforcement officers could expect that civilian interaction at the arrest site would be limited to the arrestee and any family members found at the arrest location. There was no concern, at this point, of any outside interference. FBI Agent Marcus Cain looked at the arrest warrant. "Ok, apartment 4C. The defendant's name—Luis Afanador. Let's do it."

Officer Joe Pistone, of the New Jersey State Police, held a sledge-hammer in his hand as he entered the building. Agent Cain and his partner took the stairs to the fourth floor to make sure Afanador did not somehow elude them, while the others took the elevator. The plan was for Pistone to break the lock and push open the door allowing the agents to enter first. He would then drop back with his partner to provide cover and support. The agents gathered at the door and rushed in as soon as it was broken down. Quickly making their way through the rooms, they found Afanador asleep with his wife and children in the apartment's only bedroom.

He was quickly cuffed, dressed, and out the door leaving his crying and screaming family huddled together on the couple's bed. Mrs. Martinez, the sweet older widow next door, awake and hearing the commotion, walked out into the hallway as Luis was being led away. She could hear the wailing from inside the apartment, and once the police were gone, she went in to offer comfort to those left behind.

———————◆———————

Carl Bronson pulled the SUV into the Dolan driveway, turning off the lights before doing so. The police cruiser was parked across the driveway, with the other unmarked FBI sedan directly behind it. The agents quickly exited their vehicles and made their way to the front of the house. There wsa no need for discussion, as their course of action had already been completely thought out and was now ready for execution. Two Connecticut State Troopers held a battering ram and stood ready at the front door, waiting for a signal to push forward, Anderson and Bronson behind them. Further back, Agents Hernandez and Stone stood to the left with their FBI-issued Glock model 23 semiautomatic weapons drawn and at their sides.

Diana looked at the clock on her nightstand. It was 3:48 a.m., and she was restless. She looked over at Michael and could sense for the first time in a long time that he was completely relaxed. He now appeared to be in a deep sleep. It seemed the visit with Father Paul went well, even though he told her very little. *It's ok*, she thought. *He'll open up about their meeting when he's ready*. Now fully awake, she got up to use the bathroom. Before going back to bed, she stopped at the sink, splashing cold water on her face. Turning to grab a towel she suddenly heard a loud bang from downstairs immediately followed by the wailing siren of the ADT Home Security alarm.

As soon as the State Troopers knocked the door open, they peeled off allowing the agents to rush in ahead of them. Making their way up the stairs, they quickly arrived at the master bedroom. Turning on the light, they saw Michael Dolan sitting up in bed. "Freeze mother fucker. Don't move. Hands—I want to see your hands," shouted Bronson. Michael slowly raised his hands in the air, dumbfounded by what was going on. Hernandez moved to the bed, gun still drawn, and violently pulled the covers away from him. He grabbed Michael's arm and yanked him off the bed onto the floor.

Just then Diana emerged from the bathroom. She was crying and frightened. Agent Stone turned and pointed his gun at her. "Freeze," he shouted. He immediately ran to her and taking her arm pulled Diana to the ground. Face down on the floor now, she looked at Michael who was being cuffed. Stone began running his hands up and down her body, in some sort of pat down, although she was only wearing a short nightgown and panties with no place to hide anything. The agent now asked her, "Any weapons in the house?" Diana, as best as she was capable, shook her head and said, "No." She could now hear Christina in the hallway, crying and screaming, "Mommy."

Diana turned her head slightly to one side as Stone continued to hold her down, and asked politely, "May I go to my daughter? Please."

Stone, who had straddled her in the take down, not exactly FBI protocol, released the pressure he was exerting on her backside and getting off her said coldly, "Go ahead." Diana walked out into the hallway where Christina was being comforted by what appeared to be a sympathetic police officer. Diana took her daughter into her arms and kissed her. She then realized that the security alarm siren was still blaring.

The house phone began to ring. Probably alarm central calling to check and see if everything was ok. Nothing was ok.

Diana turned to the officer and asked, "Should I answer the phone . . . maybe turn off the alarm?" Before he could answer, Bronson and Anderson emerged with a dressed Michael, escorting him out of the room and down the stairs. Seeing him in handcuffs caused Diana to start crying again. She kept Christina's face in her shoulder with an arm around the back of her head and a hand covering her eyes, who despite the restraint attempted to turn to see what was going on.

"Hon, call Phillip and Odell," he shouted to her, as he was led away through the front door. The outdoor floodlights were now on, providing a beacon in the darkness for the gathering neighbors. She ran down the steps with Christina still in her arms and went out the door onto the front lawn. A few neighbors, who had huddled together on the street, watched Michael being shoved into the back seat of an unmarked police sedan. Diana, shivering from the cold, stood in the front yard, clad only in her scant nightgown, the alarm still laring as she watched as the car carrying Michael drove away, the taillights fading in the distance quickly.

Several well-intentioned neighbors came from across the street where they stood on the front lawn with Diana as they now tried to comfort her. Katherine Hanley, ho lived directly across he street, wrapped an arm around Diana's waist and said in her Irish brogue, "Come inside dear. You and the baby will catch a death of a cold standing out here like this."

Diana tried to stop her sobbing but was unable to do so as she appeared defeated and broken. Completely frozen in place, sad and shivering from the cold, she raised an empty and dejected gaze as she was now ready to turn and walk back into the house. At that moment she saw Liz Duffy, wrapped in a plush lavender bathrobe with matching fuzzy slippers on her feet, standing near the curb. Their eyes locked. Immediately, Diana's spirits rose, wanting to put aside the pettiness and divide between them. She wanted to call out to her friend for comfort and forgiveness. She now longed to wrap her arms around Liz and say I know we both acted foolishly, it was stupid, and I forgive you. Can you forgive me? As Diana was about to call to her, she noticed a look of disdain on Liz's face. It was then that Liz Duffy turned and began to walk away, toward her own home, never to look back. Diana, wounded and tearful, watched as the bold colored robe disappeared from the light into the darkness of the predawn. Gathering her composure as best she could and comforting her daughter, Diana turned back toward the house. Walking to the front door—open and broken, she thought, *God help her, that bitch.*

CHAPTER FIFTY-FOUR

PHILLIP Richardson had called Diana back almost immediately telling her that the arraignment was scheduled for 10:00 a.m., before Judge Lois Cooley at the Federal District Courthouse in Manhattan. Thanks to a friend at the FBI, he quickly had that bit of information. He initially thought about calling Harrison but realized he would not have gotten to him in time anyway, nor did he want to give him the satisfaction. They talked just a few weeks ago about Michael's voluntary surrender should it come to that, and because he had offered his client's cooperation, Harrison certainly didn't have to arrest him in the manner he did. Harrison likely enjoyed the drama of the early morning raid, and now didn't even think enough to give Richardson the courtesy of a call to tell him the arraignment time or the name of the judge. He could have waited for Michael to call him but that would have kept Diana wondering for hours. He didn't want her to have to go through that, particularly in light of what took place earlier that morning. He thought it would not have been right, hence the call to his FBI contact. Richardson now assured Diana that he and Odell were on it and not to worry.

She thanked him, saying, "I'll see you there."

She next called her father-in-law to tell him what happened.

He said, "I'll be right over," and without waiting for a response he asked, "How's the baby?"

Diana replied, "She is better. She's a little shaken, but I tried to shield her from what was going on as best I could." She paused, "I gave her a hot bath and she is back in bed finally asleep again."

Eddy choked up and said, "My poor little girl." He then asked, "Are you ok?"

Diana began to feel the anxiety fluttering up again from the pit of her stomach. "Dad, it was horrible," she said, now trembling, her voice suddenly strained. Diana was fighting back the tears once more as she replayed the events over again in her mind.

Realizing she was on the verge of breaking down, he stopped her by saying, "I'm on the way. I'll be there in five," as he quickly hung up the phone and ran out the door.

Eddy Dolan drove as fast as he could arriving at the house in less than ten minutes. He walked in through the front door and quickly assessed the damage. He walked to the stairs and standing at the bottom step shouted, "Diana."

She replied, "Up here, Dad."

He went up to the bedroom. It was still a mess from the raid. Diana was in the bathroom. He asked simply, "You ok?"

"Yea sorry. Just want to take a shower." "Any word on Michael?"

"Yes, the arraignment is at ten. I'm going to meet the attorneys there at nine."

"At the Federal Courthouse in Manhattan, I assume," said Eddy. "Yes. Can you check in on Christina?"

"Sure. I'll start fixing that front door too."

"Thanks Dad," Diana called out, as she turned on the shower and stepped in. The hot water stung her, but it felt oddly soothing. Diana closed her eyes and thought all she wanted to do now was to wash away the filth of that FBI agent's groping hands. She pulled her face away from the steamy water, and blinking open her eyes, she broke down sobbing. *God almighty help me. I just want to get Michael out of jail and get him home. That's all I want today.*

———————◆———————

No sense taking the train into the city. Diana knew she would need to get in and out of Manhattan quickly. It was 5:50 a.m. when she left the house and knowing the tri-state area traffic patterns fairly well, she was certain the drive in would be a smooth one at this hour. She pushed her Ford Edge hard, trying to stay ahead of the traffic in an effort to make it into the city by 7:00 a.m., hoping to see Michael before the arraignment. What she didn't realize was that the Federal Courthouse building did not open its doors until 8:00 a.m. and that was for employees only. The doors to the public opened at 8:30 a.m., with the line to enter usually forming earlier.

Now just over the New York State line, Diana called Karen. It was 6:20 a.m. and she needed to tell her friend about what happened to Michael. Karen picked up on the second ring and, sounding groggy, asked, "Diana everything alright?"

No, nothing was alright. "Michael was arrested this morning. They burst into the house, guns pointed everywhere scaring everyone—it was incredible. I have never been more frightened in my life."

"Oh, my God. You poor thing. I feel so bad," she said, now coming to life. Before Diana could react, she asked, "Are you guys ok? How is Christina?"

The two talked until Diana arrived in lower Manhattan, when she said, "Let me go. I need to find a parking garage."

"Ok, you hang in there. Be strong. Give Michael my love and call me when the two of you are back in the car on the way home. I want to make sure you're both alright."

"Will do. Thanks Karen," said Diana as she abruptly hung up the phone.

Diana found a place to park and walked the three blocks to the Daniel Patrick Moynihan Federal District Courthouse. She quickly realized the building was not yet open to the public, and that it was much too early to get inside. Walking down Pearl Street in search of a coffee shop, Diana turned left onto Cardinal Hayes Place, stumbling upon St Andrew's Catholic Church. Believing it was no coincidence, she stepped inside to pray. She sat in a pew near the back of the church, knelt, and crossed herself, deep in thought. *Dear Father, please bestow your blessings upon us all . . . I humbly request that You confer upon the judge the grace of wisdom so that she may act justly. In Jesus Christ's name, I pray.*

———————◆———————

The holding cell appeared very sterile to Michael. He had been processed easily and quickly, and he now sat waiting for whatever was next. He heard the door and looked up only to see Peter Li being led in by two agents. He was placed in the cell next to his own. The cells were separated by solid walls, and although Michael could no longer see Li, he could hear him. Peter Li was talking to himself.

Michael called out, "Peter. You ok?"

Li was startled and hesitantly asked, "Who's there?"

"It's Michael Dolan. Didn't you see me when you walked in?"

"Michael, you're here too? No, I didn't see you," Li said. He then asked, "Do you know what's going on?"

"No, they haven't told me anything."

Li then said something curious, "Michael why the hell you here anyway?"

He asked, "What do you mean?" No reply. "Peter, you there?"

"Ah, we should stop talking. I bet everything we say is being recorded," murmured Li, purposefully avoiding his question.

He now looked around the cell as if he said something wrong, paranoid that someone was scrutinizing every word he was saying. He then announced, "They also arrested Joan Archer. I saw her when they were processing me. She was a mess."

"Really?" said Michael, wondering how Gerry's assistant was caught up in this whole thing.

Forty-five minutes later, Diana finished praying and lighting prayer candles. She made her way back to the courthouse, hoping to find the attorneys and get in to see Michael. Walking back, it struck her— What if they don't let him out? She never gave that possibility a consideration. Phillip said the judge would set reasonable bail, but what if she didn't? Diana wasn't sure how this really worked. When she arrived at the courthouse, she was the only one there. It was 8:10 a.m.

Sitting in the courtroom, Diana looked for Phillip and Odell. It was almost 9:15 a.m., and she was beginning to wonder if they were coming, when one of the doors opened, and Phillip Richardson walked in.

"Diana," he said. She gave a slight wave. He walked over to where she was sitting and asked, "You ok?"

"I'm fine, thanks for asking. Is Odell coming?"

"No, I'll be handling this alone. Arraignments, they're no big deal," he said without thinking how it may have sounded to her.

Maybe not a big deal for you. Diana smiled and looked at her folded hands resting on her lap and could only think to say, "Oh." She then asked, "Do you think I can see Michael?"

"No. But I'm going to lockup now. Only attorneys are permitted to speak with their clients before the arraignment. But I'll tell him you're here," said Richardson.

As he got up from the bench, Dylan Shepard from CNN walked in. He was that new hotshot reporter who reported on the Stuart Vogel and the Pharma Sales insider trading case. He also did the recent piece on Bender Capital Lending and the Perron arrest.

It was the story that ingratiated him to Harrison and the reason why the Assistant U.S. Attorney gave him a call about an hour ago concerning the developments leading to this morning's arrests.

"Phillip Richardson, what are you doing here?" Before he could answer Shepard said, "Oh, I get it. You have a horse in the race don't you."

"Dylan, I'm just on the way out . . . going downstairs. You want to walk with me?" There was no way Richardson was having this conversation in front of Diana.

"Sure, why not. Let's talk," he said.

———————◆———————

The courtroom was now full. It was 10:15 a.m. when Michael was brought up in handcuffs from lockup for his arraignment. According to Richardson, there were twenty-two defendants in the case who were being arraigned that day, and Michael was the first. Two of the agents from the early predawn raid escorted Michael into the room and seated him at the table where Richardson sat waiting. The agent uncuffed him, and Michael immediately rubbed his wrists as if the cuffs had been on too tightly. He turned and half smiled at Diana, who managed to give him a slight smile back. At the other table, only a few feet away, stood a very handsome well-dressed man, who Diana surmised could only be Assistant U.S. Attorney James Harrison. She stared at him for a moment, watching as he adjusted his tie and pulled at his shirt sleeves, appearing to want to look perfect. He turned and looked at Michael, who was now also staring at him intently. Harrison smiled at him contritely, as if he was saying, *I've got the upper hand now. Fuck you, Michael Dolan.* Diana was disgusted by his display of what could only be described as a combination of arrogance and almost uncontrollable joy. Turning away she reached for the rosary beads in her purse.

Suddenly, the door near the front of the courtroom opened and out walked Judge Cooley, making her way to the elevated bench. The court officer quickly jumped up and called the court to order, yelling, "All rise." Cooley's law clerk followed behind her holding a file. She sat down and said, "Good morning ladies and gentlemen."

The court staff, attorneys, agents, and spectators in the courtroom replied in unison, "Good morning Your Honor," as they began to sit.

Tobin stepped up to the bench and placed several documents in front of the judge, who took a few minutes to look through the papers.

She then said, "The first matter before us is The United States of America v. Michael Dolan, case number CR08-13556 -LJC; is that correct Mr. Harrison?"

"Yes, Your Honor. That is correct."

She asked, "Is Mr. Dolan present and represented by counsel?"

"Yes, Your Honor. He is present and represented by attorney Phillip Richardson," replied Harrison.

As if suddenly prompted to do so he stood and said, "Good morning Your Honor. Phillip Richardson for the defendant, Michael Dolan. My client is present and prepared to enter a not guilty plea. I am also prepared to argue for reasonable bail on his behalf, if it so pleases the court Your Honor."

"Thank you Mr. Richardson. We will hear from the government first. Mr. Harrison, if you are ready."

"Yes, Your Honor," said Harrison. He began to give a detailed reading of the indictment and the charges, at which point the court interceded and provided an explanation of the defendant's rights. She asked if he understood the charges and his rights. Michael stood. He was then asked how he pleaded. He said, "Not guilty," and it was so noted in the official court record by Cooley.

She then nodded to the attorneys and said, "Mr. Harrison you may begin."

Harrison said, "Thank you Your Honor," as he went on to argue for a two million-dollar surety bond, asserting that the severity of the crimes, as outlined in the indictment, warranted the substantial bail amount. He argued this, although the issue of bail was not typically founded only upon the crime but a threat of harm to the public and the risk of flight from the court's jurisdiction.

On this point, it appeared that Cooley was not swayed.

Harrison next asserted that the defendant, Michael Dolan, illegally garnered a large amount of money from the scheme, a long-term conspiracy in which he had an important, if not leadership role in. He also claimed that because the defendant had those financial resources, he was more likely to be a flight risk and could easily escape the court's jurisdiction, but he really did not have a basis for that claim or any other that he made that morning.

Listening to him argue, Diana thought, *My God. It's all lies.*

When Harrison was done, Judge Cooley thanked him and turned to Richardson allowing him to make a case for reasonable bail.

He stated that Michael was a family man and lifelong resident of Norwalk, Connecticut, as were his wife and daughter who lived with him. He said the Dolan family was rooted in the community where they enjoyed the love and support of both their families and many friends. He also told the court that Michael was employed locally, although it was not entirely true nor was it a lie, and that Diana was also employed near their home as an accountant, pointing out that she was a supportive and loving spouse who was present in the courtroom.

He also impressed upon Judge Cooley that Michael was a suspended member of the bar who strongly professed his innocence and was very eager to proceed with trial.

At the conclusion of the bail arguments, Cooley said, "Gentlemen, thank you. I will set bail at two hundred fifty thousand dollars and direct that the defendant post with the court a non-surety bond in said amount. The gentleman appears to be adamant in asserting his innocence, and I do not deem him to be a flight risk," said Cooley, implying that she believed Michael was not running away and that he would remain within the court's jurisdiction to face the allegations against him.

She continued, "However, if Mr. Dolan is in possession of a passport I am directing that he surrender it to his attorney. And as an officer of the court, Mr. Richardson, you will retain possession of Mr. Dolan's passport until further order."

Richardson said, "Yes, Your Honor."

He turned to Michael, giving him a delicate smile as he tried to restrain himself. He was ecstatic about the very favorable bail conditions and considered it a huge first victory.

Harrison, on the other hand, was not happy and it showed. *Fucking bleeding-heart defendant's judge.* He had the good sense to put it aside for now and to focus on getting ready for the next arraignment.

"If that is it gentlemen, the court will take a five-minute recess," said the judge as she got up to walk off the bench.

"All rise," bellowed the court officer.

Richardson turned to Michael and said, "We need to go the clerk's office and sign some paperwork."

Michael walked out of the courtroom's well that was separated by the barrister and went straight to Diana where she stood waiting for him. He put his arms around his wife and kissed her. She melted into his chest, comforted by his embrace. Richardson escorted them to the clerk's office to execute the non-surety bond, which required them to pledge the house as bail in the event Michael somehow fled the jurisdiction or failed to appear for court proceedings.

Dylan Shepard was outside on the court's steps filming for a segment scheduled to air later that day. It was an in-depth piece on Harrison, the exploding financial crisis, and this morning's arrests. He was filming footage to be edited back at the CNN studio when Richardson emerged from the courthouse with Michael and Diana. Running toward them Shepard, with microphone in hand and cameraman in tow, was describing for his audience the scheme that reached across three states and resulted in twenty-two arrests today. Turning to Richardson, he said, "Famed criminal defense lawyer, Phillip Richardson, is representing one of those defendants, Michael Dolan, attorney and Chief Compliance Officer for Bender Capital Lending, one of the lending institutions at the center of this banking crisis. He has just been arraigned here at the Federal District Court in Manhattan. Mr. Richardson any comment?" he asked, pointing the mic at him.

Richardson said, "No comment at this time," as he continued walking, trying to shield his client from the reporter with an extended right arm and hand.

Shepard drew back the mic, pushing past Richardson, and leaning in toward Michael, he asked, "Mr. Dolan any comment?"

The microphone was awkwardly shoved in Michael's direction as he stopped walking and stood there on the courthouse steps. Suddenly feeling overwhelmed by the morning's events—exhausted, enraged, and humiliated—he looked directly at the reporter and exclaimed, "Yea. It's all bullshit."

Shepard quickly pulled back the mic and appearing shocked by the response, he slowly turned to the camera saying, "Well there you have it folks. 'It's all bullshit.' Dylan Shepard reporting for CNN."

CHAPTER FIFTY-FIVE

THE traffic conditions leaving Manhattan were horrible, even by New York City standards. Ten minutes into the ride home and having only traveled a few city blocks, Diana called her father-in-law. She told him they were on the way back and that it was going to take some time as traffic was bad.

Handing the phone to Michael, Eddy anxiously asked, "Are you ok?"

Michael sensing the anxiety in his father's voice said, "Yea. I'm fine Dad. Nothing to worry about. It's over. I just want to get home."

"You sure you're alright?"

"I'm fine. What about Christina. How is she?"

"She is good. Got up a couple of hours agoand played in her room while I fixed the front door," he said.

"Dad we'll speak when I get home, ok?"

"Right, see you in a little bit," he said. Hesitating, he then said, "Michael, I love you," quickly hanging up the phone. Eddy couldn't help but get emotional, bursting into tears. Leaning forward, head down, and hands planted firmly on the kitchen table, he began to hyperventilate. He could never have imagined such a horrible thing like this happening to his son. Eddy Dolan couldn't help but wonder how this was all going to end.

———◆———

Diana next called Karen, explaining to Michael, "She wanted me to call her once we left the city. She's worried about you."

Karen answered the phone, and immediately asked, "Are you ok?"

"I'm ok," said Diana.

"How's Michael. Is he with you?"

"Yes. Here. I'll let you talk to him," said Diana, as she held out the phone for him.

Michael took the cellphone from Diana's hand and said, "Hi Karen."

"Oh my God, Michael," Karen said, as she began to whimper, "Are you ok?"

"I'm ok. Karen don't . . . I'm fine," he said, now trying to reassure her. "It's over. Today is over, thank goodness. But please stop crying," was all he could think to say.

"I'm sorry," she said. "I just needed to hear your voice and make sure you were alright."

"Thanks Karen. You're a good friend. But can I call you tonight? I have a few more calls to make. But I'm fine, I just wanted you to know that. We can talk more later, ok?"

"Sure Michael. I'm just glad you're alright, that's all."

Saying goodbye to her, Michael turned to Diana and asked, "Did you call Marco?"

Diana replied, "No." Looking at him she said, "I didn't think to call him. But then I didn't even have time. Everything happened so fast. I called your dad to come over, and on the way down here I called Karen. I needed someone to talk with while I was driving. I was nervous."

"No worry. I should call him though. He may already know. Maybe Odell called him?" Michael rubbed his forehead as he leaned back in the seat. "I better call Marco," he finally said. "He could be helpful."

———————◆———————

Arriving home, Michael was immediately greeted at the door by his father and Christina. She ran to him from the family room screaming, "Daddy," as Michael stood motionless in the foyer. Being back in the house was almost surreal, he thought, turning back to look at the broken front door.

Eddy Dolan followed his granddaughter from the kitchen with a dish towel in his hand.

Christina jumped into his arms repeating, "Daddy, daddy," as she began to sniffle.

"It's ok, honey. Daddy's home. It's ok. Everything will be ok," he said, trying to soothe her. He held her tight as she held on to him even tighter. Michael's eyes welled up with tears as Diana and Eddy also got emotional again, a little more than teary eyed themselves. Michael put Christina down Clinging to his leg, she would not let go of him as he turned to embrace his father who hugged and kissed him asking, "You alright?"

"I'm good, just want to get out of these clothes and take a shower."

Diana took Christina back into the family room. Michael headed upstairs as Eddy returned to the kitchen where he finished washing the dishes from the late morning breakfast he and Christina had eaten a little while ago.

In the bathroom, Michael stripped out of his shirt, pants, and underwear. The thought to burn his clothes foolishly crossed his mind as he felt dirty, soiled by the filth of the early morning raid on their home. Burning them wouldn't have helped the way he was feeling. He needed to cleanse his body and mind. Stepping into the steamy, hot shower, Michael began to wash away as much of it as he could.

———◆———

Diana sat with Eddy at the kitchen table, waiting for Michael to come down when her cellphone rang. It was Kelly Updike. Diana got up and said, "Dad I need to take this call. It's work." Eddy shook his head, as Diana walked out of the kitchen into the office, closing the doors behind her. Diana answered the cell phone, saying, "Kelly, hi. Is everything alright?"

"Sure, everything here is fine. But more importantly, is everything alright with you and Michael?" Before she could answer he asked again, "Diana, we are all so worried. Are you guys ok?"

"Yes, we are as good as could be expected. Back home now. It's all over."

"When you left that message this morning, I couldn't believe it. Nancy is beside herself. She's very upset. Worried for the two you." Kelly sighed and then continued. "What can we do for you? Is there anything you need? Anything we can do to help?"

"No, nothing Kelly. Thank you. I'll be at work tomorrow," said Diana.

"Diana take some time. No need to come in," said Kelly.

"I'll be in tomorrow. I have a few things I need to get done, and besides I need to stay busy. It'll help keep my mind off things."

Kelly said, "Diana, you do whatever makes you feel better. But if you want to take some time to deal with this, you can take all the time you need."

"Thanks Kelly. I'll see you tomorrow," she said hanging up the phone. Standing there she wondered what kind of reception she would receive tomorrow at work. Before she could think on it more the cellphone rang. It was Lisa D'Angelo.

———◆———

Michael came downstairs forty-five minutes later after a wash, a shave, and a change of clothes. Sitting with his wife and father in the kitchen, Diana was the first to ask, "Michael, what's next?"

"Well, I guess that Phillip and Odell will want to meet soon to discuss strategy going forward. The discovery phase is next . . . we'll get a chance to look at the evidence in the case and see what their witnesses are saying," Michael replied. "I'm really interested in seeing what Gerry told them, that no good lying fuck," he said.

Eddy responded with a wave of his hand. "Michael, people are going to lie to save their own asses; you have to expect that. I've seen it a thousand times while on the job. The trick is to plant your feet firmly and drill down into the truth, and then try and separate it from the bullshit they are feeding the feds, especially what is being said about you. I'm sure the attorneys know that. Let them do what you hired them to do."

Michael sat silently and acknowledged what his father had just said with a simple nod. He remained seated, nervously biting his lower lip. With his eyes fixed off into the distance he was thinking about how to refute the lies that were being told about him. Eddy could tell Michael was distracted by his own thoughts, and standing up, he announced that he was leaving and going home to take a shower himself. He had run over to the house this morning without washing or even combing his hair and now wanting to freshen up he said, "I'll be back in a few hours to check in on you guys. That door and frame should hold until I can pick up a new one tomorrow," he said jerking a thumb toward the foyer.

"Ok Dad. Thanks for everything, but you don't have to come back if you don't want to. You've done enough. We'll be fine." said Michael.

Diana agreeing said, "Yea Dad, thanks for everything. You're welcome to come back. I'll make dinner for all of us." She walked up to her father-in-law and put her arms around him, giving him a kiss on his cheek. "Thanks again, we love you," she added. Eddy, touched by Diana's display of affection thought, as he walked to the garage door, *Diana is a good woman. Michael is very lucky to have her. I hope he knows that.*

Michael followed him and said, "I'll walk you out, Dad," and they both made their way into the garage where Eddy had left his shoes. As they walked out of the garage toward the car in the driveway, Diana's cellphone rang again. It was her mother.

"Hi Ma," she said, picking up the phone.

"Jesus, what the hell did Michael do?" Maryann Caruso shouted through the phone. "It's all over the CNN . . . that—that young good-looking reporter, Dylan Shepard."

Before Diana could respond, she cried out, "Oh my dear Lord. Diana, what will people think? What will they say?"

CHAPTER FIFTY-SIX

THE receptionist, Patty, an older divorcee with two grown children, straightened the magazines in the rack positioned on the wall between the two leather chairs in the waiting room. Looking over at the waiting area, she realized that one thing was missing. Returning to her desk, she took the Connecticut Post newspaper out of the plastic bag, delicately dropping it on the coffee table, failing to notice the day's headline. She glanced at the clock, noting that it was almost 8:45 a.m., knowing the day would soon begin. The telephone would ring incessantly, employees would shuffle in and out, clients would appear announcing their arrival for appointments, and she would be inundated. Patty hadn't seen Diana Dolan yet, wondering if she was even coming in today. *Poor thing*, she thought, having seen the story on the news about her husband's arrest. She was shocked. Patty had met Michael three or four times, on those few occasions he had come to the office to take Diana to lunch. He seemed very nice, always smiling and making small talk. Although she had heard he was in some sort of trouble, she never imagined it was this bad. While Patty thought Michael seemed nice enough, it was now clear to her that he was not what he appeared to be. He was, what she would sometimes say, a "real piece of work." She asked herself what was a sweet, beautiful girl like Diana doing with a man like that.

Nancy walked in through the front doors and said, "Good morning Patty," as she passed her desk in the reception area. Patty waved and smiled at her as she was talking on the phone and in the middle of transferring a call. Looking down, Nancy glimpsed the newspaper sitting on the coffee table and stopped dead in her track, now completely motionless except for the sudden and rapid movement of her right hand to her gaping mouth. Picking up the paper she read the headline: *Bender Capital Attorney, Michael Dolan, and Others Indicted in Mortgage Fraud Scheme.* She folded the paper and tucked it under her arm, quickly making her way straight to Kelly's office.

Arriving at her desk, situated just outside of his office, Nancy dropped her purse into the bottom drawer while still holding onto the newspaper. Walking into Kelly's office unannounced, she saw Diana sitting in a chair in front of the desk talking with him. Stopping abruptly, Nancy immediately called out to her saying, "Come here honey," as she placed the folded paper onto a side table. She stood and smiled, invitingly holding her arms open, waiting for her friend to come to her. Diana leapt out of the chair and the two women immediately hugged tightly, both finding comfort in each other's arms. Diana was moved by Nancy's heartfelt concern and loving embrace, despite any doubts she may have had about her earlier. Without letting go, Nancy pulled her head back and asked, "Are you ok?" Before Diana could answer, she inquired, "How are Michael and the baby?"

Diana looked at her very calmly and said, "Nancy, we're ok. It's all a bit overwhelming, but we're ok. Thank God."

———◆———

Michael pulled into the parking lot at Tiny Tikes Preschool. He got out of the car and came around to the back to undo the buckle and released Christina from her car seat. He noticed heads turning in his direction as it seemed that all eyes were suddenly upon him. Immediately, he became self-conscious as he walked his daughter to the front door. It seemed that the other parents, who normally smiled good naturedly and said, "Hello," or "Morning," looked at him and quickly turned away. Keeping their heads down, they avoided eye contact and walked more hastily than usual. Michael wondered if they were trying to sidestep him or if he was just being paranoid.

Arriving at the door, Michael looked directly at the school's matron and said, "Good morning Gina."

At that moment Amy Palmer walked out of the school saying, "Goodbye Ms. Gina," as she glanced and smiled at Michael. She immediately turned her head away in what seemed to be an attempt to avoid a conversation or, at the very least, eye contact with him. Michael smiled at her, not certain what to say or do. He felt awkward and uncomfortable and wondered if Amy Palmer was feeling the same way.

The discomfort began to subside as Ms. Gina said, "Bye Amy," and the two ladies exchanged waves. Amy, however, still avoided Michael's gaze.

Putting her head back down, eyes fixated on her attendance list, Ms. Gina glanced at Christina and said, "Well hello young lady. Go on in honey, Ms. Lena is inside waiting."

Lifting her head and looking intently at Michael, she said coldly, "Mr. Dolan."

He looked at her for a moment and simply said, "Gina." He turned and slowly walked back to his car. He got in and sat there a moment feeling distressed, his mind racing. *That was not good. She could barely talk or look at me. Same with Amy and the others. What the hell. Is this how it's going to be?* Before he could give it any more thought, his phone rang. He looked at the caller ID. It was Marco.

"Hey Marco, good morning," he said answering the phone somewhat dejected.

"Hey bud, how's it going?"

"Well, just had a very uncomfortable moment at Christina's preschool. Icy cold reception from everyone. How about you?"

Marco hesitated, and avoiding Michael's remarks for the moment he asked, "How are Diana, Christina, and your dad?"

"Well, certainly Christina is oblivious to the consequences of yesterday's fuck-fest, my dad seems good, but I'm not really sure. And Diana, well she went to work. She is strong. Probably the strongest of us all," Michael said.

"I know Lisa is trying to stay on top of her as much as she can. You know, just wanting to make sure she's alright."

"Marco, tell Lisa thanks," he said. "Hey, let's get together this weekend. It might be a nice distraction."

"Good idea. Why don't you guys come down here," Marco suggested, hoping that a change of scenery would help.

"Sounds good. I'll run it by Diana."

"Michael, I was also thinking about . . . maybe, how I can help. Anyway, I thought that going forward Phillip and Odell could use a hand with the discovery and maybe trial strategy . . . and I'm thinking I can be another, you know—"

Before he could finish Michael said, "Marco, yes. Thank you. I can use your help and advice. I welcome it as a matter of fact." He waited a moment and then said jokingly, "You know how much I value your intellect." They laughed nervously knowing that the road ahead would undoubtedly prove to be a difficult one. They both knew it wouldn't be so much about Harrison proving guilt in this instance, but more about Michael demonstrating his own innocence.

He promptly added, "I'll talk to Phillip about it. I'm sure he'll welcome the help too."

"Michael, mention to Phillip that I probably should be designated 'of counsel' to his firm to maintain the attorney-client privilege. It would serve to preserve the right of confidentiality so that anything I do or we discuss isn't subject to discovery by the government," said Marco.

"Will do," he replied.

"Ok, good. But I'm sure he would know that already," Marco added. He then asked, "What do you have planned for today?"

"I'm going to see my dad. I want to make sure he's alright. We'll then probably replace the front door that was busted open and . . . well, then after that, I just want to avoid people the rest of the day."

CHAPTER FIFTY-SEVEN

THE office paralegal, Mitchell Conway, and Odell Brown were finishing their review of the documents and transcripts making up the exchange of what is known as discovery material from the U.S. Attorney's Office. The twenty-two boxes, delivered by courier weeks ago, contained the evidence the government intended to use at trial in its attempt to obtain a guilty verdict against Michael Dolan, or, alternatively, to convince him to accept a plea deal. Odell went through the government's professed evidence of guilt and organized the documents by first separating them into what he believed had evidentiary value and what didn't. The remainder of the documents went into a pile of what might be of some importance, or a pile of ones he would discuss with Phillip later. He next divided the evidence into what would be helpful in defense of the case and what might be problematic. This entire process took a week, and they were at the point of bringing in Michael to go through the FBI 302 witness statement transcripts to help separate fact from fiction in the retelling of events. He and Marco were now due to arrive at 1:00 p.m. to do just that. Once the review was complete and the lies fleshed out, Odell would further separate and organize the documents into trial notebooks. He was certain this process would be helpful in refuting the government's case. It would also be necessary to efficiently present the evidence in support of Michael's defense at trial.

It was almost noon as Odell and Mitchell continued their work in the large conference room, which was now somewhat messy with documents strewn about in piles on the table and floor. At the same time, Phillip Richardson was sheltered in the oval office. He had hunkered down early, just before 7:00 a.m., coming in to read through bank records, witness statements, and grand jury transcripts. He was enthusiastically working on trial strategy and a defense theme. He had stopped pacing the room and was now laying on the sofa with an FBI witness statement on his chest.

Having just read all of Gerry Bender's interviews, he thought, *What a piece of shit.* He was thinking about how to deal with him at trial. At the moment, he wasn't certain what to do with some of the evidence against his client, but he was sure that Bender's statements were false. *Too many inconsistences.* Richardson instinctively sensed that cross examination would flesh out all the lies. He believed the discrepancies would raise a reasonable doubt in almost any jury's minds. He was more than confident it would in this case. The conflicts in all the testimony would be part of the overall trial theme, which would also include an element of Michael's blind trust in his former friend and college roommate.

Speaking to himself, Richardson said, "A friendship betrayed by a cooperation deal with the government that was born out of self-preservation. Gerry Bender resurrected to live again . . . or some shit like that." *Damn that sounded pretty good. Needs some work but it should do,* he thought. *Good for the closing. This should play out well. Real well.*

He continued to lay on the sofa reflecting, *With friends like Gerry Bender, who needs fucking enemies?*

Before he could give the disloyalty between the once close friends anymore thought, the intercom buzzed, and Bethany, the receptionist, announced, "Mr. Richardson, your therapist, Mr. Santangelo, has arrived."

He walked over to his desk and, holding down a button on the phone, instructed her to send Bruno back to the office He hurriedly wrote down the ideas swirling around in his head. He wanted to get it down on paper before his session began. He had arranged for it a little earlier in the day since he desperately needed to unwind. The *Punisher* was just the person to loosen him up, and he was lucky to have gotten him on such short notice.

"Yes Mr. Richardson. I'll send him right back." Before Bethany could finish speaking, he had activated the mechanism that slid the wall to his office open.

Bruno Santangelo, the dim witted, muscle bound, dark haired Italian, made his way down the hall to Richardson's office, like he had done many times before. As he approached, the wall was just completing its opening cycle, and he could see Richardson standing near the desk next to the massage chair that would soon be put into use. Walking in, he made his way to where Richardson was waiting. Dropping a large black duffle bag onto the desk, Bruno turned to his client with a broad grin on his face and said, "Fucking Philly. That therapist shit gets me every time."

Bethany knew not to bother her boss while he was in a "therapy session." She had made that mistake before. So when Michael and Marco walked in almost an hour later, she immediately called Odell to let him know that they had arrived. Odell came out and greeted the men, taking them back into the conference room.

"Michael, we've been making a lot of progress going through this discovery material," said Odell. "Most importantly there are numerous inconsistencies not only in what the witnesses have said on more than one occasion when speaking to the FBI, but also with what other witnesses have said when talking about you," he said, pointing a finger at him.

Marco and Michael looked at one another and smiled, as they both believed that what Odell just told them seemed very positive. This information was consistent with what Michael had been professing all along about his innocence. It seemed the so-called witnesses couldn't get their stories straight. Michael reminded himself, *The truth has but only one version.*

Although elated at the news, Michael was troubled by the government's willingness to embrace the lies about him. He was silent for a few moments and then said, "Ok, I really need to know what Gerry is saying."

"He's certainly pointing a finger in your direction, and so are Tesler, Perron and Li."

"Peter Li?"

Odell looked at Marco and then back at Michael. He nodded his head and said, "Yes, Peter Li. Is there another Li I should know about?"

Michael looked confused and said, "No . . . of course not, no." He then added, "Jesus, that fuck," thinking back to the encounter in lockup the morning of their arrest.

Odell continued, "Anyway, their stories are disjointed and not consistent with one another. As I said before, it seems that everyone is either lying or telling their own version of the truth, however you want to call it. Gerry said you came in to replace Tesler in the conspiracy. He also claims that as an equal partner in the scheme, you benefitted from the purchase and sale of many of the properties that were being foreclosed upon, or simply transferred to the group . . . ." Odell stopped talking, distracted by the look of disgust on Michael's face as he stood there listening and shaking his head. Marco was doing the same. He now stared back at them somewhat bewildered, and sounding almost apologetic said, "Well anyway, Tesler says one thing . . . Li another, and Perron something entirely different. In any event, they're all over the place and that's good for us. You'll see when you read it yourself."

"Ok, I'll take that. Whatever," Michael said, somewhat reluctantly.

Marco asked, "What about a money trail?"

Odell nodded and said, "Yea, I'm not an accountant but looking over the bank records I see no money going out to Michael, which is a good thing as well. I think Phillip wants to hire a forensic accountant. He was going to talk to you guys about it today."

"Well, all of this sounds very positive. Room for reasonable doubt anyway," said Marco.

"That is our initial thought too, but Phillip wants you to read through the statements and drill down into the testimony, essentially pick it apart for us."

"Will do," said Michael as he moved to one end of the table and sat down. Odell slid a pile of transcripts toward him. Looking at the stack in front of him, Michael asked, "Is Phillip here?"

"He'll be joining us shortly," replied Odell.

Mitchell Conway, who disappeared from the conference room earlier, now returned with legal pads, pens, and yellow highlighters. He placed them on the table, instinctively knowing Michael and Marco would need one of each in reviewing the transcripts.

Odell said, "Thank you Mitch." He then asked offhandedly, "Do you want to take everything on this end of the table and on the floor to your office? Let's start getting this stuff ready to put into notebooks like we discussed. I'll wait here for Phillip and work with Michael and Marco on these witness statements."

Conway complied and grabbed stacks of documents from around the room, placed as many piles as he could into a box, and left.

"I want to look at all of Gerry's statements first . . . I'm sure there is no truth to anything he told the feds," declared Michael.

He and Marco began to read the 302 statements when, twenty minutes later, Phillip Richardson walked into the room looking fresh and relaxed. "Gentlemen," he said. Sitting at one end of the table, he looked to Michael and Marco seated opposite him and asked, "How are you?"

They replied, almost simultaneously, "Good."

He continued, "I'm sure Odell has filled you in, right?" Before they could respond Richardson announced, "We need to hire a forensic accountant." He waited for a reaction, not knowing they had been forewarned. Prompted by Michael's lack of response, Richardson said, "If I'm right and I think I am, the feds have a real problem. No money trail, none. Harrison can't trace any money from the conspiracy back to you. That is fucking huge." He stopped talking and glanced at Odell, who did not react.

Michael, although feeling optimistic by Richardson's enthusiasm, still had to ask, "How about Gerry's claim that I was being paid in cash? He says it right here in what looks like one of his first interviews with the FBI." He kept his focus on Phillip, as he sat with his arms folded across his chest.

"That's bullshit. It's cover for a lack of evidence," Richardson declared. He pushed back in his chair saying, "This is a very defensible case." He waited and repeated, "Very defensible."

Michael looked at Marco and turning back he asked, "Phillip, what does that mean exactly?"

Richardson smiled and said, "It means I think we can win this thing."

CHAPTER FIFTY-EIGHT

IT was shortly after 11:00 p.m. when Michael arrived home after having dinner with Marco and the attorneys at a small Italian restaurant in midtown. They celebrated the progress made on the case that day. Phillip, who had a little too much to drink, invited Michael to join him and Odell at a club in the village afterward, but he declined. Marco went back to his own office after dinner to complete some work for an upcoming trial. They had been in Richardson's law office for more than six hours, reading transcripts, discussing trial strategy, and working on a closing statement—the first step a good trial lawyer takes in preparing for a jury trial. The day was long and the results fruitful, producing what everyone believed would be a winning case. A couple glasses of wine at dinner and Michael was feeling good and now confident about their chances of a not guilty verdict.

Diana was sitting up in bed waiting for him, reading an Agatha Christie mystery novel, *The Murder at the Vicarage*, part of the Miss Marple book series. She was completely enthralled by her newfound love of fiction and reading for pleasure these days, more than she had ever done in the past.

As Michael walked into the bedroom, he asked, "Hey, what you doing?" Before she could respond he asked, "Is the baby asleep?"

Diana shook her head in the affirmative, as she placed the book on her lap asking, "How was your day?"

"Good . . . very good," he said. "I think we've put together a winning strategy."

She asked, "What do you mean?"

"Phillip and Odell think we can poke holes in the witness testimony, lots of them. They're all over the place and clearly lying. We think a jury will see right through it all." He began to undress at the foot of the bed. Continuing, he said, "That fuck Gerry said I was getting cash for my share of the so-called conspiracy proceeds. Can you believe that shit? Anyway, there is no money trail. Nothing. Not a dime coming back at me . . . obviously," he said.

Diana tried to focus on what he was saying, now distracted as he stood there clad only in his boxer briefs. She observed that he lost some weight and thought that the jogging had really paid off. He now had a shredded midsection that he was working hard at to maintain. *My husband looks pretty good, damn sexy*, she concluded. Her mind wandered back to his revelation about the weaknesses in the government's case. She now proclaimed, "Well, thank God the lies are being exposed."

Michael nodded, half listening, as he was engrossed in what he should tell her next. He suddenly declared, "Oh yeah, almost forgot. Phillip wants to hire a forensic accountant to testify at trial. He's going to have to go through all the bank records." He stopped momentarily and added, "The bad news . . . it's going to cost anywhere from twenty-five to thirty thousand dollars."

Diana thought about what he was now saying and said, "Michael, why hire someone? I can do it. You know that forensic accounting is just another name for auditing." He didn't respond, looking at her somewhat puzzled. "And don't leave your clothes there," she said, pointing to the pile at his feet. "Take them to the hamper please."

"No, I didn't know that," he said as he bent over to pick up his shirt, socks and pants. He walked to the bathroom to discard the clothes, and returning to the bedroom, he got into bed, clad only in his underwear, and settled in without saying another word.

"This way it won't cost us anything," Diana said, picking up where she left off.

He rolled over to face her and said, "Hon, you're way too close to this, don't you think?" Sliding closer to her now, he said, "A jury wouldn't find you credible because of your obvious bias. After all, you're sleeping with the defendant." Michael looked up at her trying not to laugh. They both began to chuckle as she attempted to formulate a reply, unable to do so.

Diana, giving it more thought, said, "But seriously, what does it matter? The numbers are the numbers. They don't lie. Anyway, I'll just get Kelly to do it. He is the best I know. I'm sure better than anyone Phillip can find. I can get a whole team of forensic accountants for free and I know Kelly would be happy to help."

"That makes sense. Kelly—okay. I'll talk to Phillip," he said.

Still sitting up in bed, Diana thought about the impact a foren-sic accounting expert's testimony might have on a jury. She abruptly declared, "It's not just about establishing . . . no money in, no money out."

Michael asked, "Ok, what do you mean by that?"

"Well, think about it. Gerry is claiming you were paid in cash. It's presumably untraceable, and that fact is what makes the claim difficult to refute, right?"

Michael shrugged, "I guess so."

Diana nodded and said, "Don't you see the government will tell the jury just that. No need to show a paper trail of money to you in this instance, ladies and gentlemen . . . it's cash! And by the way you have Gerry Bender's testimony to help you make sense of it all," she said angrily, stretching out her hands as if to say the evidence was now being served to the jury on a silver platter. Michael looked at her, surprised by her emotional outburst. Taking a deep breath and calming down she added, "It's a claim that is difficult to defend, but if the forensic accounting is done right it's easy to disprove. We do it by first demonstrating that our spending habits or lifestyle did not exceed the income we both earned for not only the period when you began working at Bender to the present, but also before that time. Let's say we go back to the day we got married. You know I have all our income and expenditures on spreadsheets and that I saved every receipt for tax purposes. We use all those years as a baseline to help support the data for the relevant period. Imagine, every expenditure and payment explained and properly sourced," she now said smiling.

"Ok, I'm getting it," he said. "This way there are no questions . . . no doubts about the issue of whether Michael Dolan got cash payments for his alleged role in this conspiracy."

"Exactly," Diana said approvingly.

"Ok, but what if the government asserts that the money is stowed away somewhere."

"Well, there would have been no reason to do that initially as no one appeared concerned about the money being traced back to them. It would have never come up for that reason. There was also a considerable amount of time that went by before the start of the attorney general case and the criminal investigation. Plenty of reason to spend or get rid of it if you had it. And no reason not to use it to pay for the attorneys instead of borrowing from your dad.

Everyone else was spending theirs, and I'm sure they were all living well. We audit the records of Bender Capital, the individuals, and the other businesses that the government claims were the source of ill-gotten gains to demonstrate where the money went. Once we account for all of it the jury can only conclude that you got none of it and, therefore, the allegations against you are false."

Michael looked at her in awe and said, "You know, I never thought about it that way. You're right. It's more than just money in, money out. We need to eliminate any doubt in the jurors' minds, and we use the level and consistency in our lifestyle before and after Bender to demonstrate that there aren't any unaccounted assets or funds like that fuck-head Gerry is claiming. You become the fact witness laying the foundation for all of this It's all very credible because you're an over-the-top 'type A' personality that does shit like this as a matter of routine, although nobody else in their right mind would. Once the jury finds that all the money is accounted for and that it leads to Gerry and the others only, they are left with only one conclusion."

Diana smiled again, and said, "Yes . . . yes exactly. It has to be done right and explained in the simplest terms so that the jury understands it. See, you thought I was just a big pain in the ass by my meticulous nature. Now my over-the-top personality may prove to be your salvation."

"Damn hon, you're right. And all those years I made fun of you for doing that shit. You're good . . . you're so on top of things."

She smiled at him and said, "Yeah, I am." Blushing she then said, "Now, stop talking and make love to me, Michael." She bent down and kissed him deeply and purposefully. Brushing the book from her lap and sliding down from her seated position, Diana slipped into the bed sheets to her husband's waiting arms.

CHAPTER FIFTY-NINE

PHILLIP Richardson's mood concerning the Michael Dolan case could best be described as joyful. The unabashed bliss was infectious, and Odell was equally optimistic about a very good outcome for their client. Phillip told him that he'd never seen a poorer group of cooperating government witnesses in his life. While they were all on the same page—big picture, the details were sketchy, inconsistent and not adding up. At least some, but most likely all, were lying. Their testimony, at worst, would be unreliable. At best, it would be completely unbelievable. The two attorneys imagined that Harrison knew this too. The government's case had some real problems, and Richardson now thought maybe it made sense to lay it all on the table for Harrison and his team—let the government know exactly how they would come at them, and how badly it would look once they did. He hoped this revelation would get Harrison to drop the case against Michael. After all, he did have some success doing just that with this prosecutor in the past. Richardson knew that Harrison's ego would not allow him to look bad, and he would certainly look bad once he was done cross examining these witnesses.

Richardson stared at Odell and asked, "So what do you think?"

He waited and gave it some real thought before answering. "It's risky. It tips our hand and if he doesn't bite, we have some real exposure. He then has our entire playbook, knows exactly how we're coming at him and potentially deflects our every move," he replied.

Richardson stared at him for a moment. *Well thought out. He may be right, but if Harrison senses a problem, he'll retreat. It's in his nature. After all, this is an all or nothing proposition. That's what makes it risky.* "It does tip our hand. You're right there. But, if it causes Harrison to back off . . . well then, the reward would have been worth the risk. Wouldn't you say?"

Odell looked a little annoyed and said, "Phillip, it's too risky. I don't even think you raise it as an option with Michael. After all, we need to be his voice of reason. This is a little out there," he said, pausing and waiting for pushback. Phillip simply stared and said nothing. Odell pushed on, "If you tell him there is a chance this whole thing goes away, he won't even listen to the other part of the equation . . . the severe consequences if it all goes bad." Now, trying to appease Phillip, he said, "My love, you certainly get an A+ for thinking outside of the box. I'll give you that."

Richardson knew when Odell was stroking his ego to get his way. He was not buying it. "I think we give Michael the option. Let him decide," he said, getting off the sofa and removing his hand from Odell's knee. Walking to the desk, he turned and preached to his young associate, "Without risk there is no reward." He stopped talking and looked for a reaction. Odell gave none. He continued, "You know that I've built a reputation doing the impossible. Look at Frank, for instance. He would be doing life right now if it wasn't for me."

Ignoring the urge to speak out about Frank's need for rehabilitation, Odell knew Phillip's mind was made up and, at which point, he reluctantly said, "Phillip, if you think it makes sense to do . . . I'll support you on this. But I still think it's not the best move." He looked over at Phillip and held his gaze, asking, "When do you want to talk to Michael about this?"

"Let's get him in here soon and we'll lay it all out for him. Give Marco a call too. I'm sure Michael is going to want his input on this as well. Then I'll call the U.S. Attorney's Office to set up a meeting with Harrison . . . tell him we need to talk."

CHAPTER SIXTY

THE meeting was set. Harrison was surprised, but pleased, by the phone call and Richardson's unexpected request for a talk. Immediately, he directed Angie to print out the plea agreement that he prepared months ago and attempted to force on Michael, preindictment. He would update and conform it, requiring Dolan to enter a guilty plea to one count of conspiracy, as he had done with everyone else. He instinctively knew that Phillip Richardson would want to negotiate a loss amount keeping it as low as possible to lower the sentencing guidelines range. The financial losses to the victims, along with a defendant's criminal history, is what also drove the potential sentence in these types of cases. Generally, the greater the loss—the greater the prison term. Harrison sensed this would likely be a point of contention, but something they could work out later. He would start high and Richardson predictably low. Harrison thought they would probably meet somewhere in the middle for a loss amount that would likely provide for a sentencing range of anywhere from forty-eight to fifty-four months. It was a sentence range he could live with. For now, and for this reason alone, he left the offense conduct and loss amount blank in the plea agreement. The important thing was that Richardson was willing to come in and talk a plea deal for his client and that was huge. Harrison had been more than a little concerned about the case against Dolan, but with this latest development he no longer needed to worry. Michael Dolan would soon plead guilty and that was a good thing for him.

Phillip Richardson packed a briefcase full of his notes where he outlined the many discrepancies in the witness statements knowing that almost each one failed to support the government's case. More so, it cast doubt on the entirety of the claims against his client. The preliminary analysis that was undertaken by Kelly Updike and his team on the money trail was laid out in the notes he had taken during his discussions with him and Diana.

Even though the audits of the various bank accounts were not complete, what the auditors uncovered thus far was very impactful. It was enough to take to Harrison and point out the effect it would all have not only on the case, but potentially to his career. He knew that Harrison would be most concerned about this point and would see the good sense in dropping the case against his client before he was embarrassed by it all, or even worse, disciplined for having knowingly used false testimony to obtain an indictment.

Richardson had no doubt that Harrison and the agents knew the witnesses were not telling the truth or telling their own version of it. The thought had even crossed his mind that maybe the government was orchestrating the false narrative against his client, but he dismissed it thinking that was going too far. Nobody would do such a thing, not even Harrison. Leaving the office, Odell wished him luck, still unsure if this was the right move. Although Michael was completely onboard with the strategy discussed with him and Marco numerous times, Odell continued to consider the possible outcomes. For all his thoughtful reflection, however, there was one scenario he could not anticipate.

———◆———

Getting off the elevator and making his way to the U.S. Attorney's Office, Phillip Richardson was, once again, certain that he had the upper hand. Arriving at the reception area, Angie was called to escort him back to Harrison's office where he sat waiting with FBI Agent Carl Bronson.

"Mr. Richardson, if you would follow me," Angie said softly.

Without a word, he followed behind her as he had done on many occasions before. Arriving at the office, she gave a slight knock on the door and opened it allowing Richardson to enter. Bronson was seated in front of the desk and stood as he entered the office. Extending his hand, he said, "Phillip, nice to see you."

Harrison remained seated and, without making any effort to greet Richardson, simply said, "Phillip have a seat," as he leaned backward in his chair, which was now turned to the side facing the wall instead of the desk. The blinds behind Harrison were open, allowing the afternoon light to stream in through the windows unobstructed, almost blinding Richardson as he sat down.

"James, thanks for taking this meeting. I think we have a few things to talk about concerning my client and the case you are attempting to develop against him."

"I'm always happy to accommodate counsel. You know that Phillip," Harrison responded.

At that moment, Angie closed the door and returned to her desk to print out the plea agreement and waited to be summoned back into the office. Bronson, who was now seated, looked at Richardson and was struck by the comment. *What is he talking about—developing?* Disturbed, he now said, "What do you mean? The case is fully developed and rock solid."

Harrison jumped in, stating, "Cool it Carl." He then turned to Richardson and said, "Phillip let's just get started. I know why you're here. I'm going to make this as easy as possible for you." He picked up the phone and said, "Angie, come in here." A few seconds later, Harrison's secretary reentered the office and placed a folder on the edge of the desk.

Without taking his eyes off Richardson, Harrison said, "Thank you Angie. He then directed her to wait as he straightened his chair and wrapped his left arm around her waist pulling her closer to him. He opened the folder with his right hand and tossed a copy of the plea agreement onto the desk toward Richardson, who leaned forward and took the document from the desk knowing immediately what it was.

"You think I'm here to cut a plea deal?"

Harrison looked at him dumbfounded and said, "Yea. I thought you wanted to make a deal. Why else would you come?"

Richardson tossed the agreement back onto the desk and said, "I'm not here to make a deal." He paused and said, "I'm here to tell you that moving forward with a case against Michael Dolan is a mistake and could be detrimental to your career. There is no case here, James. Your witnesses are lying. There is irreparable conflict in what they say about my client, there is no money trail leading back to him, and none of it adds up like you may think or had hoped for."

He looked at Harrison for a moment and then said, "As one attorney to another, I thought I'd come here and tell you that. I don't want you to be embarrassed and that is what is going to happen if you pursue this to trial."

Bronson shifted uncomfortably in his seat, knowing that there was more than a bit of truth to what Richardson was now saying.

Harrison was fuming, thinking, *This motherfucker*, as he continued to stare at Richardson. *Doesn't he know who I am? I'm Goddamn untouchable.* Without saying a word, Harrison reached for the plea agreement and gently placed it back in front of Richardson, somehow managing to keep his anger in check. "Why don't you think about it, while I think about what to do with your other client, Mr. Vogel. You know the matter is still under investigation. Isn't that right, Carl?" he said without shifting his gaze from Richardson.

Bronson simply nodded, unable to speak, not knowing what to make of the ongoing exchange between the two men.

Richardson implored, "Jesus, James don't do this. You know there isn't a case there. We've been down that road."

"Well Phillip, one way or another, I am going to get a conviction against someone, and who that someone is, may be entirely up to you."

"James, you can't be serious?"

"Try me," said Harrison, now leaning in toward Richardson.

"James." he paused. "Don't tell me that you're orchestrating this false narrative against my client."

Bronson unexpectedly jumped into the conversation, saying, "You got some fucking nerve . . . this is the Department of Justice, the fucking Department of Justice. What is it that you think we do here anyway?"

Richardson looked at him without commenting and redirected his attention back to Harrison. "James, we're not going to play this game, are we?"

Before Harrison could answer, Angie, who was still standing beside him, placed her hand on his shoulder and asked, "James, may I leave?"

Without looking at her and staring straight ahead at Richardson, he shook his head in the affirmative as Angie Estrada scurried out of the office.

Going immediately to her desk, she grabbed her jacket and took her purse from the bottom desk drawer, announcing to no one in particular, "I'm going to run out to the curb for a cigarette. I'll be right back." The other secretaries around her said nothing, except to take mental note of her departure. Out on the street, she reached into her purse and pulled out a cellphone. Dialing, she made the call to her father as she was instructed to do.

Hector Estrada pulled the phone from his red blazer and looked at the caller ID. It was his daughter.

"Angie, everything ok?" he asked.

"Poppy. There's a problem," she declared.

CHAPTER SIXTY-ONE

THE cheap throwaway cellphone tucked into the pocket behind the passenger front seat began to ring. Stuart Vogel pulled it out and looked at the caller ID: *Doorman.* He quickly answered the call.

Clearing his throat, he asked, "Hector, what's going on?"

Ronnie glanced back in the rearview mirror at the mention of Hector's name, and upon hearing the seriousness in his voice determined that Vogel appeared somber and focused on what had to be an important matter. He quickly turned his attention back to the road ahead of him. The Cadillac SUV was moving in an easterly direction on Meadow Lane in affluent and celebrity-filled South Hampton, New York on the way to Vogel's twelve-thousand square-foot summer home.

Hector nervously replied, "Mr. Vogel . . . you know that thing we talked about. That thing you wanted me to keep an eye on."

"Yea Hector, of course. Go ahead . . . spit it out," he implored. "You have something to tell me?"

Well, Mr. Vogel . . . we got a problem."

Five minutes later, Stuart Vogel was fully briefed on what just occurred at the U.S. Attorney's Office. He was not pleased. Ronnie continued to look back throughout the conversation, concluding that his boss seemed distressed by the discussion he was having. Before hanging up the phone, Vogel thanked Hector, telling him that he had done well. He also instructed him to tell his daughter to keep her eyes and ears open and to immediately call with any additional information. Vogel flipped the phone closed and held it against his forehead. He tried to absorb the information that Hector now delivered. He also quickly attempted to assess the possible fallout from it all.

Ronnie took another look back in the rearview mirror and asked, "Everything alright, boss?"

Vogel replied slowly, "Not sure. I'll know better in a minute."

He put down the prepaid phone and reached into his pocket for his personal cellphone. He quickly dialed Phillip Richardson's number.

Sitting in the backseat of a NYC yellow cab, Phillip Richardson was trying to wrap his head around what just happened. He was still numb from the exchange he had with James Harrison who was now pushing back and extorting or blackmailing him. Either way, he had him bent over and was driving it home hard—leveraging him for a conviction between one of two clients. Harrison was leaving it to him to choose between them. Richardson was caught off guard and completely unsure what to do next. It was a turn of events that was certainly unanticipated for all the planning and thought given to the decision to confront Harrison. He was now convinced that Harrison knew that Michael Dolan was innocent. Clearly, Harrison didn't give a shit. It seemed that Odell's intuition was right—confronting him was a bad idea. Putting his head back, Richardson closed his eyes and sighed. *Fuck, I can't believe this is happening.*

The cellphone tucked into his jacket pocket began to ring causing him to reluctantly open his eyes. He looked and immediately saw that it was Stuart Vogel calling. He sent the call to voicemail. *What Goddamn timing,* he thought as he glanced out the window and noticed the cab was now turning onto 34th Street. He considered having to tell Odell what happened, putting his head back and closing his eyes again. A moment later the cellphone rang for a second time. It was Vogel again and this time he answered it.

"Stuart, how are you?" Hesitating only momentarily, he said, "I was just thinking about you."

"Is that so," said Vogel. Before Richardson could respond, Vogel asked, "Philly, what the fuck is going on?"

Richardson nervously asked, "Stuart, what do you mean exactly?"

"I mean what the fuck just happened at the U.S. Attorney's Office . . . with that prick, Harrison?"

Jesus Christ, how did he know? I just left. "Well, you're right I was there, but on another case. Nothing to do with you or your case, Stuart," said Richardson.

"That's not my understanding. Philly, who's more important to you, me or this guy Dolan?" he asked mockingly. "Because as I see it Harrison wants this guy . . . he wants him not me. So, if anyone's going down, it better be this asshole Dolan."

He knows everything. How the fuck does he know? Shit, he's got someone inside. "Wait a minute Stuart. It's a bluff. Nothing but a bluff, believe me," he said, not knowing what else to say.

"Philly stop right fucking there. You know that's bullshit. I know that's bullshit. Harrison's got your balls in a vice, and he's going to squeeze until you give someone up. That someone isn't going to be me. You got that," he said sternly. He paused and waited for a response. There was none. He shouted, "Do you fucking understand me?"

"I understand," said Richardson.

"Good, now take care of this," said Vogel, as he hung up the phone.

The cab pulled to the curb in front of the office building. The sidewalk was now crowded with smokers huddled around a small smoking area, and pedestrians on their way to somewhere.

"Here you go. That's eighteen dollars, forty cents," said the driver.

Richardson leaned forward and handed him a twenty-dollar bill through the small opening in the plexiglass that divided them. Glimpsing the driver's identification on the dashboard he said, "Sammy, do me a favor. Drive."

Sammy Mendoza asked, "Where to?"

"I don't know . . . Central Park I guess. Just drive," said Richardson.

Mendoza slowly pulled away from the curb into the oppressive midtown traffic of 8th Avenue, moving slowly in the direction of the park. Richardson leaned his head backward and closed his eyes once again. He knew exactly what needed to be done. He knew it the moment Stuart Vogel's name appeared on his caller ID. Phillip Richardson reached into his pocket for his phone and dialed James Harrison's cellphone number. He had given it to him on the way out of the office earlier, telling Richardson to call when he decided which of his clients he liked least. As the phone rang, Harrison looked at the number and reflected. It didn't take him long to decide.

Michael, I'm sorry. Really fucking sorry. Two rings is all it took.

Harrison answered the phone, asking smugly, "So, Phillip . . . which one of your clients is it?"

CHAPTER SIXTY-TWO

URING a twenty-minute cab ride around Central Park, Phillip Richardson was able to strike a deal with Harrison that he believed Michael would embrace. He knew that the most important part of any federal plea deal in a financial crimes case was to limit the victim loss amount. It's what drove the sentence the most. To completely sell the plea deal to Michael, he needed to limit the offense conduct—his supposed role in the conspiracy—to one transaction, while simultaneously minimizing the loss amount as best as he could. With that in mind, Richardson negotiated an agreed upon loss amount that provided for a sentencing guidelines range of twenty-four to thirty months of imprisonment. It was the best he could do with Harrison, who insisted that Michael see jail time. The Federal Sentencing Reform Act of 1984 requires a judge to select a sentence within the guidelines range, with a few exceptions. A prisoner, with good behavior, in the Federal Correctional System would serve about three quarters of that sentence. Considering the agreed upon sentencing range, Michael could conceivably be out of a minimum-security facility to a half-way house somewhere in Connecticut in a little more than a year.

Richardson believed that worst case, Michael's incarceration would be short lived and very tolerable for him and his family. The more he thought about it, the better he felt. He now justified what he had done by telling himself, after all, this could go south at trial and Michael might end up with a prison sentence somewhere between ten and twenty years. Richardson was hopeful that Judge Cooley could be convinced to hand down a sentence that departed from the guidelines range, perhaps a house arrest or maybe even a probation. After all, Michael was innocent despite the intended guilty plea. If Cooley believed the facts of the case were atypical according to the sentencing guidelines act, she could depart from the guidelines and sentence outside the prescribed range.

He now thought about the mitigating factors he might present at sentencing that would enable Judge Cooley to offer up a lighter sentence. He conveniently convinced himself that this was the best course of action. This was turning out better than he had hoped. It was not only better for Michael, but also for his precious client, Stuart Vogel. With this plea deal, Harrison assured him that Vogel would not be touched. He didn't know whether to believe him, but what choice did he have.

Returning to the office, Richardson made his way directly to the oval office where he was immediately confronted by Odell. Closing the wall behind them, the two men sat next to one another on the sofa to discuss the meeting with Harrison.

Odell asked, "Have you been there all this time . . . how did it go?"

"It went well," he said. "Harrison was not buying any of it though," he quickly added. Shifting sideways and throwing his arm across the back of the sofa he touched Odell's shoulder lightly. "He wasn't going to drop the case no matter what I said. So, I did the next best thing. I worked out a very favorable plea deal."

Odell's eyes widened as he crossed his arms in front of his chest and leaned back slightly. He sat silently staring at him until he abruptly exclaimed, "A plea deal."

"A guideline range of twenty-four to thirty months, but I think I can get Michael a house arrest or maybe a probation." Richardson removed his arm from the sofa and moved it to Odell's knee. Staring at him he said, "I think it's best for the client."

Odell seemed to come undone, his entire body now shaking slightly. Leaning in and looking deeply into Phillip's eyes, his voice quivered as he whispered, "But Michael is innocent." *We told him this was going to work. The case would be dropped.*

Richardson looked at him and leaning in closer he placed his other hand atop Odell's knee and with both hands on his leg he said, "Trust me."

————◆————

It was 4:35 p.m. and Michael imagined that the meeting had to be over, yet, no word from his attorneys. He was feeling anxious as he waited for a sign, feedback, or some sort of confirmation that this nightmare was over. *Something, anything.*

Michael couldn't wait any longer. He called the office to find out what happened. The receptionist asked him to hold, and a few minutes later Odell answered, saying only, "Hello Michael."

He asked, "Odell, how did it go?" And before Odell could answer, he said, "I didn't hear from anyone . . . so, I decided to call."

Odell answered bluntly, "Michael, it didn't go as planned." *Shit, it didn't go well . . . didn't go well at all.* He then quickly added, "Phillip and I would like to come and see you and Diana tonight about eight to discuss this further. Is that ok?" Before Michael could answer he said, "I'll bring dessert. See you then."

"Eight o'clock. Ok I guess," was all he could think to say.

"Goodbye Michael," said Odell.

"See you then," said Michael, as hung up the phone somewhat confused by the exchange.

Michael called his father and asked, "Dad is it ok if the baby stays with you tonight? I've got to meet with the attorneys later . . . me and Diana. They're coming here."

"Sure, Michael do you want to bring her now? I'll feed her here, or maybe we'll go out for pizza."

"Great, thanks Dad. I'll bring her now. Be there in fifteen minutes."

Michael next called Diana to tell her that Phillip and Odell wanted to talk.

Diana asked, "Well what did they say exactly?"

"Odell told me that it didn't go as planned and they wanted to come over tonight to talk to the both of us."

Diana closed her eyes as she began to process what Michael just said. *Ok, doesn't sound good. Why would they want to meet with the both of us? It can only mean that Harrison wasn't persuaded by what Phillip or Odell had to say about the conflicting testimony or real lack of evidence. Where does that leave us?* she wondered.

"Well, ok. I'm going to come home now. I'll see you in a little bit," said Diana, who hung up the phone before Michael could respond.

Diana quickly cleared her desk, putting away every folder and client file that she was working on and placed each one into a four-drawer, light grey cabinet. She rushed out to the parking lot without talking to anyone, still thinking about this development and what it would mean going forward. It seemed to her that there wasn't a real option A jury trial now appeared to be a certainty. She called Karen from the car, who was waiting to hear from her on how the meeting went.

Answering the phone immediately, Karen said, "Hi Diana. I was just thinking about you guys." Without waiting for a response, she quickly asked, "Did you hear from the attorneys . . . how did everything go?"

"Can you come over for dinner tonight?" She, likewise, didn't wait for an answer, saying, "Phillip and Odell are coming to the house tonight. Want to talk. I'm not sure, but it seems like whatever happened today wasn't good."

Karen was silent, thinking about what Diana had just said. *The attorneys want to sit down, face to face. Clearly, they have something important to tell them.*

Diana added, "We could sure use your support . . . and, of course, your insight."

Karen now quickly said, "Yea, whatever I can do. You know I love you guys. What time?"

"I'm on my way home. Anytime is fine," said Diana.

"Well, I'm finishing up with a client. I can probably be there about six. Is that ok?"

"Perfect. See you then," said Diana, as she hung up the phone.

In the car, she reflected how difficult it had been for people to understand what they were going through. Karen was one of only a few who did. She often sat with them trying to make sense of it At other times, it was all she could do to calm their nerves and soothe their fears. For this reason alone, Diana was grateful to have a good friend like her. She was glad that Karen was going to be there tonight. On the contrary, she was not looking forward to seeing Phillip and Odell.

CHAPTER SIXTY-THREE

ARRIVING precisely at eight o'clock, Phillip and Odell pulled into the driveway in a black 1996 Jaguar XJS convertible. It was a car that was parked in a midtown garage most of the time, except when used on one of those long weekend trips to Saratoga Springs in upstate New York during the summer horse racing season. In show-room condition and with only twenty-two thousand original miles, it was one of Richardson's prized possessions.

Getting out of the car and making his way to the front door, Odell carried with him a box containing a banana cheesecake from the well-known and popular Eileen's Special Cheesecake Shop in lower Manhattan. He held it on his lap on the drive from Manhattan to Connecticut.

Dinner was over, and Karen and Diana cleared the table. Michael sat there, again thinking about his favorite wine, a bottle of Raymond Reserve, a California cabernet stowed away in the wine chiller. Diana stopped him from opening it, insisting that he wait until after the meeting. She wanted to keep their heads clear for the discussion to come. She was just beginning to brew regular coffee and also put a pot of espresso on the stove when the doorbell rang. The three of them looked at each other as Michael got up from the kitchen table and answered the door.

"Phillip. Odell. Come in," he said pleasantly, but also somewhat nervously.

Walking into the kitchen, Odell handed Diana the box that he had been holding for the last hour and said, "I hope you like banana cheesecake."

"Don't know, I've never had it, but thank you Odell," she said as she put the box down on the counter. "Phillip, Odell sit please. I'm just making coffee. Are you going to have some?"

Richardson sat down and said, "Yes, I'll have coffee. Thank you."

"I also have espresso," Diana said looking at Phillip, who put up his hand and waved, as if to say, *No espresso for me, just regular coffee please.*

Diana asked, "Odell, what about you. What can I get you?"

He thought about it and said, "I'll have an espresso," as Michael moved around the table putting either mugs or cups in front of everyone.

Cutting the cheesecake, Diana placed it in the center of the table. After setting down a stack of dishes and forks, she said, "Help yourselves, please," as she began to pour the coffee.

Everyone settled in, helping themselves to coffee and cake. There was some small talk for ten or fifteen minutes before the topic of their discussion changed to the meeting Richardson had with Harrison earlier that day.

Odell, taking a forkful of cheesecake, turned to him and getting things started, said, "Phillip why don't we go over what happened today."

Richardson looked at him, somewhat displeased for suddenly casting him in the spotlight with no way to avoid being the bearer of bad news.

Speaking slowly, he said, "Well, let me just say that Harrison is no fool. He had a plea deal waiting for me, hoping that you were prepared to fall on your sword. When I told him why I was there he appeared surprised, but I don't believe he was. He clearly knows that there are problems with the case. Although, he doesn't want to admit it, nor does he seem to care. I believe that he will go to trial with all the problems, regardless. He is willing to gamble on this one. For some reason he has it out for you Michael."

He stopped talking allowing that last part to sink in. Michael reflected on the Franklin Family Fund case.

Richardson continued, "The way he sees it, he has nothing to lose. Michael, you on the other hand, have a lot to lose. It's a risk that I think you cannot take."

The others listened intently and sat silently as Richardson continued to speak. At some point, Michael asked, "What about the fact that I'm innocent, the lies and false testimony, the lack of a money trail?"

Before he could respond, Diana added, "Phillip, what about all those things you said about Harrison's ego being too big . . . his desire to avoid looking bad? I mean, you said his sense of self-importance would prevent him from moving forward with a losing case. Isn't that what you said? What the hell happened?"

He looked at her for a moment and simply said, "I was wrong."

"Jesus," said Michael, as he looked at Diana dejectedly. Turning back to Richardson, he said, "Harrison now has our entire playbook, knows everything we know. He anticipates our every move at trial. Phillip, we're so fucked."

"Michael, exactly. That's why we accept the plea deal. Going to trial could end so very badly for you and your family. Think about the possibility of twenty years in prison. While on the other hand, your worst-case scenario is an exposure where you do about a year in a minimum-security facility and some time in a halfway house. But if we play this right, and we convince Cooley your role was *des-minimums*, then . . . well then most likely a house arrest or possibly a probation." He waited for a reaction, and not receiving one, Richardson pulled from his interior suit jacket inside pocket a copy of the plea agreement. Unfolding it, he placed it in front of Michael. Again, waiting for a reaction he added, "It's the right move."

Diana looked at Karen. They both seemed stunned. Michael appeared numb and didn't know what else to say. Diana politely excused herself, walked out of the kitchen, and went upstairs to her bedroom.

Karen looked at Michael and said, "I'm going to check on Diana," quickly following her upstairs. She was as much disturbed by the sudden change of events as Michael and Diana were, and what was expected to be good news about the meeting today, now sadly appeared very bad.

Odell watched as the women walked out of the room. He noted to himself that they were clearly upset. He felt badly for the two of them, but especially for Diana. He believed what Phillip was telling them was the best course of action. The plan now was to limit Michael's exposure and to avoid the grief and pain that came with a lengthy prison sentence. This plea deal did that. Even though Harrison was unwilling to concede completely, he did make some very big concessions in this plea agreement. It was a good deal for their client, considering the other possible outcomes.

Michael looked at the two men sitting across from him and said, "Phillip, Odell . . . I'm not sure. I think we go to trial. I'm confident we end up with a not guilty verdict."

"Hold it right there," said Richardson angrily. "Michael, what happens if Harrison convinces a jury that you're a bad guy? Remember jurors are idiots who typically overanalyze everything and already have a bias in favor of the prosecution to start with. After all, why would the government make such a claim if it wasn't true . . . and it's that kind of thinking that gets you convicted with a lengthy jail term."

"Phillip, I'm just not sure," he responded.

"Michael listen to me. If you're found guilty, do you think your wife is going to wait around for you? She can't and won't hang on until you get out of prison in ten, fifteen, or twenty years. No fucking way she can do that. She's young and beautiful, a woman with wants and desires. She needs a man, someone to take care of her and your daughter. So, she divorces you while you're rotting away in prison . . . and soon after that some other guy is fucking your wife. He's in your house, your bed, and he's fucking your wife," Richardson emphasized.

"You, well you're jerking off in the shower with six other guys, one or two who would love to fuck you in the ass. And worst of all . . . as if that's not bad enough, your daughter is calling this other guy 'daddy'. And Michael . . . look at me," he demanded. Michael turned his eyes upward, and when Richardson had his full attention, he said, "Believe me when I tell you . . . you're never going to see Christina again, because visiting you is just too fucking painful. If and when you do see her . . . she's not your little girl anymore She's a grown woman, possibly married, maybe with kids of her own. A daughter you don't know and grandchildren you've never met."

Odell looked on horrified and shocked by how Phillip was now speaking to Michael. Slipping his hand underneath the table, he placed it on Phillip's leg and squeezed his thigh, signaling *enough.*

My God Phillip, that was cruel, he thought.

The color had drained from Michael's face and he was now pale. He sat at one end of the table unable to speak. He was jumpy, his nerves getting the better of him as he now stuttered, trying to formulate a response.

Richardson stopped talking and took a deep breath, suddenly feeling exhausted. Looking away from Michael, a calm spread over him. Breaking the silence, a couple of minutes later, Phillip whispered, "That's why you take the deal."

Before Michael could respond, the women returned to the kitchen. Diana, looking melancholy, sat down and said, "Phillip. Odell. Thank you. Michael and I need to process this and get back to you." She looked at them glaringly and got up from her seat.

"Have a good night," she said.

Following Diana's cue, Michael got up and said, "Guys, let me get back to you. There is a lot to think about here."

"Ok, Michael. You two talk and get back to me next week. I may have failed to mention but we have a status conference with the judge in three weeks. Let's have a game plan in place by then. If you accept the plea deal we need to inform Harrison and Judge Cooley."

Michael looked at Phillip, saying only, "Good night."

The attorneys walked to the door, escorted by Michael, as Diana and Karen remained in the kitchen.

As Odell stepped out onto the walkway, he turned and said, "Michael, I'm sorry. I know this isn't what you expected. Believe me, Phillip is doing what he thinks is best for you and your family."

Michael did not respond, but just stood there staring at him. Not knowing what else to say, Odell put his head down and turned, walking to the driveway where Phillip stood waiting by the car.

Standing there watching them drive away, Michael began to wonder, *if this goes bad, would Diana really have no choice but to leave me, and what about Christina, what happens to her?* He closed the door, trying to shake off the thought as he began to walk back to the kitchen, where he heard Diana and Karen talking. From what he could hear, it seemed they had nothing good to say about Phillip or Odell. A soon as he entered the room, they stopped talking. Diana looked at him curiously and said, "Michael sit down. We need to talk."

CHAPTER SIXTY-FOUR

"WELL, don't stop talking on my account," said Michael, as he sat down at the table, asking for another espresso. As Diana poured him another cup, she said, "Something is not right. A few days ago, Phillip was so sure of himself, telling us this was definitely going away."

Diana walked to the stove and put down the pot. Facing Michael again she said, "He assured us that Harrison would drop the charges."

He shook his head and said, "Obviously, Phillip made a huge miscalculation, and this whole thing went sideways."

Karen skeptically asked, "Michael do you think that's what really happened?"

Diana added, "I'm not so sure."

Michael said to her, "Hon, sit down." She took a seat next to him at the table.

He took her hand and said, "I'm thinking . . . we may need to consider a plea; it seems to be the lesser of two evils."

Diana shook her head and said softly, "I don't know . . . I just don't know." She began to weep, prompting Karen to get up and throw her arms around her, squeezing tightly and refusing to let go.

Regaining her composure, Diana said, "Michael why don't you and Karen go out and relax on the patio. Open the Raymond, while I clean up the kitchen."

She observed, "It's a nice night."

Karen protested, "No . . . no, I'll help you clean up."

"Don't bother. There isn't much to do. You keep Michael company," she insisted.

Michael went to the wine chiller, grabbing the favored bottle of wine and a corkscrew.

Diana handed Karen three wineglasses and said, "Go . . . go on. I'll be out shortly."

Walking out to the patio, Michael and Karen settled into a couple of lawn chairs, with the bottle of wine and the glasses on a table between them. Through the French doors, they could see Diana rummaging around the kitchen as she cleaned up the dessert dishes and coffee cups. They sat quietly waiting for a few minutes before Karen broke the silence. "Michael really, what are you going to do?"

"Honestly Karen, I'm not sure. I really think that if we went to trial we could win. Although, Phillip and Odell are right about one thing. It would be incredibly risky. I'm just not sure."

They continued to talk for almost ten minutes before they realized the kitchen was dark and lifeless. They immediately understood that Diana decided against joining them. Michael was poised on the edge of his seat as he continued to glare at the house when he unexpectedly threw himself backward, startling Karen. Looking away, he turned his attention to the wine bottle and glasses on the table beside him and reaching for the opener, he effortlessly pulled the cork from the bottle. "No time to breathe," Michael announced, as he poured wine into two glasses, offering one to Karen. Putting a glass to his lips, he eagerly drank a generous sip knowing that the wine would never taste as good as it should, its sweetness now soured by Diana's apparent refusal to join them. Nonetheless, and without any hesitation, he took another sip and then another until the wine glass was empty.

While Michael drank unconcernedly, Karen silently contemplated the glass of wine in her hands, replaying in her head the conversation that took place earlier. *What will they do—would Michael accept the plea deal or risk it all and go to trial?*

Before she could give it more thought, he suddenly got up from his chair, now appearing very anxious, which prompted Karen to ask, "Are you ok?"

He turned his head to her and muttered, "I'm fine," as he began to walk away from her, stumbling toward the house.

He walked through the French doors into the kitchen and made his way to the foyer, quickly arriving at the stairs leading to the second floor. He paused at the bottom step, his arm carelessly slung over the banister, as he momentarily stared at a dull fluttering light coming from the master bedroom. Intoxicated and a little despondent, he unsteadily began to walk up the stairs as he considered what to say to Diana and the excuse she might offer for not coming out as promised.

Arriving at the bedroom door, he could see that his wife was lying in bed, her head propped up on a pillow, body turned slightly toward a lit candle atop the nightstand beside her. The light was softly reflecting upon her face while casting shadows onto the walls behind her, the room's gloominess triggering a sobering moment. Michael stood in the doorway unable to move, held there by the sight of her, completely focused on her trembling lips and folded hands that tightly grasped the rosary beads given to her years ago. It was only then that he realized she was fervently praying, his initial feeling of displeasure with her quickly fading.

He continued to watch her as a large tear from the corner of Diana's eye began to slowly roll down her cheek, past her chin and onto the nape of her neck.

The candle's soft light forced her anguish on him, and for the very first time, he recognized the untold emotional and physical toll this was taking on her. His self-pity and somewhat selfish preoccupation was, at long last, letting go of him.

He stared at his wife for several more minutes as she continued to pray the holy rosary, never sensing his presence. Diana, unexpectedly, gave a slight sigh and shudder as she began to sob with a whimper. Overcome with emotion, he clasped his hands to his mouth and slumped down onto one knee, also silently weeping and thinking, *My God what have I done?* After a few moments, he stood and wiped the tears from his face as the empathy he was now feeling ave way to anger. Michael slowly realized that he could no longer surrender to the fear of the unknown, as he thought, *Fuck the FBI, my attorneys, and that asshole, Harrison. From here on out, it will be all out war.* He slowly turned and walked away from the bedroom doorway so as not to disturb Diana, returning to the patio completely sobered by his thoughts.

Once outside, he grabbed the wine bottle and poured himself a glass, intent on finishing what was left. Karen, having remained seated and saying nothing, watched him as he stood near the edge of the patio looking reflectively toward the setting sun that was now scarcely over the horizon. Just then a slight breeze brushed back the trees, causing her to shiver and, in that moment, she instinctively knew that Michael had come to a decision.

Coming Soon

———◆———

Read the Conclusion of the Michael
Dolan Story

in

The Trial

Made in the USA
Columbia, SC
13 January 2019